# Banger's Ride

## An Insurgents MC Romance

## Chiah Wilder

Copyright © 2016 by Chiah Wilder
Print Edition

Editing by Hot Tree Editing
Cover design by Cheeky Covers
Proofreading by Wyrmwood Editing

All rights reserved. This book or any portion thereof may not be reproduced or used in any manner whatsoever without the express written permission of the author except for the use of brief quotations in a book review. Please purchase only authorized additions, and do not participate in or encourage piracy of copyrighted materials.

Your support of the author's rights is appreciated.

**Disclaimer:** This is a work of fiction. Names, characters, businesses, places, events and incidents are either the products of the author's imagination or used in a fictitious manner. Any resemblance to actual persons, living or dead, or actual events is purely coincidental.

I love hearing from my readers. You can email me at chiahwilder@gmail.com.

Make sure you sign up for my newsletter so you can keep up with my new releases, special sales, free short stories, and other treats only available to newsletter readers. When you sign up, you will receive a FREE hot and steamy short story. Sign up at: http://eepurl.com/bACCL1.

Visit me on facebook at www.facebook.com/Chiah-Wilder-1625397261063989

# Description

**Banger, President of the Insurgents MC, isn't looking for a woman to replace his beloved wife. Ever since she died, he's closed his heart to loving again. He satisfies his carnal pleasure with the club girls and hoodrats. It's safer that way.**

The President of the national club may have sparkling blue eyes and an infectious smile, but make no mistake, if someone crosses him or his club, he'd slit their throat in a heartbeat.

Set in his ways, tough, tattooed, and a no BS-type of man, Banger is doing just fine until he meets the sassy, curly-haired, single mom who can cook the best fried chicken he's ever tasted.

He can't get enough of her cooking…or her.

For the first time since he's been widowed, he wants a woman in his life warming his bed.

And the no-nonsense woman, who has a body made for sinning, has turned his world upside down.

**Belle Dermot is a widow with two kids whose husband left her penniless. Wanting a fresh start, she moves to Pinewood Springs and takes a job at the local diner cooking tasty, home-cooked meals.**

After finding out her husband was a cheating louse, the last thing she wants is another man in her life. She has her hands full with a rebellious teenage daughter, paying the bills, and fending off nasty accusations that she poisoned her husband.

Then she meets Banger, the muscular, handsome, and rugged biker who comes crashing into her life.

If only he wasn't so nice to her and didn't get her all hot and bothered. And why did he have to be so damn good in bed?

As hard as she tries to push him away, he keeps slipping back into her life, helping her with her problems. And Banger's not the type to let go once he decides on something. And he's decided to make Belle his. Now, he just needs her to agree to be his woman…

The Insurgents MC series are standalone romance novels. This is Banger and Belle's love story. This book contains violence, sexual assault (not graphic), strong language, and steamy/graphic sexual scenes. It describes the life and actions of an outlaw motorcycle club. If any of these issues offend you, please do not read the book. HEA. No cliffhangers! The book is intended for readers over the age of 18.

## Previous Titles in the Series:

**Hawk's Property: Insurgents Motorcycle Club Book 1**
**Jax's Dilemma: Insurgents Motorcycle Club Book 2**
**Chas's Fervor: Insurgents Motorcycle Club Book 3**
**Axe's Fall: Insurgents Motorcycle Club Book 4**

# PROLOGUE

*Lakeview, Colorado*

HAROLD DERMOT LAY in bed watching her take out his rapid-acting insulin vial, rolling it in her hands to minimize the air bubbles. He leaned his head back on his pillow, waiting for her to give him his daily shot. Her light jasmine perfume wafted around him, and Harold's groin pulled as he imagined tugging her into his arms and kissing her before they made love. Harold was in love with her, and he hoped that his dalliance with Megan had been forgiven. It was a moment of weakness. He was sixty-one years old, and when his pretty, sexy secretary had flirted with him, he'd succumbed to a passionate affair. He never meant for anyone to find out, and even though he'd broken it off with Megan, she still called him, threatening to expose their relationship.

Harold was a self-made, successful businessman, who owned a large textile company. He'd been married for fifteen years and had one adopted daughter and a son with his wife. He also had a son and daughter from his first wife, who'd died sixteen years before. Harold loved his wife, but when the fresh, twenty-three-year-old employee cozied up to him, he felt flattered, excited, and young again.

He'd never wanted anyone to find out, especially his wife, but somehow she'd become suspicious about his weekly late nights, and too many out-of-town business trips. Harold knew he was being careless, knew his wife would be devastated if she found out, but the lure of firm flesh and unbridled passion was the youth elixir his aging body craved. When he was with Megan, he wasn't a sixty-one-year-old father and husband; he was a youthful, invincible man. Megan offered him youth and new sex—a powerful aphrodisiac.

Harold heard her soft padded footsteps as she approached him. He fluttered his eyes opened and smiled at her, loving the way her dark hair fell softly around her face as she bent over to give him his shot. He normally gave himself his injections, but when she was around, she wanted to do it for him. She'd told him she loved spoiling him. A smile whispered over his lips before his teeth bit his inner cheek, preparing for the burning sting of the shot to course through his body. She pushed the needle into his abdomen. He waited for the burn. Nothing. His eyes widened.

"Did it hurt?" she asked as she brushed his forehead.

"No, just a small sting. None of the burning. I wonder why." As Harold looked into her eyes, a shiver shimmied up his spine when icy contempt glared back at him. Before he could ask her what was wrong, she walked back to the dresser, leaned against it, and faced him.

Within seconds, Harold realized he had trouble moving his eyes and fingers, followed by his arms and legs. All he could do was stare at the steely gaze boring into him. *What the hell is going on?* As hard as he tried, he couldn't open his mouth. *I can't cry for help.* He summoned all his will and tried to move his finger. *Come on, finger! Why won't you just move? I can't move. I can't yell out. I'm paralyzed!*

Panic set in as Harold's lungs tried in vain to work, to breathe. Swallowing was becoming more and more difficult. As he watched her lips turn up in a satisfied grin, he knew he was going to die. *How could she do this to me? I told her I loved her. How cunning she was to pretend she'd forgiven me.* Harold wasn't ready to die; he had a lot more living to do. He had so much more to accomplish.

She crept over to him, leaned down, and whispered in his ear, "No one fucks me over, asshole."

Black spots blurred his vision and as he slipped into unconsciousness, he realized that with a prick of a needle, his life, his essence would be snuffed out.

*What a foolish way to die.*

# Chapter One

*One year later*

"Why're you so adamant about going to Ruthie's for dinner, babe?" Hawk asked Cara as he turned the SUV into the diner's parking lot.

"Because I know chicken fried steak is one of Banger's favorites." Cara looked over her shoulder at Banger, who sat in the backseat, fiddling with his phone. "Am I right?"

"Yeah. I fuckin' love a good chicken fried steak. I like Ruthie's too, but I haven't been there in a while since the food hasn't been so good. Hope tonight's better."

"It is. Ruthie hired a new cook, and the food is excellent."

"You don't happen to know this cook, do you, Cara?" Hawk probed.

When Hawk shot a hard glance at her, Banger laughed. Judging by the way Cara was acting, he knew she was up to something, and from Hawk's expression, he knew it too. Banger didn't give a damn what she was up to; as long as the chicken fried steak kicked ass, he'd be happy.

Ruthie's diner was a landmark in Pinewood Springs. Opened in 1942, the establishment boasted tasty, home-cooked meals. Ruthie had inherited the place from her dad after he died. She was in her mid-fifties, had thrown out three husbands, and had a heart of gold. Her second husband and Banger were good friends, and that was how Banger became friends with her. She always had a good story to tell, and her tough exterior made her endearing to a lot of the bikers in the area, especially the Insurgents MC.

The diner had gone through a recent renovation, which had repaired the cracked vinyl seats and shined up all the chrome and steel. The multi-colored checkerboard floor gave a punch of color to the monochromatic black and gray of the eatery.

Cara led the two men to a large booth next to the street-front window. As she scooted in, Banger slipped into the seat across from her and Hawk. A redheaded waitress in a white uniform with pink piping set three glasses of water on the table while asking, "You want anything else to drink?" After taking their drink and dinner orders, she ambled away.

Twenty minutes later, three plates of steaming chicken fried steak smothered in brown gravy, mashed potatoes, and green beans with cherry tomatoes tantalized the trio. Banger, his eyes lighting up when the waitress set the basket of homemade buttermilk biscuits in front of him, smacked his lips. "I hope this tastes as good as it looks." He picked up his fork and knife and dove into his meal.

Hawk leaned over and kissed Cara on the cheek. "You done good, babe. This is fuckin' delicious."

"Damn good." Banger mopped up the remaining gravy on his plate with a biscuit, then wiped his mouth with a napkin and leaned back against the seat. "The best chicken fried steak I've ever tasted." He patted his stomach, a smile on his face.

Cara grinned as she placed half of her dinner on Hawk's plate, and he proceeded to eat it up. Watching Cara and Hawk together made Banger laugh, but sometimes, it reminded him how alone he was since his wife, Grace, had died six years before. Every so often, it would hit him hard, and he'd miss Grace so much it ached.

Shaking his head, he slid out of the booth and headed for the restroom. In the narrow hallway, the woman's bathroom door opened and a curvy, dark-haired woman came out, slamming right into him. Banger grabbed her arm and tugged her up as she began to fall.

"Oh, I'm so sorry," she said. Striking, electric-blue eyes met his as she lightly grazed his forearm with her fingers. Her touch was stirring, and he stared at her, wide-eyed, as a single shiver zinged through him. "I should've been looking where I was going."

He was drawn in by the mellow tone of her voice; it was like sweet honey and buttery rum. Banger raked his eyes over her body, encased in a black uniform dress with pink piping and small milky white buttons. He admired her rounded hips, her small waist, and the way the white buttons pulled tight across her large chest. Berry-stained lips and curly tendrils framed her porcelain skin. She blew away one of the stray hairs that had fallen, her warm breath washing over Banger's bearded face. Lifting her hand, she tucked the strand into her messy bun. He took a deep breath and her light, jasmine-orange scent wrapped around him, hitting him in the groin. He sucked in air while his gaze held hers.

The woman blinked rapidly, then averted her eyes, mumbling, "Sorry, again. I have to get back to work."

"Just glad you're okay," he replied in a smooth baritone.

She walked away, her delicious hips swaying with each step. Banger watched her until she turned the corner and disappeared. Standing still for a couple of minutes, he tried to make sense of his strong response to the beautiful woman. He hadn't experienced anything like that since he'd said good-bye to Grace. The club whores and the hoodrats didn't stir anything in him except lust, and when he drained his dick in them, he felt nothing afterward except physical relief.

Returning to the table, Banger glanced around to see if he could spot the pretty lady whose uniform hugged her in all the right places. She was nowhere to be seen. A tinge of disappointment wove through him as he absentmindedly wadded up the drinking straw wrapper.

"Would you like anything else? We got fresh pecan pie," the waitress said as she cleared the plates.

Upon hearing the words "pecan pie," Banger focused his attention on the waitress. "I'll have a piece with a scoop of ice cream and a cup of coffee with cream."

"Is Belle cooking tonight?" Cara asked the waitress.

"Yep."

"Can you ask her to come out for a second? I want to compliment her on the dinner."

"Don't know if she can get away, but I'll tell her."

"Tell her Cara is asking."

"Will do. I'll bring that piece of pie and coffee to you right away, sir."

Banger looked after her as she shuffled behind the counter, took out a whole pie from behind it, and cut a large slice. He could smell the fresh pecans and the brewed coffee as she came back, placing both in front of him.

The vanilla ice cream melted down onto the warm slice, sealing the nooks between the pecans. The first bite was an explosion of sweet, salty, and creamy flavors. As Banger concentrated on the amazing dessert, he heard Cara greet someone.

"The food was so good. I wanted to tell you how much we enjoyed it. Wasn't it good, Banger?"

He looked up, then stopped chewing when he met the glittering blue eyes of the woman who had sparked something in him just a few minutes before. Surprise registered on her face, and a slow smile spread over her lips.

"Belle, this is Hawk, my fiancé, and this is Banger. Guys, this is Belle."

Banger glanced at Hawk and laughed inwardly when he saw the scowl he gave Cara, and the devious smile she flashed back at him. Turning to Belle, he said, "Good to meet you. You make a great chicken fried steak. The best I've had. You make this pie?"

A cherry stain brushed across her cheeks, and she looked down. "Thanks. Yes, I baked the pie. You like it?"

"Fuckin' good."

She met his eyes. "I'm glad you like it."

An awkward silence fell between them before Cara said, "Banger is very picky about food, so the way he gobbled everything up is a huge compliment."

Belle nodded.

"You been working here long?" Banger asked, loving the way she glanced at him demurely every few seconds.

"About six months."

"Damn. If I'd known, I'd have been here sooner. I've missed all your good cooking, and your pretty face, for half a damn year."

"You're being too kind." Her laughter rang in his ears, sweet and soft, like tinkling bells, and all he could do was smile. She covered her mouth with her hand and locked her gaze with his. For a suspended second, they were connected, but then she looked away and the moment was gone.

Cara cleared her throat. "What time do you get off work, Belle?"

"In about a half hour."

Cara looked at Banger and Hawk. "Do you want to go to Blue's Belly for a drink?"

At the same time Hawk replied, "No," Banger said, "Yes."

Merriment lit up Cara's eyes. "Great. Would you like to join us, Belle? I know you don't get out much, and it'd be a nice way to unwind before you go home."

After a moment's hesitation, Belle shrugged.

"She's probably tired from being on her feet so much," Hawk said, narrowing his eyes at Cara.

"I'd like for you to come. Give us a chance to talk," Banger said as his eyes lingered on Belle's mouth.

Tugging on her silver-hoop earrings, she nodded. "Okay. Sounds like fun. Give me a little time to change outta this." She brushed her fingers over her uniform.

"Sure, you just let us know when you're ready," Cara said, a satisfied smile spreading across her face.

An hour later, they were seated at a small table at Blue's Belly, sipping their drinks and listening to a local band play classic rock covers. Cara had arranged it so Banger and Belle were seated together. If Belle wasn't so pretty and sexy, Banger would've been pissed at Cara's blatant matchmaking. He didn't have anything better to do, though, and sitting with the curvy cook beat spending the night alone at his house.

"Mmm…. This is so good," Belle said as she took a big gulp of her frozen strawberry margarita. "It's my favorite drink. What's yours?" she asked, looking at Banger.

He brought his bottle of beer up and clinked it against her drink. "Coors all the way." The way she giggled warmed him.

"I love the sugar around the rim of the glass." She stuck out her tongue and ran it over the edge, licking at the granules, then her lips.

Watching her tongue on the glass made Banger's dick twitch; he bet it could do all sorts of dirty shit to him.

"Why you looking at me like that? What are you thinking?" She playfully brushed her fingers over his hand.

"You don't wanna know what I'm thinking." His blue eyes twinkled.

"Why?"

"'Cause you'd slap my face, and I'm betting you got a damn good swing."

A blank look was soon replaced with a flush that crept across her cheeks. "Oh." She giggled nervously then broke away from his stare, stirring her drink repeatedly with the small straw.

"Didn't mean to make you nervous, but you must know you're a beautiful woman."

"I'm not nervous, just out of practice. It's been a while since I've been like this with a guy."

"Are you fucking with me? A sexy woman like you must have a bunch of guys after her."

"Not really. Anyway, I'm too busy." She took another gulp of her drink, red still the dominant color on her face.

Banger laughed and grabbed her hand. "Let's go dance. This is one of my favorite songs."

He led her to the dance floor, and they shook their bodies to Sammy Hagar's "I Can't Drive 55." As Belle moved her hips to the beat of the music, Banger felt his jeans grow tighter. The way she swayed told him she'd be all kinds of hot in bed, and for the first time in a long time, he wanted a specific woman. The fucking he did with the club whores and hoodrats didn't count—it was for physical release, nothing more—but his whole body was burning for this voluptuous woman who ignited something in him he'd thought was long gone.

When the music slowed a bit, Banger pulled Belle into his arms, pressing her close to him, loving the way her soft tits felt against his chest. They moved back and forth to the slow strains of Nazareth's "Love Hurts," her subtle floral scent driving him crazy. He wrapped his arms around her, his bulge rubbing against her, the sensation sending sparks down his spine. Belle leaned her head on his chest and put her arms around him. When his hands lowered to rest on her fleshy ass, she stiffened then shook her head. Leaning down, he whispered in her ear, "You're a sexy woman. I love the feel of your body."

"You can feel it with your arms around my waist. Take them off my butt."

Just like that, she ordered him to stop what he was doing. At first, it startled him because women never told him what to do. Hell, he and Grace had sex the first night they'd met. Since her death, the club women clamored for him; he'd been off-limits during his marriage, but they came at him like sharks, silently hoping he'd take another old lady. They couldn't do enough to please him and show him he needed their pussies. And the woman he actually craved ordered him to stop touching her tempting ass. *What the fuck?* He didn't know what to make of it.

"Your hands are still there."

It was a statement, but it worked; he abruptly moved them up and around her waist. Satisfied, she leaned her head on his chest once again. They danced the next few songs, then she said against his ear, "Let's go back to the table, my feet are killing me." Her lips just grazed his skin, and Banger ran his finger down her jawline while he nodded.

They ordered another drink just when Hawk turned to Banger. "Cara and I are cutting out. She's got an early morning hearing. I'll see you at the clubhouse tomorrow."

Banger winked and tilted his chin then turned his attention to the lovely, cocoa-haired woman who made his pulse quicken. Her tangle of curls fell a little past her shoulder, and Banger's fingers itched to wrap around the spiral strands, feeling their silkiness against his callused skin. And her full bottom lip was begging for him to suck on it while he held her close. *Damn, she's a hot one.*

"How did I miss seeing a pretty lady like you? You from Pinewood Springs?" he asked as he leaned in close, his arm pressing against hers.

She shook her mass of curls. "Lakeview. It's about an hour from here."

"Yeah, I know it. You got some great backroads for biking. I go there often during the summer. How did you end up in Pinewood?"

"My husband died a year ago, and he left me and the kids in a bad way. He always told me he'd take care of me, but he didn't." She paused, her gaze moving from his to the dance floor.

"That's tough."

When she looked at him again, her twinkling eyes had turned hard, the bluish-steel of a midwinter sky. "Yeah, it is. Anyway, my best friend, Holly, had moved here to be with her boyfriend. He's a deputy sheriff. When Harold died, and our house was foreclosed, Holly told me to get a fresh start. My kids and I moved in with her and Darren for a few months until I landed the job at Ruthie's. With the overtime, and Ruthie's generosity, I was able to afford a small bungalow on the east side of town. It's a far cry from our five-bedroom home in Lake Vista Hills, but it's good to be in a place that's all our own." She brought her drink to her lips, the hardness in her eyes softening a bit.

"How many kids you got?"

"Two. I have a daughter who is sixteen and a ten-year-old boy. They're my anchors. What about you? Were you ever caught by a lady?"

He bobbed his head up and down. "I got a daughter, Kylie. She just turned nineteen and is away at college in Crested Peak. Her mama and I were hitched for fifteen years."

"You divorced?"

"Nah. My old lady died." After six years, saying the words aloud still pulled at his heart.

Belle placed a hand over his. "I'm sorry. It must be tough."

Clenching his jaw, Banger stared straight ahead. "It is."

Silence settled around them, each lost in their memories. Grace's shining blue eyes and long, glossy blonde hair flashed in front of him. She had been a kind, beautiful woman who adored her daughter and husband. She was so clear in his mind that he felt that if he could just reach out a bit further, he could touch her, feel her warm skin and silky hair again.

"I'm glad I came out for a drink. I'm having a good time." Belle's lilting voice pushed Grace to the corners of his mind as she squeezed Banger's hand.

He squeezed back. "I'm glad I came in the diner tonight." He stroked her cheek with the back of his hand and marveled at how soft it was, like a piece of silk.

Banger relished being with a woman who made him laugh, who intrigued him, and who wasn't a few years older than his daughter. He'd become bored with the senseless chatter of the women he bedded. He had nothing in common with them, and they didn't hold his interest one iota beyond sucking him off. Being with Belle was like a breath of fresh air.

When midnight struck, Belle gathered her purse and coat. "I better go. My kids are alone, and I have to work tomorrow. It's been a nice night. Thank you."

As she rose to her feet, Banger jumped up and helped her with her coat, then lowered his head and said, "I'll walk you to your car. Just give me a sec." He texted Blade, one of the prospects, to pick him up.

As they moved through the parking lot, the icy air chilling their lungs, Banger put his arm around Belle and tugged her close to him. She didn't pull away, and they walked together until she stopped in front of a gold Honda Accord. "Here I am," she said softly.

She pulled off a glove and dug in her purse for the keys. Their breaths formed clouds around them in the bitter cold air. He took the keys from her and opened the door then swung her around so she faced him. Without hesitation, he bent down and kissed her gently on the mouth. She pushed back, a smile whispering on her lips. Banger leaned forward to capture her mouth again, but her hands on his chest held him back.

"Thank you again. I really have to go."

Banger quirked his lips. "You didn't like the kiss?"

Her eyes widened and patches of red streaked her cheeks. "You're a direct person, aren't you?"

"Fuck yeah. I don't go in for hiding what I mean. I wanna kiss you again."

She shifted from one foot to another. "There's no point in it. I had a nice time, but I don't have any time for anything more. I'm too busy working to make ends meet and taking care of my kids. A lot of times, I pull a double shift. I rarely go out for fun. Tonight was definitely an exception."

Banger drew her closer to him, her hot tequila breath warming his face. "I'm not asking you to spend your life with me. Just asking for a kiss. No harm in that, is there?"

She gave a half-shrug then tilted her head up, her gaze locking with his. He moved his hand to the back of her neck and kissed her lightly on the lips. When she pressed into him, a low growl rose from his throat and he crushed his mouth against hers, his tongue breaking through the seam of her lips then dipping into her warm, giving mouth.

Banger trailed his fingertips down her back and found her soft ass. When he cupped her rounded cheeks under her coat, he felt them flex at the same time her small moan vibrated against his mouth. The sound of her arousal lit a fire in his dick, and he pushed her against the car, his hardness poking her. Then she stiffened, pushing him back, her blue eyes watering and her face red from cold and embarrassment. His gaze lingered on her lips, swollen from his kiss. Bringing his thumb up, he ran it across her cheeks.

She panted, "I have to go," and abruptly turned and scooted into the driver's seat of her car. "Thanks again."

"I want to see you again. How about going for round two sometime this week?"

Her curls swayed from side to side. "Can't. Really, I'm too busy right now for anything more than what I already have on my plate. I'll see you if you come into the diner. I've already stayed out too long. Bye."

Banger didn't argue. "It was nice spending time with you."

Belle closed her door then blew him a kiss before taking off into the inky dark. The Accord's red taillights wavered in the misty night, and he stood watching her until he couldn't see her car anymore.

The thought of Belle and her soft lips warmed him as he made his way over to Blade's SUV parked in the far corner of the parking lot.

"Hey," Blade said as Banger slid into the passenger seat.

Banger nodded curtly, closed the door, and settled back on the heated seat. Banger wanted to see her again, hold her, smell her jasmine scent, and kiss her incredible lips. For some reason, her touch uncovered a deep desire that he thought had long been buried. With the memory of Belle on his mind, her scent on his clothes, and her taste on his lips, warmth blanketed him as the chilled wind shrouded him. There was something about her that made Banger want to know her better. Belle had intrigued him, and there was no way in hell he was going to walk away.

# Chapter Two

Belle poured herself a glass of chardonnay and sat at the kitchen table, sipping slowly as she tried to stop the fluttering in her stomach when she replayed her time with Banger. When she'd bumped into the tall man, her heart had leapt to her throat when his eyes had met hers. They were the most incredible shade of aquamarine, like the clear, tropical seas of the Pacific, and they'd pulled her in. Breaking away from them, she'd let her gaze run over his rugged, lightly tanned face. His long, honey butter-blond hair was pulled back in a ponytail, and his beard had flecks of white through it and was close to his face. His skin was slightly weathered, as if he'd spent time outdoors in the wind. The small wrinkles around his eyes crinkled when he smiled, and his deep, resonant voice melted over her like liquid chocolate. His six-foot-one frame was rugged and built, and his presence exuded strength and raw sex. Banger's chiseled cheekbones and jawline made her want to reach out and stroke them. He was definitely all male. Her pulse had raced when his eyes bored into hers, as if trying to read her soul.

When she'd gone back into the kitchen, the sound of his deep, sexy voice had echoed in her ears, and he already had her fantasizing. Then she'd seen him at the table with Cara, her daughter's attorney. She couldn't believe how nervous she'd felt when his smoldering gaze ran over her body. Banger did things with his voice and eyes that made her heart shudder. And when he'd held her while they danced, her squishy body pressed against his hard, strong one, funny sensations had tugged between her legs. When he'd kissed her, her panties dampened and her breasts ached for his touch, but she'd had to stop it. She couldn't begin to think about becoming involved with Banger because she knew she'd fall hopelessly in love with him, and a man that good-looking would surely cheat on her.

Since Harold had died, her life had been a series of upheavals. When her husband had passed away, it was the first time she'd been alone. She'd become pregnant her last year of high school with her daughter, Emily. Her boyfriend had denied any responsibility and dumped her before Emily was even born. She'd struggled to provide the basics for her daughter since her mom and dad didn't help her out, too angry at her for "ruining" herself. Not being able to afford rent and food, she'd been forced to stay at home, enduring endless lectures on how she had sinned and how she was damned.

When she'd landed a job at a tourist resort on the lake, she'd been twenty-one years old, broke, and worn down by her parents. When Harold, twenty-five years her senior, took an interest in her, she'd jumped at the opportunity to give her daughter a better life and to break away from her parents. He was a widower who'd lost his wife the year before. He had a son and daughter who were older than she, but Belle didn't care; she just wanted out of her shitty life. In six months, she and Harold were married, even though her parents threatened to disown her and his daughter, Jessica, accused her of being a "gold-digging slut."

Five years later, she'd given birth to Ethan, and Harold had been thrilled. They'd had a nice life. Harold had a successful textile company, and Belle didn't have to work. He was a good provider, and a good father. He'd adopted Emily, and their life together had run smoothly for years.

Belle loved Harold, but she was never *in* love with him. Love was overrated; she'd been in love with Emily's father, and it had left her pregnant, broke, and alone. Harold was a sickly man, who'd suffered from diabetes and hadn't taken good care of his health. He ate and drank too much, so, at the age of fifty-four, he'd been put on insulin injections to control his disease.

Belle had always made sure to be the best wife and mother she could be. She'd joined all the charity boards Harold had told her to, attended all her children's school activities, hosted wonderful dinner parties for investors interested in Harold's company, and made sure to be available sexually for her husband, even though she didn't enjoy sex very much.

She'd given Harold a good home and taken care of him, and when she'd found out he'd been cheating on her with his clichéd twenty-three-year-old secretary, her world had crumbled. He'd broken her heart. How could he have done that? After all she'd given him. She'd even put up with his bitch of a daughter, who'd consistently hated her throughout the years.

Of course, he'd admitted the affair when she'd confronted him, and he'd sworn it was nothing more than sex and freaking out about becoming old. He'd begged Belle to forgive him, to not leave him, so she said she'd stay. She didn't have a better gig, and he'd been the financial rock of the family. Then he'd died, and Belle had thought the saying that "karma is a bitch" was really true. She'd donned the obligatory black for the funeral, but her heart had been freed from the anger and disappointment she'd felt at his betrayal. His death had set her free.

Then she'd found out he'd left her and the kids penniless. He'd been bleeding the company dry, embezzling funds for the past three years. There was nothing left—even the house had three liens on it. Jessica had accused Belle of spending all her dad's money, and Belle hadn't bothered to explain the situation. She didn't want to sully Jessica's memory of her father.

Homeless, penniless, and bankrupt, Belle had moved her family to Pinewood Springs. It had been the best decision she'd made. Except for her long hours at work, she'd tried to make a normal home for her son and daughter. Her daughter hadn't dealt with her father's death very well, and she'd been acting out by drinking and ignoring her curfew. In the last year, Belle had fought with her daughter more than she had with anyone else in her whole life. She was at her wits' end with Emily. Belle really didn't know what to do.

She drained her wine glass. Being with Banger reminded her how good it could feel to be with someone attractive and sexy, but she'd have to dispel those thoughts. Her life was too busy, and she had to put her daughter back on track. She didn't have time for dating, and the last thing she had time for was to fall in love. No damn way was she going to let *that* happen.

She washed out her glass, turned off the lights, and climbed the stairs to her bedroom.

AROUND TWO O'CLOCK the following day, a loud rumble rolled to the back of the diner, and Belle looked up from a pot of bubbling beef stew just as Banger walked in. Her face flushed and a surge of adrenaline coursed through her when she saw him scoot his long, denim-clad legs into a booth. His blond hair was secured in a ponytail, and a glint bounced off the earring in his left ear. He wore a black T-shirt and from where she stood, she saw the bulge of his bicep. Not thick and ripped like he worked out, just tight and defined as though he was used to manual labor. Blue, red, black, green, and yellow ink twisted on his tanned skin as he moved his arms. When they'd gone out the previous night, Banger had worn long sleeves, so she hadn't noticed any tattoos. Watching him as he sat, the menu in his large hands, Belle held her breath in anticipation. She wanted to see his tats up close, trace them with her tongue as he explained what they meant.

*Stop it! Right. Now.*

Something searing hot splashed on her hand. Belle looked down and noticed the beef stew was boiling rapidly. Cursing under her breath, she turned the flame to low, hoping she hadn't burned the house special. And all because she couldn't keep her eyes off Banger. How stupid and juvenile was that? After all, she was a thirty-eight-year-old mother of two, hardly a young twenty-something looking for a boyfriend. She shook her head—she was acting ridiculous.

As Belle took out the homemade rolls for the stew, Ruthie came into the kitchen, her hand on her hip, her deep-set brown eyes twinkling. "Go on and take your break. Jerome can cover. You got a customer who wants to talk to you."

Belle's mouth went dry and shivers trembled up her spine. "Who?" she asked, even though she knew it was Banger. She was stalling for time so her body would calm down.

"Banger. Now go on and get." Ruthie blew on a spoon of beef stew before she took a taste. "Damn, this is good. They'll be lining up for it tonight."

Belle smiled weakly then rushed to the bathroom to make sure she didn't have flour all over her. She swiped on another layer of apricot lipstick and a smear of clear gloss, took a deep breath, and willed herself to stop shaking. She walked out toward his table.

"Hey there," she greeted him, her voice much more confident than she felt.

A huge smile cracked Banger's face, and she liked how his eyes lit up when he scanned hers. "Hiya, beautiful." He straightened against the seat and gestured for her to sit down.

She sat opposite him, their gazes locked together, neither saying anything. Belle cleared her throat. "So I must be doing something right if you're coming back so soon for another meal." Her laugh sounded forced and too high. *Damn. Get a grip. He's just a man. A gorgeous, sexy, intriguing man. Stop!*

"You're doing a lot of things right." His gaze dropped down to her chest then back to her face, and he winked at her.

Uncomfortable, she pulled out a napkin from the dispenser and began wiping the table. "You'll have to try the beef stew and homemade rolls. I'm not bragging, but they came out great." She kept wiping the table.

His warm hand stopped her frenzied movement, and her gaze shot up to his. "Pretty sure the table is more than clean."

She laughed, even though the butterflies in her stomach were twirling around. "I guess you're right." Belle leaned back stiffly against the seat, his hand still covering hers. It was nice to feel the strong warmth; it made her feel safe and comforted. *What the hell is wrong with you? So he's holding your hand. Big deal.* "Were you in the neighborhood?" she asked.

"Nope. I came here to see you."

"I usually work nights. How'd you know I'd be here?"

"Called Ruthie and asked. Her second husband and I are good friends. Have been since high school. That's how I met Ruthie, and we've been friends ever since." He squeezed her hand. "I wanted to see you again."

She swallowed hard. "You did?"

Banger stared into her eyes. "Yeah."

She slowly slid her hand from under his then pretended that someone had texted her. Even though her head was down, she was aware of his stare boring into her. She set her phone on the table then stretched out her arms, her hand knocking over his water glass. *Damnit! He makes me so nervous.*

Banger jumped up as water spilled on him. He grabbed a handful of napkins to sop up the liquid as it dripped off the table.

With her hand over her mouth, she said, "I'm so sorry. I really am. Here, let me get a rag."

"No need." Banger motioned the waitress over. "Could you take care of this mess for us?"

The waitress dried off the table and set a full glass of water in front of Banger before ambling away.

"You must think I'm terribly clumsy. First slamming into you last night in the hall, and now spilling water all over you. I'm usually careful. I don't know what's gotten into me." Her voice trailed off, and she avoided his look because she knew exactly what the problem was—him. The man made her heart flutter, her mouth go dry, and her body ache in areas that scared the crap out of her.

"I think you're pretty and cute." He took a sip of water. "I'm going to try your beef stew and rolls. Then I gotta go back to the clubhouse to do some work."

Noticing the president patch on his jacket for the first time, Belle asked, "You belong to a club?" She then spotted his one percent patch and wrinkled her nose. "You an outlaw biker?"

"Yeah. The Insurgents."

She pushed back from the table. Her only experience with a biker was Holly's brother, but she wasn't sure which club he belonged to. She knew he lived in New Mexico. When Belle had first moved to Pinewood Springs, she'd been so despondent that her friend, meaning well, had hooked her up with her brother. She'd gone on a couple of dates with him, but he'd been so pushy, he'd given her the creeps. Remembering him made her shudder. She couldn't imagine how he and Holly could be brother and sister—they were so different.

Banger looked her over. "Is that a problem for you?"

She shook her head. "Not really. You're a customer, that's all."

"Is it?" His hard gaze latched on to hers.

Diverting her eyes away, Belle nodded, releasing several strands of hair in her face. She tugged them back under her clips forcefully. The red bloom on her cheeks felt hot as she slid her fingers over them, all the while staring at the napkin dispenser.

He leaned over and said in a low voice, "Your look just told me I'm more than that." With his finger, he traced her jawline softly, and she instinctively tipped her head to the side, a small sigh escaping through her lips.

"On second thought, I'll take my meal to go. It's getting late." He motioned the waitress over and in less than ten minutes, a paper bag held a container of stew and three rolls wrapped in foil. He left the money on the table and got up.

Belle swiveled her legs from beneath the table, but before she could stand up, he grabbed hold of her wrists and pulled her up in one smooth movement, bringing her close to him. She breathed in his scent of clean freshness, letting it wrap around her like his powerful arms had done the previous night. He kissed her cheek and said against her ear, "Later, beautiful." He winked at her then strolled out of the diner, leaving Belle staring after him.

The roar of his Harley brought her out of her reverie, and Belle went back in the kitchen to prepare for the evening rush. As she busied herself, she could still feel the touch of him on her skin, knowing the flutter of excitement that ran through her as she thought of him meant bad news. He did something to her; she was drawn to him, but she didn't want to be. She had her hands full with her children. There was no way she could juggle all the crap going on and add Banger to the mix. It was too much. And he was a biker, the worst kind of man for a woman who'd been betrayed by the men in her life. Nope, she would have to keep it simple and at the diner. A few hellos and winks were about all she could handle.

The hard beat of the AC/DC song "Highway to Hell" filled the kitchen as Belle ran over to retrieve her phone. Her daughter always rolled her eyes at her mother's ringtone, but whenever she heard it, it uplifted her. Lately, she'd needed all the uplifting perks she could find.

"Hello." Belle walked back to the stove and stirred the gravy.

"Hi. Are you still at work?" Holly greeted her.

Belle marked the day she'd met Holly as one of her luckier ones. They'd met at the strawberry festival on a warm, late-summer day six years before. Belle had been manning the school booth, selling homemade fruit pies and jams, when Holly had come up. They'd struck up a conversation, and discovered they shared an interest in cooking and entertaining. Holly had been new to the area, and was feeling lonely without her friends or family. Belle had invited her to join her cooking club, and from then on they'd been close. Holly was like the sister she never had.

"Yep, still at work. I've got a couple more hours to go. What's up?"

"I'm calling you in plenty of time so you can let Emily know she has to stay with Ethan this Friday. You and I are going out for burgers. Darren has the graveyard shift, and I'm itching to go out to eat. He's been so busy that all I do is sit at home. Boring! Anyway, no excuses. We're hanging out on Friday night."

Belle laughed, but her stomach constricted when she thought about asking Emily to stay with her brother. Sometimes she was fine with it, but most of the time she gave her a real attitude. Belle thought it was simpler to stay home than have a fight with her daughter. "I'll see what Emily is up to. If she doesn't have plans, then a nice dinner out sounds good."

"You just tell her you need her to help out. Fuck, you never go out. You deserve to have some fun. Treat yourself."

"I know. You're right. If Emily can't do it, I'll see if Ethan can spend a few hours at Luke's house. I'll give Sarah a call."

"That's good. I'll let you get back to work. I'll pick you up on Friday at around seven, okay?"

"Sounds good. See you."

Belle put her phone back in her backpack. Her friend was always looking out for her, trying to make sure she didn't become too much of a homebody. If Holly didn't drag her out once in a while, Belle would never go anywhere. She needed a day away from cooking and the kids.

As the five-o'clock crowd filed in, Belle dug in her heels, preparing for a long three hours until she could go home.

PAIN SURGED UP her calves as she entered the modest, three-bedroom bungalow she rented. She knew the children were used to a lot more space, but it was all Belle could afford on the money she made at Ruthie's. She kicked off her shoes, welcoming the carpet's softness on her aching feet.

The minute she walked into her pristine kitchen, she knew Emily had not begun dinner like Belle had asked her to. She opened the refrigerator and took out the chicken she'd breaded before she went to work earlier that day. She asked so little of her daughter, yet Emily still couldn't manage to perform the simple task of making the salad and steaming the broccoli. After placing the vegetable in the steamer, she padded out to the family room. Ethan had come down while she was in the kitchen and his eyes were glued to the TV, his small hands gripping the game controller as he destroyed invaders who approached his village.

"Where's your sister?"

Without glancing at his mom, he shrugged.

"Was she here when you got home from school?"

He shook his head. Belle left the room and climbed the stairs, knocking on her daughter's bedroom door. No answer. She opened it, hoping to find her daughter sprawled out on her bed, her ear buds in, watching something silly on the computer. No such luck. Her daughter's room was just as Emily left it in the morning before she went to school. With a heavy heart, Belle went to her room to change out of her uniform.

After Ethan had gone to bed, Belle, wine glass in hand, tried for the umpteenth time to call Emily, but it went to voicemail, just as it had the many times before. Anger and worry zigzagged through her body, and by the time it hit midnight, Belle had decided to call the police. But just as she was dialing, she heard the back door bang open. Hanging up the phone, Belle leapt up from the couch and rushed toward the kitchen to confront a very stoned Emily coming into the house.

"Where the hell have you been, and why haven't you answered any of my calls?"

"What?" Emily stared at her with glassy eyes. "You called me?" She took out her phone and scrolled. "Damn. I guess I forgot to turn it back from vibrate after school. Sorry." She brushed past her mom.

Belle gripped her arm. "No way is that good enough. Why didn't you call to let me know where you were? I've been worried sick all night, and now you come home stoned off your ass?"

Emily pulled out of her mother's grasp. "Too tired. We can talk about it tomorrow." She started toward the stairs.

Belle grabbed her and turned Emily around. "We will talk about it now. You come home past your curfew, reeking of weed and booze, and you want to talk about it tomorrow? I don't think so."

"I'm tired. Leave it alone." Emily narrowed her eyes.

Belle shook her head. "I'm tired too. I've been on my feet for ten hours, and then I had to sit here and worry half the night about where you were. We're talking now." She tugged her daughter toward the living room.

Emily shoved her mom, pushing her back against the wall. "Don't ever fucking touch me again. I'm going to bed." She stomped up the stairs as Belle watched her in disbelief.

Making her way to the couch, Belle sat on it, rubbing her shoulder from where it hit the wall. She couldn't believe the daughter she'd loved and cherished had treated her with such disrespect. Covering her face with her hands, she stifled her sobs while she wondered what had happened. It seemed like Emily was growing more belligerent and for the first time, she'd been violent toward Belle. How could she stop this crazy ride her family was on? What the hell was she going to do?

# Chapter Three

The sunlight reflecting off the snow blinded Banger as he walked through the clubhouse's parking lot. When he entered, a few brothers sat around the bar, staring idly at a sports channel on the big-screen TV. He greeted them with a jerk of his chin and went to his office. Closing the door behind him, he sat down in his brown leather desk chair and closed his eyes. A bright blue gaze took center stage before the sexiest curves he hadn't seen in a long time came into focus. He couldn't get the gorgeous cook at Ruthie's out of his mind. When he went by to see her the previous day, he'd been as excited as a high school boy before he spotted her mass of dark curls. He smiled at the thought. She was a mighty fine woman, and it'd been a helluva long time since he'd been enamored with any woman other than his beloved Grace.

Pangs of guilt pricked him when he thought about Grace. He'd loved her madly, and the fact that he was thinking about another woman in a way other than sex made him feel like he was betraying her, even though he knew it was silly. It'd been six years since he'd buried Grace, yet his heart still clenched whenever he thought about her. The excruciating pain which consumed him during the first couple of years after she'd died had dissipated to a dull, ever-present ache.

He'd met Grace at a biker rally when he was twenty-five years old and she was twenty-three. The moment he saw her big, crystal-blue eyes and long blonde hair shining in the sun, he was hooked. Grace had come from a biker background—her dad belonged to the local Evergreen Dogs, a non-outlaw group. At first, her dad distrusted Banger because he was in the Insurgents, but when they'd married and given him a granddaughter, he'd learned to accept their relationship.

From the moment he met her until she died, Banger loved Grace. They had their ups and downs like any married couple, but they made a pact to stay together no matter what. And they went through a lot, especially early on when the Insurgents and the Deadly Demons were waging a turf war. Those were hard, bloody times, and Grace would always cry when he left the house to take care of club business, never knowing if he'd come back alive. She'd stuck through it, and when Banger took the reins as president and worked to stop the bloodshed, their marriage survived all the late nights he gave to the brotherhood. Because of her biker background, Grace never questioned Banger's loyalty to the Insurgents. She knew the club came first, and it was something that no citizen could *ever* understand.

Then Kylie, all pink and blonde with the sweetest blue eyes, came into their lives, and her birth brought Banger and Grace even closer. He never looked at another woman, and even though his wife would be insecure at times when he'd go to the parties where young, pretty women threw themselves at the president, he was never tempted. To him, the most beautiful woman was waiting for him at home, so the lure of easy sex never did it for him.

One rainy afternoon, Grace had taken his hand and kissed it, her blue eyes glistening, and she told him in a hushed tone that she had ovarian cancer. Banger had never been terrified of anything in his life, but those two words spread fear and darkness over him like nothing ever had. The only way he knew how to fight was with his fists, a gun, and a knife, but those didn't work with cancer. So he kept a smile on his face while he held her hand through the surgery, chemotherapy, radiation, and the last dying weeks. He had to be strong for Grace and Kylie; he didn't want them to see him cry, so he reserved those moments for when he was alone in his office.

Belle lit a fire in him he thought had been extinguished six years ago. She'd been on his mind ever since she'd slammed into him a couple of days before. He couldn't figure her out. The way she kissed him and brightened when she saw him told him she felt the spark too, but she was scared. He didn't think it was of him, per se, but maybe the idea of being with a man. Her hesitation didn't mean much—he'd still pursue her—it just made him want to know what she was hiding in her heart.

*Knock, knock.*

Startled, Banger sat up in his chair. "Come in."

Rock poked his head through the open door. "Everyone's assembled for church."

Glancing at his phone, Banger said, "Fuck, I lost track of time. I'm coming." He rose to his feet and exited with Rock at his heels.

Members crowded the meeting room, and Banger took his position at the head of the table. When he brought the gavel down, all the chattering stopped, the brothers giving their full attention to the club's president.

"We got some items we need to go over today, but first I want to introduce five new members who've joined the mother house from the defunct Kilson, Nebraska chapter." Banger turned to a group of men seated on folding chairs. "Stand up. This here is Tug, Bones, Chigger, Gator, and Hoss. Let's show them our support and welcome them."

The regular members clapped and yelled out, "Welcome," to the Nebraska Insurgents. Banger cleared his throat and slammed down the gavel again. "We got some important shit to discuss. We got approached to sell arms to a Mexican group called the United Revolutionary Army."

"Who the fuck are they?" Rags asked.

"I was getting to that, if you can be fucking patient. They're a leftist guerrilla movement in Mexico. They need arms for their operation in the states of…." Banger squinted at the piece of paper in front of him. *Fuck. I'm gonna have to get me some reading glasses. I can't see shit.* He handed the paper to Hawk.

"Let's see… They operate in the Mexican states of Guerrero, Oaxaca, and Veracruz. They're looking for a supplier, and they got our name from Liam." Hawk turned to Banger, sitting down once the president nodded to him.

Banger stood up. "As you know, we've backed away from this illegal shit since we're making a fuck-load of money with our dispensaries and grow sites." He laughed. Thinking of how much money the club was pulling in by growing and selling marijuana legally always made him shake his head. The irony was too great. "We also got a good revenue from our other businesses, and the new strip mall is bringing in a sizable amount in rent, so we don't need to do this deal. If we decide to do it, it'll bring in a shitload of money, and we could use it to build a larger strip mall in east Pinewood."

"How much are we talking here?" Axe asked.

"'Bout four million plus. We'll ask for five, but we'll settle on four." Banger nodded as the members whistled and clapped their hands. "Yeah, a fuckin' load of money at one time. If we do supply the arms, we make money and help a group of rebels fight their fuckin' government, the drug cartels, and gangs. The idea is that it'll make life better for the masses. The cons are that we can be double-crossed by this group. We don't know them, never worked with them, but they do come recommended by Liam. We've worked with Liam for years supplying arms for the Irish and African rebels. Another thing is we could bring the heat down on the club. For the last several years, the ATF has left us the fuck alone. Not sure we want them sniffing around the club again."

"But it's a shitload of dough. Fuck the ATF, they won't have anything on us. Let's vote," Throttle said as several members voiced their agreement.

"And we get to help kick another government in the ass. Fucking anarchists," Chas chimed in.

The Insurgents lived by their own rules and despised all governments. To say they were non-conformists was an understatement. If the opportunity came up to make a lot of money, the Insurgents were down for it. Flipping the middle finger at the government was a bonus.

"Let's put it to a vote. All in favor of making a shitload of money *and* kicking the Mexican government in the ass, say 'aye.'"

"Don't forget the motherfuckin' drug cartels. I'd pay to have their asses shot," Axe said, eliciting a round of applause from the membership.

"So is it 'aye' or 'nay'?" Banger asked.

The "ayes" bounced off the walls.

"Then it's a go. Hawk and I will get the ball rolling on this. Church over."

The members clomped out of the room. Hawk turned to join them when Banger said, "Hawk, hold up a second. I want to go over some particulars."

Hawk nodded, and the two waited until the members left to have some fun and drinks in the great room.

"I'll go with you when we finalize the deal. The president of the United Revolutionary Army is coming and out of respect, I need to go."

"Okay, that's cool. I'll let you know the details as soon as I have them. I'll get on it right away." Hawk glanced at his phone. "Anything else you wanna go over? I gotta get back to the shop. A customer is coming to pick up his custom bike, and I wanted to add a few last touches."

Banger rubbed his face with his hand. "How does Cara know Belle?"

"Belle?"

"You know, the cook at Ruthie's."

"Oh, yeah. Fuck, I meant to tell you that I'm sorry my old lady meddled in your business. I had no idea Cara was matchmaking when we went. The cook's daughter has some minor shit going on with the law, and Cara's her attorney. I told her to leave you the fuck alone, but you know Cara—the more I tell her not to do something, the more she wants to do it. Fuck."

"No need to apologize. Your old lady is one clever woman. I liked Belle, but not so sure it's mutual. I think it is, but she's acting fuckin' skittish." Banger shrugged.

"You starting to pine for this one? Fuck, you even got the pansy-ass shrug going." Hawk laughed, and Banger joined in, even though dormant feelings stirred inside him.

He and Hawk walked together to the great room before Hawk clapped him on the shoulder. "Gotta go, man."

Banger nodded while he looked around the room. Groups of men talked, drank, and groped the club whores and hoodrats who had come to party. He spotted a bunch of scantily clad women who were only a few years older than Kylie, and a sadness like he hadn't felt in a long time gripped and squeezed his heart.

"I'm heading out too," he said to Hawk. For reasons he couldn't articulate, he didn't want to spend another night drinking Jack and beer, screwing a woman who was young enough to be his daughter, and talking bullshit with the brothers. He just couldn't do it. Not that night. He walked out with Hawk and, with shoulders slumped and head bent, he approached his Harley.

"Hey, do you wanna come to the shop with me? I could use your eye with this custom job."

Banger jerked his head up. "Sure. I'd love to see the way you're customizing the dude's Harley. Fuck, you've been working on it for a couple weeks now."

"Yeah. It's been a fuckin' good time." Hawk put on his black gloves. "After I close up, why don't you come over to my place for dinner? Cara's making lasagna."

Banger's eyes lit up. "I'll take you up on the offer. You two still playing musical houses?"

"Fuck, yeah. Her parents, especially her mom, wouldn't be cool if they knew we were living together. I can't wait for the bullshit to stop. I go along with it to keep the peace."

"When will the house you're building be ready?" Banger swung his leg over his bike and settled on the leather seat.

"We just hired Baylee to design it. After we get married, we'll sell both our houses and move in. Can't fuckin' wait."

They revved their engines and took off toward downtown Pinewood Springs.

A few hours later, Banger sat comfortably on the couch in front of a blazing fireplace, munching on the cheese and crackers Cara had set out on the coffee table. He took a swig of his beer and popped in a few cashews as he looked around the room. Once Hawk's domain, Cara had definitely added her feminine touch, with dried floral arrangements and punches of pink decorative accents. He snorted, knowing how Hawk must hate the additions.

"Do you want another beer?" Cara asked as she set down a plate of salami, pickles, green and black olives, and roasted red peppers.

"Sure do, thanks. Fuck, this looks good." He leaned over and grabbed a few slices of salami.

He watched Cara go into the kitchen and saw Hawk loop his arm around her as she passed him, bringing her close. She giggled and Hawk brought his mouth down on hers. As Banger watched them kissing passionately, a stab of loneliness pierced through him. In that instant, the ache he'd carried in his heart since Grace had died was acute, and the back of his eyes burned. *What the fuck is up with me?* He turned around and stared into the fire.

Hawk came over with a bottle of Coors and handed it to him. Banger, grateful for the distraction from his thoughts, took a long pull of his beer. He and Hawk talked Harleys until Cara told them to come for dinner.

After dinner, Banger leaned back and said, "Damn, woman, I love how you cook. You make the best lasagna."

"I bet Belle makes a great lasagna. She told me she loves to cook and bake."

Banger saw the "leave it the fuck alone" look Hawk gave Cara, and he chuckled under his breath. "I'd love to taste Belle's lasagna. She makes a damn good beef stew. I stopped in yesterday to see her and I got me a bowl. Fuckin' good."

"You went to see Belle?" Cara gave Hawk a satisfied smirk, and Banger saw him shake his head. "How's she doing?"

"Seemed okay. She told me she's got her hands full right now with all the shit going on in her life."

"She worries about her daughter. Emily got into some trouble. I can't reveal the particulars about the case, but I can tell you that Belle is a wonderful mother who loves both her kids dearly. She's had problems with her daughter since her husband died."

"Yeah, that shit can mess with kids. Fuck, it messes with grown-ups. I'm glad Kylie fared as good as she did."

"You were fuckin' there for her one hundred percent. You blew all the brothers away by your dedication to Kylie," Hawk said.

"Even with all the love you can give, kids can lose their way. Just glad my Kylie did okay." Banger finished his glass of red wine.

"Are you going to see Belle again?" Cara asked.

Banger shrugged. "Maybe." *What the fuck am I saying? Damn right I'm gonna see her again.*

"You should give her a chance. She's a bit jittery about men right now. I'm not sure why, but you shouldn't give up." Cara gathered the dishes from the table.

Banger guffawed. "I'm not the type who gives up. When I see something I want, I go for it. Just haven't made up my mind if I want her or not." *You lying sack of shit. You can't wait to get your ass to the diner to see her again. Fuckin' pathetic. Hawk's right, you're a pansy-ass.* He laughed again as he poured himself some more wine.

Finishing their lemon cake on the couch in the family room, Banger stood up then swayed as the effects of too much alcohol overcame him. Hawk rushed over to steady his president.

"Whoa, man, you better crash in one of the spare rooms. You're in no shape to ride home."

"I think you're right." Banger glanced at Cara who smiled at him, nodding in agreement.

Hawk showed him to the guest room on the main floor. Banger had crashed many evenings at Hawk's after Grace had died, but it'd been a while since he'd drunk too much to ride. Hawk made sure he was okay, then closed the door and left. The room was nicely decorated in southwest designs and colors. He shucked off his boots and clothes then slipped under the sheets, bringing the down comforter up under his chin. He was glad he stayed over. Something inside of him didn't want to go back to his dark, quiet house. At least not that night.

He closed his eyes and let sleep set in.

# Chapter Four

At nine o'clock in the morning, Belle sat at the kitchen table waiting for Holly to come by for their morning walk. Unless the weather was really bad, she tried to walk at least three times a week with Holly. Her friend lived only about a mile from Belle, and that made it convenient for whenever she needed Holly to stay with Ethan. Emily got along very well with her, and the two of them would often go shopping together. Belle was happy that at least Emily had one adult woman with whom she connected, especially since the two of them had been having a lot of problems.

After a brisk walk in the frigid air, Belle placed two cups on the table and filled them with steaming coffee as Holly sat down at the table.

"How are things going with you and Emily?" asked Holly.

"Not so good. We had a terrible fight last night." Belle wrapped her fingers around her coffee cup. "She was so angry at me. She shoved me." Her voice lowered to a whisper. "I can't believe she did that."

"You gotta be kidding."

"I wish I were." Belle's voice hitched.

"Shit, that must be tough."

She looked at Holly. "I gotta be honest here, I don't know what I'm gonna do with Emily. If it were just the two of us, I would deal with it, but I have Ethan to think about. All the stress is making it terrible for him. I know if Harold were here, Emily wouldn't be acting this way at all. It's just so unfair to Ethan, that's all."

"Yeah, she was always close to her dad. Harold was actually good for something."

"I wish he were here to tell me what to do. He had a way with Emily. It's funny, because I have such mixed feelings about Harold. I hated him for cheating on me, but I loved him for being a good dad and supporting me in raising the kids."

Holly shook her head. "Damn, men can be so loving to their kids but shits to the women in their lives. I lucked out when I met Darren, but all my exes are assholes." She grabbed Belle's hand and stared at her. "Harold was a fucking idiot to have cheated on you. You're a great mother, and you were a fantastic wife—don't ever forget that. It seems like the more you do for a man, the more he takes advantage of you."

Belle squeezed her friend then smiled weakly. "Thanks. Okay, poor-little-me conversation is over."

"Just remember that Emily is having a hard time because she's missing her dad and doesn't know how to deal with it. Add being a teenager on top of it, and it has to be tough for her. Remember back when you were her age. It sucked, right?"

Belle shrugged. "My parents were very strict, so for most of my life with them, I felt like a caged bird with clipped wings. I would never cuss them out or even think of shoving them against a wall. I give Emily what I never had—freedom. She can go out with friends, go on dates, and listen to whatever music she likes. But she still resents me. I don't know what to do."

"The problem is, as much as you didn't have any freedom, you've given too much of it to Emily. She needs more supervision. With you working so much overtime, Emily can do whatever the hell she wants, and you're not around to watch her. Some kids need more supervision and a man in the house." Holly leaned back in her chair. "You know, if you want to diffuse the tension, maybe it'd be better for Emily to come and live with me and Darren until the end of the semester. We're just talking five months. It'd give her a chance to miss you and Ethan, plus it'd give her more structure. You could have quality time with Ethan. It'd ease up the tensions in the house."

Belle stood up and placed her coffee cup in the sink. It was sweet of Holly to try and help her out, but how could she let her daughter live away from her? She loved Emily so much, but it did bother her that she'd been so aggressive the previous night. Belle hoped it was an isolated incident, but Emily hadn't apologized to her earlier in the morning when she'd left for school.

"I know this is a hard decision for you. I'm just trying to help. I've always gotten along fine with Emily. I'm worried about you because I've never seen you this tense. You're more stressed out than you were when Harold died."

"Things are rough right now. It isn't all Emily. Our financial situation is always on my mind. It seems I never have enough to pay everything at the end of the month. I feel awful that I can't take the kids on a trip, or even to a fucking movie." Belle pulled her shoulders back. "But I know things will get better. Life has a way of turning out great when we least expect it. It'll all be good."

"I hope so. Just think about what I said. The offer is open any time." Holly walked over to the back door.

"Thanks. I will. I've got to get to work. We'll talk soon. Thanks for listening."

Holly smiled and left out the back. Belle ran upstairs to change into her uniform then headed to Ruthie's Diner.

Throughout her shift, she looked out the pass-through window, watching for Banger, but he never showed up. A knot formed in her stomach. Why hadn't he come? Maybe she shouldn't have rebuffed him the last time she'd seen him, but she knew his type—he was a man looking for a good time. If she didn't have all the crap going on with Emily, she may have been interested in having some fun with Banger. But the way her life was, having fun wasn't an option.

A gust of icy wind wove its way into the kitchen. Belle rushed over and looked out to see who'd come into the diner. When she spotted an elderly couple, her heart sank. *I'm acting like a fool. So what if he doesn't come in? He probably has several women he's playing. I have enough going on that I don't need to be obsessing over a playboy biker.*

She put the final touches on a three-layer chocolate raspberry fudge cake.

"Mmm… That sure looks good." Jerome gave her a wide grin, exposing the gaps from his missing teeth.

She smiled warmly at her colleague. Jerome was the other cook for the diner. He was a sweet man around her age, although his deep wrinkles and blotchy skin made him appear much older. He was a reliable employee, and Belle loved him for that, especially when her feet ached from standing for nine or ten hours.

"Try a piece. I prepped everything for tonight," Belle said as she grabbed her purse and coat.

"Should be a quiet night since they have a rodeo over at Rutger's barn."

"I didn't know that was this week. I guess a lot of people go to it."

"You bet. It ain't a big one, but it's enough to bring out a bunch of folks. You gonna go?"

"Nope. The only thing I want to do is soak my feet. Damn, they're killing me."

While she put on her coat, a long rumble shook the windows of the diner. Her heart leapt, and she ran to the picture window with a big smile on her face, only to quickly have it wiped away. Instead of Banger on the bike, Holly's brother killed the engine. She turned quickly, dashing to the kitchen before slipping out the back door.

She set her tote bag and extra groceries Ruthie insisted she take in her trunk. She hated handouts, but she needed the food so she took them, grateful to Ruthie for her compassion. She closed the trunk, then jumped when she saw a man leaning against the hood of her car. Her heart sank.

"Hi, Craig. Are you looking for Holly?"

"Fuck, I told you my name is Scorpion. Craig left a long time ago."

"I refuse to call anyone Scorpion." She laughed lightly, but she was weary, and she wanted to go home.

He came up to her and pulled her to him. "You'll call me Scorpion, got it?" His eyes flashed as he scanned her face.

Her stomach churned. "I was only joking, *Scorpion.*" She turned toward her car door, gently pushing him away. Out of the corner of her eye, she saw him staring at her with a hard look. *He's probably trying to figure out if I'm being sincere or a smartass. I can't stand this guy.*

Scorpion spun her around, his grip tight on her arms. "Don't ever fuckin' forget it. You don't wanna piss me off, do you?" He ran his finger across her cheek, his ragged nail scratching her. "You gonna give me a kiss?"

Before Belle could answer, he leaned down, his mouth inches from hers. She wriggled away, and his mouth landed on her cheek. "What are you doing at the diner? Are you looking for Holly?"

He was staring at her mouth. "No. I'm meeting her at the bank across the street. I need to get something notarized. I came over here to see you. You're looking fuckin' hot." He unabashedly checked her out, leering at her from head to toe.

Belle cringed, feeling dirty when his eyes skimmed over her body. When Banger had checked her out, she'd been energized, tingly, like a teenager. *Why am I thinking of him? I need to concentrate on Craig, because he's looking at me in a creepy way. I have to get outta here.* She twisted around, clutching the door handle, slowly opening it. "I have to get home to my kids. I'm already late." She slid her leg into the car.

"I'm gonna be in town for a couple of days. Let's hook up and have some fun." He moved closer to her again.

She threw herself in the driver's seat. "I'm working too many shifts. Maybe next time, okay?" She feigned a sweet, innocent smile.

He glared at her before shifting back on his heels, and she grabbed the handle and closed and locked the door. Scorpion's eyes narrowed and he moved toward the front of her car, leaning against the hood, his eyes fixed on her.

Belle started the vehicle, putting it in gear. She drove forward. Scorpion jumped away. "What the fuck?" he yelled.

Smiling, she waved at him as she left the parking lot. When he disappeared from her rearview mirror, she finally breathed, her heart pounding. She couldn't stand Holly's creepy brother. Cursing herself for ever going out with him, she hoped it'd be a long time before she ran into him again. She'd never wanted to in the first place, but Holly kept insisting, and Belle relented just to shut her friend up. Now she regretted her decision.

When she entered the house, the comforting aroma of her barbecue pork and potato casserole greeted her, making the house smell homey and cozy. Happy that Emily remembered to put the dinner in the oven, Belle stood in the small kitchen, letting the warmth envelop her. She padded into the living room, and tenderness spread to her core when she spotted Emily, cross-legged on the sofa, and Ethan, kneeling on the floor, playing a video game together.

"Hi, Mom," Ethan said, his eyes never leaving the TV screen.

"Hey, Mom," Emily greeted, her own eyes unblinking as her fingers moved over the game controller.

"Hey, you two. Thanks for putting the casserole in the oven."

"Sure, Mom."

Belle smiled, her heart bursting. She went upstairs to change, happy the evening would be spent with the daughter she used to know before Harold died and everything turned to shit.

After a pleasant dinner filled with lively conversation and laughter, Belle stretched out on the couch, a glass of white wine on the coffee table next to her. If she could just find a way to have more nights like that evening, then she could breathe again.

She stared at the blue flame in the gas fireplace and a sense of loneliness shrouded her. She wished she had someone to talk to, to share the day's events, to hold her and tell her it would all be okay. She hadn't been intimate with a man for over a year and a half. The last six months before Harold died, he'd told her he was too sick or too tired each time she'd tried to initiate lovemaking, and she'd believed him, like a fool. Then she'd found out that he'd been banging his secretary, and she'd seen red. Knowing that he'd ignored his wife and lavished his attention and love on someone else had gnawed at her. As she recalled the shock, the anger, and the hurt his betrayal had caused her, bitterness rose in her throat. *How could he have done that to me? I never looked at another man during our marriage.*

Emily's biological father had turned out to be a loser, and Harold had too. She was so done with men. It was less painful to fantasize and touch herself than trust a man. Her fantasies always consisted of a tall, handsome man with dark eyes, but lately, the dark eyes had turned to smiling blue ones with small crinkles at the corners. She shook her head and picked up the remote, turning on the TV. She definitely didn't want to go *there*. Aimlessly, she stared at the flickering screen until she fell asleep on the couch.

# Chapter Five

"Belle's working the swing shift," Ruthie said as she set a large slice of apple pie in front of Banger.

"Did I ask?"

"No, but you wanna. I've seen more of you in the last couple of weeks than I have all year." Ruthie stood with her hands on her hips, grinning at Banger. "Belle's a nice woman."

"Didn't ask that either."

"You're a hard man," she said, winking.

"Won't argue with you on that. Pie's good."

"Belle made it last night before heading out. Since she's been here, business is back on track. I couldn't wait to get rid of Jimbo. He was a lazy ass who liked his booze too much. He ran so many of my customers off. And the ones I tried after I canned him made Jimbo look like a gourmet chef. I lucked out when Belle answered my ad."

A blast of icy air swooshed inside as a group of four entered the diner.

"I gotta get this," Ruthie said, nodding toward the group. She shuffled away.

Banger took a sip of his steaming coffee and savored the fresh-roasted taste. A good cup of coffee with a tasty piece of apple pie was a slice of heaven, especially on a frosty morning. He glanced up at the clock, whose two hands were a fork and spoon, noting that it was only nine thirty in the morning. Belle's shift didn't start for another four-and-a-half hours. He'd do some business at the club, drop in on Hawk's shop to see if he needed any help, then see how the day went.

He wanted to see Belle again and make her eyes sparkle. The sound of her laughter echoed in his brain. This woman tugged at him; it was like she was a magnet pulling him to her. It was a bit unnerving, but a level of comfort also surrounded the feeling.

After draining his coffee, he rose to his feet and placed his money on the table. As he headed out, he waved to Ruthie. "See ya."

"Tonight's special is pot roast," she said as he opened the door.

"Not sure I'll be back."

"You'll be back."

He could hear the smile in her voice. He didn't answer because she was right—he'd be back, and he couldn't wait to see the dark-haired Belle.

★ ★ ★

BELLE RUSHED AROUND, finishing up the laundry then putting the final touches to the casserole she'd made for her children's dinner. She hated working the swing shift because she missed dinnertime with her kids. When she was growing up, it had been the most important part of the day. It was when her family all came together and talked about their day, shared funny stories and laughter. When she'd been married to Harold, she'd made it a point that they all sat down to dinner as a family. No phones, no TV, only family time, talking to each other. The two years before Harold had died, he'd started missing dinners, using new mergers and work as an excuse. He'd done it several times a month, but she hadn't been suspicious; she'd known he was trying to expand the company, and he totally used that to his advantage. How naïve she had been.

The phone rang and she jumped, cursing it for its intrusion on her reveries. As a screeching tune played, she wondered why she'd let Emily change her ringtone. She answered the phone.

"Is Mrs. Dermot there?"

"This is she."

"Hello, this is Mr. Campbell, the principal at Pinewood Springs High."

Belle's stomach twisted.

"I'd like to meet with you this afternoon, if possible."

"Can I ask why?"

"It's about your daughter and her many absences from school. I think it's better if we meet rather than do this on the phone."

Belle turned white as her hand grasped her neck. *Emily is skipping school? What the hell is she doing when she's supposed to be in school? Why can't I just have one day free from all bullshit?*

"I'm sorry, Mr. Campbell. I'm not able to meet with you this afternoon because I have to work. I can't skip my job. I'm available tomorrow morning, if that works okay with your schedule."

"Does nine thirty tomorrow morning work for you, Mrs. Dermot?"

"Yes, that'll be fine. I'll see you then."

"Thank you, Mrs. Dermot. Goodbye."

Belle hung up the phone then rubbed her temples. That one phone call had dashed any glimmer of hope of them having a happy family. The last thing she wanted to deal with right then was all that. She decided she'd talk to Emily after she went to the meeting with the principal the following morning; she didn't want to rock the boat and have Emily storm out, because then Ethan would be all alone that night. She didn't have a backup plan for anyone to stay with Ethan, so she'd pretend like everything was okay between her and her daughter until after the school meeting.

As she finished her last touches of makeup before heading to work, she wished her life was easier and not such a roller coaster ride. Under her breath, she cursed Harold for spending all their money and leaving her and the kids with nothing. The way she felt right then, all she could think about was how life sucked big time. With a frustrated sigh, she grabbed her tote and car keys, locking the door as she headed to her job.

When Belle arrived at Ruthie's, every booth, table, and stool was occupied. She was happy when she saw how busy the diner was, because then she wouldn't have to think about her daughter and all the problems that came with it.

At around seven thirty that evening, she heard the low rumble of a motorcycle. Thinking it may be Scorpion again, her heart sank and her stomach twisted in knots. She knew she couldn't deal with him right then. When the door opened, she couldn't help but look through the pass-through window, the heaviness of her heart disappearing when she saw Banger's imposing figure enter the diner. Her insides tingled when she saw his strong, broad shoulders as he slipped out of his leather jacket. His eyes went directly to hers, and she felt a strong pull to him—a connection. She'd never felt anything like it before. The intensity of it thrilled and frightened her at the same time.

Belle turned away and busied herself with stirring several pots on the big gas burners. About twenty minutes later, she went over to Banger's table to say hello. When she approached, she saw his eyes slide up and down her body. Crimson streaked her cheeks, and a sweet sensation pulled between her legs.

"How are you? I haven't seen you in a few days. I was hoping you'd stop by tonight," Belle said softly.

"Were you?" Banger's eyes lingered on her mouth. "I'm doing okay. What about you?"

Belle sighed and tucked the stray hairs behind her ears. "I could be better. Just having a rough time with my daughter right now."

"Yeah, I know how it can be. Raising a teenage daughter on your own is a real challenge. I've raised Kylie single-handedly since my wife died, and I gotta say, we had some trying times."

"I just don't know what to do with Emily. I wish I could be at home and spend more time with her and Ethan, but I have to work. Most of the time, I have to pick up overtime to make ends meet. It's just the way it is. I just wish she understood what I'm doing to keep our family together."

Banger reached over and held her hand, squeezing it lightly. "When they're young like that and going through whatever teenagers go through, they never understand. Give it some time. When she gets older, she'll know what you did for her and her brother, and she'll love you even more for it."

"I hope so." Belle gently stroked Banger's cheek. "Thanks for listening. I needed to unload. I gotta get back. My break's over."

Banger nodded. "Best damn pot roast I've had in a long time." He winked at her.

Smiling, she said, "Glad you like it. I love cooking for people who really enjoy what I make. It just seems like every time I see you, you make me feel better."

With that, Belle went back to the kitchen, pulling out vegetables from the refrigerator and chopping them to prepare for the next morning.

After she was finished, she bent over to pull out a sack of potatoes from the cupboard when she heard a low whistle. She jerked up and spun around, her eyes falling on Banger, who was leaning against the doorway, his hungry gaze slowly riding up her body. "That's what I like. A beautiful woman with curves I can hold onto."

Belle blushed as she pulled her dress down then crossed her arms over her chest. She wasn't used to male attention. Scorpion gave her attention in a creepy way, but with Banger, it was different. It didn't make her feel uncomfortable. His attention made her stomach flutter and her core tingle.

"I don't think you're supposed to be back here," she said.

"What I should and shouldn't do has never stopped me." His deep laugh skimmed over her, leaving goose bumps in its wake. "I just came by to say that I'm taking off. I gotta go back to the club. I want to see you again. When's your day off? I'd love to take you out to dinner and spend some time with you."

"I'm off on Friday, but already have plans with Holly."

"What's your next day off?"

She smiled. "Sunday, but I'll be busy with my kids. It's just really hard right now for me to make any plans outside of my family and my really good friend. I'm sorry, I wish I could offer more. The timing just isn't right, I guess."

Banger narrowed his eyes. "I gotta go. Later." He turned around and walked away. When he left the diner, he didn't give a backward glance.

Belle felt a terrible ache in the pit of her stomach. *Why did I just turn him down?* She wanted to be with him, but she was terrified of being hurt by another man again. She didn't trust men anymore, but with Banger she felt comfortable, even though she barely knew him. She deserved some time to herself, especially since she'd been so stressed with her daughter. Thinking about Emily made her heart sink. How could she even think about going out with Banger when her home life was in such disarray?

Belle sighed and started peeling the potatoes.

★ ★ ★

BANGER RODE TO the clubhouse, the icy night air whipping around him. He was madder than hell, and he couldn't wait to down a few shots to cool his fire. What the fuck was her problem? He knew she was attracted to him, but damn, Belle had some shit going on that she didn't want to share with him. Why the hell he was bothering with her, he didn't know. Maybe she was still in love with her dead husband, but the way she looked at him told him she was ready to love again. Something was holding her back, and he should just move on. He didn't need that kind of shit in his life. Damn, Belle was complicated, and not at all like Grace. With Grace, they'd seen each other, were attracted to each other, and fucked like rabbits six hours after meeting. None of this complicated bullshit.

Banger entered the great room at the clubhouse, the heat and smoke curling around him as he made his way to the bar. After he downed his third shot of Jack, a woman about thirty years old approached him. He recognized her from a few months back when she came to the clubhouse to party with the brothers. He'd been with her a few times, but he couldn't remember her name, only that she liked it in the ass. She planted a big kiss on his cheek as she rubbed her tits against his arm.

"Hiya, sexy." She licked his earlobe.

Banger nodded. Running his eyes over her, her short skirt and barely there top made his groin pull. *What the hell. I need a good fucking.* He hadn't been with a woman since he'd laid eyes on Belle. He grabbed the woman by the hand and took her to his room upstairs. Once inside, she stripped down to her thong and unzipped his jeans. His semi-hard dick flopped out. She placed her hand on it, rubbing it while she pushed her tits into his face. Nothing. He wasn't getting harder. He pushed her away. "Sorry, darling, this just isn't going to be."

"Just give me a chance, baby." She kneaded his shoulders. "You're so tense right now. I can relax you. I can give you a good time. Haven't I always treated you good?"

Banger stood up, went to the door, and opened it, his eyes fixed on hers. "Yeah, real good to me, but it's not gonna happen. It's not you. I just got a dark-haired woman on my mind. This was all a mistake."

The blonde walked out, blowing him a kiss before he closed the door. Banger walked over to the bed, lay down, and closed his eyes, Belle's smiling face burning in his mind.

# Chapter Six

The following morning, Belle went to her daughter's school to see the principal. She sat in the brown leather chair in front of his desk and waited until he finished his phone call, wringing her hands over and over in her lap. When he finished, Mr. Campbell turned to her and smiled. "It's nice to meet you, Mrs. Dermot."

"It's nice meeting you as well. So, what's going on with my daughter?"

"Emily has had seven unexcused absences this month. I have no choice but to turn her over to the school board for habitual truancy."

"What does that mean?" Belle's head was spinning.

"It means that Emily will have to go before the Truancy Court. She could end up getting juvenile detention, home arrest, or have a suspended sentence."

Belle hung her head down. Tears slipped out of her eyes and trickled down her cheeks, dropping onto her hands in her lap. "I don't know what to say. I thought she was coming to school. I don't know what more I can do. I'm a single mom and I have to work long hours. I'm doing the best I can to provide for my family, but I feel like I'm giving my daughter up in the process. Can't you give her another chance? Please don't turn this over to the courts. I'll make sure she comes to school. I'll do whatever it takes to get her back on track."

"I feel for you, Mrs. Dermot. It's tough raising children on your own, and even harder when money is tight. The problem is, this is the second warning. I sent a letter home last semester because Emily was missing too much school."

"A letter? I don't remember getting a letter."

The principal opened a file on his desk and pulled out a letter, handing it to Belle. She took it from him and scanned it. Her eyes dropped down to her signature on the letter, and she knew immediately it had been forged. She felt like someone had punched her in the stomach. "That's not my signature," she whispered.

"I figured as much. I wish there was something more I could do, Mrs. Dermot, but I am bound by the law. I have no choice but to report your daughter as a habitual truant. I am sorry." He looked at her, and Belle saw empathy in his eyes.

"What happens now?" she asked him.

"I think you should get your daughter a lawyer. I always recommend that to parents."

Belle thanked him and left, then headed straight to Cara's office. After she told Cara about the situation, she leaned back in the chair, saying a prayer that the young attorney could help her and her daughter.

"I can help you with the truancy case, but it isn't as easy as Emily just getting detention. In some cases, depending a lot on the judge, a truant kid could be removed from the home."

Sudden coldness hit her to the core as she asked in a shaky, disbelieving voice, "Removed from the home? They would take Emily away from me?"

Cara nodded. "I really wouldn't have brought that up, but Judge Richter is the one presiding over the truancy cases now. He's a tough SOB, and his tendency is to blame parents for everything their kids do. Of course, I'll fight hard for Emily and for you, but she has to be prepared that she may go to detention. I'll try hard to get home arrest for her, and I'll fight even harder for her to stay in the home with you. But Judge Richter isn't going to like the fact that she doesn't have much supervision in the home due to the number of hours you work."

"This is insane! I don't want to work as many hours as I do, but I don't have a goddamned choice. If I don't work, I don't make money. If I don't make money, we don't have a house or food. How can he sit there on the bench, acting so high and mighty with his big salary, and pass judgment on parents who work hard to give their children a home? I can't believe this is happening."

"I know. He doesn't get it, but we're stuck with him. I'll do my best to fight for you, to explain your situation, and tell him that you have a handle on it now that you're aware of the problem. I'm not saying he's going to take Emily away, but I just wanted you to be prepared that it could happen."

"If he takes Emily from me, where would she go?"

Cara said in a soft voice, "Foster care."

Breathlessness overtook Belle, and she gripped the sides of her head as if to cover her ears. "*Foster care?*" She said the two words as though they were dirty, disgusting, and not relevant to her and her family.

"Unless Emily can stay with a family member or friend who can offer supervision. But again, I'm not saying this is going to happen. It's just a possibility, especially in Judge Richter's court."

Spreading her fingers out in a fan against her breastbone, Belle said, "Okay. I just have to think about all this. It's too much right now to absorb. How much is this going to cost me?"

"Nothing. I'll do the case pro bono. Leave everything up to me, but make sure that from today on, Emily goes to school every day. If she misses one day without an excuse, there's not much I can do to help her. You may want to think about an alternative if the judge decides to pull her from the home."

With glistening eyes, Belle said in a low voice, "I want to pay you something. I don't want handouts, and I don't want to be a charity case. I insist on paying you something."

"It's okay, really. You're paying me for Emily's other case, so it's all good. I don't regard this as a charity case. You have more than enough on your plate right now, Belle, I'm sure you don't need anything more."

Taking a tissue from her purse, Belle dabbed the corners of her eyes. She rose to her feet, walked over to Cara, and extended her hand. Cara shook it, and Belle smiled and whispered, "Thank you so much. I appreciate this more than you'll ever know." She turned around and left the office.

When she arrived home after work that evening, she saw Emily sitting on the couch, staring at the computer screen.

Belle sat in the chair opposite the couch, and said in an even voice, "I have to talk to you about something."

Emily jerked her head up, stared at her mother, and shrugged.

"Your principal called me in this morning for a meeting. It seems that you've been skipping school. You've already skipped seven times this past month." Belle smoothed out the wrinkle in her uniform. "You want to tell me what's going on?"

Emily's jaw clenched and her eyes narrowed. "Why should I bother to tell you anything? I can see you already made up your mind, and you're siding with him."

"I'm not siding with anyone. I heard his side of the story this morning. Now, I want to hear yours. Have you skipped school?"

"Of course I skipped school. I hate it there! You're the one who dragged us to Pinewood Springs. You made me give up my friends and our home. When dad was around, things were so much better, but since you took over, everything has gone to shit. I hate it here. I hate my life. I hate you!" Emily jumped up from the couch, ran up the stairs, and slammed her bedroom door.

Belle dashed after her, stopping in front of her door. She knocked. "Open the door, Emily."

"Just leave me the fuck alone."

"Emily, I told you to open the door. Now." Belle stood by the door and heard her daughter sobbing. Her heart broke, but anger also flowed within her. If only she could take Emily in her arms as she used to when she was a young girl and tell her that everything would be all right. It seemed so simple back then: a hug, her fingers through her daughter's hair, and all was good. How had life changed so drastically? "Emily, I'm still waiting for you to open the door."

Something large crashed against the door. "I told you to leave me the fuck alone. If you don't, then I'm breaking everything in the room."

Before Belle answered, she heard whimpering coming from Ethan's room. She walked over to his door and knocked on it. There was no answer. Trying the knob, she turned it and entered. Ethan, sitting at the head of his bed, curled up in a ball, shook like a leaf. In that instant, her heart shattered into a million pieces. She dashed over to him and pulled him into her arms. His small arms hugged her waist, and he nestled his head against her chest. As she stroked his head, she whispered, "Shh… It's going to be okay. Don't worry about anything; I'll always be here for you. Your sister and I are just going through a rough patch right now, but it has nothing to do with you. We both love you. It's all okay."

Ethan clung to her as she ran her fingers through his hair, rocking back and forth until he fell asleep. She placed him on his pillow and covered him with his sheets and comforter, happy that he had calmed down and everything was all right with him again.

*It's so unfair to put Ethan through all this stress. I don't know how to handle Emily. Maybe I can't control her. Maybe it's too late for us. I just know I can't subject Ethan to this anymore.* A pang of guilt stabbed her as she realized that, for the past year, it had all been about Emily—helping, placating, and understanding her—while Ethan seemed unscathed, but that night told her a different story. She had to think of Ethan and not only Emily. Not wanting to leave him, she sat in the rocking chair and watched her son sleep.

As the minutes turned into hours, Belle wrestled with the reality that she may lose her daughter to foster care. Holly's offer of Emily living with her and Darren for the rest of the school year started sounding like a good alternative. The problem was she didn't know how Emily would respond to it. What if she thought Belle was trying to get rid of her, discard her like a piece of trash? Would she ever understand her mother's actions, or would she hate her for the rest of her life? Belle wasn't sure what she was going to do, but she knew she would never give her daughter up to an impersonal system that treated children like collateral. If Emily couldn't live with her, then she'd live with Holly—someone she knew and cared about.

Belle bent over and grabbed the afghan on top of the trunk at the foot of Ethan's bad, wrapping it around her shoulders. She leaned her head against the rocking chair and closed her eyes, welcoming the darkness sleep brought.

# Chapter Seven

Friday night had finally arrived, and Belle was excited to go out and have a night on her own. After work, she took Ethan to his friend Luke's house for a sleepover and dropped Emily off at Chelsea's house, where she'd spend the night. Belle spoke to Chelsea's parents just to make sure everything was legitimate so worrying about Emily wouldn't ruin her night.

Satisfied that her kids were settled in, Belle rushed home to get ready before Holly came to pick her up. After showering and applying her makeup, Belle put on a black skirt a couple of inches above her knee, a black fitted sweater with silver metallic threads running through it, and mid-calf black boots with round silver studs, buckles, and a chunky three-inch heel. She checked herself out in the full-length mirror on her closet door and thought she didn't look half bad. It'd been a long time since she'd dressed up to go out on the town. Having a free night felt like going on a vacation to her, and she may need a couple of margaritas to loosen her up, but she planned on having a good time. When she heard Holly's car horn, she fluffed up her hair, grabbed her evening bag, and went out to meet her.

Belle could see the bright yellow sign with the black lettering which read Burgers & Beer Joint a couple blocks before Holly turned into the restaurant's parking lot. The lot was almost full, and several people milled in front of the restaurant. Belle and Holly entered through oversized glass doors, and the heat from the kitchen surrounded them. The restaurant looked like a modern, urban eatery, with its glossed oak hardwood floors and red brick walls. Rich brown leather booths and wooden tables were scattered around the restaurant. Large planters of green plants and dried branches added warmth to the place. A long, wooden bar, complemented by bronzed barstools with rust leather cushions, was the focal point. There were ten beer taps pouring the best locally brewed beers from Colorado and New Mexico. Overhead, classic rock tunes played, drowned out by the din of chatter, clanging pots and pans, and raucous laughter.

The place was packed, and the wait was thirty minutes. Belle and Holly went to the bar and ordered a couple of beers. After she took a sip from her mug, Belle looked around the restaurant. "This doesn't look much like a beer joint. When you told me were going to a beer and burger joint, I expected some hole in the wall." Belle laughed. "This is the fanciest burger joint I've ever been to."

"I know. The name gives you a different impression from the inside. This is a new place. Just opened three months ago. I heard the burgers are awesome."

Half an hour later, Belle and Holly were shown to their table. Holly ordered a simple cheeseburger, and Belle ordered one of the signature burgers made with cream cheese and sliced pickled jalapeños.

"Scorpion called me today, and he talked a lot about you. You know, I think my brother has the hots for you." Holly brought her beer to her lips.

"Isn't it weird for you to call your brother 'Scorpion' when he's been 'Craig' your whole life?"

"At first, it was, but he's been going by Scorpion for a long time now." She shrugged. "I guess I'm just used to it. Anyway, my brother can be a sweet guy. I know he comes off as being a badass, but he can be nice to the people he cares about. I know he really wants to get to know you better."

Belle wasn't sure what to say, so she took a slow, long pull on her beer as she formed her answer in her head. "I'm sure your brother is very nice." *Not. I think he's a real jerk.* "But I'm not interested in dating anyone right now. I have so much going on with work and my kids that I don't have any energy left over for anything else. The timing just isn't right."

Holly stared at Belle, making her feel uncomfortable. She fidgeted in her chair and pretended to be engrossed in reading the label on the beer bottle. "You know, you're going to have to get over trying to be Superwoman. There's nothing wrong with having some time to yourself and going out with a nice guy. My brother's really into you, and you could do worse, believe me."

"It's just not the right time." Belle was grateful that their food arrived at that moment, since it diverted her friend's attention.

The burgers were delicious, and Belle couldn't figure out what seasoning she tasted that made hers more than just a juicy hamburger. She wished she could go into the kitchen and ask the chef, but she'd bet he wouldn't divulge his secret. As they finished their meal, Belle had to order the raspberry velvet cheesecake sundae, because it just sounded so good. When the waitress placed it in front of her, she dug in, savoring the richness of cheesecake and vanilla ice cream with a burst of raspberry. Holly helped her with the last few bites.

"This meal was fantastic. I'm so glad we came here. I'm going to call Luke's and Chelsea's parents just to check in and make sure the kids are okay."

Belle spoke briefly to both sets of parents, happy that everything was going all right. For the first time in a long time, she relaxed. She glanced around the restaurant, looking at the patrons and noticing many of them were coupled, a stab of loneliness gripping her momentarily. She missed the intimacy and fun of being a couple.

"I'll be right back. I'm going to the ladies' room," said Holly. "Don't let them take away the dessert. I'm not done with it yet." She smiled and left the table.

While Belle waited for Holly to return, the waiter brought over a strawberry margarita, and before she could say anything, he said, "Compliments of the gentleman at the bar."

Belle slowly turned around and her eyes met Banger's. Her pulse raced as a wide grin spread across her face. He tipped his beer bottle to her, smiled, and winked at her. Nodding, she raised her glass to him. *Damn, he's hot in his denim and leather.* He exuded danger—that sense of the feral barely concealed below the surface. His impossibly handsome face, lean and muscular physique, and blond hair pulled back in a ponytail gave her a rush that went straight between her legs. The silver arrow earring dangling from his ear shimmered under the lights. For a split second, she yearned to go over to him, lean close, and lick his earlobe, and feel the earring hit against her chin. They held each other's gazes, and the connection she felt when she looked at him was stronger than ever. The current that ran between them was like a live wire, electrifying her skin. It was like they were the only two people in the restaurant, his stare boring into her, and her body tingling and misbehaving.

"The bathroom is so cool. The stall doors and walls are bronze and copper. An awesome effect. I've never seen anything like it." Holly flopped down in her chair and motioned the waiter over.

Belle broke the stare between her and Banger, turning her head and focusing on what Holly was saying. As Holly continued to gush about the bathroom, Belle tuned her out. She could feel Banger's eyes on her, and the thrill of knowing he was watching her made her tremble. When the waiter came over, Holly ordered another drink and Belle scooted her chair back, saying, "I've got to see this bathroom you keep talking about. I'll be right back." She stood up and glanced at the bar, disappointment setting in when she saw Banger was gone, and his seat was taken by a young man who had his girlfriend on his lap.

After checking out the bronze and copper décor of the ladies' room, she reapplied her lipstick and exited. As she walked back to her table, an arm looped around her waist. "You look pretty tonight," a gravelly voice said next to her ear.

Recognizing Banger's voice, Belle placed her hand on top of his, smiled, and half-turned, her eyes latching onto his. "Thanks for the drink. Are you here alone?" The minute she asked the question, she regretted it. She didn't want him to think she cared as much as she did.

His low chuckle washed over her. "Yeah, I'm here alone. Here with your best friend?"

She bobbed her head up and down. He pulled her closer against him, tightening his arms around her waist, and she loved the feel of him, and his crisp, fresh scent. But people kept bumping into them, since they were standing at the entrance to the hallway leading to the bathrooms.

"I think we're in the way." She laughed. "You want to join us?"

"Lead the way."

When they arrived at the table, Belle saw Holly's surprised look, and she also noticed how her friend raked her eyes over Banger. Belle's muscles tightened, and she possessively placed her hands around his bicep. Smiling, he turned his head and kissed her cheek. He pulled her chair out, and Belle sat down then gestured the waiter for another round of drinks.

"Who is this deliciously handsome man?" Holly said as she touched Banger's forearm.

"The name's Banger." His lips curled in a half-smile.

The waiter placed the drinks in front of the trio. Holly lifted her beer to her lips, opening them wide and closing them tightly around the bottle, moving it up and down. She took a gulp, then smiled at Banger and said, "You must be good at banging, right? Is that how you got your name?"

Belle couldn't believe how her friend was blatantly flirting with Banger. She wasn't normally the jealous type, but she was ready to grab her friend by the hair and give her a good shake. She knew Holly was a flirt, so why was it bothering her so much this time? Part of it was that Holly was always giving her shit about what an asshole Harold had been for cheating on her, but it also was because Holly knew Banger was with Belle, and she didn't seem to care about that. Belle couldn't believe it.

Shaking his head, Banger pulled his arm away from Holly's touch and placed his hand over Belle's, giving her his full attention. Belle smiled at him, and from the corner of her eyes, she noticed Holly looked somewhat pissed. When Banger placed his hand on Belle's neck and drew her closer to him, Holly coughed loudly as if to distract him. Not missing a beat, he crushed his lips on Belle's, and a single shiver went from her head to her pulsing sex.

"Excuse me, I'm choking here," Holly said in an irritated voice.

Belle pulled back and looked at Holly. "What's wrong?"

"Just that I couldn't get my breath. It would've been nice if you would've at least pretended like you care."

Belle opened her mouth to answer, but Banger said, "You look fine to me. If you were choking for real, you'd be blue in the face and down on the floor 'bout now." He turned his attention back to Belle.

Holly's eyes narrowed as she covered her mouth with her hand, and Belle bit her inner cheek to keep from laughing. Her friend's childish attempt for attention pissed her off. She had no idea why Holly was acting like this. Maybe she and Darren weren't getting along as well as she pretended they were, or maybe she was mad because Belle wasn't interested in her brother. The reason didn't really matter; Holly knew Banger was interested in Belle, and she was trying to thwart it. The fact that Banger did not flirt back with her friend, simply kept his focus on her, raised him up several notches in Belle's eyes.

The restaurant began to close, and Belle wished the night would go on forever. She had such a great time, and bumping into Banger unexpectedly made her evening extra special. She hated to admit it, but she liked him a lot. She wasn't sure if it was the alcohol, but she wanted to get to know him a whole lot better.

Outside, the frosty air pinched their faces, and the wind murmured as the snow fell like confetti to the ground. Under the bright street lights, snowflakes glittered as the swirl of white curled around them.

Belle pulled her coat tighter around her. "Brr… It's cold out."

Banger put his arm around her, drawing her to him. "I'll warm you up." He kissed her cheek, and her stomach did a flip-flop. She wanted to be with him, and she didn't care about how she'd feel the next day—all that mattered was the moment. She snuggled closer to him.

"I'm taking Belle home," Banger said.

Holly snorted. "You're being pretty presumptuous, aren't you?"

"Don't think I am." He looked at Belle. "Am I?"

She shook her head and glanced at Holly. "I'll call you tomorrow. Drive safely."

Banger led Belle to his SUV, and she waved to Holly, who stood staring at the couple. From the way Holly's lips were pressed together, Belle knew she was angry, but she didn't know why her friend cared if she went home with Banger. After all, wasn't Holly the one who was always telling her she should meet somebody? Belle refused to feel guilty; Holly was a grown woman, and she'd just have to deal with it.

Belle sat in the car with the heat going full blast while Banger cleaned the snow off his car. Nervous excitement weaved through her. She had the house to herself for the first time in years. Should she invite him in? She'd been stressed for so long, and she'd had such a long week, she deserved to get laid. She assumed Banger was only looking for fun, but at least he was nice and made her feel like she was the only woman in the room whenever he was around.

Frigid air filled the car when Banger opened the door and slid into the driver's seat. He took off his black gloves, leaned over, and pulled her to him. He brushed his lips against hers, gently licking the seam. She parted them, and he sucked her upper lip between his while he threaded his fingers through her hair. She moaned, her hand around his neck drawing him closer to her. He released her upper lip then lightly licked both before he captured her lower lip between his. Butterflies fluttered in her stomach, and her heart warmed with each stroke of his tongue.

Pulled into the moment, she dipped her tongue into his mouth, curling it around his while he squeezed her thigh.

"That's it, baby. Fuck, you taste and feel so good," he muttered, holding her face close to his while he rubbed his nose against hers.

"I love the way you kiss me," Belle whispered.

He groaned then plunged his tongue into her warm and willing mouth, running circles with hers as she did the same. Their seductive dance left her breathless and lightheaded before she pulled away, nestling her head in the crook of his neck. He felt his way around her body as he pulled her coat open. She gasped as his hand on her stockinged thigh lit a flame between her legs.

"Are your panties wet?" he rasped, his voice sending electric waves through her.

"Real wet." She looked up at him, slowly running her tongue across her lips.

He sucked in his breath. "Fuck."

"Let's go to my place for a nightcap." A smile pulled at the corners of her mouth.

Banger squeezed her inner thigh, then captured her mouth with his. He kissed her hard and deep while he swallowed her whimpers of pleasure. Drawing back, he gazed at her, his blue eyes dark with lust. A single jolt of intense desire skated up her spine.

"Let's go, beautiful."

As he drove toward her house, she rested her head against his shoulder, knowing that once he entered her home, she would be forever changed.

# Chapter Eight

Belle led Banger into the small living room, gesturing for him to sit on the couch. He placed his jacket on the couch's arm and plopped down. She turned on the gas fireplace, trying to quell her twitchy muscles. What was she thinking by asking him over? She hadn't been with another man in years. Shuddering, she willed herself to take deep, calm breaths.

"Need some help?" he asked in a low voice that spread goose bumps over her arms.

Looking over her shoulder, she caught his mischievous grin, which made her giddy with desire. "I'm good." She pushed up, grasping the mantel for support. "I'll get you a beer." She shuffled to the kitchen then grabbed onto the countertop, trying to calm her erratically beating heart. *You can do this, Belle. He's obviously interested, so don't let your self-doubt ruin it.*

She'd put on a few pounds over the past few years, but she wasn't obsessed about it like Holly was whenever she'd gained a couple. Belle always struggled with her weight, and when she'd married Harold, she'd come to accept her natural curves and shape of her body. But at the moment, she was insecure because Banger was so good-looking and fit. What if he found her soft flesh a turn-off? Clothes could be deceiving, and girdles did wonders on hiding some of the fleshiness of her size fourteen body. What possessed her to invite him in? She wasn't ready for—

"You comin' back?" Banger's voice interrupted her thoughts. Taking a deep breath, she hurriedly grabbed a couple of bottles of beer and walked into the living room.

"Here you go," she said as she handed him one.

He took it, then grasped her hand and pulled her down on top of him, his arms wrapping tightly around her when she landed on his lap. "Love the way you feel in my arms," he said as he gripped her hips.

"Do you?" The tip of her tongue peeked out between her teeth.

A low growl rumbled from his throat, and he pushed her face toward his then darted his tongue out, licking the tip of hers. "Fuck, babe, you make me all kinds of crazy." His hand moved to her ass, and she nearly jumped out of her skin when he gave her fleshy cheek a hard squeeze. "I like *this*." He nibbled at her lower lip, teasing at it, tugging it between his teeth.

She moaned softly and wiggled in his lap, her cheeks becoming crimson when she felt something hard forcing its way up. Placing his fingers under her chin, he turned her face toward his, winked, and said huskily, "See what you do to me? My head is filled with nasty ideas about the things I want to do to you."

Belle swallowed hard, unable to speak. She hadn't been with a man for over a year, and her need was bubbling beneath the surface. Her body flushed with heat as she pulled away then settled herself close to him as she curled her feet under her. Reaching over to the coffee table, she grabbed her beer, welcoming the cold liquid as it slid down her throat, cooling her heated body.

"I was surprised to see you at the restaurant tonight." She had to steer the conversation away from sex. She needed a few more beers in her to still her nerves.

A wide grin spread across his rosy face as he playfully tweaked her nose. "You wanna take it down a few notches? That's cool. The Insurgents own the burger joint."

"For real? I didn't think a motorcycle club would have such a nice restaurant." She placed her hand on his thigh.

He glanced at her hand, then his gaze slowly rose up to her face. "We're a classy bunch of guys." He laughed and kissed her lightly on the lips. "We own the whole fuckin' strip mall. It was built this past summer."

"That's so interesting. I know you have a strip club and a tattoo parlor. I mean, all motorcycle clubs have them, right? Aren't those the standard things a club owns? Everyone knows bikers love to watch women strip and they love tattoos, so the two go together. I never thought a club would own a sleek restaurant like the burger one, and a whole strip mall. Who would've thought it?" She knew she was rambling, but she couldn't stop. The way his eyes pulled her in was dangerously sexy.

"We got a strip bar and an ink shop," he said with a bemused smile on his face.

After she took a sip of beer, he went in for a kiss, and she welcomed the exploring swirls of his tongue. Pressing into him, her breasts rubbed against his chest, her nipples pulsing with desire. She moved back and forth, pushing them against him as tingles of pleasure zinged down between her legs.

His baritone chuckle set her on fire. "Let me help you with that," he said as he pinched her aching buds. He captured her moan of pleasure in his mouth, and her whole body was a live wire. She wanted to have sex with him. Now.

Pushing him away, she gripped his hand then stood up, taking him with her. "Let's go upstairs," she whispered.

When they were in her room, she led him to her queen-sized bed. He pulled her close and buried his face in the space between her ear and neck, his beard scratching her. Nibbling her soft skin, he murmured against it, "You're so fuckin' soft and beautiful." His warm breath tickled her skin.

His hands roamed over her hips then landed on her thighs, slowly inching their way under her skirt until they landed on her pulsing mound. She squeezed her eyes shut as his fingers rubbed her wet clit through her panties, choking back her moan of sheer pleasure.

"You like that?" he rasped, placing her hand on his crotch. After she unzipped his jeans, his hardness punched out, and she stroked it—his skin was hot and soft. Low groans from his throat sent sparks through her, and she boldly squeezed his dick, running her thumb over his smooth head, the beads of pre-come coating her fingertip.

Banger cupped his hands under her ass and lifted her off the floor. "Oh!" she gasped. He laid her gently on the bed, then whipped off his T-shirt, revealing hard, tight muscles and a flat, tapered waist. She gaped at him; she'd never seen a body like his up close and personal. Her mouth watered—he was delicious-looking. He took off his boots, and when he pulled his jeans off, the corded muscles in his legs flexed, and the swell of his firm ass cheeks lit a raging fire in her. He was magnificent, and he was all hers for the night.

Smiling, his blue eyes dark with hunger, he lay next to her on his side, propped up on his elbow. With his fingertip, he lightly traced her jawline, moving down her neck and arms, goose bumps rising with each stroke. In spite of the heat raging inside her, she shivered. When he came to the bottom of her shirt, he tugged it up, the palm of his cool hand refreshing against her heated skin. "Take this off. I wanna see your tits."

Belle's stomach did a somersault. Slowly, she pushed her top up and over her head, revealing her breasts contained in a black lace bra. Banger whistled softly, his eyes fixed on her creamy, rounded swells. She blushed, instinctively crossing her arms over them. Sucking in his breath, he gently unfolded her arms then bent down and kissed each breast. A deep shiver ran from her nipples to her throbbing mound.

"Fuck, I figured they'd be beautiful, but not like this." He licked his lips and dipped his tongue between her tits while his hands massaged them, pinching the beaded nipples.

"Feels so good," she breathed as he played with her swollen breasts.

He unfastened her bra, grunting as they spilled out against his chest. Burying his face in them, he muttered, "Fuckin' love your tits, babe."

Belle sighed, embarrassment creeping over her. Harold had never been very vocal during lovemaking, and he certainly never said words like "tits" or "fuck." She didn't know what to say when Banger said those things, and what surprised her was that she was getting turned on by his dirty talk.

"Let's take your skirt off so I can see your pussy shining through your panties."

"Pussy" made her body pulse like crazy. Each filthy word he uttered, each stroke, each kiss made her putty in his hands. The way her body was burning and humming, she'd do anything he wanted. Kicking off her boots, she slid her skirt down, her sheer black panties barely covering her sex.

"Beautiful." He cupped her wetness then slipped his hand inside her panties, burying his fingers between her swollen folds.

*Holy fuck!* The way Banger rubbed his fingers between her throbbing lips, just brushing her clit, drove her wild. She arched her back, grinding her mound against his hand. *I'm acting like a slut, but I can't help it. I'm on fire. I need him to touch me* there.

Banger withdrew his hand, and disappointment spread over her. With one hard tug, he rid her of her panties. She lay naked before his probing gaze, and she suddenly felt shame. Grabbing the sheet, she pulled it over her then reached next to her to turn off the light. He captured her hand, preventing her from switching off the lamp.

"Why you covering up? I don't fuck in the dark. I want to watch you come as I fuck you." He lifted her chin up. "What the hell, beautiful?"

Belle turned her head to get away from his probing stare. "I'm used to doing it in the dark."

"That's real sad to hear. Tonight, that's gonna change."

She shifted, pulling the sheet tighter around her. "Okay, but we'll do it under the sheets."

"What the hell? You expect me to fuck you without seeing your beautiful body? No goddamned way."

She bit the inside of her cheek, then caught his gaze. "I'm a little overweight. It's been real stressful for the last few years, and I let myself go. I used to be a perfect size eight, but—"

His mouth on hers silenced her while his hand caressed her cheek.

He shifted, hovering over her, his eyes locking with hers. "You can't be serious. Don't you know you're fuckin' gorgeous?"

She shrugged.

"Baby, I think you have a sexy, beautiful body that I can't wait to taste and touch. So take the fuckin' sheet away so I can see it." He tore the green floral sheet away from her, then smashed his lips on hers, kissing her deep and hot. Her discomfort melted away with each plunge of his tongue in her mouth, and she craved him with a hunger that was insatiable, a passion that burned hotter than fire.

He moved his mouth, bestowing feathery kisses over her face before slowly trailing his lips over her ears, taking her earlobe between his teeth and sucking it. Tingles skated across her body as each lick from his delicious tongue made her nerves explode. He brushed his hand over her skin, nibbling her neck and shoulders, whispering, "You're so soft and beautiful. Each time I look at you or touch you, I'm so damn turned on." She squirmed under his touch, his firm hands snaking up her belly as he stippled fiery kisses on her sensitive skin.

*What in God's name is he doing to me? I'm ready to come just from his touch. Oh, fuck!* Belle pulled out his leather tie and dug her hands into his thick hair. It felt amazing, like sinking her hands in soft, lush fur. Everything about him threw her body in overdrive.

When his trail of kisses and nips hit her inner thighs, Belle was a quivering mess. She skimmed her fingertips across his shoulders. "You're so sexy."

He raised his head, his desire-filled eyes locking with hers. Sticking out his tongue, he dipped his head between her legs then traced light, wet circles on her inner thighs, his gaze never leaving hers. With a painfully slow pace, he inched his tongue toward the aching heat between her legs, while his fingers pushed open her lips, revealing her slick, dusty-rose folds.

"I like that you're wet for me. Can't wait to taste you."

Belle held her breath as she watched Banger's tongue glide over her pussy. With his elbows planted at shoulder width, her lips open and exposed, his eyes staring into hers, he swiped his tongue in one long and slow lick from her sensitive opening to her clit. Her body jumped as though it had received an electric shock. Up and down, he used slow, steady rhythmic licks, and with each stroke, he growled. "Fuck, you taste good." The reverberations from his deep voice against her sensitive sex, and the way he was enjoying eating her out, drove her wild. Grabbing his hair, she tugged at it. "You're driving me crazy. It feels too good. I want you inside me."

"I'm getting there, but I want to taste you some more. Let me see you play with your tits while I eat you."

Aroused beyond belief, Belle cupped her breasts and squeezed them, the tip of her index finger flicking across her reddened bead.

"Fuckin' hot," Banger breathed as he slipped his finger into her.

While she played with her breasts, she watched as he pulled his finger in and out of her while steadily stroking her clit. When he blew across her glistening pussy, it spasmed with excitement, making her scream, "Fuck, it feels so good!" And when his steady strokes on her sweet spot intensified, she moaned, "Yes, right there. Don't stop."

When he curled his finger inside her, stroking her G-spot as his tongue worked her clit, her orgasm ripped through her with such force that it took her breath away. The raw, primal scream she emitted startled her, as well as the clawing on Banger's shoulders. Total ecstasy spread over her, and as she began to catch her breath, his lips on hers made her feel wanted.

"Damn, that was epic," she panted.

"You ain't seen nothing yet." Banger sucked on her rigid nipples then trailed his mouth to her belly button, licking around it. Putting his arms under her legs, he raised them as he positioned himself between them. He pushed them further up toward her shoulders until her back was curved and her glistening pussy was fully exposed.

"I'm gonna fuck you like you've never been fucked. You like it hard?"

Still regaining her breath, Belle nodded. Banger shoved two fingers inside her as he leaned over and sucked her tits again. His digits were stretching and twisting inside her heated wetness, and she whimpered in pleasure.

"You like that? Your cunt likes being full. Wait 'til my cock gets in there."

She bucked her hips toward him as he grabbed a condom from the back pocket of his jeans crumpled next to him, and deftly rolled it on. He slid his wet fingers from her heat and placed them in his mouth, sucking on the juice that covered them. Then he leaned over and kissed her deep so she tasted herself on his tongue.

"I promise it will be so good," he whispered in her ear, before he pushed back on his heels. With his hands on her legs, he plunged his cock inside her hot depths. "Fuck." His voice was hoarse with lust.

He thrust in and out of her, each time harder, faster. She gasped from the sweet agony while she ground her hips hotly against him, taking every inch of his pulsing cock deep in her. "Oh, Banger. Damnit!"

"You feel fuckin' amazing," he grunted as he slammed into her, his hips meeting hers.

She watched as he pulled in and out of her, stretching her wider, his dick gleaming with her juices. Every inch of her body burned, like a giant torch was inside her. When his legs tightened, she knew he was ready to come. She let herself go, her orgasm washing over her in searing waves of intense pleasure. Their grunts and moans filled the room, and the musky scent of their arousal surrounded them.

Banger collapsed on top of her, his panting sweet music to her ears. She stroked his back with one hand, while the other tightened around his waist. Tears rolled down the corners of her eyes. What they had shared had been so intense. More intense than anything she'd ever shared with her husband. *How can that be? I barely know Banger, yet I felt so connected with him, like our bodies were one.* He kissed her neck then her lips and rolled off her, drawing her close to his side. She pillowed her head on his chest and he lightly tickled her shoulder.

"You know how to fuck, babe." He kissed her head.

"You know a thing or two yourself." She giggled.

Pressing her closer, he leaned down and she tilted her head, meeting his mouth. They kissed and cuddled for a while before they fell asleep in each other's arms, her heart dancing like the snowflakes outside the window.

# Chapter Nine

THE HEADY AROMA of dark-roasted coffee woke Banger up the following morning. When he turned on his side, an empty spot greeted him. He rolled over again on his back, his arms crossed under his head, and smiled widely; he felt great. The night before had been the best fuck he'd had since Grace had died. He definitely wanted to see more of Belle and get to know her even better. She was wild, like she hadn't had sex since her old man died, which he couldn't believe. A sexy woman like her probably didn't go through much of a dry spell, but he'd like it a lot if he were her first post-marital fuck.

He lazily swung his legs to the side of the bed, pushed himself up, and went into the bathroom to get ready. After he was finished, he ambled down the stairs and went into the kitchen. Belle sat at the table reading the *Pinewood Springs Gazette* as she sipped a cup of coffee. He came up behind her, bent down, and nuzzled her neck. Her soft laugh, and the way she skimmed her fingers over his hands, ignited a fire in him. He slipped his hand down her neck, grazing her collarbone with his thumb, until his hand molded over her breast. When his callused finger pad glided across her nipple, she moaned and pushed her head back against him.

"Baby, I got a burn going on here," he rasped in her ear.

She squirmed in her chair and raised her arms, clasping them behind his neck, and tugged him down toward her. They fused their lips together while Banger's hands squeezed, pinched, and caressed her tits. He pivoted around to her side then dropped on his knees, his lips never leaving hers. A loud beep startled them, and she quickly broke their embrace.

"That's probably Ethan," she mumbled as she looked at her phone. "Yeah, that's him. He's wondering where I am. Wants to come home." She gave a half-shrug then stood from the chair.

"You gonna leave me like this?" He took her hand and plastered it on his crotch, loving the way her eyes widened and a sly smile formed on her lips.

"No choice. I gotta go."

"You gonna disappoint me?" Banger drew her closer to him, his face in her hair, breathing in her scent.

"You're a big boy—I know you can handle a bit of disappointment. But I have a little boy who's going to be crushed if I don't pick him up." She kissed him lightly on the cheek, patted his shoulder, and texted her son.

Catching her gaze, he said, "You're a good mama, and a fine woman." He gave her a warm hug. "What about you coming over to my place tonight after work?"

"No, that won't work. I have to be with my kids. Last night was my night off, and we had plans to watch a movie and have some popcorn."

"I'd like to meet your kids. I guess I'm asking for an invitation."

"It's too soon. I don't know how they would react. When we get to know each other better, then yes, I'd love for you to meet my kids." She placed her coffee cup in the sink. "And I'd like to meet Kylie someday. You want a quick cup of coffee before I leave?"

He stood in front of her, grabbing her arms and pinning her against the sink as his mouth crushed hers. "This is the only thing I want. Your kisses light me up. Fuck, woman. You do something to me, and it's something I fuckin' love."

She kissed him back, and they stood in the little kitchen lost in each other's embrace. Another beep. Belle gently pushed him back. "I have to go. I don't want to, but I have to."

"I don't mean to be keeping you from your son. It's just that you're so damn irresistible. I can't be in the same room with you without touching and kissing you. I better get out of here or neither of us is going anywhere. Here," he handed his phone to her, "put in your number." After she finished punching it in, she gave his phone back. He gave her one more kiss then walked to the front door. "I'll call you." He opened the door and walked out into the swirling snow, but he didn't notice the cold because he was still hot from Belle's kisses.

Banger drove to the clubhouse: he didn't feel like going to an empty house. When he entered the great room, he sauntered over to the pool table and asked Bear if he wanted to shoot a game. Bear nodded and took two cue sticks down while Banger racked the balls in the triangle. As they played, some of the brothers came over to watch and have a few beers. Jax wandered in and tilted his chin to Banger as he approached the pool table.

"Hey, how's it goin'?" Jax asked.

Banger, still on a high from being with Belle earlier, smiled. "Couldn't be better."

Bear raised his eyebrows. "You got something you wanna share?"

Bending down low as he gauged his shot, Banger shook his head. "Nope. Six ball in the left pocket." The cue stick hit the ball, and the group of members watched as it rolled into the left pocket.

"Fuckin' good shot." Jax gulped down his beer as Banger made the next one too.

Ten minutes later, Banger scooped up the money he won from Bear, who clapped him on the shoulder and said, "Good game."

As Banger put the money in his wallet, Jax asked, "I'm having a poker game at my house tonight. Who wants in?"

"Count me in," Banger said.

"Me too," Bear replied.

All in all, seven brothers told Jax they'd be at his house at six o'clock that evening. Banger told them he'd see them later that night, then he strode to his office to do some work.

★ ★ ★

THE BROTHERS SAT around the poker table in Jax's basement, smoking weed, guzzling beer, and shoving peanuts into their mouths. The basement was perfect for a good poker game: full bar, small kitchen, and a stash of weed that would last them a week. The blazing fire in the large, stone fireplace kept out the winter chill. When they were in the middle of their game, they heard the patter of footsteps on the stairway, and as Banger and several members looked toward it, Cherri and Paisley came into view. Cherri carried a large, steaming pot, and Paisley had two wrapped crackers in her chubby hand.

"I hope you guys are hungry," Cherri said as she set the pot of chili down on the table. "I'll go grab some bowls in the kitchen."

Paisley went over to Jax and handed him the crackers, then she placed her hands on his thigh. Jax swept her up in his arms, sitting her on his lap. She grinned at the rough bikers who sat around the table. Banger, seated next to Jax, ran his hand over her downy hair, saying, "You're a real cutie." Paisley's white-blonde hair, big blue eyes, and red, chubby cheeks reminded him of Kylie when she was the toddler's age. It tickled him every time he saw Paisley, and it also made him sad because those times with Kylie and Grace were over forever.

Cherri ladled out the chili into the bowls and set them in front of each of the brothers. She placed a basket full of crackers in the middle of the table along with several smaller bowls of onions, shredded cheese, and sour cream. "Enjoy." She smiled and bent over to pick up Paisley from Jax's lap. He put his hand behind Cherri's neck and kissed her deeply before she took Paisley and walked up the stairs.

An hour later, Banger took out his phone, noticing he didn't have any reception in the basement. "Count me out on this hand. I gotta go use the phone." When he came upstairs, he spotted Cherri lying on the couch with Paisley tucked in to her side, watching *My Little Pony* cartoons. For a moment, his mind flashed back to a rainy afternoon when he had just come back from a long ride. He'd walked into the family room and saw Grace lying on the couch with Kylie curled in her arms, watching a cartoon. When he saw them, he knew his life was complete. Little did he know that Kylie would lose her mother before she started high school, and he would lose his beloved wife before he hit forty. If he had known that, he would've cherished the moments even more than he did.

Paisley's shrill laughter brought him back to the present, and he softly walked to the laundry room and closed the door. He dialed Belle's number.

"Hey, there," he said when her cheerful voice caressed over him.

"Hi. What are you up to?" she asked.

"I'm at Jax's house with some of the brothers playing poker." He cleared his throat. "I was thinking 'bout you."

"That's nice." Her breathless laugh hit him in the dick. "I'm coated in flour from rolling out a bunch of pie crusts."

"Sounds like we could figure out something nasty to do with that." A pause then he heard her swallow. That got to her and he liked it. A lot. "Let me come by after you get off work."

"I'd like that, but remember I'm spending tonight with my kids. I'm going to leave as soon as I finish the pies."

"I'm sure your kids would understand if you got home a little late. You need some time for yourself."

"I took time for myself last night. Ethan has already picked out the movie. Anyway, I need to make sure Emily doesn't pull anything. I'm sorry."

"What about after they're asleep? I can come over and keep you company."

Her sigh whispered over the phone. "That won't be possible. I have to think of my kids."

"What about me? I need to be with you. Fuck, I got a hard-on just talking to you. I need you to take care of it."

"What? Are you serious?"

"Yeah, I am. I need you, Belle."

She didn't answer, and at first Banger thought he'd lost the connection, but then he heard her cluck her tongue. "I told you, it won't work. Either you understand or you don't. I have to get back to work."

Banger poked his tongue lightly into his cheeks and inhaled a long breath as the heat rose in his body. He wasn't used to women telling him no, and he didn't fucking like it one bit. He'd be damned if he was going to beg her like some lovesick asshole. *Fuck that.* "Don't sweat it. Call me when you want to hang. Gotta go."

"Are you mad at me because I'm spending time with my kids?"

"Nope." But he was, even though his gut told him he was being unreasonable. He needed Belle, and it pissed him off that she didn't seem to need him as much. *I should just move on and stick with the club whores and hoodrats. I don't need a woman with baggage. Fuck.*

"You sound mad. It's not that I don't want to be with you, it's just that my kids have to come first. You must understand that since you have a daughter."

"Said I wasn't mad. You better get back to your pies. Call me." He hung up, his face tight. He wanted nothing better than to put his hand through the laundry room wall. This was bullshit. Belle was a fucking good time in bed, and he should leave it like that. He didn't want the bullshit drama of her life. Hell, he didn't even know *what* he wanted. He still loved Grace, but Belle stirred something in him that both excited and scared him at the same time. He left the laundry room and headed downstairs to play a few more rounds of poker.

After they'd played their umpteenth hand, Banger stood up and called it a night. The others agreed, and they walked out into the frigid night air. As the icy cold slapped his face, Banger cursed. He hated the snowy weather because he couldn't ride his bike and had to take the cage. Of course, there were the crazy bikers who took chances on the ice and snow with their Harleys, but they were mostly the young ones. He remembered being stupid like that when he was young, but when Kylie had been born, he'd changed his reckless, impulsive lifestyle. Having her in his life made him think differently; he had to be smart and stay safe for her.

When he arrived at his house, he lit a fire then grabbed a beer from the fridge. Throwing his leather jacket on the couch, he switched on his

CD player and flopped in the overstuffed chair in front of the fireplace. The haunting strains of Buffalo Springfield's "For What It's Worth" filled the room. The blaze of the fire softly lit the pictures of Grace which adorned the walls, the fireplace mantel, and the bookcases. A few framed photos of Banger, Grace, and Kylie at Sturgis and on family trips caught Banger's eyes, bringing back a flood of memories.

A piercing memory of the last six months of his wife's life squeezed his heart as he remembered the slow death that had robbed him of her a little each day. He recalled when she'd held his strong hand in her weak and pale one and had told him that, when she died, she didn't want him to sit around and mope.

"You're young, sexy, and virile, and you deserve to love again, even if you can be a pain in the ass sometimes." Her voice echoed in his mind, bringing a smile to his lips. "Find a woman to love again. I don't want you chasing the club or party girls every weekend. I'll haunt your ass if you do." She laughed then broke into a coughing fit.

"Don't talk about this shit, sweetheart. You're not going anywhere."

Her blue eyes misted as she brought his hand to her colorless lips, kissing it. "Promise me that you'll find another woman and marry again. I don't want you alone."

"I got Kylie. No more of this shit, woman."

"Promise. Please." Her eyes pleaded with him, and he hung his head. Grudgingly, he agreed, but he'd never wanted to admit that his wife was going to die.

When she died, the last thing on his mind was meeting another woman and loving her. Banger's loss was great, his desire to plug the hole in his heart intense, and it felt good to have someone by his side again, even if it were only for a few hours each night. So he lost himself in mindless pussy, and the younger the woman, the more likely nothing would come out of it. He did the opposite of what he'd promised Grace.

And now, he'd met Belle, who was beautiful, sexy, and complicated, but being in his home surrounded by memories, he realized he still loved Grace. Belle stirred something in him, but it was lust, not love. He didn't think he could care for Belle in that way; it would be as though he were betraying Grace, minimizing what they'd had. But damn, he wanted to see the pretty, curvy cook again. She was a great bed warmer, and it beat the club women.

As the lilting guitar riffs from Pink Floyd's "Wish You Were Here" played, Banger lifted his glass to one of his favorite pictures of Grace—leaning against his Harley with rosy cheeks, a warm smile, and a mischievous twinkle in her eyes. A deep feeling of sadness washed over him. "Love you, Gracie," he said, then took a long pull on his beer, his eyes never leaving her picture.

# Chapter Ten

Jessica Dermot Hoskins sighed loudly as she punched in the prompts from the Lakeview Police Department. She was a few years younger than her stepmother, Belle Dermot, and she resented her from the moment her dad had brought her into the home. How her father could've married someone that young was something she would never understand. Belle had tried to be a friend to her, but Jessica couldn't stand the woman, so she spent as little time in the house as possible. Jessica had been married for ten years, with two young boys who had rarely seen their grandfather. The last thing Jessica wanted to do was bring her kids around Belle. She'd told her father many times if he wanted to see his grandkids he had to make the effort to come to her house or meet them somewhere.

He did it the first few years, but then the visits became more infrequent, until she rarely saw her father. He called her for her birthday, and of course there was always a standing invitation for Thanksgiving and Christmas, but she never went. Sometimes her father would give her money when she told him that she and her husband, Bert, were in a bad way. He never expected her to pay it back, and she was grateful for that. She had expected to inherit quite a nice sum of money when her father had passed away, and was outraged when there was no money left. She blamed Belle one hundred percent for squandering her father's money.

"Lakeview Police Department, how may I help you?" a gruff voice asked.

"I need to talk to someone in homicide," Jessica replied.

"Homicide? Are you in any danger?"

"No. I want to talk to somebody about a possible homicide. My dad died under mysterious circumstances. I need to talk to a detective."

"I'll patch you through to Detective Sanders."

Jessica filed her nails as she waited for the detective to pick up the phone.

"Detective Sanders, how can I help you?" a deep, raspy voice asked.

"Hi. My name is Jessica Dermot Hoskins, and my father was Harold Dermot. He died over a year ago, but I found something very unusual in the storage unit that he and my stepmother had."

"You say your dad died over a year ago? Was his death ruled natural?"

"Yes, but what I found in the storage unit made me wonder about his death. I always had a nagging suspicion that things weren't the way they seemed. My dad was sixty-one years old, and even though he suffered from diabetes, he was still a strong, healthy man. He was fine one day, and the next he died. It never sat well with me or my brother."

"Did you tell the police your suspicions at the time of his death?"

"No. I wanted to, but my brother told me not to. He didn't want to rock the boat, and when he saw how upset our stepmother was, he told me to leave it alone."

"Okay. What was this thing you found in the storage unit?"

"A syringe, but not the type my dad used for his insulin shots. It's a different one. I've never seen anything like it before, and it was wrapped in plastic and hidden in one of the boxes inside a small purse that I'm sure belongs to my stepmother. I want it to be tested. I was gonna send it to the lab myself, but I thought I should call the police and see if they wanted to look at it."

"How do you know your stepmom put it there?"

"She had to. The only one who has access to the storage unit besides me and my brother is my stepmother. She moved all my dad's stuff and she didn't want us to help at all. It was found among the boxes she moved from his house, ones full of books and papers. It's like she was trying to hide it, you know?"

"Well, what you're telling me is anybody could have planted it there, even you. Do you have anything else to go on besides this syringe you found and your own opinion?"

"No, but I know she was somehow involved in my dad's death. I don't believe for one minute that he died of natural causes. And she squandered all his money. She probably killed him thinking he had a large insurance policy. He had one, but he cashed it out without her knowledge."

"How much was the policy for?"

"Two million."

"Did your dad have any other insurance policies?"

"He had one where my brother and I were the beneficiaries. The policy was for one million."

"You got that much money when your dad died?"

"No," she whispered. "He cashed that one out too."

Jessica held her breath as she heard the detective's fingers clacking on the keyboard. She hoped he would look into her father's death because she knew something wasn't right. She'd always known.

"Well, I need to get the syringe from you so we can take a look at it, see what comes up. Of course, I have to run it by my superior. If he says to go for it, I'll go see your stepmother and ask some questions. But as it stands now, your dad's death was ruled as natural causes. It will take a hell of a lot more than a syringe to open up a murder investigation on his death. Now, I need to get some particulars from you and more information...."

Half an hour later, Jessica opened a can of Diet Coke and took a large gulp, the cold stream of liquid soothing her throat. She stared out the kitchen window and saw her two boys playing with the dog in the backyard. She narrowed her eyes, and ice ran through her veins. The bitch would get what she deserved. Jessica had been screwed out of her inheritance, and she wasn't too happy about it. She had a strong suspicion Belle knew exactly where the money was that everyone said her father had embezzled from the company, and Jessica would pry it out of the bitch. She'd make sure she and her family received the money they were entitled to. Belle Dermot wouldn't get away with a damn thing, she'd make sure of that.

★ ★ ★

DETECTIVE SANDERS SCRATCHED his head as he left Chief Garcia's office. He thought it was a long shot looking into the death of Harold Dermot. After all, his death certificate indicated he'd died from a heart attack. Sighing, he sat down and plugged Belle Dermot's name into the search engine. A smiling blue-eyed, dark-haired woman popped up, and he took note that she now lived in Pinewood Springs. He'd pay her a visit, just to see if he could read anything between the lines. He wasn't sure what Jessica's angle was. Her dislike of her stepmother came over the phone loud and clear and being a seasoned detective, he knew not to believe what people told him.

He had been to Pinewood Springs several years before, and knew it would be a pleasant drive over there, if it didn't snow like hell. Printing out Belle's picture, he placed it in a file he had started and made a note to himself to contact her within the next few weeks.

He'd meet Jessica over at the storage unit to retrieve this syringe, then he'd make out a lab report and send it off. Detective Sanders wasn't too sure if anything would come out of this, but his instinct told him something was amiss. He would just have to wait for things to play out. But he was very curious to see what the widow would have to say to him when he paid her a visit.

# Chapter Eleven

"Are you going out with that guy who bought us drinks on Friday night?" Holly asked as she stirred her coffee.

"I think so," Belle said.

"What does that mean?"

"We've hooked up a couple of times, and he keeps coming in here. He's asked me out for dinner. I slept with him. Hell, I don't know what that is. I was married for fifteen years. I don't know what I'm doing."

"Hey, back up. You had *sex* with him? For you, that's huge."

Belle groaned. "I know, but it felt so right. I wanted to be with him. *I'm* the one who initiated it. He probably thinks I'm a slut." She wiped her hands on the pink apron around her waist. "But the man knows how to please a woman. Hot damn." Giggling, she covered her mouth with her hands as wisps of red streaked her face.

"That good?" Holly asked, her eyebrow raised.

Belle bobbed her head up and down, curly tendrils of hair bouncing around her face.

"When you're finished with him, I'll have to try him out."

Belle's stomach twisted as she recalled how her friend had blatantly flirted with Banger at the burger restaurant. "Aren't things going well with Darren?"

"Things are fine with us, but he works long hours, and he can't satisfy my needs all the time. Having something on the side would be perfect."

"Are you serious? Darren adores you. You can't do that to him. Talk to him about what's bothering you. Anyway, Banger is off-limits." Belle gave her friend a hard stare.

Holly busted out laughing. "Damn, you can be so provincial sometimes. I was only joking, although I have to admit your guy looks real good. Holy shit. Is there anything on him but hard muscle?"

"Sometimes, you're too crazy. And the man is pure muscle. So sexy...."

"He looks like a biker."

"He is. He rides a Harley and he's president of the Insurgents MC."

Holly paled. "He's the *president* of the club? Fuck, his club and my brother's are rivals. We definitely don't want the two of them bumping into each other. Make sure you don't tell either one that you know the other."

"That seems silly."

"That's the way it works with one-percenters. My brother is a Deadly Demon, and the Demons and Insurgents were at war for years."

"War?"

"Yeah, just like in Iraq and shit. Like bombing each other's clubhouses and torturing and killing each other. It was a war between them for a long time."

A knot formed in the pit of her stomach as Holly spoke. She couldn't believe what her friend was telling her. The man she knew couldn't be capable of such things, could he? He seemed easygoing and cheerful. She'd seen hardness in his eyes, but she just figured he didn't like being pushed around, and since he was president, he was used to being in control and having people listen to him.

"Belle, are you listening to me?" Holly's stern voice pulled Belle out of her thoughts.

"Yes. I was just thinking about what you're saying. Are they still in a war?" It sounded so alien for her to ask the question. People didn't really live like that, did they?

"No, they called a truce and it's been relatively calm. The Insurgents control Colorado and the Deadly Demons have New Mexico. The Insurgents lucked out when Colorado legalized marijuana. They're making a shitload of money, and it's all done legally. My brother is always broke, and the Demons are always on the lookout to make more money."

"How does your brother's club make money?"

Holly shrugged. "It's club business, so no one's talking."

"I can relate to not having enough money. It's been such a struggle since Harold died."

"It sucks that he squandered everything."

"I couldn't believe it. He always told me that the kids and I would be taken care of. He cashed out his life insurance policy six months before he died. All I was left with were mountains of bills, but you know all that, I don't want to rehash it. I just can't believe how he changed in the months before his death. His company was his life, and to embezzle from it and run it into the ground was so not like Harold. I guess the woman he'd fallen for cast some kind of spell over him. Some men just do not handle aging very well."

"He was a dirtbag. You deserved better. Leaving you penniless was wrong."

"I hold onto the thought that he would have straightened it all out if he hadn't died. You know, he didn't think he was going to die." Belle broke up the napkin she had in her hands into tiny pieces. "I didn't think he was going to die either. I know that sounds stupid, because he wasn't in the best health, but I pictured him living another twenty years. When I found out he'd cheated on me, I was devastated." Her breath hitched and her eyes glistened.

Holly patted her friend's hand. "Don't go there. It's been over a year and a half. You gave him everything, and he did that shit to you? The bastard got what he deserved. He spared you the humiliation of being a cliché—older wife gets left for a younger model. You need to forget him."

"When I found out about Harold screwing around behind my back with his secretary, I felt like someone had hit me in the head with an axe. Everything I believed to be true was suddenly called into question." Belle leaned back and stared out at the sun's rays bouncing off the pristine snow. "I always thought we had a good marriage. We didn't have sex very much, especially the year before he died, but I figured he just wasn't in the best health and worked too much. He had a lot on his mind. Little did I know he was getting it from some home-wrecking bitch."

"I'm telling you that he didn't deserve you. You have to put this behind you."

"I do, most of the time, but this thing with Banger has stirred up all kinds of insecurities. I mean, I've survived, but I'm very guarded. I guess I'm jaded. I think men are jerks looking to have a good time until they get bored, then they'll go on to the next woman. I no longer believe that love is forever, and I realize that things may not work out, no matter how good they seem to be."

"Men can fucking suck. That's why you gotta live for the moment. If you see a hot guy and want to screw, go for it. I mean, Darren and I love each other, but sometimes it's not enough. All that Cinderella shit we had forced down our throats growing up just made us open to a bunch of hurt when we hooked up with men. Look at you. You thought Harold was your Prince Charming, and he screwed you big time. Rose-colored glasses are fucked."

Belle giggled. "You're even more jaded than I am. Harold was never my Prince Charming, but I thought we had mutual love and respect for each other. Hell, we raised two kids together and shared the same bed for fifteen years. You'd think loyalty would've come into play at some point, or communication." She sighed and looked at the wall clock. "It doesn't fucking make any difference now. I better get back to work. My break was over like ten minutes ago."

Belle slid out of the booth and smoothed down her uniform then retied her pink apron with lime green polka dots. The apron always made her smile because it reminded her of a slice of watermelon on a lazy, summer afternoon. Whenever it was freezing out, she'd take out her "summer" apron and wear it, and it would lift her mood immediately. Belle collected aprons—five trunks full of them attested to her obsession.

As she walked away from the table, Holly asked, "So, you going out with the sexy president again?"

Banger's smiling blue eyes with the fine lines around them flashed in her mind. "Probably. Talk to you later." She walked back to the kitchen to start making the dinner specials: tamale pie and chicken breast casserole with stuffing.

As she worked, she grappled with the idea of Banger; she liked him a lot, maybe too much. What she loved was that, when they were together, she wasn't a mom or a widow. She was Belle, a woman who was having a good time during a small slice of her hectic life. All the crap with Emily made her so anxious and sad because, above everything else, she wanted the best for her and Ethan, but her daughter didn't believe it. She didn't know how to reach Emily; it was as though the two of them were in a vacuum being sucked away from each other in opposite directions. How she wanted her little girl back, the one who'd hug her, who wanted to spend time with her. How had things gone so bad between them?

Since Banger had slipped into her life, he was the only thing that made all the stress tolerable. She shook her head. *Crazy.*

When the clock struck six, Belle hurriedly gathered her purse and coat. She took her phone out of her purse and glanced at it to see if she'd received any calls she hadn't heard. Nothing. More specifically, there weren't any calls from Banger. She hadn't heard from him since he'd called her and tried to coax her to go out with him after work. It wasn't that she didn't want to—she simply couldn't. She'd promised Ethan and Emily they would spend time together and watch a movie. He'd seemed pissed when he hung up the phone, but he didn't understand how hard it was with the kids. She couldn't just leave them and go off with him like they didn't exist.

She put on her gloves and trudged to her car, the snow crunching under her feet. Maybe he would call. If he didn't, she'd text him the following day. She slid in the driver's seat and drove slowly home. When she pulled into the driveway, she noticed her daughter's bedroom was dark. Belle's chest tightened and her pulse raced as she walked through the back door into the kitchen. She saw the flickering lights in the living room, and knew Ethan was sitting transfixed in front of the TV, playing his video games.

"Is your sister home?" Belle called out.

"Nah," her son replied.

She took out her cell phone and dialed her daughter's number. No answer. She sent a text asking Emily to let her know that she was okay and what time she'd be home. Nothing. Rubbing the back of her neck, an empty feeling formed in the pit of Belle's stomach. Forcing herself not to jump to conclusions, she opened the refrigerator and took out some eggs, ham, and potatoes for dinner.

As Ethan relayed the events of his day, Belle pretended to listen, but her thoughts were scattered as she wondered where Emily was. Irrational fears shimmied up her nerves, and by the time dinner was over, she was a basket case.

"Do you want to watch me play, Mom?" Ethan asked.

"Sure, in a minute. Why don't you set things up and I'll just finish clearing?"

She attempted four more times to contact Emily by phone and by text, but silence was all that greeted her. As much as she tried not to, she was freaking out. What if Emily were hurt? What if something bad happened to her?

She called Holly and told her she hadn't heard from Emily and she was scared something had happened to her.

"You need to chill. Emily's done this before, you know that. Wait a few more hours, and if she doesn't come home then call me back."

"I can't just sit here and do nothing. I'm going to call the police." Belle brought her fingertips to her throbbing temples and rubbed them.

"Hang on, here's Darren."

"Hiya, Belle. Hear Emily's giving you some trouble again."

A sob caught in her throat. "I don't know where she is. If I keep calling her, she eventually calls or texts me, but she hasn't contacted me at all. I'm going to call the police."

"They won't take a report until it's been twenty-four hours. I know it's hard to do, but just sit tight. She'll come home, you'll see."

"But she hasn't responded even though I've called and texted her many times."

"Maybe her phone's battery died, or she has it on silent. There are a lot of reasons why she may not be answering her phone. Just try not to think of the negative ones."

Belle was on pins and needles from the time she hung up with Darren until her daughter came home drunk at two in the morning.

"Where have you been?" she asked Emily.

"Out."

"I know *that*. You're drunk."

"Good observation, Mom."

Not wanting to wake Ethan up, Belle said, "We'll discuss this in the morning. Go on up to bed."

As she watched her daughter stumble up the stairs, anger battled sadness within her. Too wired to sleep, she made a cup of tea and stared into the gas burner's flame. Sitting at the kitchen table, she sipped her tea, tears rolling down her face as the minutes turned to hours.

# Chapter Twelve

During church, the arms deal with the United Revolutionary Army was firmed up. It would go down in four weeks, Banger choosing Hawk, Rock, Chas, Throttle, Tug, Chigger, Jax, Bear, and Axe to meet with the guns dealer to secure the shipment. Banger, Hawk, and a few more brothers would meet with the guerrilla group to exchange weapons for money. It should go smoothly, but in the murky world of arms dealing, nothing was guaranteed. For that reason, Banger assigned the present Sergeant-At-Arms, Rock, and the past one, Jax, to accompany him and Hawk.

After church, Banger headed to the great room to grab a beer. Looking around the room, he inhaled deep, satisfied breaths. The brotherhood had come a long way since he'd joined. When he'd signed up to be part of the Insurgents family, the club was in the throes of a turf war with the Deadly Demons. Bloodshed, lockdowns, and badges sniffing up their asses had been the norm.

He took a long pull on his beer, happy that the chaos had ended. For the past six years, things had calmed down substantially. Club life wasn't all rainbows and shit, but at least the turf wars with the Deadly Demons had been settled. The badges left the club alone since the Insurgents kept hard drugs out of the county. It was a tenuous relationship, but it'd been working for the past several years.

Banger couldn't complain; the club had enjoyed a long period of relative peace, and the money it was making from its businesses and dispensaries shocked him at times. The one problem he could see on the horizon was the fucking Skull Crushers MC. They'd tried shit in the Insurgents' county during the summer, but he knew they'd be back.

Punks who rode bikes thought that was what made a brotherhood. They were so damn wrong. The assholes in Skull Crushers were young punks who wanted to do whatever the fuck they wanted regardless of whose territory they were in. There was no way in hell he'd let Skull Crushers get anywhere near Pinewood Springs again. He'd make sure to wipe them out if they tried any more shit on Insurgents' turf. What bothered Banger was that the young MC was causing hell down south in Puebla, where the Insurgents' affiliate club, Night Rebels, had claim. He'd have to call the prez, Steel, and find out if he needed more muscle to teach the punks respect.

A ping interrupted his musings. Glancing down at his phone, he saw Kylie's smiling picture flash on his screen.

**Kylie:** *Hi, Dad. Whatcha doing?*

**Banger:** *Just got out of church. Having a beer. How are you?*

**Kylie:** *Good. Aced my Spanish test!*

Banger's chest puffed.

**Banger:** *Been telling you for years you're smart. Now you know your old man was right. ;) When you coming to visit?*

**Kylie:** *Soon. Just wanted to say hi.*

**Banger:** *Hi.*

**Kylie:** *Oh, Dad. :-D See ya.*

**Banger:** *Later.*

Just when he'd laid his phone down, another ping sounded. Smiling, he picked it up, and was surprised it wasn't Kylie. He opened the message.

**Belle:** *How r u?*

A wide smile crossed his face. He'd wondered if she'd contact him. He'd been pissed at her a couple of days before and had decided to cool it for a while, but when he saw her text, a funny feeling punched him in his gut.

**Banger:** *Good. You?*

**Belle:** *Busy and tired. The usual. :)*

Banger motioned Blade to give him another beer. He ran his hand over the top of his head then stared at his phone.

**Belle:** *U still there?*

**Banger:** *Ya.*

**Belle:** *Thought u left.*

**Banger:** *No. Still here.*

**Belle:** *We ok?*

**Banger:** *Don't know. R we?*

**Belle:** *I'm ok. Hope u understand I have kids who need me.*

**Banger:** *I do. I'm taking you out. I'm not taking no for an answer.*

**Belle:** *I want to go out. I don't know if I can get someone to watch Ethan.*

**Banger:** *No worries. I'll get an old lady to do it.*

**Belle:** *How old??*

Banger guffawed, and a few brothers looked his way. *Damn, this woman is green. Fuckin' love the challenge!*

**Banger:** *Old lady is someone's woman. I'll take care of it.*

**Belle:** *Get someone without a record. K?*

Shaking his head, he guzzled the rest of his beer.

**Banger:** *Trust me. I'll pick you up at 7:30.*

**Belle:** *K. Do I need to do anything?*

**Banger:** *Wear something sexy.*

**Belle:** :) I meant re: babysitter.

**Banger:** Nope. Also, plan on a late night. ;)

**Belle:** See u.

**Banger:** Right.

Belle's naiveté tickled him. He was going to have all kinds of fun with this one. Glancing around, he spotted Hawk talking with some of the brothers. He strode over to him.

"Gotta talk to you," Banger said, a big-ass smile plastered on his face.

"Sure. What's up? And what's with the smile? Did you just have a great blowjob?"

"Aiming to. You and Cara doin' anything tonight?"

Hawk shook his head. "Nah. You wanna do somethin'?"

"I'm doin' something with Belle, and I need Cara to sit with her son."

Hawk threw his head back and laughed. "Fuck, that's classic. Yeah, she'll stay with the kid. It'll serve her right for butting into your personal life."

"I'm fuckin' glad she did."

Hawk clapped Banger on the back. "You givin' up easy pussy?"

"Not sure yet, but I'm enjoying Belle's company."

"I'm sure you are. I haven't seen you smile like that in years. Fuck, go for it."

Banger gripped Hawk's upper arm and gave it a tight squeeze, tilting his chin. He was closer to Hawk than any of the other brothers in the club. Hell, he was closer to him than his own siblings. From the day Hawk joined up years back, they'd been tight. "Tell Cara to get to Belle's around seven o'clock."

Hawk nodded, and Banger turned around and walked out. The ice covering the parking lot shined and looked like a clear lake. Poking his head back into the great room, he motioned Puck to come over, the prospect dashing over immediately. "Throw some damn rock salt on the parking lot. Someone's gonna break their ass." Puck bobbed his head up and down and ran off to retrieve the bag of ice melt.

Banger went out to his car and drove off, a thread of excitement weaving its way around him. He was going to see Belle in a few hours, and it turned him way the hell on, but it also pissed him off that he was so excited about it. She was just a woman, after all—a woman with a pretty face, round tits, and a fleshy ass. What was the big deal? Stacked women with great asses came into the club all the time to party with the brothers. But they weren't Belle. For reasons he couldn't articulate, he only wanted *her* face, tits, and ass, and her curves tempted the fuck out of him. Damn, this dark-haired woman had him all mixed up, but he couldn't wait to see her later that night.

★ ★ ★

WHEN BANGER ARRIVED at Belle's at seven thirty, Cara was there along with Hawk. "When did you start babysitting?" Banger ribbed him as he sat on the couch in the living room, waiting for Belle.

"I didn't have anything else to do. Anyway, I didn't want Cara being alone."

Banger shook his head. "Totally pussy-whipped. You can't leave your old lady alone for one night?"

Hawk ran his eyes over Banger's dress shirt. His usual T-shirt and jeans had been replaced with a gray pin-striped shirt and black dress pants. Hawk smirked. "From the looks of you, you're only a few steps away from being pussy-whipped yourself."

Before Banger could answer, Belle walked in the room. Banger rose, sucking in his breath as his gaze riveted on her face, then moved over her body slowly, taking in the royal blue dress that hugged all her curves so seductively. When his eyes met hers, something intense flared between them, and they stood staring at each other, neither one speaking or moving.

"Is Cara up in Ethan's room?" Hawk's deep voice invaded their intimate moment.

Belle cleared her throat. "Uh… yeah, she is. You can go on up. He's showing her something on his computer." She smiled warmly at Banger. "Hi."

In two strides, Banger was close to her, his head bent low as he breathed in her jasmine scent. "Hi, beautiful," he whispered hoarsely. Placing his hand on her neck, he felt her shiver, and his pants grew tighter. He brushed her hair out of the way, gently kissing her neck before he trailed his lips up to her ear, and breathed, "Seeing you in your tight-as-fuck dress makes my fingers itch to dig into your sweet, sexy body, babe." The sound of her hushed sigh went straight to his groin.

In a small voice, she said, "We better get going."

He wrapped his arm around her waist and gave her a quick kiss on her lips. "Let's roll."

The restaurant Banger chose was an intimate, rustic one, nestled in the mountains on the outskirts of Pinewood Springs. A raging fire in the fireplace welcomed patrons as they entered. Wrought iron chandeliers with muted lights cast a romantic ambience, and the dark hardwood floors, burgundy leather chairs and wood tables lent an air of coziness to the place. Paintings of the Old West—cowboys on bucking broncos, and old steam trains twisting around tracks in a lush valley surrounded by tall, snow-capped mountain peaks—decorated the earth-tone walls. From the piano bar, easy listening music spilled into the restaurant.

As they sat at a table for two, Belle sipping a glass of white wine while Banger drank a beer, he thought she was the most beautiful woman he had ever seen. In some ways, she was like his Grace—soft-spoken, kind, and mischievous—and in other ways she was different—naïve, stubborn, and fiery. He took her in, loving her curly hair which flowed around her like a wild sea.

"You never been around a biker before, have you?" He smiled at her as his hand covered hers.

She ran her fingers over her wine stem, casting her eyes away from him. "I… uh… Why are you asking me that?"

Searching her face, he thought he detected a slight uneasiness in it. "Just that you didn't know what an old lady was, and you always seem surprised when I say things to you. Just seems like I'm the only biker you know. It's cool. I was just asking." He squeezed her hand.

She took a gulp of wine. "I didn't know you guys call your wives old ladies. It doesn't sound like something a woman would want to be called. And you are so… blunt. I'm not sure if that's because you're a biker, or that's just you."

He winked at her. "A bit of both. I tell it like I see and feel. If me telling you that I like your tits is 'blunt,' then you'll have to get used to me. If I see a pretty woman and like her stuff, you can bet I'm gonna fuckin' tell her."

Belle blushed, and he reached out and cupped her chin. "You are such a sweet, hot woman. I love the way you get red when I tell you stuff. Fuck, you hit some buttons in me, pretty lady." Banger brought her hand to his lips and kissed it.

After dining on New York strip steaks, loaded baked potatoes, and asparagus with a Dijon-lemon sauce, they settled into a corner booth in the piano bar. The place was small, seating only about forty people, and the distinct scent of leather and brandy wafted around the patrons. There were several people sitting on the stools circling the mahogany baby grand as the thin, wiry-haired pianist's slender fingers danced over the keys while he crooned "Margaritaville."

The waitress placed their drinks in front of them—a red port for Belle and a double shot of Jack for Banger. He wrapped his arm around her shoulders, drawing her closer to him. He breathed her scent in deeply, letting it spread through him, exciting the hell out of him; her smell was intoxicating. Cupping her chin, he tilted it, her eyes moving upward to his mouth as his face neared hers. His tongue traced the soft fullness of her lips then he moved his mouth over hers, devouring it. Panting, her large breasts rubbed against him with each breath she took. A hot jolt of desire burned through him and he pressed her even closer, his hand molding around the full swell of her breast; he loved the feel of its weight in his palm.

Pushing his hand away, she murmured against his lips, "We're in a public place. I can't do this."

Banger gazed into her gleaming eyes. "Fuck, woman, I can't help myself. You're so beautiful. Since I first saw you in your sexy dress, you've been driving me wild." He gripped her hand and set it on his hard, pulsing dick. "See what you're doing to me?"

With the heel of her palm, she massaged it under the table, and he groaned in her ear. Each touch moved him closer to throwing her down and fucking her good and hard, not giving a shit who was watching. He wasn't shy to fucking in public; he did it often at the club during the parties—as many of the brothers did—but it was only to relieve a throbbing itch. With Belle, he wanted to consume her, ravage her, do nasty things to her he'd never done with anyone else. She was fucking driving him crazy.

"Let's dance," she whispered, pulling away from him.

"Now?" he rasped.

Smiling sweetly, a wicked gleam in her eye, she nodded. "Now." She scooted out of the booth.

On the tiny dance floor, he held her close to him, desire throbbing in his dick. He rubbed his hardness against her, remembering that he hadn't done that since high school. His hands rested on her rounded hips and, sinking his finger into their softness, he inhaled sharply, knowing that before the night ended, he'd be gripping them tight as he fucked her from behind. Holding Belle—her tits pressed against him, her arms clamped around his waist, and her incredibly soft body moving under his hands—was a moment he wished he could freeze. He hadn't felt this turned on or enthralled with a woman since Grace had passed. He didn't know what the hell was going on, but he knew he was enjoying it.

As they swayed to the music, they held each other close, like a vine wound around a trellis. From the soft sounds Belle made, Banger knew she was just as turned on as he was, and the way she rubbed her pussy against his leg torched his dick so much that he moved her back toward the table, picked up their jackets, and escorted her out. She followed his lead, her arm never leaving his waist, her face flushed with heated desire. He loved the rosy sheen on her face and neck, and decided that burning-with-need pink had become his favorite color.

When they entered the car, Banger kissed her deeply, then said against her lips, "I need you real bad."

"We can't go to my house. I can't bring a man home in front of my kids. I mean, they haven't met you yet."

He nuzzled her neck. "You gonna keep me hidden from them forever?"

"No," she moaned. "It's just not the right time. I'm having a bunch of problems with my daughter."

"Not tonight, baby. You texted Cara and she said your girl was home. You gotta have some fun too."

Belle moved back and looked straight in Banger's eyes. He saw hunger and determination brimming in them. "I want to be with you, just not at my house. Are *you* going to make this happen?"

He crushed her to him. "Fuck, woman. Let's go." He switched on the engine and screeched out of the parking lot.

Banger opened the door, allowing Belle to go inside his home. He'd had a raging hard-on for too long, and his sweet Belle was going to take care of it. He forwent the niceties of offering her a drink or engaging in small conversation and pulled her straight into his bedroom, swinging her around so her back faced him. He ran his hands over her curves, growling while he softly bit her shoulder. Reaching down, he tugged at the hem of her spandex dress and peeled it off like a wrapper from a rich, delectable chocolate. "Fuck," he growled when he scanned her big tits encased in a plunging, sheer bra, the matching panties barely concealing her sweet pussy.

In one quick movement, her bra was off and he was crushing her breasts in his hands while she whimpered and wiggled her ass against his hardness. When she reached around, placing her arms on his lower back, her tits jutted out, and he swore he was going to shoot his load before he made it inside her silky wetness. "Beautiful, my cock wants inside you something fierce." Skating down her stomach, his hand slipped inside her panties and he tucked his fingers into her slick folds. A satisfied grunt broke through his lips. "You want my cock in you too. Fuck, that's hot."

"Damn, you make me so wet." She spun around to face him and kissed him deeply.

Banger guided her to his bed before quickly taking off his clothes. Opening the drawer in his nightstand, he took out a foil packet. He started to rip it open when Belle sat up and took it from him. Holding his eyes in a seductive stare, she placed the packet between her white teeth and slowly tore it open, the compressed sheath falling into her hand. Placing her hand on his ass, she moved him closer then licked the beads of pre-come from his glistening head before rolling on the covering.

When her warm tongue hit his crown, he had to pinch the base of his dick so he wouldn't come. She was making him all kinds of crazy. Leaning over, he breathed in jasmine with fresh citrus mingled with the musk of her arousal. He kissed her deep, hard, and wet, and her squirming body under his caressed his dick. Bringing his mouth down to her tits, he hungrily sucked and nipped on her taut nipples, his thumb brushing back and forth against her sweet spot, drawing cries of pleasure from her that drove him wild.

Placing both hands on her hips, he flipped her over. "Get on your knees," he commanded. "I'm gonna fuck you like you've never been fucked."

Belle scrambled to her hands and knees, her breasts swaying as she wiggled her ass against his hard dick. Watching her jiggle, Banger bent down and softy bit the flesh while his hands kneaded the rounded globes. "You've got the kind of ass that brings men to their knees, beautiful. Fuck." He squeezed hard then lightly smacked her ass cheek. "I love this ass."

Belle's moans and whispered sighs egged Banger on, and he kissed her lower back while his hands cupped her hanging tits. Pulling down on her hard nipples, he moved his dick up and down the length of her wet mound. "You want it now?" he asked hoarsely.

"Yeah. Now."

He separated her legs with his knee, her glistening sex making his mouth water. Rubbing her clit with his hand, he rammed his cock inside her soft wetness. His dick felt so good encased in her hot walls. He pummeled in and out, his finger rubbing the side of her hard nub. Belle arched her back, and it made him crazier. With one hand, he caught her hair, pulling it back until she groaned in pleasure. He rode her hard, and her ass pounded back into him, urging him to go faster, harder, deeper. When she screamed out his name, her warmth gripping him like a vise, he knew she was on the waves of ecstasy. His muscles contracted tightly, his body jerking forward as his hips thrusted. He could feel his seed rising up from his balls, then an intense pleasure broke through, like a burst of electricity zapping every part of his body, making him twitch as he felt his come shooting out into the sheath. "Fuck. Belle. Fuck!"

Her arms tightened around his neck, pulling her close to him, and he kissed her breathless, his tongue slipping in and winding around hers. His body relaxed as he buried his head in the crook of her neck, a warm, drowsy feeling spreading over him. He rolled over, taking Belle with him to nestle in his side. "Fuck, that was intense, baby." He kissed the side of her head.

"Wow. Just wow." She lightly kissed his chest as her finger traced patterns over it.

They lay together for a long while, Banger dozing for a bit. He couldn't believe how intense it had been. He hadn't felt this good since the last time he and Belle had fucked.

Belle stirred next to him, and he gripped her tighter. "I have to go," she said in a low voice.

He didn't say anything. He didn't want her to go; he wanted her to spend the night with him, smell her sweet perfume as he drifted off to sleep, and have her again in the morning. If he kept holding her, maybe she'd fall asleep.

She pushed up. *Fuck it.* He reluctantly rose, dressed, and held her close as they left his house.

When they walked into Belle's house, Banger saw Cara jump away from Hawk, who was zipping up his jeans. "We didn't hear you come in," Cara said as she smoothed down her hair.

"Yeah, I saw that." Banger smiled, and he laughed inwardly when he noticed red streaks fanning out on Cara's cheeks.

"So, Emily and Ethan didn't give you much trouble?" Belle asked as she took out her wallet.

"Not at all, and put that away. I'm not taking any money. If you need help with watching Ethan, let me know. I think Hawk will come again too, even though Ethan beat him at a couple of video games." Cara and Belle laughed while Hawk narrowed his eyes.

Banger clasped Hawk's shoulder. "You're gonna have to practice before coming back. You don't want the brothers knowing an eleven-year-old kicked your ass."

Hawk grumbled something inaudible. Turning to Cara, he drew her to him. "We gotta go." The couple walked out into the freezing night.

"Thanks again," Belle called out to them. Turning toward Banger, she grasped his hand. "I had a wonderful time. Thanks."

"No need to thank me. I had the best fuckin' time in a long while." He yanked her into his arms and kissed her.

"Mom?" a small voice said.

Belle jerked away from Banger, and he looked up to see a boy with a mop of dark, curly hair and blue eyes staring at him from halfway down the stairs.

Belle rushed to her son. "What's wrong, baby?"

"My stomach doesn't feel so good," he answered, his eyes on Banger.

Belle put her hand on his forehead. "You feel warm. Let's get back in bed, and I'll take your temperature and give you something for your tummy."

Ethan nodded then pointed at Banger. "Who's he?"

Panic streaked across her face as she looked at Banger. Clearing his throat, he said, "I'm Banger. You must be Ethan." He moved toward the stairs. "I'm a friend of your mother's. She tells me you have quite a baseball collection."

A half-smile tugged at the corner of his lips. "I do. I have, like a hundred cards." He looked down at his feet. "Do you like baseball?" Banger heard the hesitancy in his voice.

"Oh, yeah. I was about your age when I started collecting 'em."

Ethan glanced up, his eyes on Banger's face. "You must have thousands 'cause you been doing it for a long time."

Banger laughed. "I have a lot. Thousands? Nah. I'm old, but not that old."

Belle's laugh tickled his heart, and the frenzied look in her eyes softened. "Ethan has some very valuable cards." She ran her hand through her son's mop of hair.

"Yeah? I'd like to see them sometime. I'd like to show you mine, too."

"Really. Okay. Can I, Mom?" Ethan's earnest face made both Belle and Banger laugh.

She hugged her son. "Of course, but right now, you have to get back in bed, and I need to take your temperature."

His small shoulders slumped. "All right." He turned and started to climb the stairs then swiveled halfway around and said, "Nice meeting you. When I feel better, you can come back and see my baseball cards. Bring yours too."

"Sounds like a plan. Now, go on and do like your mama asked you to. You listen to her and you'll be feeling better in no time." Banger jerked his chin at the boy.

"Okay. Good night." Ethan trudged up the rest of the stairs and padded to his room.

Belle came down and grabbed Banger, kissing him deeply. "Thank you," she breathed, her breath scorching his skin.

"For what?"

"For that—making Ethan feel comfortable. You're a sweet man, even though you want everyone to think you aren't."

"Fuck, baby, if that's all it takes to warm you up, I'm all in." He kissed her hard. "I like your boy. He looks like you—he's got your hair and cute upturned nose." Banger kissed the tip of her nose.

She hugged him, then Banger pulled away, lightly pinching her chin. "Go take care of your son. I'll call you."

On his way home, he cranked up the radio and sang along to Scorpions' "Rock You Like A Hurricane," heat radiating through his chest. He liked the boy, and he *really* liked the mom.

Turning his engine off, he jumped from the car and went into his house. In the bedroom, he stared at the mussed-up bed, then walked over to it. He picked up the pillow and inhaled her scent of jasmine on the pillowcase. Sitting on the edge of the bed, his eyes landed on his and Grace's wedding picture on the bedroom dresser. A jab seized his heart, and he darted his eyes from the picture to the bed. Sighing, he shuffled over to the dresser and picked up the photograph, staring at the love and happiness in his and Grace's eyes. An image of Belle's electric blue orbs and infectious smile filled his mind. Slowly, he opened the drawer, placing the wedding picture in it.

He walked to the kitchen and grabbed a beer while images of Grace and Belle ran through his mind. After draining the bottle, he went back to the bedroom and stripped down to his boxers. Before slipping between the sheets, he looked back at the dresser and the empty spot where his wedding picture had been. He rubbed his eyes, and a thickness formed in his throat. Ambling back to the dresser, he took the photo out, placing it back in its spot, then flopped into bed, the scent of Belle all around him. As he closed his eyes, Belle's laughter, soft body, and curly hair danced across his brain, not Grace's. His heart soared when he thought of the time he had spent with Belle that night.

Sucking in his breath, his temples pounding, he got up and put his wedding picture back in the dresser drawer, then went back to bed. With the scent of Belle in his nose and the taste of her still on his tongue, he fell into a deep slumber.

# Chapter Thirteen

The week flew by, and Belle was busy at work and taking care of Ethan. He ended up staying home from school for one week, and Belle wasn't able to take off more than one day at work, so she'd asked Holly to help out. Belle didn't know what she'd ever do without Holly, who was always there, offering to lend a hand.

Emily, of course, had been more trouble than help during the previous week, and her attitude and lack of responsibility had made Belle come to a decision. As hard as it was for her to admit, she had no control over her daughter. Because of her long hours at work, there was a major lack of supervision in her home, so Belle made the decision that, before the judge could take Emily away and place her in foster care, she would go live with Holly and Darren.

She knew her decision was going to be met with hostility, bitterness, and hate from Emily, but she'd hoped that her daughter would understand that this was the best thing for her. It wouldn't be for more than the school year, and Belle hoped Emily wouldn't hate her for the rest of her life. Belle didn't know how she could make her daughter understand that deciding to let her stay with Holly was Belle's only guarantee that the court wouldn't put Emily in foster care, and that she would get the supervision she needed.

There was so much stress on Belle, but the silver lining—besides her son—was Banger. Although, she had to admit she was pretty freaked out when she'd gone to his home and had seen that it was nothing more than a shrine to his dead wife. He'd told her that it had been six years since his wife had died, yet he still had her everywhere in the house. Belle was positive that if she'd looked in the closets or the drawers, his wife's clothes would have been in them. It was like the house had been frozen in time. Seeing that made her wonder if Banger would ever be able to give himself wholeheartedly to a woman. She had a hunch he just wanted someone to warm his bed, to fill the void his wife's death had opened in his life.

The way he had enshrined her memory in his home, how he said his wife's name, told her that he'd loved the woman very much. How could she ever compete with her? A past love could never be matched, and Belle was up against a woman who would never grow old. She had to compete with rosy-hued memories that would keep gaining luster as time went on, while she would grow old, gaining lines and sunspots on her face as time marched forward. Grace was eternally immortalized in youth in Banger's mind.

Perhaps Belle would still be the grieving widow, if she hadn't found out about Harold's cheating. Although she'd never been in love with him the way Banger was with Grace, she did love and care for him. When she'd found out he'd been sleeping with another woman, it had broken her heart, and she still wasn't over it entirely. But Banger made her feel happy and alive, the sex with him was mind-blowing, something she really needed to relieve all the tension in her life.

Maybe she was overthinking this whole situation with Banger. She wasn't even sure she wanted to be more than what they were. From the look around his house, he wasn't ready to bring another woman into his life, but she didn't think she was ready to bring another man into hers either. The last thing she wanted was her heart to be broken again. She would rather miss out on love than plunge into the deep waters of a relationship. She didn't want to drown, and from the way her body responded to Banger, and the way she felt when they were together, she knew she could fall head over heels in love. It was better to have a good time and keep it light rather than throwing caution to the wind.

She could push her feelings down; she wasn't the young girl who had blindly given her heart and body to Jake back in high school. She had fallen in love too quickly and too completely with him, and he'd taken everything, then called her a slut when she told him she was pregnant with Emily. His good-bye to her was a black eye and a split lip. She had been so in love with Jake and he'd hurt her so badly, and never even came by to see his daughter.

Then she'd met Harold and they'd married. Even though she hadn't been head over heels for him like she had been with Jake, she'd cared for Harold and promised herself she'd make him a good wife and give him a good home. And she had, for fifteen years, but then she'd learned of his betrayal. She'd been hurt and so angry that she'd sworn he'd pay. Something had snapped inside her, and she'd decided she wasn't going to let another man trample on her heart. Then he'd died, and a sense of relief had come over her. The thought of him with another woman would never be again, and that had calmed her, soothed her sadness *and* her anger.

No, she was done giving herself to any man. Light and easy, that's what she'd do, and from the looks of his house, Banger wasn't ready to do anything more than that either.

Picking up the phone, she dialed Holly. "Hey, Holly. Just a quick call to ask if you want to get together on Saturday for coffee while Ethan's at the movies with his friends."

"What time?"

"Is one o'clock good?"

"Yeah, that's fine. Can I ask what it's about?"

"It's about Emily. I think I'm going to take you up on your offer and have her stay with you until the semester's over. I just wanted to get together with you to go over the details."

There was a short pause before Holly spoke. "I know how hard this is for you, but I think you're making the right decision. One o'clock is fine on Saturday."

"Great. We'll talk then."

Belle put the phone in her pocket and went into the ladies' room, locking the door behind her. Leaning against the beige-tiled wall, she covered her face and sobbed.

★ ★ ★

When she returned home from work, Belle found Ethan in front of the TV playing one of his video games. He had called earlier in the day to tell her that he was feeling great but was starving because he hadn't eaten hardly anything for the past week. He'd begged his mom that morning to let him have a pizza for dinner, and she'd reluctantly agreed. Emily had gone out with friends again, and Belle said a silent prayer that she would be home at a decent hour, and sober.

"Hi, Mom. Having pizza, right?"

"How are you feeling, sweetheart? I just want to make sure you're ready." She walked over to Ethan and placed a hand on his forehead. "You're not running a fever anymore. I'll order the pizza, but I don't want you to overdo it by eating too much. I'll just go upstairs and change, then place the order."

"Mom, can Banger come over to join us? I want to show him my baseball cards, and I want to see his too."

"I can call him. I think he'd like to come over and see your cards."

Belle trudged up the stairs and sent a quick text to Banger asking if he wanted to join her and Ethan for pizza and possibly a movie. His quick response made her smile. All of a sudden, her feet didn't hurt as much, and she felt giddy. She'd get to spend an evening with her son and Banger. In that moment, it didn't get any better.

A half hour later, Banger and Ethan were on the couch exchanging baseball cards, laughing, and telling each other anecdotes about the players. A warmth spread over her as she watched her son chattering with Banger, his face lit up like a Christmas tree and his hands flying all around as they always did when he was excited. She smiled; it felt good to have a man around and hearing Ethan talk about the things he used to with his dad. She knew her son really missed that.

Belle excused herself and went into the kitchen to make a big salad to go with the pizza. She sliced the carrots and radishes, then cubed the mozzarella cheese, adding all of it to a bowl of romaine lettuce, pepperoni, salami, and Italian peppers. Pouring a homemade creamy Italian dressing she had whipped up, she tossed the salad, then quickly dashed to the door when the bell rang. The pizza guy handed her two steaming boxes, and she reached for her purse. Before she could pay though, Banger handed money to the delivery guy. As she took out a twenty from her wallet, she said, "Banger, I don't want you to pay. I invited you for dinner."

"Put your money away, woman. I've never let a woman pay for anything, and I'm sure as hell not gonna start now."

"But I want to pay. You're my guest."

The delivery man stood in front of them, holding two twenty dollar bills. "So, what do you guys want me to do here?"

"Take my twenty. Keep the change. Thank you." Belle took the pizza boxes from the guy.

Glaring at the delivery man, Banger said, "Give the lady back her twenty. Best you move on now."

Wide-eyed, the young guy hurriedly gave Belle her money back, turned around, and sprinted to his car. Banger closed the door, leaning in to place a kiss on her lips. He pulled away and winked. She shook her head, her eyes twinkling, and left to bring the salad and plates.

After filling up the salad bowls, she squeezed in between Banger and Ethan, nibbling on a slice of pepperoni and green pepper pizza. "You want to put a movie on, Ethan?"

"Yeah." Turning toward Banger, he asked, "Have you ever seen the movie *Field of Dreams*? It was my dad's and my favorite movie. We always watched it together, especially on pizza nights." Ethan jumped up to grab the DVD.

Banger put his beer bottle down on the coffee table. "No, I don't think I've ever seen that movie. It sounds like it's about baseball."

Ethan nodded emphatically.

"Then it's a go for me."

Belle sat quietly, watching the exchange between Ethan and Banger. She knew it meant something to her son to share his favorite movie with someone other than his father. Behind her eyes, unshed tears burned, and she grasped Banger's hand and squeezed it tightly. He squeezed back and rubbed his knee against hers, and she placed a kiss on his cheek. When Ethan sat back down next to her, she put her arms around him, clasping his shoulder. Ethan glanced affirmatively at Banger then said, "Aw, Mom."

By the time the movie was over, they had gone through two pizzas, a large bowl of salad, and three bowls of popcorn. Belle chided herself for letting Ethan talk her into all the popcorn, but he was having such a good time and she hadn't seen him so animated for a long while.

Ethan yawned and cushioned his head against his mother's arm.

"You tired, sweetheart?"

"Uh-huh."

"Let's go up to bed."

As she began to rise, Ethan said, "Mom, you don't have to go up with me. I'm not sick anymore." He padded toward the stairs then stopped and looked at Banger. "Good night. Thanks for showing me your cards."

"Sure. You have some kick-ass cards in your collection. Loved seeing 'em."

Ethan ran up the stairs, yelling, "'Night, Mom!"

Belle stood to pick up the plates, but Banger grasped her wrists, pulling her down on him. Laughing, she pushed him away. "Stop. I have to clear the dishes. It'll take a few minutes to clean up then I'll be back."

"The dishes can wait 'til later, because I'm not going one more minute without my lips on yours." His mouth covered hers and a tingle of excitement rushed up her spine as she melted under his kiss. "Do you know how hard it was sitting next to you, feeling the heat of your body? And fuck, your sweet scent wrapped right around my cock. It was fuckin' hard for me not to be able to touch you like a man wants to touch a woman. I need you, beautiful."

"I need you too, but we can't go all the way with Ethan upstairs."

"Then I guess we'll have to make out like two horny teenagers." He ran his finger down the side of her face, past her neck, stopping at her cleavage. Locking their gazes, his lips grazed against hers, teasing her with a kiss that didn't come.

Goose bumps pricked her skin as she pressed closer, his clove and leather scent driving her crazy. He pushed a few strands of hair off her forehead then touched his lips to it, kissing her softly. She shuddered, and his low chuckle electrified her. She loved his gravelly, baritone voice; it was the type made for whispering nasty things in her ear.

Just as Banger glided his hand into Belle's damp panties, the front door opened and she scrambled to sit up. Emily stumbled in, and Belle twisted out of Banger's arms and went to her daughter.

"You broke your curfew again. You know, Emily, I'm damn sick and tired of this. You're grounded. Now, go up to your room."

Emily laughed bitterly. "Shut the fuck up! I'm done with you telling me what to do. I'm done with all the shit in this house."

"How dare you speak to me like that! I'm your mother, you will not speak to me that way, do you understand me? You're tired of the shit in this house? Well, I'm sick and tired of your attitude, laziness, and disrespect. We'll talk about this in the morning. Go to your room."

"I'll say and do whatever the fuck I want. I'm sick of you, and living in this piece-of-shit rental." Emily drew closer to her mom and raised her hand as if to strike her. But before she could bring it down, a strong grip stopped it.

Banger said, in a deep, stern voice, "Don't even think about it, missy."

"Who the fuck are you?" Emily snapped.

"I'm the one who's gonna make sure you respect your mama."

She looked at Belle. "Mom?"

Belle said softly, "It's okay, Banger. You can let go. Emily, this is my friend, Banger."

Emily looked Banger up and down as he stepped back, disgust spreading across her face. "Seriously, Mom? I don't think so."

Banger crossed his arms. "Nobody here is asking for your approval. I'm just telling you that I don't like the way you're talking to your mom, and I'm not gonna sit here and watch you hurt her."

"I don't think this is your business." Emily turned away, as if dismissing him.

"When I care 'bout someone, I don't let her get hurt, even if it's her fuckin' brat who's doin' the hurtin'. No one does that shit when I'm around." Anger flashed in his ice-blue eyes. "No one," he hissed.

Belle's stomach tightened, and she shook like a leaf as she watched the exchange between her daughter and Banger. She tried to say something, but the words were caught in her throat. *Emily had been ready to* hit *me.*

Emily looked down and mumbled, "I wasn't going to hurt my mom."

"From the tears in her eyes and the way she's shaking, I'd say you already did."

In a low voice, Emily said, "I didn't mean it, Mom." She pushed past her and ran up the stairs.

When Belle heard her bedroom door close, she turned to Banger and said, "I appreciate your intentions, but I'd rather you not reprimand my daughter. That's my job and responsibility."

"Agreed, but it didn't seem like you had a handle on it. Your daughter has a mouth on her, and you need to rein her in or she's gonna get in some big trouble."

Her jaw tightened. "I know that. She's just having a real hard time since her father died. We used to live in a big house and she attended private schools. Money was never a problem, and I was always at home. Her life was so different from what it is now. It's been a hard adjustment on her." Belle wrung her hands together and said softly, "On all of us."

Banger took her hands and brought them to his lips, kissing them. "Some changes in life are harder than others. It fuckin' sucks when we get a curveball thrown at us, but we gotta deal with it and move forward. She's had over a year to come to terms with her new life. Being disrespectful to her mama shouldn't be acceptable under any circumstances. And if I weren't here, the kid would've hit you. Who the fuck hits their mom?"

A sob she'd been holding in since the whole incident began finally escaped. He tugged her to him and wrapped his arms around her, holding her close and tight as her body heaved up and down. They stood like that for several minutes, and all the stress and bitterness she'd been holding in for a long time seeped out of her. Being in Banger's arms, his hand rubbing her back, her face buried in his shoulder, gave her more comfort than she'd known since even before her husband died. As he held her, she felt as though everything would be okay.

Finally, she pulled away and grabbed a few tissues from the box on the table in the foyer. After blowing her nose, she said, "Thanks for helping me through my meltdown. I'm ashamed you had to see all the family drama."

"No need to thank me or be embarrassed. Families got all kinds of shit goin' on. The key is to get a handle on it." He locked eyes with her. "You know I'm here for you. Never hesitate to ask. You gonna be okay?"

She nodded. "I think it's best if you go. I hope you understand."

"I get it, but if you have problems with *her,* you call me. Got it?"

"Okay." She leaned in to him and kissed him deeply, breathing in his scent, wishing he could stay the night. She wanted nothing more than to fall asleep snugly in his arms.

"I'll call you tomorrow."

She tilted her chin then he left. Despite the frigid night air, Belle stood on the porch watching Banger's SUV fade into the hazy darkness. Emptiness seized her and with a sigh, she closed the front door.

# Chapter Fourteen

Banger couldn't get Belle out of his mind. He was all kinds of messed up about her, and he wanted to give whatever they had a chance. All he knew was that when he was with Belle, the hole, which had been in his heart since Grace died, was not so empty anymore. He liked being with her, and even though she had some major shit going on with her daughter, she always had a smile on her face.

*Fuck, her daughter is out of line. The bitch needs to be taught respect.* Banger couldn't believe the way she'd yelled at her mom, and she would've hit her if he hadn't been there to stop it. *Fuck that shit!* He knew it wasn't his place to intervene in family matters, but if she had struck Belle, he would've gone ballistic. He couldn't imagine kids hitting their parents. Where he came from, that shit didn't happen. His mom had been the long-suffering wife of the cruel sonofabitch who was his father. Banger's dad didn't use his fists on his wife, only his words and his sick games, like openly flaunting his whores in front of her.

Banger remembered one morning when he'd been about seven years old, waking up to the strong scent of cheap perfume. It hadn't smelled like his mother, and when he'd open his sleepy eyes, he'd seen a heavily made-up woman looking down on him. It had scared the shit out of him, and he'd thought it was the Fifty-Foot Woman from the sci-fi movie he, his brother, and two sisters had watched with their mom the night before. He'd thrown the covers over his eyes only to have them pulled back down by the woman. She had on a real tight dress and a ton of silver and gold chains around her neck and wrists. She'd asked him if he was Big Ray's son. He'd nodded. She'd laughed huskily then coughed, spit falling on him. She'd sounded like his grandpa Bill who'd wheezed and coughed as he'd smoked his cigarettes while his grandma yelled at him to stop his goddamned smoking or he'd die.

Before he could have said anything else, the door had banged open and his dad filled the doorway, his figure tall and menacing. He'd glared at the woman then at his son. He'd asked her what the fuck she was doing in the room, and if she preferred small peckers to his big, throbbing one. Then his dad had cupped his pants, and a deep, throaty laugh passed through the woman's lips. She'd walked over to his dad and rubbed her body against his while she put her hand over his big dick. Banger had closed his eyes, and he heard his dad laugh. Soon, the laugh had given way to moans and groans. When he'd peeked through his squinted eyes, he saw the woman kneeling in front of his dad, doing something to him, something which must have been good because his dad had a big grin on his face as the woman's head moved back and forth quickly. Then his dad had groaned and yelled, "Fuck!"

At that moment, he'd heard his mother say, "In front of your son, you bastard."

"Better he learn what women are good for at a young age. Ain't that right, boy?"

Banger had pretended to be asleep, but he knew his dad, mom, and the strange woman knew he was awake.

Later that morning, Banger and his siblings had sat at the breakfast table along with his dad and the heavily made-up woman while his mother ran about fussing with the breakfast, catering to all of them like she was the servant and the woman stinking of cheap perfume was the lady of the house.

The incident had been burned in his mind and, years later, after one of his more severe beatings from his dad, Banger had realized how fucked up his family was. His father liked to impose corporal punishment on his two sons, but he'd never laid a finger on his daughters or his wife. To Banger, it seemed like he made up for all his frustrations on the boys.

When he had turned fifteen, and his dad took out his belt for the thousandth time, Banger had grabbed the buckle before it hit his back. It had been the first time he'd stood up to his dad. Shock registered in his old man's eyes, then anger. Banger had met his dad's stare, only Banger's had reflected cold rage. His father had backed down, and he'd never touched him again. A year later, Banger left and found himself at the Insurgents' clubhouse.

Even with all the hate he'd felt for his father, he'd never once struck him. He would never have thought of hitting the sonofabitch unless he'd tried to beat his mother or sisters. Belle's daughter had thought nothing of raising her hand to strike her mother. Belle hadn't hit her daughter or physically threatened her; all she'd done was told Emily she was grounded. He shook his head. That was all kinds of fucked. He wanted to help, but he knew it was something he couldn't get involved in unless Belle asked. This shit they had was between them.

His phone pinged and he looked down at it, a rush of joy shooting through him.

**Kylie:** *I'm on my way to PWS with a couple of friends. Will be there in an hr.*

**Banger:** *Great surprise. Can't wait to see you.*

**Kylie:** *Me too. Will talk soon. :)*

Banger couldn't wait to see his daughter, who hadn't been home since Christmas break. Nerves gripped his stomach when he wondered what Kylie would think when she walked in the house and saw a lot of the photographs of Grace put away. He hadn't told her about Belle because he wasn't even sure how he felt about the curvy cook, and he didn't want to say too much to his daughter if things didn't turn out. Banger was sure that Kylie wouldn't be too happy to see the changes he'd made in the house, but he'd talk to her, try to explain that he had to move forward. That it was what Grace had wanted.

An hour later, Banger could hear the pulsing base from one of the heavy metal CDs Kylie always listened to in her car. She had grown up surrounded by music from Black Sabbath, Judas Priest, Megadeth,

Scorpions, and a whole slew of other bands. She really hadn't had a choice, since she had been born to parents who were major headbangers. Instead of rebelling when she became a teenager by choosing something different, she embraced all the music her parents loved, and it had become her favorite as well.

Banger walked into the garage, a big smile on his face, and went over to hug his daughter. Kylie wrapped her arms around her dad's neck and gave him a big kiss on his cheek. "Hi, Dad." She pushed back and scanned his face. "You're good. You look more relaxed than I've seen you in a long time. Did you start meditating like I suggested?"

"Nope. I'm just finding some time to take it easy. You know, enjoying some things that I haven't done in a long time."

"Really? Like what?"

"We'll talk about it later. It's damn cold in this garage, let's get inside." Turning to look at the other two girls climbing out of Kylie's car, he said, "I'm Banger."

Kylie introduced her friends to her dad, and he grabbed their luggage and showed them into the house. When they went into the family room, he heard Kylie gasp. He kept walking to the guest room and put the suitcases on the floor.

"Dad? What happened to all the photographs of Mom?"

Banger shuffled into the family room and came up behind his daughter. "There are still pictures of your mother in here."

"Yeah, like three. What happened to the others?"

"I put them away," he said softly.

"Why?" Surprise and hurt were etched on her face.

"Because it's time for me to start living again. Your mom would've wanted it."

Kylie pursed her lips together and crossed her arms over her chest. "There's a reason why you did this. I was just here Christmas and everything was the same, and now it's all different. I don't believe for one minute that you woke up one day and decided you wanted to start living again. What do you think you've been doing for the last six years?

You've been here breathing, partying at the club, going to Sturgis, and a bunch of other stuff too. Mom's the one who's not here. You've been doing plenty of living, and you just decided *now* to put away Mom's pictures?"

Banger clenched his jaw. "You're away at school, you're young, and you got your own life to live. I'm the one left here in the house, and it's just time for me to move forward." He put his arm around her shoulders, but she twisted away. "Kylie, don't be that way."

Kylie's friends had just come in, and she grabbed their hands and said, "Let's go." She swiveled around and rushed toward the back door.

"Where you going?"

"To the clubhouse." Then she slammed the door.

Banger stood in the family room listening to Kylie rev the motor of her car before she peeled out of the garage and zoomed off. He knew she'd be upset and in retrospect, he probably should've told her about the changes he was making. Maybe he should've mentioned that he'd been seeing Belle, but he didn't want to go there yet because he knew Kylie would be upset. What was the point in stressing her about something if it were going nowhere?

He sighed and walked out of the room.

★ ★ ★

When Banger walked into the clubhouse a couple hours later, he saw Kylie seated on the barstool. Her legs crossed, she was laughing and leaning in to Jerry, who had a hungry look in his eyes as he stared at her. Banger's muscles twitched and he clenched his fists as the boiling anger burned in the pit of his stomach. He yelled, "Why the fuck are you talkin' to my daughter?"

Jerry jumped back and rushed away, and Kylie narrowed her eyes. "What is your problem, Dad? I've known these guys since I was a kid. You telling me I can't talk to them anymore?"

Banger walked up to her. "I'm not saying you can't talk to Hawk, Bear, Throttle, or some of the other older brothers. You've know them since you were a kid. Jerry and the younger ones, you haven't known them for that long. Anyway, I don't like the way he was looking at you. You stay away from him. You got that?"

"Aren't you being a hypocrite? You're telling me I can't talk to Jerry or some of the younger brothers, but you can freely hang with the club whores and the hoodrats?"

In his steely voice, Banger said, "That's different. You've become a real smartass since you went away to college. How would you like for me to drag your ass back home to learn some manners again? You don't tell *me* what the fuck I can do. I tell *you* what the fuck *you* can do. And I'm saying you don't hang with Jerry. This is not open for discussion."

Kylie blinked hard. "I'm sorry, Dad. I was out of line. Jerry and I just talk when I come into the club, it's no big deal. I guess it took me by surprise that Mom's pictures are gone. It makes me sad and angry." Kylie looked down at her hands in her lap.

Banger placed his hand on her shoulder. "I'm not worried about you, okay? I just don't like the way Jerry looks at you. Remember, I know how bikers are. I'm sorry I didn't tell you about putting some of the pictures away before you came up. I know you're angry, and that's okay. I know you're sad, but you have to respect that I need to do this in order to move forward. Your mom wanted me to do this, but I couldn't for such a long time."

Kylie leaned against her dad, laid her head on his shoulder, and wrapped her arm around his waist. He rubbed his hand up and down her back, then said, "Go grab your friends. I'm taking you out to dinner at the burger joint. Go on now, it's all good."

★ ★ ★

THE FOLLOWING MORNING, Banger came into the kitchen and smiled when he saw Kylie at the stove scrambling eggs for breakfast. He pulled out the kitchen chair and she turned around, narrowing her eyes when she saw him. Banger sat down and reached for the orange juice, pouring himself a full glass. "It's like old times, seeing you making my breakfast.

I've missed you." He took a large gulp and wiped his mouth with a napkin. "Just seems like everything moves so fast. Sometimes I'm out of breath just trying keep up with the passing of time."

"I've missed being home too, but I do love college." Kylie placed a plate of scrambled eggs, bacon, and hash browns in front of her father. "Who's Belle?"

He jerked his head back. "A friend, why?"

Kylie shrugged, her eyes fixed on his. "She called while you were in the shower."

Banger glanced at the kitchen counter and saw his phone on it. *That's where I left the fucking phone.* "You checking up on me?"

"Your phone rang, and I picked it up to make sure it wasn't one of the brothers. I've done that ever since I can remember. I saw her name flash on the screen."

Banger nodded. "Belle's a cook over at Ruthie's diner, and we've been hanging out for the past few weeks. She's a nice lady. You have to meet her sometime."

Kylie wrinkled her brow, and twisted her hair around her fingers. "Now I know why you put the pictures away. You've met someone and you're airbrushing Mom out of your life. You can put away all the pictures, knickknacks, and anything else Mom ever had in this house, but you'll never take her away from me. Even though you're trying to." Kylie's voice broke.

Banger stood up and pulled his daughter into his embrace, cradling her head against his shoulder. Pangs of guilt and stabs of heartbreak assaulted him as Kylie sniffled. "I'm not trying to get rid of your mom's memory, in this house or in my heart. I loved your mother, and I will never stop loving her. I know this is hard for you to understand because you've been used to everything being the same for so long, but I have to go on with my life. Since your mother died, I've been a lonely man. She didn't want me to be lonely, but I was so heartbroken when she left us, and I had to raise you all on my own and didn't know what the fuck I was doing, so I ignored how alone I was. Just because I'm going out with

Belle doesn't mean I will ever forget your mother. It also doesn't mean that I don't love her because I do, very much, and I always will.

"You're young and away at college, and you're experiencing new things in your life, as you should. It would be unrealistic for you to expect me to live my life on my own and sad. Belle makes me feel happy in a way that a man should be." Gripping Kylie's shoulders, he pushed her back a little, then placed his hand under her chin and lifted her head so she would look at him. "I'm hoping you understand where I'm coming from. Don't ever think for one second that I don't cherish and love your mother. She will always be in my heart."

Kylie wiped her nose. "It's hard for me to accept right now because it's all so new, but I can tell you've been alone for a long time. I know things haven't been the same for you since Mom died. I guess all I can say right now is that I'll try to understand, but you have to appreciate that this is really hard for me."

"That's fair. I don't want you to think the last six years have been awful for me either. Raising you, getting to know you in a way that I would probably never have if your mom had lived, has brought me more happiness than I can ever tell you. It's just that a man needs certain things, let's leave it at that. And I do want you to meet Belle."

Kylie nodded. "I'd like to meet her, but not right now. I need some time with all this." She chewed her cuticle as she looked at her dad. "Do you love her?" she asked in a barely audible voice.

Banger shrugged. "Don't know. I feel good when we're together."

Kylie hugged him. "Now your eggs are cold." She pointed to his plate on the table. "I'll zap them in the microwave for a few seconds." She nudged her father toward his chair.

Kylie's two friends walked in, and the three of them decided they wanted to go shopping at the mall. His daughter placed his piping-hot breakfast in front of him, gave him a quick kiss on the cheek, and smiled broadly when he handed her his credit card. Giggling and chattering, the three girls left, and silence shrouded him.

As he ate his meal, he thought about Kylie's question. Did he love

Belle? He wasn't sure, but he knew he liked her a lot and wanted to spend time with her. He loved fucking her, and he'd be sad if he didn't see her again. But love… He didn't think so. Even though he had put some of Grace's pictures away and told Kylie that he was ready to move forward, he still felt like he was betraying Grace when he was with Belle. He knew that was fucked up, but that's just the way it was. It also didn't help that Belle was holding something back; she acted like she didn't trust him. He wasn't sure what was going on with her, but he suspected it was more than just having an out-of-control teenager in the home. He had plans to get together with her the following night, and he sure as hell was going to find out why she kept pushing him away. It was time for her to lay her cards on the table.

He took a sip of his coffee as he stared out the kitchen window, watching the snowflakes cling to the windowpanes.

★ ★ ★

BANGER WATCHED BELLE as she spoke in hushed tones to her daughter on the phone. The glow from the fire crackling in the large stone fireplace softened the crease in her brow. In the firelight, her brown hair shined like melted chocolate. She was beautiful, and he was glad that they were seated away from the crowds at the restaurant. Since Big Rocky's was the club's other restaurant, he didn't want to bump into a lot of the brothers. He wanted to be alone and share the night with Belle. There would be time for her to meet the brothers, go to a club party, and experience the thrill of a bike rally, but that night was only for the two of them.

"Everything good with your kids?" Banger asked as Belle laid her phone on the table.

"Thankfully, yes." Her shoulders slumped a bit. "What's new with you? We haven't spoken in a few days. I called yesterday, but you didn't pick up. Did you get my message?" Belle looked him in the eye, and he took her hand. What could he say? He should have called her back the previous day, but his feelings were all mixed up.

"Yeah, I got your message. I was busy. Kylie's in town with two of her friends."

"Really? Why didn't you tell me? I'd love to meet her."

Banger cleared his throat. "Didn't know she was comin' 'til she was on her way. She and her two friends came to ski. They're doing an overnight tonight in Aspen, left real early this morning. She'll be heading back after the Aspen trip. Maybe next time she's home, I can get the two of you together." One thing Banger had learned during his forty-six years was not to tell the *whole* story to a woman unless he wanted hysterics and drama. Anyway, no sense in upsetting Belle over the way Kylie was feeling. He didn't even know if they'd be together by the time her summer break started.

"I'm sure they'll have a wonderful time. I'd like to meet your daughter, so when she's ready, let me know." She slipped her hand away from Banger's then touched the base of her throat.

"Why'd you take your hand away? You don't want me touching you tonight?"

Belle turned her eyes away from him. "That's silly. I wasn't aware that I moved it away from yours. It's not a big deal, is it?"

"Look at me." Banger caught her gaze when her eyes locked with him. "What's going on with you? I feel like you're keeping your distance from me. What the fuck?"

"I'm not." She motioned the waitress to bring her another glass of chardonnay. "You're being overly sensitive."

"Never been accused of *that* before." Leaning back, he grabbed his whiskey and downed it. "How'd you get along with your husband?"

At first, Banger didn't think she'd heard him, then she blew out a long breath, tucked her hair behind her ears, and placed her elbows on the table, her chin resting on her hands. "It was all right for a long time, but toward the end of our marriage, Harold cheated on me. I probably would have left him if he hadn't died." She smiled.

"Was it just an affair, or did he love the bitch?"

Belle's eyes widened as a large smile spread over her lips. "Good description. She *was* a bitch, and I don't know if he was in love with her. I know he was in love with the way her youth made him feel. I never met her, but I'd speak to her on the phone when I'd call his office. She knew I was his wife, and she fucked him anyway. Harold later told me she was twenty-three years old." She shrugged.

Banger didn't bother to tell her that his world called all women "bitches"; he didn't think she'd understand it. "Was that his first time, or was that the first time he got caught?"

Belle winced. "He swore he'd never cheated on me before, but I didn't believe him. I'd suspected he was seeing someone even before he hooked up with his secretary. I guess now it doesn't matter."

"So, that's why you push me back? You think I'm gonna hurt you like your old man did? Fuck, woman, I'm not anyone but me, and I don't cheat if I care about a woman. The minute I met Grace, I stopped fucking around. Hell, I never looked at another woman the whole time I was married. I get that your old man did shit behind your back, but you can't compare me to him."

"I can't help being jaded by it. You tell me you're not that way, and you're asking me to believe you. Harold told me the same thing, and I did believe him, but it was all one big goddamned lie. I know bikers have a rep for screwing around." A half-smile brushed across her lips. "How many women have you been with since your wife died?"

Banger shook his head. "What difference does it make? How many women I've fucked doesn't mean shit. The bitches were there to take my mind off shit, that's all." Why was she asking him *that*? The past years of fucking different women didn't mean squat. He couldn't even remember most of their names or even how they'd looked. For him, they'd all blended into one big pussy.

"Wow, that many." She stared down at her hands.

Banger rubbed his hand over his face. Cupping her chin, he made her look at him. "I told you, none of those women meant anything to me. At the club, easy pussy is everywhere. The club whores are there to pleasure the brothers. It doesn't mean shit to the men or to the women."

In a soft voice, she said, "If you're trying to win me over, you're blowing it."

He laughed. "I just want you to know that I'm not the cheatin' type of man. Many are. There're members who fuck all the time behind their old ladies' backs, but not me. I'm not that way." He smacked his lips as the waiter placed a steaming plate of beef brisket and hot links smothered in barbecue sauce. "Now that we got that settled, let's eat."

Belle picked up her fork and took a bite of mashed potatoes. "Yum. The chef put a hint of horseradish with the sour cream before he whipped them up. Delicious. I'll have to try that at the diner."

After the large meal, they sipped a shot of Amaretto, and Banger leaned over and kissed Belle full on the lips. He reached behind her neck, drawing her mouth closer to his, and he slipped his tongue between her lips. Desire teased his stomach. When she pulled away, he frowned.

"Something's been on my mind since I went over to your house a couple weeks ago."

He raised his eyebrows, taking in her apprehensive look. "Speak your mind."

She licked her lips several times before speaking. "Don't take this the wrong way, but I don't think you're over Grace yet. I can't give you my heart for fear it'll be shattered. I don't want to be a bed warmer. I don't think I have the personality to be one. I don't sleep around, and when I've given myself to someone, it means something to me." She tapped her index finger against her lips.

Banger scrunched his face. "You think that's all you are to me? A fuckin' bed warmer? If that were the case, I wouldn't be sitting here with you at the restaurant. A bed warmer is for fuckin' only. We got a helluva lot more than that. I enjoy your company, and I want to find out a lot more 'bout you." He brought her hand up, resting it on his cheek.

"You have to admit, your house is a shrine to Grace."

"Maybe I didn't have a reason to change anything once she died." He winked at her. "Kylie is in Aspen, Ethan and Emily are crashing at their friends' houses, so it seems fitting that we should take advantage of the situation." Moving her hair away from her neck, he whispered, "Let's go to my place."

He felt her stiffen under his touch. "I don't feel comfortable with all the pictures of your wife staring at me. I understand and respect that you want them, and I'd never, *ever* tell you to take them down, but I feel like an intruder. For reasons I don't even understand, I feel like I'm being disrespectful to Grace."

He placed a hand on either side of her face, forcing her to look at him. "That isn't the case at all. As a matter of fact, Grace would like you if she were here." He gently kissed her mouth, murmuring, "I want to spend the night with you. I want to feel your skin against mine when I fall asleep, and when I wake up. I fuckin' need you, babe."

After a bit of coaxing, Belle finally agreed to go home with Banger, and he knew she was expecting to see the house the way it was the previous time she'd been there. When he led her into the family room, he heard her gasp behind him as he bent over to light the wood in the fireplace. Before he had a chance to stand, Belle knelt beside him, brushing the side of his face with kisses as delicate as a butterfly's wings. He pivoted around, his arms encircling her waist and drew her in, his lips hungry for hers. When her lips pressed against his, the tip of her tongue pushed against the seam, lighting his brain on fire, and causing molten desire to flow through him. Her arms reached up and tangled around his strong neck, and he held her so close to him that their breaths mingled.

Breaking away, she panted, "Why didn't you tell me?"

"And miss out on *this*?" His voice was husky even though his eyes smiled. He kissed her again, pulling her head back so he could delve in deeper, her moans echoing down his throat. In one fluid movement, he stood, taking Belle with him. He led her to his bedroom, and he saw her eyes glance at the dresser, looking for the wedding photo. When it wasn't there, her kiss intensified, and Banger pushed her gently on the bed, staring down at her as he ripped off his shirt. She lay there, her tits pushing up and down from her heavy breathing, her eyes smoldering with an intense fire. He inhaled sharply, he couldn't pull his gaze away from her; he needed to lose himself in her lush body.

"Take your top off," he ordered, his breath erratic.

She obeyed, unbuttoning the small, green pearls slowly, her eyes locked with his. His dick was on fire as she teased him with each button she undid. She was fucking teasing him, and he loved it. He forced himself to stand still and watch as she slipped her top down her shoulders and then her arms, revealing her rounded breasts covered in a gold, lacy bra. He clenched his teeth as she reached behind her then the straps of her bra slid down, and she removed her bra. From where he stood, he could see her hard nipples and the puckering of the skin around them. He wanted to bite them and suck them deeply in his mouth, but he held back and watched her unbutton her jeans, scooting off the bed while she slowly tugged them over her hips, thighs, and calves. Her jeans laid pooled around her feet, and she stepped out of them, standing before him in the sexiest panties he'd ever seen on a woman.

"Play with your tits for me," he demanded, and she cupped her breasts and kneaded them with her hands. She threw her head back and her lips parted, and Banger wanted those lips around his cock so badly, but he just watched as she pinched and flicked her long nail over he hard buds.

"You like watching me touch myself? You want to know what I like?"

"Yeah. It's hot seeing you play with your big tits."

"I like the way you touch them."

Her gaze never left his, and his jean had grown uncomfortable. "Slip off your panties. I want to see your sweet pussy."

With a wicked smile, Belle glided her panties down her legs then stepped out of them. Her skin shone in the golden glow of the lamp, and the moonlight bathed her in brilliance. She was so gorgeous, and he wanted to jump her, consume her, fuck her so hard she wouldn't be able to walk. Belle had grabbed him by the balls, and he was so enjoying the ride.

His staring must have made her self-conscious because she crossed her arms over her chest, hiding her lovely tits. "Uncross your arms. I want to see all of you."

Slowly she uncrossed them, but she fidgeted in place. "You like what you see?" There was a tinge of self-doubt in her voice.

How in the hell could she not see that he was loving what he saw? He nodded and walked toward her. Bending down, he took hungry possession of her mouth, his tongue plundering her dark recesses. His ferocity must have taken her by surprise, because she lost her balance, but his strong arm held her, drawing her close to him, as he continued his frenzied assault. Each whimper of pleasure went straight to his cock and fired every nerve in his body, and he cupped her ass cheeks tightly in his hands, his fingers digging into her soft flesh.

As they kissed, Belle unzipped his jeans, and when her warm fingers curled around his pulsing cock, a low growl came from deep in his throat. He moved his hand to her pussy, dripping with her juices, and he buried his finger deep in her folds, stroking her until he felt her sweet spot harden. As he touched her, he felt her hot skin tremble beneath his hands, and he inhaled the scent of her arousal—she was ready for him.

"Turn around so your ass is facing me." He nudged her around.

When she was standing in front of him, his eyes ran up the length of her, lingering on her ass and the small of her back. He leaned over and traced a slow, wet trail from the back of her neck all the way down to her quivering ass cheeks.

"Bend over," he demanded.

Belle bent over, her delicious ass cheeks spreading showing him her rosy, glistening pussy. He almost lost his load looking at how beautiful she was. Kneeling down, he spread her globes even farther then with one, long swipe, he ran his tongue from her wet slit to the top of her clit.

"Oh, God, Banger," she moaned, squirming under his touch.

"You like that? I bet it feels real good, huh?" He slipped two fingers into her, and her legs bucked. He drank her, savoring her scent and taste as he slid his tongue over her again and again.

When her legs tightened, he knew she was on the precipice, so he pulled the nightstand drawer and grabbed a foil packet. Ripping it open with his teeth, he hurriedly rolled it on. He wanted her in the worst way—her taste, scent, and feel of her skin next to his drove him fucking wild.

"Bend over," he rasped.

Belle complied, her hands holding on the chair next to the nightstand.

"Spread those sexy legs wider." He was pressed against her back, breathing in her ear. He grabbed her tits and massaged them, pulling the nipples down hard as she groaned and shook under his touch. Stepping back he took in the way her breasts were slightly swaying as they hung down, her ass was flexing—from excitement, he guessed—and he swollen pussy was shining wet. *Fucking awesome!*

He took his dick and rubbed it in her juiciness, then with one hard roll of his hips, he entered her wet heat. Her loud gasp filled his ears and pushed him on. He slammed into her over and over, smacking her jiggling ass, squeezing her bouncing tits, and stroking her sweet nub.

Hard. Deep. Rough.

"You want more?" he grunted as his hips thrust against her, and her ass pushed back and wiggled against him.

"Yeah. Feels so good. Damn."

He kissed her back then pushed harder and rougher, loving the way the walls of her pussy clamped around him. It was the best fucking feeling, it was like being burned alive with the sweetest heat. Wrapping his hand around her thick hair, he pulled her head back, and she screamed out, "Damn, I'm coming. Oh, I'm coming!" She writhed and moaned as her legs quivered and her heated walls clenched around his hardness like a vise. Her panting and shaking wrapped around him, and the pressure within him began to build until he couldn't hold it in anymore, crossing the threshold into an insane explosion.

As his hot seed spurted into the sheath, he dug his fingers into her hips, holding on for dear life. With his head tilted back, his eyes closed, he grunted, "Fuck, woman. Fuck!"

Leaning down, he kissed the top of her back as he stroked her sides. Belle's whole body was still shaking, and she was short of breath as she came. Banger's face was soaked, and when he pulled out, her legs gave out, and he caught her and placed her on the bed, lying down beside her.

He curled his arms around her, and her short pants became more normal as they lay together basking in the pleasure of their union. "You're somethin', you know that?" He threaded his fingers through her hair, kissing her lightly.

"You bring out the sexy woman I always wanted to be in bed." She kissed his shoulder.

Drowsiness overcame him, and he held her close, his eyelids heavy, his body sated. *This woman makes me feel things I thought had died with Grace.* And that was the last thought he had before sleep overtook him.

# Chapter Fifteen

Several days later, Banger called church in order to finalize the plans for the arms deal. Hawk and his crew had secured the various weapons sooner than they thought possible.

Banger slammed the gavel on the table. "Shut the fuck up! We got shit to go over. First thing is: who the fuck beat the shit outta the two citizens at Steelers on Saturday night?" Steelers was a popular bar and restaurant frequented by bikers. Every so often, citizens would show up to down a few drinks, watch the fights on the big-screen TVs, or hit on the women who hung around waiting for some fun with a biker.

Several eyes turned to Rock, who leaned against the concrete wall, a scowl on his face.

"You done that shit? Did you have a reason, or were you just bored?" Banger asked while the membership laughed.

"The fuckers were messing with a chick who only wanted biker cock. I told them to back off, and they challenged me. I fuckin' warned them." Rock grumbled, his voice laced with a Cajun accent. The Sergeant-At-Arms hailed from Lafayette, Louisiana, and had joined up with the Insurgents six years past. He was a man of few words, preferring to act rather than talk. After Jax had been stripped of the position, the club unanimously voted Rock to take over, and he rose to the occasion.

"Were there many citizen witnesses?" Banger asked as he shuffled through some papers Hawk had handed him.

"Nah. Mostly bikers. No one's fuckin' snitching."

Banger looked at Axe. "You, Jax, Chas, PJ, and Rags pay a private visit to the assholes. Make sure they understand what happens to people who testify against an Insurgent. That should solve the problem. If it doesn't, we'll have to make them disappear. These fuckin' citizens come to our bars pretending to be badass. It gets them in trouble every time." He stared at Rock then Axe. "I don't want this shit blowin' up in our faces. Take care of it. Fast."

Rock grunted while Axe tilted his chin up. Banger knew he could count on them to bury the incident in whatever way was necessary. "All right. Let's talk about when we deliver the goods to the Mexicans. And those—" he pointed to the rocket launchers and AK-47s spread out on the table "—are beauties."

"I brought a few of them here to show everyone where their money was going." Hawk smiled. "We got all the stuff in the storehouse."

As they discussed the day and time the assigned group would meet up with the Mexican revolutionaries, Bruiser's loud, angry voice silenced the room. "Who the fuck are you and why are you in here?"

Banger looked in the direction Bruiser was pointing, and he stepped back a couple of steps. A flush of adrenaline tingled through his body as his steely blue eyes landed on Belle, who stood inside the room staring at the weapons on the table. Banger gave the gavel to Hawk. "Take over," he growled, then he walked over to Belle, yanked her hard, and dragged her out of the room, the door slamming behind them.

When he pushed Belle into a small room, he pounced on her. "What the fuck are you doing here?" Sour bile rose in his throat as heat flushed through his body.

Beads of sweat were visible on her forehead. "I came to see you. I thought it'd be a nice surprise for you. I see now it wasn't." She looked down at her feet.

"What were you doing in the room where we were having church?" His nostrils flared.

"Church? I don't know what you're talking about. I was looking for you, and I heard your voice, so I went in to see you." She grasped his hand, but he pulled away.

"You fuckin' never do shit like that, woman. What the fuck is the matter with you? What did you hear? How long were you standing there? You tell me what the fuck you heard and saw. Now!"

Belle backed away from him, but he moved toward her. "I'm sorry. I really am. I didn't mean any harm. I didn't hear or see anything."

"Bullshit! I saw you staring at the table. Fuck, Belle. Fuck!"

She brought her fingers to her lips; her face had turned white as snow. "Okay, I saw some guns. They looked like machine guns, but I don't know why they were there. I didn't hear you say anything about them. I only came to see you. I knocked on the door, but no one answered, and I heard your voice. It's all a misunderstanding. You have to believe me. You have to." Her voice hitched, and her eyes glimmered with tears threatening to spill over.

Banger eyed her, his insides battling with him. Was she telling him the truth? How much did she hear? He pressed his lips together in a grimace. Should he believe her?

She ran her finger up his arm. It was a soft and intimate gesture which set off a small spark in him. Looking at him with pleading eyes, she said softly, "Please, you have to believe me. I was looking for you. I didn't know it would be a problem if I went into the room. I really am sorry."

"You *never* fuckin' enter a room when the members are having church. Never."

She nodded. "I know that now, and I'll never do it again." She took out a tissue and dabbed at the corners of her eyes. That small gesture twisted his heart. *Fuck, I've got a soft spot for her.*

A loud knock on the door made her jump, and he gripped her elbow to keep her from falling down. "Come in," Banger said.

Rock stuck his head in. "You need me to take care of her?"

Banger shook his head. "It was an accident. She doesn't know shit."

He saw the glimmer of surprise flash in the Sergeant-At-Arm's black eyes. *Fuck, he's figuring I'm thinking with my cock instead of my head. What a fuckin' mess.* "You can go."

Rock jerked his chin and closed the door.

"What did he mean by 'take care' of me?" Belle asked in a low voice.

"We don't like people knowing our club business. You're damn lucky I got a soft spot for you. Fuck, Belle, don't wander around the clubhouse again. If you come to see me, sit your ass in the bar and fuckin' wait for me. You just can't go bursting in on church." He ran his hand through his hair. "Fuck."

"I've told you I'm sorry, and I'm getting pissed now. It happened. I didn't mean it. Let's move on, okay? How in the hell am I supposed to know the rules around here? And what the fuck is 'church,' anyway? Where I come from, church usually involves a minister."

Banger watched the color come back to her face as she raised her voice. A small smile curled the corners of his lips. She was a feisty one, he had to give her that. Reaching out, he looped his arms around her waist and brought her close to him. "Church is what we call a meeting."

"Then why in the hell don't you say 'meeting'?" Her eyes flashed at him, and he viewed her small outburst of anger with amusement. He playfully pinched her ass as he silenced her with a kiss.

"Next time, just text me that you're comin'. It'll eliminate all kinds of problems." He hugged her.

She shook her head. "*Next time*? You've got to be kidding."

He laughed. "Be a good girl, and wait for me out by the bar. Get yourself a drink. We'll be done with church in a bit." He kissed her again, feeling her tension seep away as she sank into his hold.

After he made sure Belle was sitting on the barstool and had a glass of white wine, he returned to the meeting room. Angry scowls and low grumblings met his entrance.

"Who the fuck is she? Bitches know they aren't supposed to disturb church," Throttle said, his eyes narrowed.

Banger cleared his throat. "She's a friend of mine. She's a citizen. I'm the only biker she knows. We gotta give her a break 'cause she had no idea." He glanced around the room, sensing the group's disapproval as to how he handled the situation. They wanted to spill blood—Belle's—and he couldn't do it. He'd trusted her explanation. If he wanted to keep seeing her—and he fucking did—he'd *have* to trust her on this one.

"Anyone got a problem as to how I'm fuckin' dealing with what happened?" His eyes had turned to frost as he stared each of the members in the eye. No one said a word. "Didn't think so. Now, let's get back to firming up the plans so we can finish up and get some beer." *And I can have some prime pussy.*

They focused their attention on the details of the arms deal that was going to net the club a cool four million.

★ ★ ★

THE FOLLOWING AFTERNOON, Belle dropped Emily off at Holly's. She'd explained the situation to her daughter, but Emily had accused her of being a bad mother, and she was giving her the silent treatment. Belle's stomach had been knotted up since the previous day when Banger had yelled at her for walking into a room. The ludicrousness of it amazed her. He'd acted like she'd discovered some long-lost secret; it was ridiculous. She hadn't heard anything. She *did* wonder what all the guns were doing on the table, but she had no idea what they were up to. At long last, Banger had finally believed her, and they'd had great make-up sex, but the veiled threats from the evil eyes the members had given her when they'd walked into the great room after their "church" made her body shake.

Driving to Holly's house, Belle's eyelids were hot and her chest ached. She hated sending Emily away, but she had no other choice. Her only hope was that Emily would see it her way one day.

When they arrived at Holly and Darren's house, Emily jumped out of the car, lugging her suitcase behind her without so much as a glance back at her mother. Belle watched her daughter with dull, wet eyes. Two years past, she never would have imagined this scenario. After waving to Holly and yelling, "I love you, Emily," to her daughter, she exhaled and with a heavy heart, she drove away.

Later that evening, she called Holly to see how Emily was doing. Holly said she was fine, and they were watching a chick flick together. Belle was happy, but a thread of jealousy wove around her as she wished that it were she and Emily watching the movie instead of Holly.

After her phone call, Belle texted her daughter.

**Belle:** *I love u.*♥♥♥

There was no reply. Tears stung at the backs of her eyes.

"Mom? Is Banger coming with us to the movies?" Ethan's excited voice broke through her teary veil.

Wiping her eyes quickly, she nodded. "Yes. He's picking us up in about fifteen minutes. Are you happy he's coming?"

Ethan bobbed his head up and down. "You bet. I like him. He gave me one of his really cool baseball cards when he was over the last time. He told me when the weather got nicer, we'd throw the baseball." Her son's eyes shone with anticipation.

She smiled warmly. "I'm glad you're getting along with him." Belle pulled her son to her and hugged him. "You know I love you very much, don't you?" She kissed his cheek.

He stiffened and pulled away. "I know, Mom."

She held his gaze. "I love you and your sister more than anything." She paused then lowered her voice. "For complicated reasons, your sister had to move to Aunt Holly's for a short time. She'll be back for the summer. I didn't want her to go." Her voice hitched.

Ethan shifted from one foot to the next as he shoved his hands in his jeans' pockets. "I know, Mom. Emily's coming back, but it is quieter without her. There isn't any yelling. I'm gonna wait for Banger in the family room." He scampered away.

Belle sat staring at the kitchen wall until Banger came over, bringing excitement and joy with his presence.

At the movies, with Banger's arm around her, her son's eyes bright as he laughed at all the silly parts in the film, and a bucket of popcorn among them, Belle let the sadness and guilt recess to the corners of her mind, enjoying the happiness which spread through her. Ethan was having a wonderful time, and he and Banger had a connection which thrilled her to no end. Life could be good if she focused on the simple things: a night at the movies.

Ethan laughed and rehashed all his favorite scenes from the movie. As Banger spoke with Ethan, he caught her eye and winked—a single shiver rode down her spine. Ethan and Banger played a video game before he went up to bed. When Belle came downstairs, Banger pulled her toward him and wrapped her close, and in his arms, she felt like she was in a cocoon—safe and protected from everything.

He kissed her forehead. "I know today was rough on you. Deciding to send your daughter to your friend's house to protect her is the bravest thing a mother can do. You made the right choice."

"Then why is my heart breaking?"

"Sometimes, making the right decision hurts. Your daughter's lucky to have you as her mother."

Belle looked up at him then put her arm around his neck, pulling him down to her. She crushed her mouth over his. "You're a special man," she breathed against his lips. "Can you stay the night?"

With a twinkle in his eye, he nodded then kissed her deep. Breaking away from him, she stood then took his hand, leading him upstairs to her room. Banger stripped down to his boxers and climbed in bed, his eyes never leaving her face. Before she slipped in beside him, she took out her phone and texted Emily.

**Belle:** *Nite, honey. I love u.*

She knew Emily wouldn't respond, that she would need more time. Belle would keep texting and calling her no matter how many times her daughter ignored her. She set down her phone and scooted close to Banger, curling her arm around him. She looked up at him and he bent his head low, his warm breath ghosting across her face before he kissed her. Soft and slow, as his hands slid down to her hips. Heat engulfed her as desire replaced tension, and she let herself be lost in Banger's scent, his taste, and his touch. . . .

# Chapter Sixteen

"Belle, someone wants to see you out front!" Ruthie yelled as she grabbed the plates under the hot lights. "Take ten."

Belle wiped her hands on a dish towel, smoothed down her hair, and wandered out to the eating area. She looked around expecting to see Banger, but she didn't see anyone she knew. Glancing at Ruthie, she followed the woman's tilting head and spotted a young, dark-haired woman sitting at a small booth. Belle didn't recognize her. "*She* wants to see me?" Ruthie nodded then shrugged as she set the plates in front of the patrons seated at the counter.

Belle's stomach twisted. She hoped it wasn't someone from social services doing an assessment for the truancy court. Every time her phone rang with a number she didn't recognize, or someone she didn't know approached her, she always thought it was bad news about her daughter. Inhaling deeply, she walked over to the young woman. A sweet jasmine scent wafted around Belle, startling her. The young brunette wore the same perfume as she. Maybe that was a good sign. She stood by the table, the sense of dread not as pervasive as it'd been as she walked to the table.

"I'm Belle. You asked to see me?"

The woman assessed her with cold, flat eyes then wrinkled her nose. "*You're* Belle Dermot?" She curled her lip. "Figures."

Belle's face tightened. "Who are you?"

The woman placed a slender hand under her chin. "I'm the woman your husband was fucking." A forced smile exposed perfect white teeth.

Belle grabbed the edge of the table to steady herself. The woman's statement hit her right in the gut, and she was lightheaded. Had she heard correctly? "My husband has been dead for more than a year. I don't know you, and I have nothing to say to you." Her voice dripped ice.

"I'm not here to tell you all the details, I just want my share of the money. Harold made me a lot of promises he didn't keep. He promised me a large amount of money. I'm here to get my share." Her brown eyes bored into Belle.

Belle couldn't believe the audacity of this woman dressed in expensive designer clothes, carrying a Chanel purse that probably could feed Belle and her kids for three months. It seemed like she'd already received more than enough of her share from Harold—there was no way a secretary salary bought her outfit. As her pulse sped up, heat crept up her neck, reddening her skin in its wake. "You have a lot of nerve. You come here after all this time *demanding* money from me, you stupid tramp?"

"I would've come sooner, but I left town for a while right after Harold died. I've only now returned. The point is, Harold was planning to leave you so we could be married."

"I don't believe you! Harold told me he broke it off with you."

"You *would* believe that. Anyway, like I said, I'm not here to give you all the sexy details. I just want what he promised me."

Belle laughed dryly. "You can have everything I received." She shook her head when she noticed the woman's eyes shining with greed. "I have the list of creditors who were discharged in my bankruptcy. Will that do? Get the fuck out of here."

Belle turned to leave when the woman grabbed her wrist. Belle jerked her hand out of the lady's grip. "Don't you ever fucking touch me," she hissed. The young girl pulled away.

"Where did all the money Harold embezzled from the company go? Do you think I believe this 'poor widow' shit you're dishing? No fucking way. I'm going to get what's owed me, one way or another. No one screws me over."

"Seems like Harold screwed us both over. Get out and leave me the fuck alone. If you don't, I can make sure you will." She narrowed her eyes.

"This woman giving you a problem?" Ruthie said as she came up behind Belle.

"No, she was just leaving."

The pretty girl jutted her chin out, defiance etched on her face. "I'll leave when I want." She tossed her head, her long hair falling over her shoulders. "You can't tell me to leave. You don't own the place."

"But I do. Come on, missy, haul your designer-clad ass outta here. I don't need business from people like you." Ruthie stood with her legs spread out and her hands on her hips. "Go on, get outta here before I throw you out, and I'm not known to be gentle."

Harold's former mistress glared at the two women then stood up, shoving past them. Without a backward glance, she slid into a cherry-red Mustang convertible and took off.

"You okay? Why don't you have a seat and drink something. You look mighty upset." Ruthie handed Belle a glass of water.

Shaking her head, she drank slowly, the cool liquid soothing the burn in her throat. "I'm okay, really. That bitch was the woman my husband had an affair with. I always wondered how she looked. Damn, she's only about seven years older than Emily. Why are men such pigs?"

"'Cause they got that goddamned dick that's always looking for a new hole to stick. I been through three husbands and they were all good for nothing. I can't believe the fucking nerve of that woman. She came just to hurt you. Your man's been gone for a while, so she came to throw her young ass in your face. I should've thrown the bitch out on her butt."

Belle smiled, a warm glow replacing the angry fire that had burned in her only a few minutes earlier. She had only known Ruthie for less than a year, yet the kind, rough-around-the-edges woman had her back. "She wanted money. That's a bigger joke than Harold fucking a woman less than half his age."

"Money? Why the fuck would you give it to her if you had it?"

She shrugged. "People are all kinds of fucked up. I hope I don't see her again. I have enough shit to deal with."

"If she bothers you again, you let me know. I'll set her straight. Better yet, tell Banger. The Insurgents will make sure she gets the message loud and clear." Ruthie laughed.

"I think I can handle it, but I'll keep your offer in mind. I better get back to work. I'm sure Jerome is freaking out about now."

While she deep fried the Thursday night special—fried chicken—she couldn't help but think about all the money Harold had embezzled from the textile company. The shareholders had been livid, and she had several insurance and stock investigators questioning her for months before they were satisfied that she knew nothing. She'd been shocked to learn that Harold had stolen close to two million dollars. What had he done with it? She sighed. How could a man who told her he loved her almost daily betray her and leave her and their kids penniless? She'd been duped, and she had no plans of giving herself to Banger or any other man completely. Men could not be trusted. Period.

When her shift ended, she couldn't wait to go home and put her feet up. Even though money was tight, she'd order pizza for her and Ethan; the last thing she had the energy for was to make dinner. After that woman came into the diner, Belle's day had deteriorated with one mishap after another in the kitchen, and she couldn't get the woman's bitchy face from her mind. She couldn't erase the images of the pretty woman's lithe legs around Harold's waist as he grunted and pushed into her.

The doorbell interrupted the slideshow playing out in her mind. "Is that the pizza already?" Ethan yelled down from his room.

"I don't think so. I just called in the order less than five minutes ago." Belle trudged to the door. "I'll call you if it is." She opened the door and stared into the face of a man dressed in a tweed jacket and yellow tie. "May I help you?"

The man pulled out a badge, and Belle's heart dropped to her stomach. *Something's happened to Emily. Oh, no. God, please let her be safe. Please let—*

"Mrs. Belle Dermot?"

"Yes," she whispered.

"I'm Detective Sanders from the Lakeview Police Department. I have a few questions I'd like to ask you. May I come in?"

Trying to unlock the screen door with trembling fingers proved to be nearly impossible. She smiled weakly then took several gulps of air, forcing herself to calm down. She finally unlocked the door. "Come in. Is this about Emily?" She led the detective to the living room, gesturing him to sit down. She sat on the couch, opposite him. "Well, is it?"

"Emily?"

"My daughter. That *is* why you're here, isn't it?"

"No, ma'am. I'm here to ask you some questions about the death of your husband, Harold Dermot." He reached inside his jacket and took out a small notepad and a pen.

"Harold? He's been dead for over a year. I don't understand." *What is it about today that makes all these people come out of the woodwork asking about Harold?*

"Can you recount the details surrounding your husband's death?"

The questioning went back and forth for about ten minutes, and it seemed to Belle as though the detective was hinting that Harold's death may not have been due to natural causes. She rubbed her pounding temples.

"Can you tell me about the syringe that was found hidden in your silk bag among Harold's papers in your storage unit?"

All of a sudden, she felt her body overheating. "Um… silk purse? I don't know what you're talking about."

Detective Sanders showed her the picture of the purse and syringe he had retrieved from the storage unit after Jessica Dermot Hoskins had called him. "Do you recognize anything in the photograph?"

Belle tried hard to focus, but her eyes were playing tricks on her and everything was blurry. She rubbed them hard, then looked at the photo, concentrating. "Uh… The purse is mine, but I don't recognize the syringe. It isn't like any of the ones my husband used for his insulin shots. What does this mean?"

The detective continued playing a cat and mouse game with her, asking questions that indicated Harold's death was suspicious, and even that she may have been involved. When she asked him what was going on, he only replied with circular answers.

"I've told you for the umpteenth time, like I told the investigators who came around after my husband passed, I don't know anything about the money. Do you really think I'd have gone bankrupt and live like this—" Belle swept her outstretched arm "—if I had the money? I certainly wouldn't be working ten-hour shifts on my feet at a diner."

The doorbell rang, and Belle paid the pizza delivery man. "Pizza's here," she called at the bottom of the stairs. The detective stood up, thanking her for answering his questions. Ethan dashed down the stairs then stopped abruptly when he saw Detective Sanders. Belle placed her hand on Ethan's shoulder. "This is my son, Ethan," she said.

He nodded to Ethan. "I'll let you know if I have any more questions," he stated as he opened the screen door.

"Ethan, take the pizza to the kitchen. You can start without me." She followed the detective out. Hugging her arms around her, she shivered in the cold, evening air. "You know, a woman came to the diner today to see me. She said she had been my husband's mistress." A brush of red crossed her cheeks. "She wanted money. She seemed angry that I didn't have any. You should talk to her."

Belle then gave the particulars to Sanders about her encounter. She watched him as he drove off in a dark blue Chevy Impala, his questions echoing in her head. *He thinks Harold was murdered. Who in the hell told him about the syringe? I bet it was that snooping bitch, Jessica. She's been a pain in my ass since I married Harold. Fuck!*

"Mom, aren't you gonna eat?"

"Coming." Belle walked inside the house and closed the door, shutting out the cold.

# Chapter Seventeen

"I FUCKIN' NEED money. When are we gonna kill the bitch?"

A soft voice with a steel edge replied, "When the time is right. We can't rush this. You wanna get caught? Haven't I delivered on all the others?"

"Yeah," he grumbled. "How much we getting this time?"

"We're looking at a million."

"Each time we eliminate someone, the price goes up. I fuckin' like that."

"We just have to be sure that we play it smart. I don't want any cops sniffing around.

The deep voice laughed. "I'm good at making things look like an accident. I've had a shitload of practice." They both laughed.

"We gotta be careful about being seen together too much. There's a detective snooping around asking all sorts of questions. He's trying to dig up a bunch of shit."

"Any chance he'll find out the old man didn't go the natural way?"

"I'm hoping he will. I know the Lakeview Police Department is incompetent, but maybe this detective has half a brain. Once he finds out it's succinylcholine in the syringe, the grieving widow will be the prime suspect. It works out perfectly. We just need to put some distance between us and the investigation. I'll let you know when the time is right."

"Okay. I guess I can rob a couple of liquor stores while I wait."

"Don't do anything stupid. I don't want you in the slammer. I'll front you some money to hold you over."

"Sounds good. I'll be in touch."

The person with the soft voice smiled. In about three months, Belle Dermot would be dead.

# Chapter Eighteen

Belle waved at Cara as she rushed down the hallway of the courthouse, her heels clacking on the polished floors. "Sorry I'm late," she breathed as she flopped down on the wooden bench outside the truancy courtroom.

"No worries," Cara said as she leafed through several papers. "This is the report from the school. It's not very good. It seems like Emily missed a lot of school last semester too. The judge isn't going to like that. It's good Emily is in a home with supervision."

"You don't think the judge will take her out of Holly and Darren's home, do you?"

Cara shook her head. "As long as I can show that Emily has supervision and structure, then he'll leave her with them. Judges don't want to put kids in the foster care system, so we should be fine."

A tall man in a sheriff's uniform opened the courtroom door. Cara squeezed Belle's hand. "We're first on the calendar, let's go in. It's going to be all right."

Thousands of butterflies fluttered in Belle's stomach, and a wave of nausea washed over her. She followed the young lawyer into the courtroom and sat on the bench in the first row. When the door clicked open loudly, she looked back and saw Emily, Holly, and Darren walk in. "Hi, Emily," she said.

Without acknowledging her, Emily sat on a bench across from her mother. Holly came over and hugged her, saying in a low voice, "It's going to be okay." Belle's lips quivered, and she nodded.

Cara motioned for Emily to join her at the table she sat at, her notebook and law books strewn over it. Emily walked by her mother, her eyes staring straight ahead, and she jerked as though she'd been stung by a bee when Belle reached out and touched her hand. Emily took a seat next to Cara, her back to her mother. When the judge came in, everyone stood up, and Emily glanced over her shoulder at Holly and Darren, smiling slightly. Belle's heart twisted.

After the school board presented its evidence, Cara introduced several documents and had Emily, Belle, Darren, and Holly take the stand. Before sentencing, Cara argued against suspension and detention in a juvenile facility.

Judge Rickers cleared his voice and looked over his glasses, which were perched on the middle of his nose, at Emily. He chewed her out for her indifference, her lack of regard for the rules, and her insolence. He ordered her to complete a ten-day detention. Instead of sending her away to juvenile detention, he told her he'd allow in-home detention, and she could follow along with her class online. From where Belle sat, she saw her daughter's tight face, her dull eyes staring past the judge.

Judge Rickers took his glasses off and peered at Belle. "You have shirked your responsibility in providing a home for your daughter that fosters good habits, responsibility, and respect. You must take the brunt of her truancy and disregard for rules because you are the parent and you set the example. Unfortunately, the examples you have set have not been good ones. You are never home, you are cavorting with the president of an outlaw biker gang, and you have left your daughter to basically raise herself. Shame on you! If you did not have the kindness of your friends, who graciously offered to take your daughter in and give her a home with structure and supervision, you would have lost your daughter today. I will order a review hearing in forty-five days to see how the truant is doing in school and in her new home situation." He looked to the court clerk to announce the date then tapped his gavel. "Court is adjourned."

Belle sat speechless, her body shaking as raw pain coursed through her. Wide eyes blinked away briny tears before the world turned into a blur, all sounds, sights, and smells gone. She was an incompetent mother. She was to blame for the way Emily was turning out. How could that be? She loved her daughter and only wanted the best for her.

Cara's hand on her shoulder pulled her back into the courtroom. Emily walked past her, and Belle called out, "Emily, I'll call you. I love you." Her daughter went over to Holly, who glanced at Belle, half-shrugged, then put her arm around Emily and walked out of the courtroom.

"Belle, don't you dare believe a word that asshole judge said to you," Cara whispered in her ear. "He's a jerk and a bully. He's got some major hostility toward women. Don't pay attention. You're a great mom."

Belle smiled weakly. "My own daughter won't even look at me, my son is stuck in after-school care now, and I see more of Jerome and Ruthie than I do my family. Yeah, I'm a great mom."

"You're doing the best you can."

"I'm not looking for any adulations, and I'm not feeling sorry for myself. It is what it is, and I have to keep going on for Ethan." She followed Cara out of the courtroom. "How did the judge know about Banger?"

"I was surprised when he said that. I guess the school board's investigators really dig deep. Seems like a silly waste of taxpayers' money on a truancy charge."

After Belle said good-bye to Cara, she texted Banger:

**Belle:** *U doing anything tonight?*

**Banger:** *Spending it with you.*

She beamed, a funny feeling skipping across her heart.

**Belle:** *I'm making baked macaroni and cheese with smoked bacon, a tomato and radish salad, and country biscuits. Comfort food fest. I need it.*

**Banger:** *You okay?*

**Belle:** *No. Court today. Feeling the blues.*

**Banger:** *Did the judge fuck up?*

**Belle:** *No, I did.*

**Banger:** *No fucking way. The system always fucks up. Not the people.*

**Belle:** *:) Thx for that. Be over at 6:30. Bye.*

**Banger:** *Can I come earlier?*

She sighed. She craved a slice of quiet where she could wallow without talking, thinking, or feeling—alone time to simply be. Ethan wouldn't be home from Luke's until six.

**Belle:** *6:30 works out fine. See u.*

She knew Banger would be thinking she was still distancing herself from him, and he'd be right. But for the time being, that was the best she could give him.

★ ★ ★

AFTER DINNER, SHE watched with mild amusement as Banger and Ethan battled the zombies in a new game he'd brought over for her son. Every so often, Banger would glance over to her, his hand gently squeezing her knee, concern brimming in his eyes. He was sweet, and she'd tried real hard to be cheery and perky at dinner, but the truth was she didn't fucking feel cheery or perky, and he'd just have to deal with it.

They watched a few episodes of *Goosebumps* then Ethan went up to his room to finish his homework and read. Banger put his arm around her, drawing her in to him, his hand tilting her head back so he could kiss her. At first, he brushed his lips across hers gently, but then he took her bottom lip and sucked it between his teeth. She broke away from his mouth and burrowed in the crook of his arm, her head pillowed on his chest. She heard his heart thumping, felt his chest rise and fall with each breath. His scent of cloves and leather comforted her.

He threaded his fingers through her hair. "What's the matter, baby? Do you wanna talk about it?"

She squeezed him tighter. "No. I just want you to hold me. Nothing more." She felt him bend down before his warm lips touched her head, kissing it. As they watched the figures flick across the TV screen, her eyelids grew heavy, and with the steady rhythm of Banger's heart, she fell fast asleep in his arms.

# Chapter Nineteen

Banger kicked the metal filing cabinet next to his desk, denting it with his steel-toed boot. "Fuck! What the hell happened?" He stared at Hawk, who sat with an impassive face watching the president kick and bang against the office furniture. Banger leaned against the wall, sweat beads rolling down the side of his face. "Tell me what the fuck happened."

"The Mexican group called off the deal. They told me they got a better one at a cheaper price. They asked if we wanted to match it, and I told them to fuck off. We had a goddamned deal with them, and they call it off at the last fuckin' minute?"

"Did Liam know any of this?" Banger asked as he began to cool down.

"He swears he didn't know shit. He was just as surprised about the whole thing as I was." Hawk shook his head. "Something doesn't ring right with this."

"You're fuckin' right about that. Someone pulled the goddamned deal from under us."

"We got a mole." Hawk rubbed his face.

Banger blew out a long breath. "Fucking right. Damn! Who else knows about this in the club?"

"Just you."

Affection spread over Banger. Hawk was a brother to the end; he could always trust and depend on him to do what was in the best interest for the brotherhood. "Good. Let's keep the knowledge to a bare-ass minimum. I want to know who the fuck gave the assholes a better deal, and when we find out, I suspect we'll find our mole. You do your computer research magic, and I'll have Rock, Axe, Tug, and Chigger dig around."

"Maybe we shouldn't have the new guys know 'bout this yet. I think we should go with Chas and Bear instead of Tug and Chigger."

Banger rubbed his chin, his beard scratching his fingers. "You could be right, but Tug, Chigger, and I go way back. They were the ones feeding me all the shit 'bout Dustin running the Kilson chapter into the ground. They're cool."

"If you trust them, then I'll take your word. I don't know 'em. I'm the type who doesn't trust anyone unless they prove themselves first."

"They're cool. Tell 'em all the bare minimum, and you do a lot of the shit behind the scenes. I wanna know who betrayed the club, and when I do, I'm gonna fuckin' make sure we invoke the Insurgents' justice—slow and painful death."

Hawk rose to his feet. "I'm with you on this all the way, brother. I'll let you know when I find anything out."

After Hawk closed the door, Banger slumped down in his chair. The mother club had been lucky for the past twenty years—that had been the last time a brother had betrayed them. The guy had been a skinny, wiry one, always sweating and darting his eyes all around, thus earning him the name Nerves. It'd turned out he was a Deadly Demon, and when the club had found out, the fuckin' snitch pleaded for death after five days of systematic torture. Banger ground his teeth. When he flushed out the snitch, he'd make the eventual death of Nerves seem like a walk in the park. No one fucked with him or his club.

★ ★ ★

LATER IN THE day, Banger decided he needed a break, and he wanted to see Belle. After a rough few days, Belle had seemed to relax a bit, and they were back to laughing and fucking, which made him relaxed.

When he arrived at the diner, he noticed a wicked-looking Harley parked out front. He went over and admired it, wondering who it belonged to. The scent of freshly brewing coffee and baking bread tantalized him, and he realized how hungry he was. He bent over and looked through the serving station window, but he didn't see Belle. Figuring she was in the ladies' room, he sat at the counter and fiddled with the sugar packets, his eyes glancing every so often at the doorway leading to the kitchen.

"What can I get you, handsome?" Ruthie asked as she walked behind the counter. "Coffee and a slice of pie? Belle made a delicious banana cream pie. I can't keep up with the demand."

"I'll take a slice of it. Where's Belle?"

"She's out back. She's on break, but she should be back in a few minutes."

Banger rose from his chair. "Pour me a cup of coffee. I'll be back in a minute." He walked through a small corridor then pushed open the back screen door. He stopped dead in his tracks, the muscles in his neck tightening as he saw Belle leaning against her car and a big guy towering over her. Spotting the patch of a grinning skull with snakes crawling out of its eyes, his ears pounded, and his fists clenched and unclenched. The Deadly Demons' logo mocked him, and a guttural roar burst from his throat as he rushed up to the rival club member, whirled him around, and punched him in the face, knocking him to the ground. Blood gushed from Scorpion's nose, and before he could move, Banger kicked his side savagely, his low grunt music to Banger's ears.

Wiping his bloodied knuckles on his jeans, Banger stood back and with an agility that could rival a panther, Scorpion leapt up. Throwing his body weight into it, Scorpion's fist slammed into Banger's jaw, and the club president tasted metal as blood pooled in his mouth.

"Fucking asshole!" Banger said as he wiped the trickling blood from the corner of his mouth. With both hands, he grasped Scorpion's head and brought his knee up to his face; there was a blunt crack and Banger released his head. Crimson escaped from Scorpion's nostrils and, reaching into his cut, he whipped out a knife. Banger slid his hand into his boot and pulled out a gleaming one as well. Belle screamed.

From behind him, he heard the screen door creak open and slam, then Ruthie yelling, "What the hell is going on?"

As he and Scorpion crouched low, circling each other, he heard Belle say, "They're fighting. I'm afraid Banger's going to be hurt. We have to call the police."

Ruthie's loud voice rose above the pulsing in his ears. "The police don't need to be involved in this. Banger can take care of himself."

Scorpion lunged toward Banger, and in the second that his knife grazed Banger's forearm, the club president grabbed hold of Scorpion's wrist, twisting it behind his back until the Deadly Demon screamed in pain. Banger drew his fist back and ploughed it in the asshole's stomach, dropping him to the ground. Then he pushed his knee into the Demon's chest and pummeled his face with tight, angry fists, blood humming in his veins.

"Stop it, Banger! You're going to kill him." Belle's voice screeched over him, and he looked down at Scorpion's bloody face, the swelling just beginning to make his distorted features more grotesque.

He jumped up and marched over to Belle, his eyes narrowed. "Woman, we gotta talk!"

Nodding toward Scorpion, Ruthie asked, "Is he dead?"

"Nah. Just fucked up. Throw a bucket of water on him. Belle will be back in twenty." Before Ruthie answered, he yanked Belle's arm and dragged her with him to the side of the diner, near the alley.

Letting her go, he stared at her, and he could feel her fear radiating from her. "How long you been fuckin' a Deadly Demon?"

Belle's eyes widened as she brought her hand in front of her mouth. "I'm not fucking him."

"Do you know him? The truth, woman!"

Belle nodded, her eyes cast downward.

Banger growled and slammed his bruised fist against the diner's brick wall. "Why the fuck didn't you tell me you were with a Deadly Demon? That's something I needed to know. You fuckin' told me you didn't know any bikers, and I catch you with that piece of shit? Why'd you lie to me?"

"Scorpion is Holly's brother," she said.

A bitter tang rose up his throat when he heard her say *his* name. "What the fuck does that have to do with you lying to me? Did you go out with him?"

Belle grimaced and raised her head up and down. His muscles tensed, and it felt like a million ants were crawling on his skin. She took a step toward him. "It meant nothing. I never liked him. I thought he was a creep. Holly pushed him on me, and I did it to please her. I only went out with him twice, and nothing happened. I didn't know a Deadly Demon from an Insurgent. When I told Holly you were the president of the Insurgents, she told me not to tell you about her brother because your clubs were rivals. I didn't lie to hurt you, I lied to keep the peace." She reached out and touched his hand. He jerked away from her.

Images of Belle standing inside the room when they were having church a couple of weeks before flooded his mind. He tilted his head while mentally weighing the evidence: she had seen the guns, she'd heard what the club was talking about, the Mexicans called off the deal, and someone betrayed the Insurgents. A knot formed in his belly. "*You* told the fuckin' Demon about the shit you heard at the meeting, didn't you?" Blankness covered her face. *Fuck, she's a good actress.*

"I don't know what you're talking about. I've already told you that whatever you all were talking about didn't sink in."

"You're fucking lying." He crossed his arms around his chest and took a few more steps away from her.

"Banger, please, listen to me. This is all a big misunderstanding. I'm sorry I didn't tell you about Scorpion, but Holly told me it would cause a lot of problems. I didn't mean to hurt you. I don't know what you're talking about with the club. Please, calm down and think reasonably. I let you into my home, my life. You know me."

"I thought I did. I was wrong." Pointing at her, he hissed, "No one fucks with my club. We're through." He turned around and stormed to his Harley, her pleas bouncing off him. He revved the engine and blasted away from the diner.

When he arrived at the club, all eyes were on his battered face, and he waved all questions away. Clutching a bottle of whiskey, he trudged upstairs to his room on the third floor. On each step, he cursed himself for letting the curvy, dark-haired vixen grab his cock and his heart. Deciding he was through with her, he collapsed on the bed, twisting open the bottle of booze. He took a deep drink, relishing the sting of the whiskey as it coated his throat. The late-afternoon rays flooded his west-facing room. He slammed the blinds shut then flopped back on the bed. Squeezing his eyes shut to block out his suspicions, thoughts still swam through his mind. If Belle turned out to be the snitch, he'd have to slit her pretty, soft throat. A hard iciness crushed his heart.

*Fuck!*

# Chapter Twenty

Even though Banger had left, Belle stood watching the street, hoping he'd come to his senses and return. She couldn't believe what had just happened. And for him to suspect her of telling Scorpion stuff about the Insurgents was insane. Banger had been so angry, hurt, and disgusted with her; she'd seen it on his face, heard it in the tone of his voice. She shouldn't have lied to him. She'd wanted to tell him, but Holly made it sound like it would be World War III if she did. But lying to him had made everything between them terrible. Images of the fight haunted her, and she'd been repulsed by the viciousness of it. Banger had always been so sweet with her and Ethan, but the man who beat Scorpion to a pulp frightened yet titillated her. And what the hell was up with *that*?

Although, Belle had been glad Banger came when he did, because Scorpion was forcing himself on her, and he wasn't taking her protests seriously.

Behind her, Scorpion moaned, and Belle, fearful he'd come for her, hurriedly walked past him and entered the diner. She picked up her phone and dialed Holly.

"You have to come here and get your brother. Banger caught him pinning me up against my car, and he went ballistic."

"What? Is Scorpion okay?"

"I think so. He's on the driveway behind the diner. He's pretty banged up."

"How could you let this happen? Do you get off on men fighting over you? I told you not to let that asshole Insurgent catch you and Scorpion together. You're a stupid, naïve woman. Grow the fuck up!"

While Holly ranted, Belle wondered if she woke up this morning with a sign on her back that said, "Punching Bag." Tiredness weaved through every fiber in her body, and her legs felt like Jell-O. Grabbing a chair, she dragged it close to her and collapsed in it. She wanted to jump off the never-ending merry-go-round her life had been on for two years.

Interrupting Holly's tirade, Belle said, "Holly, come pick up your brother. I have to go." She disconnected the call.

Ruthie came over and rubbed Belle's neck. "You're too tense. I called someone in. Go home and relax. You look beat."

"I can't believe what happened. Banger is so mad at me."

"I've known Banger a long time, and he's a softie with the women in his life."

"I'm not a woman in his life. I think we were getting to that point, but then this shit with Scorpion came up, and now he's dumped me." Her voice broke.

"Don't worry too much 'bout that. It wounded his pride, seeing you with Scorpion. A man's pride is everything. He'll come around, you just wait and see." She pulled out another banana cream pie from the refrigerator. "I could kick myself in the ass for telling him you were out back. Shit, I didn't know Scorpion was back there with you. Sorry, Belle."

Belle shook her head. "I'm glad you told him. Scorpion was forcing himself on me, and I couldn't push him away. I didn't think it'd end like this though. I'll take you up on your offer to leave early. I'll see you tomorrow afternoon."

As she gathered her things, Holly blustered in. "Where's Scorpion?" Belle pointed to the back door. "Come on, and bring some warm rags." Holly dashed out.

Belle trudged out back, a few wet rags in her hand. She saw Scorpion leaning against her car, smoking a joint. He glanced up when the screen door banged behind her. "Your fuckin' boyfriend is a dead man. Tell him that, you fuckin' cunt."

Belle didn't come any closer. "Do you want the rags, Holly?"

She came over then stopped when her brother snarled, "I'm fine. I'm fuckin' outta here." He slammed his fist on the hood of Belle's car, then glared at her. "You and me ain't finished yet. Remember that." He stared at her with the eye that wasn't swollen shut, sending shudders of dread through her, and then he was gone. Belle blew out a breath.

"I'm sorry for the things I said to you on the phone," Holly said. "I was so upset and worried when you said my brother got in a fight, I said some nasty things to you. Let me buy you a drink. I think we both need to unwind a bit before going back home."

Belle agreed, and the two women headed to Billy's Tavern, a few storefronts away from the diner. Sitting at a table in the dimly lit neighborhood bar, Belle sipped her white wine—it tasted like vinegar. She recounted the events to Holly, leaving out the part where Banger suspected her and that he'd dumped her. Even as she thought of it, she winced from the pain of loneliness the idea of him being out of her life brought.

"How's Emily been doing?"

"Great. She's adjusted nicely to living with me and Darren, and we're both making sure she goes to school."

Belle smiled. "I'm glad. Tell her I said hi." She then proceeded to tell Holly about Harold's ex-mistress coming to see her.

"Was she pretty?" Holly asked before she took a sip of her beer.

"Yeah, she was. And young. She came looking for the money."

"Did she have a good figure?"

"Uh… yeah. Why?"

"Just wondering. You should've scratched the bitch's eyes out. What a slut."

"As long as I don't see her anymore, she could be a pin-up girl, and I couldn't care less."

"So, she didn't get any money from Harold?" A gleeful spark flashed in her eye.

"I wouldn't say that. When Harold confessed his affair to me, he told me that he had lavished her with trips, jewelry, clothes, and expensive dinners. Anyway, all that's in the past. I don't care anymore." *I only care about Banger, and how I can make it right between us again.* "Oh, and it seems like Jessica is spreading lies about me. You know, she always hated me for marrying her father."

For the next hour, the two friends chatted about their lives, their sorrows, and their joys. Belle didn't dare tell Holly that one of the biggest joys of her life since Harold died was meeting Banger. A rawness chafed her, and the pain was acute. She couldn't imagine not hearing Banger's voice anymore or seeing his twinkling eyes. He had invaded her life, and she couldn't let him go with the bitterness he had against her burning inside him. She had to make him understand. She missed him, and it hadn't even been two hours.

When Belle arrived home, sadness and emptiness shrouded her. She texted Emily, as she did every night.

**Belle:** *Nite, honey. I love u.*♥

As always, there was no answer.
She drew in a sharp breath and texted Banger.

**Belle:** *I'm thinking of u. Wish u were here. Text me.*

She stared at the phone for a long time, her insides tense in anticipation of the familiar *ping,* but its silence taunted her. She glided under the sheets, hugging the pillow next to her—it still smelled of Banger's aftershave. Pulling the comforter over her head, she buried her face in the pillow while her sobs consumed her.

# Chapter Twenty-One

*One month later*

ON HER BREAK, Belle sat on the low concrete wall, welcoming the warm spring breeze as it caressed her. She tilted her head toward the sky, feeling the heat of the sunlight. The scent of evergreens and spruces was in the air with their new growth, and the air vibrated with birdsong, bees, and the beginning of life. As she knew too well, the budding life around her could be short-lived with a blanket of snow. For that reason, she basked in the moments of early spring.

Her phone pinged and she looked down, a smile spreading over her face. It was from Emily, telling her that she had a great day at school. She had slowly begun communicating with her mother, and Belle said silent prayers every day in thanks. She would see her daughter on Saturday at the chili cook-off in Clermont Park. Every March, Pinewood Springs High School put on the fundraising event. If the weather was bad, it was held in the school's gym. In good weather, it was held at Clermont Park, and Belle had her fingers crossed that the lovely days they had been experiencing would continue until Saturday.

She was excited about the cook-off because the first prize was one thousand dollars, and the second and third cash prizes were still pretty decent. She could really use the money. For the past few weeks, she'd been cooking and tasting, using Ethan as her chili-tasting guinea pig. She laughed, recalling how, for the past several days, he would run to his room whenever he'd hear her start pulling the chili pot from underneath the stove.

The last time she'd heard from Banger was that horrible day when he'd beaten the shit out of Scorpion. He still came to the diner, but instead of calling Ruthie to find out when her shift was like he used to, he'd call to find out when she *wouldn't* be at work. The ache in her heart was not as strong as it was at first, but the lump in her throat still flared up whenever the diner's front door opened and she peered through the service window, hoping to see his twinkling blue eyes.

Each time she heard a motorcycle, her heart leapt, wondering if she'd see him with his blond hair blowing in the wind, his strong legs hugging the bike. But she never did. He'd done a good job of extracting himself from her life.

Belle had stopped calling and texting him a few weeks back. She still couldn't believe that what they may have had was short-circuited by an association she'd had with a rival club. The one she really felt sorry for was Ethan. In the beginning, he'd kept asking about Banger, but now he barely asked at all. Children could be very resilient at times.

She hadn't seen nor heard from Scorpion since that terrible day, and she wasn't complaining about that. All in all, her life had been moving forward, but she still missed Banger like crazy, even though she didn't admit it to anyone but herself.

She glanced at the time on her phone, then pushed up and walked into the kitchen to begin cooking the evening special—chili.

★ ★ ★

ON SATURDAY, THE weather was perfect, and all the vendors set up their booths early in the morning. The contestants for the cook-off also had their own chili booths, and Belle recruited Holly and Ruthie to help her dish out chili to the hungry festival-goers.

A few hours into the fundraiser, Belle spotted several men in leather jackets with the Insurgents' name and logo. Her heart skipped a few beats as she scanned the crowd, looking for a tall man with ocean-blue eyes and long, blond hair. She wondered if he were going to be there, or boycott it because he'd figured she would be.

Cara walked up to the booth with a woman who had flaming red hair and the cutest baby in tow. "Hey, Belle. Smells good," Cara said, pointing to the chili simmering in a pot. "I saw Emily with a couple of her friends. How are you two doing?"

"Better. At least we're talking now. That's a start."

Cara moved to the side, allowing the redheaded woman to come into full view. "Belle, this is Addie."

Addie smiled and held out her hand. "It's nice meeting you. I gotta try your chili—it smells awesome."

"Coming right up. Your daughter's beautiful. How old is she?"

"Thank you. Hope will be nine months in two weeks. I can't believe how fast she's growing." She bent over the stroller and ran her fingers through her daughter's bright red hair. "I better get two more cups for my husband and son."

Belle filled up three large cups, securing lids on them before she handed them to Addie. "Let me help you with those," Cara said as she took the containers.

"Hawk with you?" Belle asked as Cara turned to leave.

"Yeah." She leaned in close. "Banger's here too."

A surge of adrenaline shot through her, as her mouth went dry and her pulse sped up. "Oh." From Cara's devilish grin, Belle knew she wasn't fooling her with her feigned cool demeanor. "Did you want to take some chili to Hawk?"

"I'll be back in a bit. I'm going to help Addie get situated. See you."

Belle stirred the chili absentmindedly as she watched Cara and Addie disappear into the crowd. *Banger's here! I hope he comes over to see me.*

All morning, she served chili while scanning the crowd for the handsome biker. He was nowhere to be seen. She resigned herself to the fact that he was dissing her, and she'd be damned if she was going to spend all day moping about it. She had a cook-off to win, and she spotted the five judges heading to her booth.

Belle watched the judges' faces as they sampled her chili, and swore she'd seen sheer delight gleaming in three pairs of eyes. They thanked her, made notes on their sheet of paper secured on a clipboard, and moved away. When they parted, she spotted Banger talking with some men about ten feet from her booth. She bent over and put on her sunglasses so she could spy on him without fear of being caught.

He pretended to be engrossed in the conversation with his other club members, but she saw him peeking at her from the corner of his eye. Loving it, she decided to ignore him, which was easy to do since her booth was so damn busy. Several men she knew from the diner came over and chatted and flirted with her, and she noticed Banger shooting daggers at them. How he thought he had a right to be mad about men flirting with her when they weren't together was beyond her. She wondered if all bikers were as difficult as Banger.

After half an hour of playing "pretend I'm not looking at you," Banger strolled over to the booth, greeting Ruthie with a big smile and acting as though Belle didn't exist. "Hi, Ruthie. How you holding up?"

He chitchatted with her boss, and Belle, hopping mad, pretended to be engrossed in a conversation with one of the truckers who always came to the diner. He was sweet on her and asked her out at least four times a week, even though she'd always decline. He loved to talk, and normally she'd find an excuse to dodge a lengthy conversation with him, but at the moment, he was a godsend. When the guy placed his hand on hers, Belle thought she heard a growl. She ignored it. Finally running out of breath, the trucker said his good-byes and sauntered away.

Belle overheard Ruthie say to Banger, "You gotta try some of the chili. Here." She handed him a cup and a plastic spoon.

Out of the corner of her eye, Belle saw him take a big spoonful of the mixture. His eyes lit up. "Fuck, this is good." He glanced at Belle, and she turned to him and smiled. He ran his eyes over her, then smiled back. The thrill of his gaze tingled over her skin. He tipped his head to her and moved away, planting himself against a tree directly across from her booth, watching her every move.

An hour later, Ethan came up with a couple of his friends. "I saw Emily, Mom. She said to say hi to you, and she was gonna come by soon."

Warmth spread through Belle when she heard the words. She

couldn't wait to see her daughter, having missed her so much the past few months. A loud voice came over a crackling speaker. The votes had been tallied, and the judges had made their decision. "The third runner-up of the Pinewood Springs fundraising chili cook-off is Pearl Gunthe." Cheers and claps echoed among the festival patrons. "The second runner-up is Susie Evans. And the winner of the chili cook-off is Belle Dermot. Let's give these ladies a loud round of applause. And for all of you who didn't win this year, keep cooking and we'll see you next year. Could the winners please come to the judges' tent to collect their prize money? Thank you."

When she heard her name, Belle squealed and jumped up and down, and Ethan ran over screaming and hugging his mom before he and his friends ran around in circles, laughing and shoving each other. Ruthie and Holly made all kinds of noise as they congratulated their friend on her win. From the sidelines, Banger came up to her and also congratulated her. She was so happy to have won that she grabbed Banger and hugged him. When she realized what she'd done, she broke away, muttering, "Sorry."

Banger pulled her back into him and hugged her, whispering in her ear, "I've missed you, woman."

She pushed away. "I've missed you too."

"What are we going to do about it?"

She shrugged.

Banger took her hands in his. "Let's go to your house and talk."

"I'm not up for it tonight. You can't just decide you want to hang out with me tonight and then I don't hear from you. I won't let you do that to me, and I most definitely won't let you do that to Ethan. When you left me, I was sad, I was hurt, but I got over it. Ethan was the one you hurt the most. He couldn't understand why you left *him*. You didn't even fucking call him to say good-bye. That was a crock of shit." He circled his arms around her and pulled her close, but she twisted away from him. "I have to collect my prize money. I do want to see you again, but not tonight. Call me sometime."

Leaving Holly and Ruthie in charge of the booth, she went to the judges' tent to pick up the check. It took all of her strength not to agree to have him come over to her house after the festival, but she wanted him to know that it wasn't that easy to get her back. In her opinion, he'd acted like an asshole, and she wasn't going to let him jump back into her life whenever he decided he wanted to.

On the way back to her booth, Emily crossed her path. "Congratulations, Mom. That's so cool that you won first place. I always told you that you made the best chili." Emily played with her hair, braiding and un-braiding a small strand. "How've you been?"

"I've been okay. I've missed you. I can't wait for the school semester to end so you can come back home. How are you doing?"

Emily raised her shoulders up and down. "Okay, I guess. I gotta whole new set of friends. I think you'll like them." She twisted her hair around her finger. "I guess things are okay. I gotta go now. See you."

"I'll call you soon. Take care of yourself." Belle wanted to grab her daughter and hug her tightly, tell her how much she loved her, but she knew it would be too much too soon. She had to go back to the way it had been when Emily was a small child, with baby steps. That's how they would build a relationship again—one step at a time.

★ ★ ★

The following morning, Belle was awakened from a deep sleep. *Knock. Knock. Knock.*

She glanced at her phone which read four thirty in the morning. Her bleary eyes stared at the large numbers as another knock echoed through the quiet house. She grabbed her robe and leapt out of bed, running down the stairs, her heartbeats pounding against her chest. *Please, please, don't let this be about Emily.* She swung the door open and her eyes landed on Banger, but her brain couldn't grasp that he was the one making all the ruckus.

"What in the hell are you doing here at four thirty in the morning? Are you drunk?" She pulled her robe tighter around her as the early morning chill seeped in through the open door.

"Nope. Open up."

She unlatched the screen door and let him in, closing the door behind him. "Explain yourself, and it better be damned good."

"Get dressed, then get Ethan up and dressed 'cause I'm taking you both trout fishing."

Belle heard his words, but in her sleep-fogged mind she didn't understand. "We're doing what?"

Banger laughed. "Trout fishing. You're not too swift in the morning, are you?"

"I'd say the crack of dawn is usually not the best time for me. There's no way you're dragging Ethan and me to freeze our asses in a boat on a lake. No way."

Banger's smile disappeared.

"Mom, I wanna go. Please?" Ethan said from the top of the stairs.

Belle groaned, and Banger's smile reappeared. "I guess we're going fishing, woman." She looked from Ethan's hopeful eyes to Banger's sparkling ones, and she sighed. "Yeah, I guess I'm going to freeze my ass on the lake."

★ ★ ★

TEETH CHATTERING FOR a good three hours wasn't exactly Belle's idea of a good time, but she'd endure the cold, the icy wind, and her gnawing stomach again just to see the way Ethan's face lit up every time he reeled in a trout. He was having the time of his life, and it was all due to Banger. Fishing, baseball cards, and playing video games were things Ethan liked to do, but she didn't have the time to do any of it with him. She didn't know a thing about fishing, and all she knew about baseball was that a player hit the ball with the bat. Ethan needed someone like Banger in his life. The two of them got along so well together, and it warmed her all over.

The morning had heated up, and the sun shined over them as Banger loaded the ice chest full of fish in the back of his SUV. "Are we going to eat them?" Ethan asked as he slipped in the backseat, slamming the door behind him.

"Yep, but we gotta clean 'em first, and I'm gonna show you how to do that. I'm taking us to one of my favorite spots in the area. I want to share it with two of my favorite people."

"Wow. Are we really your favorite people?" Ethan asked.

"You and my daughter, Kylie." He looked in the rearview mirror and winked.

"If we're your favorite people, why did you stop coming around?"

Belle felt Banger stiffen beside her, and she took a perverse pleasure in it. Now he could figure out how to explain his absence from Ethan. Banger cleared his throat. "Sometimes, things happen. It had nothing to do with you, but I guess you kinda got lost in the shuffle. Didn't mean anything by it, I want you to know that. I'm not bullshitting you, kid."

Ethan seemed satisfied with Banger's answer, and he busied himself by playing a game on his phone, Belle listening to the intermittent bells and pings. As they drove over the rocky terrain, Banger slipped his hand inside hers and held it tightly. Calmness washed over her as they drove in silence, each happy to be in the other's presence.

They pulled into a clearing among the evergreen and aspen trees, and as soon as the car stopped, Ethan jumped out, running toward a gurgling creek. "Be careful," Belle called out after him. She bent down to gather her tote and jacket, and when she rose, Banger planted a kiss on her cheek. She turned her head and smiled at his lopsided grin, the one she was sure landed him in a lot of women's beds. He cupped her chin, tilted her head back, and kissed her softly on the lips.

"The water's cold," Ethan said as he crouched down by the creek.

Breaking away from Banger, Belle pushed out of the car and sprinted to her son. "You're too close. The water is really flowing. I don't want you to fall in."

"Hey, come over here. I need some help cleaning the fish," Banger said.

Ethan and Belle walked over to where Banger had set up a few chairs, a table, and piles of wood. After starting the fire, Banger brought the ice chest with the newly caught fish over to the table and told Ethan to start setting the trout on the table so they could clean them. Belle watched in amusement as her son's face wrinkled in concentration, Banger's fingers flying as he scaled, cleaned, deboned, and rinsed the fish as fast as Ethan placed them on the table. Neither of them spoke, as all their energy was given to the task at hand. From the way her son's eyes danced when he glanced at Banger, Belle knew he was having the time of his life.

Banger moved his head up and jerked it at a chest near the campfire. "Take out the frying pan, put a little oil in it, and place it on the cooking grate over the fire. We're almost ready to fry these fillets."

When she opened the chest, she smiled as it revealed not only the frying pan and oil, but rolls, oranges, potato chips, chocolate sandwich cookies, a spatula, utensils, and napkins. She pulled out the frying pan and oil, placing the greased pan on the cooking grate. Banger brought the aluminum platter piled with fish over to the fire. "Be right back. I'm gonna wash my hands." She watched him go over to the creek, crouch down, and wash up, Ethan standing beside him.

There was nothing like eating freshly caught fish grilled over a fire; it was delicious. And when Banger brought out a bottle of chardonnay, the icy reserve around her heart began to melt, but she reminded herself of the solitary confinement he'd put her in for a month just because she knew a man from a rival club. As the day passed, she realized he'd gone out of his way to give her and Ethan a special day in different ways, and she was finding it more difficult to stay mad at him.

After gorging on fish and potato chips, they went for a walk. Slim shafts of the sun's rays pierced through the evergreen forest as they walked, their footsteps muted by the pine needles, which carpeted the ground. The light spring wind ruffled her hair, and she took out an elastic tie and gathered her tresses in a ponytail. The scent of honeyed sap from the pine trees floated in the air, and in the distance, she heard the oozing rush of the creek.

Ethan ran ahead, stopping every so often to retrieve something from the forest floor to add to his collection. Banger slipped his arm around her waist, and she slammed into him when he abruptly stopped, his strong arm holding her steady. He nuzzled his nose against her neck. "Fuck, baby, I've missed your scent… and your taste." He nipped the sensitive spot right below her neck, and a current of desire sparked so intensely that she gasped, her gaze locking onto his hungered one. "I missed you and the boy." He threw her a cosmic smile, and it landed right between her legs.

"We missed you as well." Belle nuzzled against his face; his graying beard was soft as a light breeze. With the tip of her tongue, she traced the outline of his lips. He groaned and caught her mouth, plunging his tongue deep inside. She responded and their tongues fluttered and stroked each other's, their passion growing. When he glided his hand down the sides of her body to her ass, firmly cupping her cheeks, sparks of sensation zinged through her. She craved his touch, his taste—his everything.

Ethan's laugh brought her out of her aroused state. She whispered against Banger's lips, "Not here with Ethan." He kissed her, pressing her closer to him. She turned her head and saw Ethan on his haunches, scrutinizing something on the ground. "What are you looking at, honey?" she said.

"This big ant hole. There must be millions of them, and they're all so busy coming and going. It's totally cool."

She and Banger, hand in hand, walked over to see what all the fascination was about. They both agreed that watching the ants as they worked was pretty cool.

As the sun dipped and sherbet orange and pink streaks covered the sky, Banger packed up all the stuff he'd brought while Belle helped Ethan find the "perfect rock" for his collection. As they drove, "Hotel California" by the Eagles played on the classic rock station Banger always listened to. Belle watched as flashes of green zipped past them, and she concluded that the day had been perfect. She never imagined that dragging her ass out in the cold at the crack of dawn could have turned into one of her favorite days. Covering Banger's hand with hers, she stroked it lightly, then looked into his gentle eyes and smiled.

When they arrived at her home, Ethan rushed inside and climbed the stairs to his room. Belle faced Banger. "I can't thank you enough for today. I had a wonderful time, and I know Ethan was in heaven." She brushed a kiss on his lips.

He leaned his forehead against hers. "You gonna invite me in?"

Longing pulled at her heart, her breasts, and her pulsing mound, but she remembered how hurt she had been when he'd dropped her cold, and how humiliated she'd felt when her calls and texts had gone unanswered. "Soon, but I'm not quite ready to give you all of me. You know, you hurt me just at the time when I was beginning to trust you." She smoothed down his T-shirt. "I need some time. I hope you can understand."

Banger nodded, his hands on her hips. "I understand. I don't like it, but I get it." He tugged her to him and kissed her deep and wet. Pulling back, he took her chin between his callused fingers and pinched it lightly. "I'll call you." He kissed her forehead then walked to his SUV. She watched the red taillights until they disappeared into the night.

# Chapter Twenty-Two

Leaning back in his office chair, hands behind his head and feet on top of the desk, the buzz that had been vibrating in him since he'd seen Belle at the chili cook-off continued to electrify him. Having Belle back in his life made everything seem brighter, happier, and just plain fucking good. A couple of weeks before, the club had found out that the Deadly Demons weren't involved in snagging the arms deal out from under the Insurgents. It seemed that whoever struck the deal had covered themselves in several layers of brokers, and Hawk continued to work on piercing the veil. Once the club found out where the leak had come from, blood would flow, and Banger couldn't wait to be the one to draw the first drop.

He'd wanted to call Belle the moment he'd found out the Deadly Demons hadn't been involved, but the image of the fucker's body crushed against hers stopped him. She'd lied to him, and Banger had doubted her lame excuse for the deceit. Night after night, he'd stared at his phone, rereading her texts, listening to her voice messages, wishing he could purge the image of Belle and Scorpion. But he couldn't, so he turned off his phone, watched too much television, drank too much Jack, and hung out too much at Dream House, watching the dancers shake their asses and tits—always seeing Belle's face instead of theirs.

When Ruthie told him that Scorpion had been forcing himself onto Belle when Banger saw them, he'd felt like a fucking fool. He'd been so quick to judge her, but there was something about her that made his blood boil whenever any man looked at her. He'd been protective of Grace, but not like he was with Belle. He couldn't understand it. He'd wanted to call her, but he hadn't. Then, after Ruthie had told him he was a "stubborn old man who didn't know a good woman when he saw one," she'd let him know that Belle would be at the chili cook-off. He chuckled at the memory.

When he'd seen Belle dishing out chili, her long hair swishing, her sweater tight around her fantastic tits, he'd decided he needed her in his life. It had been hell for him during the month they hadn't seen each other. Back in with her, he wasn't surprised she was putting up defenses. She wanted him to jump through hoops for her, and he'd gladly do it. Hell, he'd jump over fucking canyons for her—she was worth it.

A knock on the door drew Banger out of his reverie. "Come in."

Tug poked his head in. "Badge is here to see you."

Banger raised his eyebrows. "What the fuck for?"

Tug shrugged. "He didn't say. Said he wanted to talk to you 'bout something. You want me to tell him to get the fuck outta our club?"

"Nah. Tell him to come in."

Detective Sanders entered the office, and Banger eyed him suspiciously. He hated badges, and he didn't need any of them sticking their noses around his club. Maybe this was a new transfer who wanted to show his boss he was on top of crime, so he came snooping around the one-percenter club. *Fuck that.*

"I'm Detective Sanders with the Lakeview Police Department. I'd like to ask you a few questions."

Banger stared at him, his face stony. An awkward pause ensued. "Do you mind if I sit down?" Sanders asked, as he plunked down on the leather chair in front of the club president's desk. Banger still stared without saying a word.

"Do you know a Belle Dermot?

*Fuck, I didn't expect* that. "Why do you wanna know?"

"I just need to ask you some questions about her. How long have you known her?"

"I didn't tell you I knew her."

The detective sighed, then took out a tissue and wiped his nose. "Damn cold," he offered. "Do you know Belle Dermot?"

"Again, why you asking?"

"Our department is looking into her husband's death as a possible homicide."

Banger stared at the middle-aged man impassively. *Damn, she may have offed her hubby? She's got a lot of fuckin' spunk.* "I don't know shit."

"But you do know her?"

"What I know is this 'conversation' is fuckin' over." Banger jerked his chin at the door. "Don't slam it on your way out."

Detective Sanders stared at Banger, and the president could see the pulse beating away on the badge's neck. Silence engulfed them as they sat, staring at each other, neither giving an inch. Finally, the detective looked down at his notepad. "If you're protecting her in any way, I'd suggest you rethink it."

"I'd suggest you get the fuck outta my office. You're wasting my time with this bullshit. Do you need me to call one of the brothers to show you the way out?" A flat smile curled around his lips.

Slowly, Sanders stood up, taking his time to put away his notepad and pen. He threw his card on the desk, and Banger picked it up, throwing it in the trash while his narrowed eyes never left the detective's face. Sanders walked out, slamming the door behind him.

*I wonder if she eliminated her old man.* He chuckled. *Fuck, I better not cheat on her.* He appreciated that she didn't take any shit from any man. Even though he was dying to be back in her pussy, he liked that she hadn't taken him back in her bed. She was a challenge.

He grabbed his phone.

**Banger:** *I'm coming to the diner for dinner.*

**Belle:** *The special is fried chicken.*

**Banger:** *Fuck, it's my lucky night. Two of my favorite things, you and fried chicken.*

**Belle:** *Sweet. :) Gotta go. Later.*

★ ★ ★

WHEN HE ENTERED the diner, the scent of freshly baked sweet berry pie wrapped around him. He waved at Ruthie, who was chatting up a customer at the counter, as he headed for the kitchen. The first thing he saw when he walked in was Belle's shapely legs and rounded ass as she bent over, flouring a mountain of chicken legs. Sneaking up behind her, he circled his arms around her waist and kissed her damp neck.

"Oh!" she squealed, whirling around.

"Hey, beautiful." He leaned in for a kiss but she backed away, her butt bumping into the prep table.

"Not now. I'm coated in flour, corn meal, and oil." She wrinkled her nose.

"Those are some of my favorite flavors." He licked the base of her neck.

"You're crazy," she said, her eyes glowing.

"'Bout you." He peppered her neck with feather-light kisses.

Laughing, she nudged him away. "I have to finish flouring the chicken. I was hoping you'd come in for dinner. I had you in mind when I planned tonight's special." She placed several drumsticks on the large cookie sheet, rolling them in the flour and cornmeal mixture. "I'll come out and see you for a bit after I get things under control." She gave him a quick peck on his cheek then began cracking eggs into a large bowl.

"See you in a bit." Banger smacked her ass then rubbed it lightly, before he headed out to snag a table.

Stella, a new waitress who wore her uniform tight around her bust, placed a steaming plate of fried chicken, mashed potatoes, buttered corn, and green beans with crumbled bacon. He sank his teeth into the crispy, coated chicken, and his stomach sang. *Damn, she's a good cook!* The explosion of flavor and texture had Banger on a high as his taste buds hummed. As he was finishing the last morsels on his plate, Belle slid into the booth, opposite him.

"Best fuckin' fried chicken I've ever had, woman." He licked his fingers then tore open a packet of wipes and cleaned his hands. He pushed his empty plate to the side, sipped his coffee, and took her hands in his. Clearing his throat, he looked her in the eyes and said, "I acted like a fuckin' asshole in not calling you. When I saw that fucker's body against yours, I exploded."

"But it wasn't—"

"Let me finish. I acted before I asked. I have a habit of doing that. Hell, I've been using my fists and might most of my life, so asking first never occurs to me. Grace used to accuse me of that." He shook his head, a smile skating across his lips as memories filtered in. "Anyway, what I'm saying is that I'd understand if you kicked me in the balls and told me to never come back. 'Course, I wouldn't listen, but I'd get it if you did that."

She raised her eyebrows and cocked her head. "I should do that. A whole month without hearing from you? Do you know how fucking pissed I was? And you didn't even return *my* calls or texts. You've just got too damn much machismo. Male pride does it every time. And, for your information, I never had anything with Scorpion. I was trying to push him off me."

Banger's eyes twinkled. "I know that. I admit I was a fuckin' fool, and I don't do that very often." Bringing her hands to his lips, he looked at her. "Fuck, woman, you make me do and say shit I'm not used to. I want you back in my life."

A wide grin spread across Belle's face. "That's where I want to be, but no more bullshit. You got a problem, you talk to me. I don't want this nonsense where you give me the silent treatment, even if it has to do with the club."

"I'll keep that in mind, but club business remains with the club. Only the brothers know. Don't ever ask me about what's going on with the club, and never make me choose. If you get that part of it, we'll do all right."

"I guess I have a lot to learn about your club and how it works."

"If you wanna be with me, you gotta get to know my world. It's different from yours. I'm gonna tell you, it'll be a challenge for both of us 'cause I never been with a citizen woman before. My Grace came from a biker background, and she knew the score and importance of the club for me. She respected my position as president, and let me do what I had to do."

"I can't say that I understand the club because I don't even know enough about it to tell whether or not I do, but I know I care about you. I get that you're president of the Insurgents, and I have no intention of interfering in any of your club business. I guess time will tell if we fit in each other's worlds."

"Guess you're right 'bout that. I know I want to spend time with you and get to know you better. I also want to get to know your kids better too. That means something."

"It does," she said softly.

He gazed into Belle's brimming eyes. "So, we're good again?"

She nodded.

Stella set a piece of berry pie in front of him and refilled his mug. While he stirred cream into his coffee, he said, "A fuckin' badge came by to see me today."

Scrunching her forehead, she said, "Badge?"

"Fuckin' cop. He was asking questions 'bout you." Banger looked intently at her to gauge her reaction.

She grimaced. "Was his name Detective Sanders?" Banger nodded curtly. "Damn. He has some stupid notion that my husband was killed, and that I did it. I mean, he didn't come out and tell me that, but I can read between the lines. What did you tell him?"

"Nothing. I don't talk to fuckin' badges." He took a forkful of pie in his mouth, savoring the burst of blueberry, strawberry, and raspberry flavors. "Did you?"

Her eyes widened. "Did I what?"

"Kill him." He said it matter-of-factly. He and killing weren't strangers; it was as much a part of his world as a nine-to-five job was in the citizens'.

An incredulous stare met his gaze. "No! How could you ask me that?"

"Just wondering. I know you said you'd been cheated on. Deep emotions can make people do all kinds of shit they ordinarily wouldn't do." He brought his coffee cup to his lips. "Shit happens." He took a gulp.

Wiping her now sweaty forehead, Belle looked down at the table. "Well, I didn't. I could never *do* something like that." She raised her eyes to meet his. "It's my bitchy stepdaughter who's started all this. She's always hated me, and she thought she'd get a large amount of money when her dad died. At the funeral, she had the nerve to accuse me of spending all the money, then, in the next breath, she accused me of stashing it somewhere. Can you imagine that? I was upset, my kids were devastated over their dad's death, and she's yelling at me about money. Incredible." She rubbed her temples with the tips of her fingers.

"You got a headache?" When she nodded, he took out a couple aspirins from the inside of his leather jacket. He always kept it with him to help ease the chronic back pain he'd sustained in a motorcycle accident when he'd been much younger. "Here you go." He handed Belle the pills.

After swallowing the aspirin, she said in a low voice, "Harold stole a helluva lot of money from his company, but neither I nor the insurance investigators could ever find it. I can't imagine what he did with it."

"Yeah, something's not right there. Maybe someone *did* kill him, for the money. Seems fucked up that it's disappeared."

"Since the detective came to see me, I've been thinking the same thing. I can't imagine someone killing Harold, though. It's too awful." Belle then told Banger about her husband's mistress coming to see her.

"That must've hurt. What a fuckin' cunt." He smiled when Belle blushed.

"It really didn't. I'm over that. I just couldn't believe her nerve."

"Maybe she's got something to do with offing your old man."

"You think? It was strange for her to find me after all this time. I wonder…."

"Never know." Banger caressed her hand.

"I better get back to work. I'm way over my break time."

"We gonna spend some time together after you get out of work?"

"I'd like to, but I have to pick up Ethan from his friend's house."

"Can't the boy stay longer, or spend the night?"

Belle nodded. "Let me see what Ethan wants to do. I'll let you know."

"Text me. I'm meeting a couple of brothers for a beer, but you say the word and I'll come over." He stood up and helped Belle out of the booth. Crushing her to him, he breathed, "I need you."

"Me too," she whispered.

Her answer curled around his dick; he needed her so badly. If he didn't leave soon, he'd be pitching a tent. "Call me." He watched her hips move seductively from side to side as she went to the kitchen. He walked out into the cool evening air, the light breeze carrying the faint smell of pine and car exhaust fumes. The green trees and bushes looked almost black as they blended into the ever-darkening night, and the cloudless sky offered an unfettered view of the glittering stars. Banger revved his engine, its rumble piercing through the busy silence of the town.

# Chapter Twenty-Three

By candlelight, Belle's skin glowed like the sunset's blush on a crystalline lake. She'd grouped the flickering flames together in each corner of her bedroom. Standing by the bed, she tingled as Banger's eyes, darkened in the candlelight, lingered on her mouth, then slowly glided to her cleavage, down to her hips and legs then back up again until his hunger-filled eyes locked with hers. The thrill of his gaze skated over her skin, and she shivered when he said huskily, "Get over here."

She came to him, his strong arms engulfing her. Holding her face in his hands, he threaded his fingers in her hair, pulling at the roots, slowly tilting her head back. He placed his lips on hers, giving her a deep, lasting kiss that dampened her panties and drove her wild with desire. When he broke away, she saw his eyes sparkle and lips curve up into a smile. She smiled back, her craving burning between her legs.

He led her to the bed and he sat at the edge, tugging her on his lap so she straddled him. Sweeping her hair away from her neck, he kissed and nibbled on the sensitive spot right below her ear—the one that made her toes curl. She moaned and tipped her head to the left, exposing more of her delicate flesh to his sensuous mouth.

"You like that, beautiful?" he growled, his breath tickling her sensitive skin.

"Mmm…."

"I'm gonna put my mouth all over your sweet body. I'll start here." He traced his finger lightly over her shoulder. "Then go here—" he moved it to her collarbone "—and here." He nestled it between her breasts as he drew her earlobe between his lips, gently sucking it.

Belle squirmed and circled her hands around his neck, her index finger looping under his leather tie, unfastening it. Long, blond hair fell on his back, and she ran her digits through it, loving the feel of its silky strands.

He moved his hands under her top, shoving it up and over her head, then he buried his tongue in her cleavage, the light, wet strokes fueling the fire between her legs. Deftly, he unhooked her bra and her tits bounced out, hitting his face. He growled and cupped them in his hands while his mouth sucked and pulled her aching nipples. She moaned and arched her back, pushing the nipple deeper into his mouth. Squirming, his hard dick rubbed against her throbbing sex, and she rubbed her leg against his length, massaging it. His sharp intake of breath turned her way on, and all she could think of was his hand on her clit and his dick inside her.

"Gonna have to ask you to quit squirming so much. It feels fuckin' fantastic, but I don't wanna come yet. I want to taste you before I put my cock inside your warm pussy." He sucked harder on her nipples, the jolts of pleasure zinging across every nerve in her body. "You like what I'm doing to you?"

"God, yes. It's so good."

"You feel so fuckin' soft. Damn, I could play with your tits all day."

With his strong arms, Banger swiveled her around, laying her on the bed. Blowing on her belly, her skin vibrated with electrified gratification. He held her gaze as he slowly unzipped her pants then pulled them down and off, leaving only her panties.

"Fuck, you're gorgeous," he rasped, running beneath the fabric all the way down to her wet folds.

When he slid off her panties, he spread her legs and massaged her swollen outer lips gently. She sucked in her breath, her heartbeats erratically pounding against her chest. She needed him to fuck her. Now. Reaching down, she grabbed a fistful of his hair, guiding his head to her aching mound. "Touch it."

"Not yet, babe." His teasing tongue scorched her belly, hips, and inner thighs. Each time it threatened to lick her *there*, it flitted away, making the heat curled within her tighten to the breaking point.

"Please," she whispered, pushing his face closer to her throbbing sex.

He chuckled then teased her by brushing her swollen lips lightly as he moved his tormenting mouth to her other thigh, nipping and kissing it. *What a bastard!* To calm herself, she focused on Bryan Adams's raspy vocals for "(Everything I Do) I Do It for You" coming from her CD player on the nightstand. *Kaboom!* It was like lightning had struck within her, singeing her to the core. Intense pleasure wove between her shivering nerves. She looked down and caught Banger's smoldering gaze, watched his flattened tongue swipe her pussy from the back right up to the top while his finger rubbed the side of her hardened bud.

"Fuck! That feels amazing," she panted.

"You taste amazing."

"Take your shirt off," she said as she tugged it up. "I want to feel your skin against mine."

He whipped his shirt off, kicked off his boots, then scrambled out of his pants, a small condom packet secured in his hands. His thick cock pulsed, and her insides clenched just from the thought of it entering her. Rolling the sheath over his hardness, he placed himself snuggly between her legs, his hand on either side of her thighs, his face buried in her mound. He inhaled deeply, his nose against her sweet spot. "I love smelling how much you want me. And fuck, you're wet." He buried his tongue in her rosy folds.

"I can't believe how good your tongue feels against my body," she breathed.

"And I can't believe how fuckin' good you taste and feel, babe."

Banger ignited an intense fire within her, scorching every inch of her body. No man had ever done that before. He took her out of herself, to a deeper level where all her senses were heightened, and her desire was off the charts.

"You want my fingers in your wet pussy?" he asked.

Words stuck in her throat, so she moaned instead of answering. He pushed her legs further open, to the point she thought she would be split in two, then he placed a finger on her heated opening and rubbed back and forth. She clenched her thighs against his face, holding him prisoner between her legs. The last thing she wanted him to do was stop his exquisite torture. Then he pushed his finger inside her wetness, and it pulsed around it. In and out he pushed, and she craned her neck to watch him. His face buried in her pussy, his corded shoulder and back muscles flexing as he licked and finger-fucked her, and his firm ass moving in rhythm with his mouth, sent her over the edge. Her orgasm washed over her in searing euphoric waves.

"Fuck, Banger." she said in a raw, hoarse voice she didn't recognize.

"I love watching you come. It's hot as fuck." He leaned down and kissed around her belly as his hand played with her tit.

Placing her hand behind his neck, she pulled him to her, crushing his mouth against hers. This man made her *feel* so much. She couldn't get enough of him; she wanted to devour him, suck him into her. He drove her fucking wild, and she loved it.

He leaned back on his knees and placed his hands on her hips, flipping her over. Scooting down, he rose from the bed then dragged her close to the edge. Standing behind her, he ordered, "Get on all fours." After she complied, he spread her wider, and she locked her gaze with his as she looked over her shoulder. With his palm on her back, he pushed her down a bit, causing her ass to hike up. He leaned over and kissed her shoulder, whispering, "You're so sexy." Her insides melted.

Still locking eyes, he rubbed her dripping mound before he dropped to his knees, using his hands to push apart her ass cheeks. "Fuckin' beautiful," she heard him say. His tongue entered her slit, darting inside her over and over while his expert finger stroked her clit, and she almost lost it. When he ran a finger drenched in juices over her puckered rosette, she tightened.

"Ever been fucked in the ass?" he asked as he nipped her rounded cheeks.

"No." She swallowed as fear climbed inside her.

"That's too bad. You got a great ass for fucking. You okay if I play with it? I won't go in, I'll just touch it. You tell me if you like it."

"Okay, but don't put your thing in there."

He laughed. "You mean my cock? I won't do it until you want me to." He bit her cheeks, then smacked them while his finger rubbed and pressed against her small opening.

Breathing deeply, she realized she was excited by what he was doing, but her fear of him going further, especially since he was so big, kept her from wanting anything more. "It feels good, but I still don't want you going in."

Still looking at him, she saw him licking his lips before he spread her cheeks again, then ran his cock between her folds, his sheath glistening with her juices. "Here it comes, beautiful." He burst through, and Belle yelled out as her silky walls clasped around his cock. He shoved in and out, his hips swiveling to make it deeper and more pleasurable for her, and she pushed back each time he pulled out. The fusion of their bodies as they moved together in perfect rhythm drove her insane. Soon, her moans, his grunts, and the sound of their bodies slapping into each other drowned out the music, and Belle felt Banger's legs tighten at the same time her pussy did.

"Fuck, Belle. Fuck!" Banger growled as his fingers dug into her fleshy hips.

"Banger!" Her pussy convulsed and her body exploded into a million sparks, zapping sheer ecstasy from her curled toes to the top of her head. She buried her face in the mattress, her groans and screams muted by the thick comforter. Her whole body shook, and she feared her wobbly legs would collapse.

Banger moved the hair away from her neck and kissed her before he pulled out and threw away his condom. When he came back to the bed, she was still in the same position, unable to move. He gently turned her around, tucking her in to his side. "That was fuckin' awesome," he said against her forehead before kissing it.

Still breathless, she craned her head and kissed his chin then held him tightly. *Make-up sex fucking rocks!*

Snuggled beside him, comfort and security enveloped her, and she drifted off to sleep.

## Chapter Twenty-Four

"Find out who the fuck hit us up at the Weed Station and bring him to me." Banger's nostrils flared as his face turned bright red. "How the fuck did this happen?" He stared at Rock, waiting for an answer.

Rock uncrossed his massive arms and pushed himself from the wall with his boot heel. "It was an inside job, for sure. The fucker knew shit 'bout the place no one else knew 'cept the brotherhood. He knew the hours of the store, where the safe was, and when we take out the money. Yeah. The dead man also knew the combo to the alarm system. I'm questioning the employees."

"They'd be fuckin' suicidal if they stole from us. I don't think it's any of them," Jax said. The membership rumbled in agreement.

Banger scrubbed his face, his body rigid. "I want to find out who the fuck did this and fast. We can't let this shit slide by. We gotta find the fucker. This is the number one priority for the club." Banger looked around at the brothers, wondering who the mole was. He didn't think for one moment that it was an outsider. Only two people knew the combination to the safe, him and Hawk, and he trusted Hawk with his life. "That's all I got. Church over. Go get drunk."

An angry tension fell over the brothers as they clamored out the door, heading to the great room to throw back a few beers and shots. Banger took Hawk aside and waited until the room was clear before he spoke. "There's a goddamn traitor in the club. Fuck!"

A deep scowl crossed Hawk's face. "Agreed. We need to flush the fucker out by setting him up. I can guarantee that, whoever it is, he's not working alone. There's some other club or something behind him. I'm putting my money on the newest members. I haven't trusted them from the start."

Banger leaned against the wall and let out a long breath. "I'd hate to think it was one or more of them. Fuck, we go back a long way, but maybe I let those feelings get in the way when I embraced them into the club so quickly. I've known those guys for twenty-plus years. Shit."

"You knew Dustin a long time too," Hawk said quietly. Banger threw him a dirty look. "I'm just sayin'. You let that shit in Kilson go on longer than it should have before throwing their asses outta the Insurgents. Maybe you're doing the same shit with these guys." Hawk stared at the president.

Clenching his jaw, Banger nodded. "Maybe, but I'd also hate to think it's one of our own brothers. Fuck! A brother betraying the brotherhood is fucked. This shit has to be stopped. Now."

"I'm sure there's a connection between the club losing the arms deal and the theft."

"I'm thinking the same thing, and the common denominator is money. Whoever is doing this shit is money-driven, so that'll be the bait. Let's get the buzz around the club that we have a ton of money from a private arms deal, and we're gonna keep it for a while before we distribute it. We'll make it known, indirectly, that the dough will be in the safe at the clubhouse for about a week 'til we transfer it to the safe house. We'll take Rock, Axe, Chas, and Bear into our confidence for surveillance. Let's see who shows up there next week. I gotta find this fucker, and when I do, I'm gonna kill him. No one fucks the club over."

"Sounds like a plan. When do you want to bring Rock and the others into it?"

"Let's give it a few days. Then we'll bring them in and spread the shit about the money."

"Sounds good. Fuck, it gives me a bad taste to know a brother's betrayed the club. Damn!" Hawk opened the door. "You coming? We both need a few shots."

"Yeah. I'm comin'." The president and his VP walked to the great room with a heavy gait, their shoulders tight.

A few hours into nightfall, Banger received a frantic call from Belle. Between her tears and stuttering, he couldn't figure out what the hell the problem was. He understood enough that it had to do with Emily, but he couldn't grasp what she'd done. "Babe, you gotta calm down, because I can't understand a fuckin' word you're saying. Tell me slowly what the fuck's up with your daughter."

Belle hiccupped over the phone, and he heard her inhale and exhale several times before answering. "She's run away. Holly called me, and she doesn't know where she is. Emily has never run away before. What if something happens to her?" Her voice thinned out.

"I'll find her for you, but you gotta stay calm."

"I never should have let her stay with Holly. This is my fault. Emily thinks I don't love her because I sent her away. What the fuck am I going to do if she gets hurt? I can't—"

"Belle, stop. You're getting worked up again, and it's not helping shit for you to be freakin' out. I need you to calm down if I'm gonna help you. Okay?" A few more hiccups crackled over the phone then a long sigh. "Belle?"

"I'm okay. I'm freaking out, but I'm okay. Please, find her. Please."

"Does she have a boyfriend?"

"Not that I know of. I asked Holly the same thing, and she told me no."

"Who's her best friend?"

"Chelsea."

"Good. Give me the girl's full name and address. You sit tight. I'm sending Cara and Addie to keep you company while I search for her."

After finally calming Belle down, Banger arranged for the two old ladies to sit with Belle and keep her calm while he found her daughter. Enlisting the help of Rock and Puck, the threesome started their Harleys and blasted into the chilly night.

Chelsea proved to be a fountain of information, especially when she saw the three tatted and muscular bikers whose soft-spoken words held an undercurrent of danger. She relayed the fact that Emily had met a man who was a good ten years older than she, and they hung out a lot at his place. The trio thanked her and left a terrified Chelsea standing on her moonlit porch.

The Harleys parked in front of a run-down bungalow with several beat-up cars in the front yard. The gate creaked when Banger pushed it open, and he and the others walked toward the door, their boots catching every so often on the broken sidewalk. In one long stride, Banger leapt onto the porch, opened the broken-down screen door, and pounded on the inner one.

A medium-sized man opened the door, his eyes widening as he scanned the threesome in front of him. He looked to be around twenty-six years old. His head was shaved, he was shirtless, and his arms were covered in tattoos of dragons, snakes, and a busty, half-naked woman swigging a bottle of beer. "What do you want?"

"Emily. Get her now and there's no trouble. It's fuckin' simple."

"Who? I don't know who the fuck you're talking about. Get off my porch."

Banger fixed his stare on the man right before he threw a punch to his stomach. The man bent over, groaning. "Maybe you didn't hear me so good. Get Emily. I don't like fuckin' repeating myself."

Gasping for air, the doubled-over man shook his head.

Banger pushed his way in. "He needs some persuasion," he said, his eyes locking with Rock's. The Sergeant-At-Arms grinned, exposing straight, white teeth. Banger moved aside as Rock's fist met the man's jaw.

"Fuck!" the guy sputtered as he fell to his knees. "She's in my room, hiding in the closet. I don't have anything with you guys." He rubbed his jaw. "No bitch's worth this."

"You're right there. No bitch is worth shit." Rock placed his heavy boot on the man's hips and pushed him down.

Banger tried a couple of doors before he found the bedroom. He went over to the closet and threw open the door. Emily was curled up in the corner, glaring at him.

"Get the fuck out," Banger ordered.

"No fucking way, asshole."

The skin on his arms prickled, and a burning rage rushed to his head. He stared at her, breathing deeply, trying to quell the rage which threatened to explode. After a couple of minutes, he hissed, "Get out, or I'll drag you out."

"Just because you're fucking my mom doesn't give you the right to tell me what to do." She defiantly tipped her chin up.

"You, *missy,* don't have the fuckin' right to hurt and worry your mama. Now, get your ass outta there." Before she could answer, Banger grabbed her by the hands and dragged her out as she kicked and cussed at him.

He held the flailing Emily until she tired herself out. Looking at him with a gleam of hatred, she said, "Just leave me alone. You don't know anything about me. My mom tells you how she loves me, but she doesn't. She dumped me at Aunt Holly's. She fucking threw me out."

"She fuckin' saved your ass from foster care."

Emily stopped screaming and looked at him. "Foster care?"

He told her what he knew, what Belle had shared with him. "Do you know how fuckin' hard it is for a parent to send their child away just to protect them? Fuck, you don't know shit. Talk to your mama and fix whatever shit you two got going. I came to get you and I did, so now I'm takin' you to your mother."

Fixing her eyes on the floor, she mumbled, "I didn't know. Why didn't she tell me?"

"I don't know why the fuck you two aren't talkin'. I'm no fuckin' shrink. Now, let's go. Oh, and the asshole gave you up in no time. You don't need a pussy like that."

On the way out, Banger leaned down and snarled in Emily's boyfriend's face. "Don't even think of calling or seeing her again. The law can get you for stat rape, but I'll get you for not fuckin' listening to me." He punched him in the stomach again, smiling as the guy grunted and crumpled over. "Let's get the fuck outta here," Banger said, as they walked down the pathway toward their Harleys, Emily sandwiched between them.

He watched Emily trudge up the driveway to her house, head hanging down. Belle had flung open the door the minute Banger had turned off the engine. He felt a twitch in his groin when he saw her curvaceous figure outlined by the glow of the amber porch light. She stood there, chewing on her fingernail. As he approached, he saw her puffy, red eyes smile through the veil of tears.

"Emily," she said, as she hugged her daughter tightly. Looking over the girl's shoulder, she mouthed, "Thank you," to him. He jerked his head then pulled back, letting mother and daughter go inside. He turned to look at Rock and Puck who patiently straddled their bikes. "You can go." Without answering, the two men took off. Banger sat on one of the porch steps. The light from the neighboring homes flickered like an old movie reel on the ground, which appeared to be swallowed up by the inky darkness of the night. He jerked around when he heard the screen door open.

"You want to come in?" Belle asked in a low voice.

"You got stuff to talk about with your kid."

"I know, but I'd like you to come in."

He rose to his feet and walked in, placing a quick kiss on her lips. "Talk to her. I'll watch TV." He went into the living room, plunked down on the couch, and turned the set on.

After a long time, Belle came into the living room and sat next to Banger. Noticing her swollen eyelids and red nose, he stroked her cheek. "You two work some shit out?"

"A little. Emily told me she wants to come back home, so I called Holly and told her. For some reason, she acted pissed. Anyway, I want my daughter with me. If the judge doesn't like it, then I'll have to deal with it. The biggest thing is that Emily asked to come home *and* she's agreed to go to family counseling. That is huge." Her voice hitched, and she stopped to blow her nose. "Thanks for bringing her home."

"No need to thank me. I'm glad you two are getting shit out in the open. I know you have to do it. When Grace died, I couldn't talk to Kylie about it. Fuck, I didn't know what to say, so I pretended everything was fine when it wasn't. My sister finally told me I had to talk to the girl, and be there for her no matter what. It wasn't easy, but we got through it." He folded his arm around her, pulling her into the crook of his arm, then kissed her forehead.

Belle snuggled closer to him, and he breathed in her floral scent, which always got his cock going. But even though he wanted to be inside her, he knew what she needed was his comfort. So he gave it to her. He sat there quietly holding her, listening to her stuffy-nose breaths, feeling her soft hair tucked under his jaw, as he watched the blue flames curling and swaying in the fireplace.

# Chapter Twenty-Five

After she dropped her kids off at their schools, Belle went back home and poured herself a cup of coffee, then sat down at the table to eat a slice of coffee cake she'd picked up from the bakery. She had cancelled her weekly walk with Holly, not in the mood to rehash Emily's decision to return home. Belle had been elated when Emily had told her she wanted to come home, and she couldn't understand why Holly seemed so angry about it—after all, Emily wasn't *her* daughter. Holly had had an attitude with Belle ever since they went to the burger restaurant and Belle had bumped into Banger. And when they'd reconciled following his month-long silent treatment, Holly had been so pissed at her that she hadn't spoken to her for a week. It seemed strange, but Belle remembered when Holly had become angry at her for forgiving Harold when he'd had an affair with his secretary. Belle appreciated her friend's concern, but she'd wished several times that she'd just fucking butt out.

As she finished the last morsel of cake, her phone rang. Hoping it was Banger, she picked up.

"Hello."

"You're not going to get away with it. I know you killed my dad, you greedy, vindictive bitch. I'm going to make sure you spend the rest of your life behind bars." The voice of one of her least favorite persons assaulted her ears.

"Jessica, I didn't kill your father. You're being ridiculous, and you know it. Are you that angry about not getting any money from your father's estate? I told you he was broke when he died. You need—"

"I need to have you pay for killing my dad," Jessica snarled. "I found the syringe, and when they do the tests, the cops will believe me. I never believed he died of a heart attack, and you refused to have an autopsy, even though I wanted it."

"Jessica, your father would never have wanted that. The doctor said it was a heart attack. What more do you want? There's no money at all. I don't have a clue what he did with the millions he stole from the company. If I did, I would give you and your brother your share. You need to move on."

"You'd like me to just forget the whole thing, wouldn't you? Well, I won't. I'm going to make sure you get everything that's coming to you. You think you can get away with this?"

Belle pressed the disconnect button. Her quiet time had been ruined by Jessica's call. She had thought Jessica would have grown weary from her vendetta against her, but she hadn't. From their conversation, it seemed she was more crazed and obsessed than ever. Her malevolent accusations were making Belle's life miserable, and having the detective snooping into her life was embarrassing.

Belle shook her head. Jessica had always been a spoiled girl; her father had placated her childish tantrums even though she'd been married with children. Belle hadn't said much since it wasn't her business, but she'd thought he was crazy to give in to her demands all the time. Harold had given Jessica a shitload of money over the years, and now she blamed Belle for the money being gone. The woman was a nutcase.

The phone rang again, and Belle ignored it. She was done with Jessica Dermot Hoskins, and if she kept bothering her, Belle would just have to make sure she stopped. The nut job was out of control, and it was high time someone pulled the reins in.

# Chapter Twenty-Six

A FEW DAYS later, Belle tried to tame her mass of curls before Banger came by to pick her up. He'd called earlier that morning, telling her to be ready in an hour because she was spending her day off with him. Her insides sang, and when she hung up, she immediately arranged for Emily to pick up Ethan at his school.

Since starting family counseling, she and Emily were working through some issues, and even though they had a long way to go, they were at least speaking to each other civilly. For Belle, that was a huge plus, and she'd hoped that all the darkness, the bitterness, and the hatred would eventually dissipate and they both could be whole again.

She heard Banger's cams from a block away, and her skin tingled with anticipation. She'd never ridden on the back of a motorcycle before, and even though it was something she'd always wanted to try, she never had. When she and Banger had first hooked up, it was too snowy and icy to ride on the back of his bike. It was now spring, and they were back together, so she'd been bugging him about being his "biker chick" on the back of his Harley. When he'd told her he was coming by on his powerful machine, she was beyond thrilled.

Closing and locking the door behind her, Belle waved at Banger and hurried down the sidewalk. "I can't wait to feel the wind in my hair," she said as she hugged him.

"I can't wait to feel your tits pressed against my back. It's fuckin' awesome to have a woman wrapped around you while you're flying." He handed her an orange bandanna. "Put this on to keep your hair from going crazy. You got a lot of hair, woman."

She did her best to tuck her thick tresses under the scarf before she grabbed hold of his thigh and swung on, positioning herself until she felt comfortable and balanced. He instructed her on what to do, and as he spoke, fear coiled around her. Maybe this wasn't such a good idea. Before she could debate it with herself any further, she let out a squeal and held onto Banger's waist for dear life as the Harley let out a pane-shattering roar. They were off.

When they cleared the town and turned onto the mountain roads, Banger disregarded the speed limits, and Belle held her breath. It felt like the bike was propelled by the wind, and the landscape blurred past her; the budding trees, tufts of new grass, and the butterflies' kaleidoscopic wings were nothing more than a smudge on her field of vision. The sunshine was strong and almost had a touch of summer to it. The feeling of soaring through the air was exhilarating, and Belle clung tightly around Banger's waist, the faint smell of oil and cloves winding around her. He had braided his hair, and she leaned her cheek against its golden softness. On the bike, careening through back roads, her body pressed against his, Belle felt complete.

They slowed as they passed through Larkspur Village, veering toward a narrow road at the outskirts of town. The Harley twisted and turned around the road until they pulled into a dirt lot, Banger cutting the engine before swinging his leg over the seat. He put out his hand and helped Belle off the bike, holding her as she crumpled into his arms. "Oh," she gasped as her hands crashed against his chest. "My legs are like Jell-O."

"First time, babe." Banger winked at her. "You'll get used to it, but I think I like you like this." He bent down and kissed her deeply. "Loved feeling you behind me. Did you like it?"

"Yeah. It totally kicked ass." She hopelessly tried to smooth her tangled hair down as she looked around the small dirt lot. "What are we doing here?"

Clasping her hand in his, he tugged her along. "I'll show you."

They walked up a flight of stone stairs, a wooden ticket booth at the top to their right. "Wait here," he said as he strode over to the stall. He came back with two tickets and led her to another long flight of stairs. At the top, Belle saw buckets attached to a cable wire and a yellow sign stating, "Aerial Tramway."

"We're going in *that?*" She pointed to a brightly painted red tram.

"Yep. I love it up here, and I wanted to share it with you." He handed the ticket to an older man, who sat on a metal folding chair, chewing a cigar butt.

"Is it safe?" she whispered to Banger.

He threw his head back and laughed, then snagged her around her waist and led her into the metal car. Coming up behind them, a group of four huffed loudly. Banger turned to the ticket man and handed him a hundred dollar bill. "I don't want anyone riding with me and my woman." The man nodded then opened the steel door, latching it shut after the couple settled in.

The tram glided high above the tree tops, and the spectacular views of the Rocky Mountains took her breath away. The jagged high peaks were still covered in winter's snow, and evergreens, blue spruce trees, and blooming wildflowers wove around the mountains like threads in a tapestry. Belle stood in front of Banger, enveloped in his arms, his breath warm on her neck. "This is gorgeous," she murmured, spotting the lone flight of a gliding eagle.

"Glad you like it. There's a place we can eat at when we get to the end."

The ride was too short, and Belle reluctantly left the tram and followed Banger into a small gift shop that had an eating area in the back. The shop had windows all around, and the couple settled in a booth, Banger seated next to Belle. She rubbed his arm with hers, then kissed him tenderly. He placed his hand on her thigh and squeezed while he kissed her back, drawing her lower lip between his. Desire flushed through her and she placed her hand on his crotch, his dick hard under her palm.

"You want anything to drink?" the teenage waitress asked.

She pulled away, immediately missing his lips on hers. "A glass of water and iced tea, please."

"Coors on tap."

The waitress shuffled away. For the next hour, they enjoyed the spectacular vistas, a wonderful lunch of burgers and fries, and the unhurried closeness of each other. After they finished, Belle bought a book about history and critters of the area for Ethan, and pretty silver leaf earrings for Emily, as well as a couple of T-shirts for them. When she was checking out, she noticed bags of peanuts near the register. "Are these for feeding the animals?" she asked the clerk.

The thin man with wire glasses and gray hair smiled. "Mostly the chipmunks and squirrels."

"I'll take a bag." She joined Banger outside on the observation platform. "I got peanuts to feed the squirrels." While she threw the nuts to the fattest squirrels she'd ever seen, Banger grinned and rubbed her back. After the bag was empty, he suggested they head back, since some dark clouds in the distance were forming. The weather in the Rockies could change in a snap, so they wound their way down the deck's stairs and waited to board the tram.

On the way back, they shared their metal car with another couple who were visiting from Texas. They kept chatting with them, and Belle answered while Banger stared at them stony-faced. After they alighted from the red car, she and Banger walked over to the Harley and mounted it. Soon, they were riding against the wind. She knew he wanted to beat the thunderstorm that was threatening, but twenty minutes after they'd left, she felt the first drops of rain on her skin. Banger turned his head toward her and said something that was stolen by the rush of the wind. She shrugged and buried her face in his back.

As the rain came down harder, Banger turned off and rode a couple of miles then stopped in front of a dilapidated shack. He tugged her off the bike, and they ran into the wooden hut. The scent of rain was dark and heady, and Belle looked out the cracked glass pane at the black clouds sprawled across the sky, billowing in from the west. She shivered, the warm wind from earlier in the day having turned damp and chilled. A boom of thunder rolled over the boughs of the swaying trees, then a ragged line of silver split the sky before the rain poured down, its drops sounding like bullets on the rusted tin roof of the shack.

Banger came up behind her and drew her into his arms, kissing her neck in the spot that made her wild with desire. She moaned as he nipped and kissed her tender skin, and when his hand slipped under her top, she clenched her legs and whimpered. He unclasped her bra then cupped her heavy breasts, grazing their stiffening nipples with his thumb. She drew in her breath as he turned her around and lifted her top, exposing her tits. He bent down and sucked her hard bud into his mouth, and an exquisite streak of pleasure went straight to her aching pussy.

"Oh, Banger," she murmured against his hair, as she buried her face in it. The sound of his mouth as he sucked and licked her breasts drove her mad with desire. She reached down and caught his zipper, but he stopped her.

"Babe, I'm pleasuring you."

"But I want to touch you," she breathed into his neck.

He chuckled then let go of her hand, and she unzipped his jeans. He groaned when her fingers tightened around his hardness. Her mouth watered just thinking about taking it into her mouth and sucking every last drop of him deep into her throat. Lowering herself, she kneeled in front of him and swirled her tongue over the glistening tip. He jerked his head back. "Fuck, baby, you're killing me."

After tugging his jeans down, she continued licking and stroking his dick while he pinched and pulled her nipples, a sweet pain spreading between her legs. She took in more of him, her lips closing tightly around him as she slid her mouth up and down over his cock. He placed his hands against her head, moving it faster as his hips pushed him further down her throat.

"I love watching you suck me off," he grunted, pushing his dick deeper into her mouth.

She looked up, and his smoldering gaze met hers. With a gentle touch, she scratched and cupped his balls, tugging at them very gently. Feeling them contract, she knew he was close, so she lightly pressed her knuckle against the spot right behind his balls. His feral growl pushed her to knead the area a little harder while he fucked her mouth faster. When he threw his head back, eyes closed, she pressed his bundle of feel-good receptors a little harder until a warm stream spurted down her throat while he blurted out her name in a raw, primitive voice.

She kept him in her mouth until he took a small step back, then she released his warm dick for him to tuck into his jeans until the next time. He handed her a tissue and she wiped her mouth. Then he placed his hands under her arms and pulled her close, hugging her as he kissed her neck and shoulders.

"What the hell did you do to me? Fuck, babe. I've never come like that before." He hugged her tighter, and she relished the feel of his arms around her.

"The rain seems to have stopped, at least for now," she murmured against his shoulder as she laid her head on it.

"We better take advantage of it and get moving," he said in her ear, sucking on her earlobe.

"You keep doing that and we'll never leave this place," she joked. She broke away, picked up her purse, and hooked her arm through his as they left the abandoned shack. "Look," she exclaimed, pointing at a double rainbow, its band of color shimmering against the gray sky.

After Banger dried off the seat, they hopped on and headed back to Pinewood Springs. As they rode, Belle realized that she'd fallen hopelessly and completely in love with him. She wasn't sure exactly when it'd happened. It could have been when she'd gone to his house again and had seen his wife's pictures were gone, or the night he'd brought Emily home when she'd run away. There were so many moments they'd shared, the good and the bad, and they'd all slipped into the corners of her heart, filling it until it was overflowing with love. She didn't know if he loved her, but she didn't care. Riding on the back of his bike, her body pressed against his, the wind blowing through her hair, she felt total happiness. No matter what happened, she'd never forget this feeling. It would be etched on her heart forever.

# Chapter Twenty-Seven

He was impatient and he needed money fast. Waiting around for the "right time" drove him fucking crazy. If it were up to him, he'd have already taken care of the dark-haired bitch, and he'd be invested in some premium coke. All he could do was buy the street shit just because he wasn't calling the shots. Walking over to the window, he slammed down the blinds, shutting out the morning sun. He picked up his phone on the first beat of his tune. "This shit's gotta happen now. I'm tired of waiting around."

Soft laughter fell on his ears, and instead of soothing him as it always did, it pissed him off even more. He seethed in silence. "You have to be patient for just a bit longer. The plans are all in motion, I swear, and soon, we'll be rolling in money."

He snorted. "We fucking better be. What about that bitch whose mouth is flapping nonstop to the cops? Have they talked to you?"

"They did, and I wasn't happy about that. I was cool as ever, and they seemed satisfied with what I told them, but the bitch has become a pain in my ass. No one knows about you, so you're in the clear. I can handle myself."

"Just give me the word and the bitch is dead. Who the fuck is she again?"

"Harold's daughter. If I didn't have other plans for her, I'd have you kill the cunt."

"If anything changes, just give me the word." He lit a roach, inhaling deeply. "I'm broke."

Her exasperated sigh filled his ear. "Again?"

"Yeah, that's why we gotta do this shit soon. I'm coming to Pinewood Springs."

"Don't. You should stay away. I don't want to be seen with you around town. Let's keep it cool, okay?"

"You're not thinking of double-crossing me are you?" His brows knitted together.

"Of course not. Anyway, I need you to help. I can't do this all by myself."

"I'm just fucking climbing the walls."

"You're on call. When I give you the word, you come. It's not too much longer. Shit, that fucking pesky detective is back for another round of questions. I could strangle Harold's daughter. What a fucking bitch. I gotta go. I'll call you." There was a pause. "Stay cool, okay?"

"Easy for you to say. Call me."

He hung up and tapped his fingers on the nightstand in his modest room. If the pace didn't pick up soon, he'd have to take things in his own hands.

★ ★ ★

As BELLE PLACED the boxes of tomato sauce and sliced peaches—another gift from Ruthie—in her trunk, her phone pinged. She looked at the screen, expecting it to be from either her children or Banger, but it was from an unknown number. She closed the trunk and settled into the front seat of her Honda, then opened the text.

**Unknown:** *You bitch. Why the fuck did you send the cops after me?*

Belle looked around the parking area, grateful that daylight savings had kicked in and it was approaching twilight even though it was eight o'clock. She instinctively locked her car doors then stared at the text. She had no idea who it was from. The only person she'd told the detective about was Harold's old mistress. She was so not in the mood for this.

**Belle:** *I don't know who this is.*

**Unknown:** *The woman your husband loved. You know my name,* *you used to call his work often enough.*

**Belle:** *I have nothing to say to you. If you had nothing to do with my husband's death, then you shouldn't mind talking to the cops. I'm done with you. Don't contact me again.*

**Megan:** *You're such a pathetic, jealous bitch. I can see why Harold came to my bed. He loved me, not you.*

Belle shook her head, determined not to be sucked into this juvenile "conversation." She simply hit Delete when the next text came through. Rubbing her temples, she switched on the ignition and pulled into the street. On the way home, Belle wondered why Megan was so mad about the detective asking her questions regarding Harold's death and her relationship with him. If she were innocent, why would it bother her? What did she have to hide?

When she turned down her street, the leafy green trees on both sides were dark against the setting sun, their lengthened shadows melting into the twilight. Streetlights lit the sidewalks, a smudgy pool of yellow glowing around each one. The sun was dipping behind the crest of the mountains, and the sky was awash with colors found during the height of autumn. To the east, Belle could see chips of light winking against the darkening sky. In the warm amber glow, she spotted Banger's bike parked next to the curb, and her insides lurched. She pulled into the driveway, reapplied her lipstick, attempted to smooth down her hair, and went inside her home.

From the sound of their voices, Belle knew they were in the middle of a video game. She set down her purse and keys and quietly padded into the living room. When she saw the two of them transfixed by the screen, she smiled. It was too cute: Banger on the couch, his face taut, eyes unblinking, and Ethan cross-legged on the floor, his shoulders hunched, brow furrowed. She watched them for several minutes until Banger darted his eyes to her, a huge smile spreading over his face which lit her heart. She nodded and mouthed, "When you're finished," and went upstairs to shower and change.

When she came back downstairs, they had finished their game, and Ethan was excitedly telling Banger about joining Little League for the summer. Belle walked in and ruffled her son's hair, receiving an "oh, Mom" look. Then she leaned over and kissed Banger, who gave her a "want to fuck" look. "Who won the game?" she asked.

"Who else?" Banger grimaced and pointed to Ethan, who was sporting a huge grin.

"Has anyone eaten?" Belle questioned.

"I just had a peanut butter and jelly sandwich when I got home. Emily's in the kitchen deciding what to eat," Ethan replied.

Belle walked into the kitchen and saw her daughter leafing through take-out menus. "Anything look good?"

"I'm sick of pizza, but Indian sounds good. What do you think, Mom?"

"I love Indian. Let's see what the guys want. If they want something else, we can order from two places."

She and Emily went into the living room, and everyone decided on Indian food. When the delivery arrived, they sat around the kitchen table, eating and talking like a normal family. Emily even talked about school and how much fun she was having being in the spring play. It was a perfect evening, and Belle wished she could freeze the moment.

"Mom, Chelsea and I are going to a movie tonight. Is that cool?" Emily asked as she helped clear the table.

Belle's stomach churned. "Are you done with your homework?"

Emily nodded.

"It's fine. Please be sure to be home by eleven o'clock—your weeknight curfew, okay?"

"Uh-huh."

"Are you picking Chelsea up?"

"No, she's picking me up in about forty minutes. I better change my clothes." Emily rushed out of the kitchen, her footsteps on the stairs loud and fast.

Banger came over to Belle and rubbed her shoulders. "It'll be fine.

They're just going to a movie."

She placed her fingers against her throat. "I hope she's not lying to me. I can't help but think the worst."

Banger turned her around, kissed her, and held her close to him. She rested her head on his shoulder, and the stress dissipated a bit. *I'm so glad he's in my life.* They stood and held each other until Ethan asked if they wanted to watch a movie. Belle pushed back from Banger after kissing him deeply. They walked together into the other room, finding Ethan sitting on the floor with several DVDs sprawled around him.

After much thought, Ethan picked an action picture, which made Belle groan inwardly, but she could tell by the smile in his eyes that Banger thought it was a good choice. As they watched the movie, Emily ran down the stairs then poked her head into the living room. "I'm off," she said.

"Bye. Have a good time." Belle had to bite her inner cheek to keep from adding, "And remember your curfew." She wanted to show her daughter that she trusted her, even though a large part of her didn't. She hoped Emily wouldn't disappoint her.

After the movie and a few games of *Sorry*, Ethan went up to his room to sleep. He and Banger had really hit it off, and Belle was bursting with happiness. She could never be involved with a man if her children disliked him. Emily was still wary of Banger, but she did tell Belle that she was okay with her mom dating him—she just didn't want him acting like he was her dad. When Belle told him what Emily had said, he chuckled, stating, "I already got a daughter who's a handful. I don't need another one." Belle hoped in time Emily would warm up to Banger a bit more.

The minute he heard Ethan's door close, he had his arms around Belle, his mouth on hers. She giggled and whispered, "We have to be careful. I don't want Ethan coming down and catching us."

He nodded, his gaze riveted on her face before it slowly moved over her body. There was a tingling in the pit of her stomach. Pulling her close to him, he brought his finger up and starting at her forehead, he lightly ran it over her face. The mere touch sent a warming shiver through her. She tilted her head back and his finger swept over her neck, her shoulders, and landed on the sensitive spot between her collarbones. She whimpered then held her breath as his butterfly kisses flitted over her neck, cleavage, and arms. "I love how soft you are," he breathed into her tingling skin, as he continued caressing her.

She moved her face toward his to capture his mouth, but he turned away, preferring to lavish small kisses over her sensitive body. When his lips pressed to her neck, right under her ear, the jolt of his touch made her heart race. He took her hands and turned them over, tracing long, slow patterns over her palms with his tongue. She groaned and closed her eyes, letting herself become caught up in the sensations which were exploding over every inch of her body.

His mouth was back on her neck, his hand tangled in her hair as he licked, sucked, and kissed her deeply. "I fuckin' love how your hair feels in my hands," he whispered. His lips seared a path from her neck to her cleavage while his hands slipped under her knit top, exploring the hollows of her back. Every part of her quivered as he continued to seduce her. She gasped loudly when his hand dipped into her leggings, kneading her ass cheeks. Belle ran her fingers up and down his muscular arms, squeezing his biceps as she leaned down and licked the tattoos on them.

Raising his head, he held her closer, and she felt his uneven breathing on her cheek. Placing his hand on the side of her face, he turned her so they were directly facing each other. His tongue traced the soft fullness of her bottom lip, sending shivers of desire racing through her. Then his mouth covered hers hungrily and the kiss fused them together, like soldering heat joining metal. His tongue slipped in and swirled around hers, and their breaths mingled while they tasted and consumed each other. He swallowed her moans and she his grunts, and the power of their kiss made her dizzy. She pulled away, seeing the hunger and tenderness in his piercing blue eyes.

"Woman, you get me all fuckin' worked up." He tugged her closer to him, and she buried her face in his neck. "I think about you all the time."

She looked up and kissed his chin. "That makes two of us. You know I'm crazy about you, don't you?"

He looked down at her, his eyes soft and bright. "Good to know. I'm pretty crazy 'bout you too. You make me feel stuff I haven't felt for a long time. I like having you in my life."

Belle held her breath as she waited for him to continue. Then she heard Emily come in through the back door. She broke away from Banger and smoothed her hair down. Emily walked in the room and dropped onto a chair.

"How was the movie?" Belle asked, her skin still scorching from his touch.

"Good." She eyed Banger then her mom. "Mom, can I talk to you about something? It's personal." She twisted a strand of hair around her finger. "It's about Jared, a boy I like."

Belle cleared her throat. "Of course, Banger and I were just ready to call it a night." She glanced at him, and he gave her a half-smile, regret shining in his eyes.

He stood up. "Your mom's right. I gotta go." He walked to the door and Belle followed him.

She went out on the porch with him, tugging him back when he started to walk down the stairs. "Sorry." She nuzzled her face against his chest.

"Family comes first. I get it." He kissed her.

"You're not mad, are you?"

"Nope." He walked down the stairs and headed to his Harley. Halfway down the sidewalk, he turned to her and said, "I want you to meet Kylie. She'll be coming home in a couple of weeks. Time you two met." He swung his leg over his bike, broke the stillness of the neighborhood with his cams, then he was gone.

Belle jumped up and down on the porch. *Yes!* She went inside and sat on the couch. Looking at Emily, she said, "Now, tell me what's going on with this boy."

# Chapter Twenty-Eight

Banger couldn't get Belle out of his mind. He had a stack of paperwork to go through on his desk, and all he could think about was Belle. He had it bad for her, and it felt right. He'd been in love before; it was a wonderful thing, and he knew how it felt. Everything about Belle was perfect, and that could mean only one thing—he was in love. He'd been ready to tell her when her daughter walked in the previous night. Talk about shitty timing. Banger was pretty sure she had some strong feelings for him too, only he wasn't sure if she loved him.

Ethan was a pretty cool kid, and Banger got a kick out of playing video games with him and talking baseball. He was like the son he never had. If he had to be honest, Emily was a pain in the ass, and he could foresee some problems with her down the road, but he had to give the girl some credit—she was trying real hard.

He picked up his phone and sent a text to Kylie.

*Banger: I want you to come home next weekend. We gotta talk.*

*Kylie: R u okay? Ur not sick or anything…?*

*Banger: No, I'm good.*

*Kylie: Then what?*

*Banger: Gotta talk in person, not over a fucking text.*

A very long pause ensued, and Banger didn't think she was going to respond. He figured she may be in class or in the middle of doing something. He turned to the stack of papers on his desk and began shuffling through them when his phone pinged.

*Kylie: Is it about that lady u've been seeing?*

Banger scrubbed his face with his fist and sat staring at her text. He didn't want to tell Kylie over a fucking phone how he felt. Maybe he didn't have to tell her he loved Belle, only that he wanted her to meet his woman, but Kylie was bright. She wouldn't buy that shit for a minute—she knew him too well.

**Banger:** *Yeah.*

**Kylie:** *Ur not going to marry her, r u????*

**Banger:** *Dunno. Not sure how she feels about me. I told you, I don't want to do this on the phone.*

**Kylie:** *Not sure I want to meet her. Let me think about it. K?*

Banger sighed, but he knew this was hard on Kylie. For the past six years, it had just been the two of them, and they'd been each other's comfort when Grace had died. He'd let her call the shots on this one, he didn't want to force anything on her. But he hoped she'd give Belle a chance.

**Banger:** *Ok. You let me know if you come down. Love you.*

**Kylie:** *Love u too, Dad.*

Banger stared out the window at the aspen trees, the leaves a new vivid green that only the springtime could bring. Evergreen trees, dotting the parking lot around the clubhouse, towered over the aspens. From an open window, he heard the swift rush of the creek which ran behind the property.

A knock on his door drew his attention away from the window. The doorknob turned right when he said, "Come in."

Hawk sauntered in and took a seat, a scowl creasing his brow. "I found out who underbid us. The fuckin' Demon Riders."

Banger's eyes narrowed as his anger grew. "You sure?" Hawk nodded. "Fuck!" Banger slammed his fist on the desk. "I shoulda had you kill that sonofabitch, Dustin, and that piece of shit, Shack, when you guys went to close their sorry-ass club down. Fuck!" Banger was angry at himself for letting a friendship of twenty-plus years cloud his judgment. He blamed himself for all the problems his club was going through. He also knew that the traitor or traitors were among the newest members to have joined.

"I know you're thinking what I am," Hawk said as he leaned forward in his chair. "Dustin and Shack have been itching to get back at us, and they placed a fuckin' mole in our club. I don't know if it's all of them, or two of them, or only one, but I know it's someone in the fucking group."

"Fuck, Hawk, you were right when you told me not to trust them. Shit, I thought they were loyal. I've known the brothers for a long time. We went through hell and back when we were fighting with the fucking Deadly Demons. Damn, I can't believe they'd betray their club. Fuck!" He pounded his fist again on the desk.

"We're gonna find out soon. I set all the cameras up, and Rock, Chas, Axe, and Bear have been taking turns watching. Nothing yet, but I believe that's all gonna change. I arranged for a family dinner tonight out in the yard. Mostly everyone will be outside. Usually, the club is swimming with people except when we have a rally. I want to get this shit over with, so I think having everyone mostly outside will bring the piece of shit inside."

"Good. When the fuckers go in to steal the money, get them, and call me. I wanna be the first to take a crack at them. Now that I remember, Chigger, Tugs, and Hoss did time in the pen for safe cracking. They robbed some banks and stores in towns in Nebraska and northern Colorado. I bet it's them. Fuck, they stayed with me and Grace when they'd come to Pinewood. How could I forget about the safe-cracking shit? Damn, I'm getting soft."

Hawk chuckled. "You're not soft. You didn't think of it because it never crossed your mind that your long-time brothers would betray you. Hell, you were tight with them before they even met Dustin."

"Yeah, I'm the one who introduced them all to each other, gave them the charter in Kilson to run. Fuck. I shoulda killed Dustin when I had the chance."

"Tonight, you can do it vicariously."

Hawk and Banger laughed.

Soon, it would be a showdown.

★ ★ ★

THE FAMILY DINNER was in full force out in the yard, and Banger could hear the squeals of laughter from the children as he slipped in through the back door into the club. It was pretty quiet inside since everyone was outside eating, drinking, throwing horseshoes, and listening to classic rock pumping from the speakers.

Banger had each of the brothers in on the setup circulate in the yard, so as not to cause suspicion. His jaw tightened as he went into the back room where the video equipment was set up. It caused him pain and frustration to think that a brother would betray the club, and it was even worse to think it was a brother and a friend. Each member should be able to trust the others with their lives, but he knew shit like this happened when greed, power, and revenge were involved. Each brother knew before they joined what happened to snitches—a slow, painful death.

Two hours later, nightfall crept in, covering the lightness of the blue sky and swallowing the shadows with its encroaching darkness. The brightly colored lanterns the old ladies had strung along the tall, steel fence danced in the gentle breeze. Banger knew time was running out. Soon, the breeze would turn cold, and the women, children, and brothers would make their way into the clubhouse. If the window of opportunity were lost, they'd have to keep a vigil until the fuckers were caught.

Hawk slipped into the room, along with Rock and Axe. "Anything?" Hawk asked.

Banger shook his head. Then out from the shadows, a figure appeared, tentatively taking steps as he jerked his head around, as if to see if anyone had followed him in. The infrared recording devices clearly showed Tug's face. Banger's heart became stone. Part of him was relieved that it was only one traitor, but that was still one too many. They waited for him to crack open the safe—Hawk had changed the combination to an easy one for the setup—take out the marked money, stuff it in a backpack, and walk out.

"Let's roll, we got a motherfuckin' snitch to kill," Banger said icily.

They split up, with a couple going out into the yard, a couple staying in the clubhouse, and Rock and Axe checking out the parking lot. Banger's phone pinged.

**Axe:** *We caught the fucker trying to take off on his bike. We got him in the hole.*

**Banger:** *I'm there in five.*

Nodding at Hawk, they took off and met up with Axe, Rock, Bear, and Chas. When they entered the hole—a concrete room built under the barn on the property—Tug was trussed up and hanging from a low beam, his face bloodied. Banger jerked his head to Rock, who promptly lowered the snitch. When Banger was face to face with him, he spat in Tug's face. "You piece of shit!" He threw a full punch into Tug's belly and the man gasped and gaped for air, like a fish out of water. "Dustin and Shack put you up to this, didn't they? You fucking sonofabitch!" Banger punched him again, that time more viciously, all his rage and hurt contained in that one punch. Tug coughed up blood. Banger walked away from the hanging man, saying to the others, "Find out who else was in on this. I know the fucker wasn't acting alone. I'll be back." He walked out, closing the steel doors behind him.

A couple of hours later, he went back to the room and saw Tug covered in blood with lacerations all over his body, strategically placed to cause pain but not lead to a quick death. Rock was smeared in blood from the waist up. He turned to Banger and said, "The fucker admitted he worked with Dustin and Shack, but the others who joined with him weren't involved. Seems like his loyalty has always been with the motherfuckers you threw outta the Insurgents. He was sent here to get money to fund the Demon Riders."

Banger jutted his chin out, his muscles tense and rigid. He blamed himself for all this, despite what Hawk said. He'd let friendship get in the way of what was best for the club, and he swore to himself he'd *never* let it happen again. "He's got an Insurgents back tattoo. Burn it off."

Rock nodded and picked up the blowtorch in the corner of the room. Members who'd been in the Insurgents for ten years or more earned the right to have the club's logo tattooed on their backs. If a member snitched, the customary punishment among one-percenters was to burn off the club's logo. Rock approached Tug, who weakly held up his head when he heard the blowtorch ignite. With fear in his eyes, he shuddered, then drew his last breath. Rock stood with the canister in his hands. "Lucky sonofabitch," he said.

"Yeah. Clean up and make sure he's never found," Banger ordered.

In silence, he and Hawk trudged back to the clubhouse, the moonlight splashing down on the ground illuminating their way back. A heaviness weighed on them. Killing a brother, even a snitch, was always difficult.

# Chapter Twenty-Nine

On Saturday, Banger went over to Belle's house. He'd told her he was taking her and the kids to Burgers & Beer Joint for dinner. When he arrived, Belle was sitting on the porch on a lawn chair as Ethan ran toward him.

"Wow, your motorcycle is so cool. Can I go for a ride?" He ran his small hands over the chrome and leather, wrapping his fingers around the handlebars.

Belle came over and Banger hooked his arm around her waist, pulling her close and kissing her. "How are you?" he asked as he squeezed her.

"Great… now." She pressed herself closer to him.

*Fuck, she feels good in my arms. And the way she smells gives me a hard-on all the time.*

"Can Banger take me for a ride, Mom? Please?"

Belle looked at Banger, and he could see the fear and concern in her eyes. "It's your call, babe. I'll be real careful with him. Just take him around a few blocks, that's all."

"Please?" Ethan said again.

Belle sighed. "Okay, but you have to hold on real tight, and only three blocks." She shifted her eyes to Banger's. "Okay?"

"Yep, got it. Come on, kid, I'll help you on." Banger settled a very happy and excited Ethan on the seat. Then he started the bike and they were off.

He went slowly so Ethan could savor the short ride. The small arms around Banger's waist reminded him of when he used to take Kylie for spins around the neighborhood, with a fretful Grace waiting on the front lawn as Belle did now for her son.

He rounded the corner and parked in front of the house, Belle standing in the same place she'd been when they'd left fifteen minutes before. He'd actually taken Ethan around five blocks, but he knew Belle would forgive him since her son had the biggest, goofiest grin he'd ever seen.

Banger helped Ethan off the bike, and he chattered incessantly to his mom about how much fun it was, and how he felt like he was part of the wind. It was fun listening to him, as it reminded Banger of how he felt when he'd first rode on his uncle's bike when he was eight years old. That first ride hooked him for life, and he couldn't wait until he was old enough to buy his own bike.

"Did you say 'thank you' to Banger?" Belle asked as Ethan started to run up the walk.

"Thanks. I had fun." Ethan turned to his mom. "Can I go again?"

"We'll see. Go wash your hands and tell your sister we're ready to go out to dinner."

Ethan dashed up the stairs and ran into the house, the screen door banging behind him. Banger placed his hands on Belle's hips and guided her to his bike, pushing her back so she leaned against it. "You know what I want to do to you on my bike?" he whispered in her ear as he nibbled it.

"What?"

"Peel off your clothes, lay you on the seat, and lick every inch of you before I taste your pussy." He gently bit her lobe.

"Then what?"

"Then I'll spread you wide and put my cock right up your sweet cunt." He nipped her neck, moving toward her shoulder.

"You do like to talk dirty," she said.

"You inspire me, babe." He placed his hand behind her head and pushed her face toward his.

She laughed. "That was pretty cheesy."

"What do you want? I'm not a fuckin' poet." He covered her mouth with his. Every time he kissed her was like the first time. He loved tasting her, and gliding his hands over her soft, sexy body.

The creaking screen door made her break away from him, and he cursed inwardly. He'd love to take her back to his place and make love to her, but he knew that wouldn't be possible. She didn't want him to spend the night because of her kids, and he understood that; it may be awkward for her if her kids heard her screaming her brains out. Each time they made love, she'd scream so loud he'd considered wearing ear plugs, but he didn't think it would sit well with her.

Ethan and Emily went over to their mother's Honda. Banger held out his hand. "Give me the keys, I'll drive." She handed them to him, and soon they were on their way to the Insurgents' burger joint.

While they enjoyed their meal, Ethan did most of the talking, and Belle kept sliding her foot up and down Banger's leg, driving him wild. If she didn't stop being so wickedly sexy, he'd have to haul her off to her cramped Honda and fuck her good and hard while the kids ate dessert.

The waitress came over and cleared their plates, asking if they wanted anything else. Belle and Banger decided to share the cheesecake with strawberries while Emily chose a chocolate sundae, and Ethan picked a scoop of vanilla ice cream.

They were almost finished when a guy around twenty years old came up to the table, glaring at Emily.

"Why the fuck don't you pick up your phone?"

Emily glanced at him and took a sip of water. "You need to go away."

"Why aren't you answering my calls or texts?" he demanded.

"'Cause I don't want to talk to you. Easy to figure out, Chad. Duh."

Belle said, "You're disturbing our family, and I don't like the way you're talking to my daughter. Please leave."

Chad glared at Belle, his eyes flashing. "Shut the fuck up, bitch." Belle gasped and, before anyone could react, Banger had the guy in a choke hold.

"You fuckin' need to learn respect." He tightened his grip, and Chad clawed at his arm. "Apologize to the lady and her daughter." *Another asshole. Damn, just how many guys has Emily been seeing? And Holly was supposed to be supervising? Fuck that.*

Chad looked to two men who were standing to the side of him, and it was the first time Banger noticed the asshole had a couple of buddies with him. The friends started to come toward Chad, but Banger saw them stare at the Insurgents patch on his cut before they stepped back. Out of nowhere, Throttle came over to Banger. "You need some help with this?"

He glared at the extra guys. "I will if these assholes don't get the hell out of here now." Banger dragged Chad out, and his friends quickly followed. He shoved Chad hard, and the young man fell to the pavement, glowering at Banger. "Stay the fuck outta my restaurant. You and your fuckin' friends need to get the hell away from here. If I ever find out you're bothering Emily again, you'll have to deal with me."

"And me," Throttle's deep voice growled from behind Banger.

"She's not worth shit," Chad said, pulling his shoulders back and strolling to his car. Banger bit the urge to give him a swift kick in the ass to move him along. When they left, Banger and Throttle went back in the restaurant.

"What the hell went down?" Throttle asked.

"The fucker was disrespecting my woman and her daughter. I don't like that shit."

Throttle lifted his eyebrows. "Your *woman*? What the fuck?"

"I've been seeing someone. Her name is Belle. Come on over, I'll introduce you."

"Fuck, whoa. If you're gonna introduce me that must mean it's serious."

Banger looked at him. "It is. Come on."

"Who was that man, Emily?" Belle said.

"Someone who doesn't know respect," Banger answered as he approached the table.

"Emily?"

"He's a loser, Mom. He's a friend of a friend, and he became obsessed with me after I went out with him a few times. I didn't like him, so I moved on. I guess he didn't. Anyway, you know I like Jared."

"You went out with him? He's at least five years older than you. When did you go with him?"

"When I was at Aunt Holly's. She actually encouraged it. She's pretty cool."

Trying to diffuse an escalating situation, Banger pointed to Throttle. "Hey, this is one of my brothers, Throttle. This is Belle, Ethan, and Emily."

Throttle smiled broadly when he saw Belle, and Banger wanted to punch him in the face because he knew what that face meant; he'd seen it too many times when Throttle was on the prowl for a hoodrat or club whore. Belle laughed at his jokes and listened to his stories as he pulled up a chair to join them, but all the while her soft, warm foot kept teasing the shit out of Banger.

He noticed Emily kept sneaking peeks at him, and when he'd catch her eye, she'd avert her gaze. Later, as they walked through the lot to their car, Emily came up next to him and said in a low voice, "Thanks for taking care of that creep. It was cool that you'd do that for me."

"No worries." Banger held her gaze for a few seconds then turned away, knowing they'd reached an understanding. He grasped Belle's hand, clutching it.

When they arrived home, Ethan and Emily went to their rooms, and Banger and Belle sat outside on the porch necking like a couple of teenagers for a long time. "Woman, I need to be with you."

"I know. I'll try to see if I can arrange for the kids to do sleepovers. I don't trust leaving Emily alone. She needs supervision."

"I get it, but we need to have some time too."

"I'll find the time, I promise."

He took her in his arms and kissed her deep and wet before he climbed on his bike and went home.

★ ★ ★

THE DINER WAS unusually slow, and Belle sat backward on one of the stools at the counter, facing the street. She relished the pocket of quiet, knowing it was only temporary until the lunch crowd filed in. Across the street, a bright bakery sign beckoned passersby, while a pet store's front window displayed adorable puppies romping with each other, oblivious to the onlookers. A newspaper dispenser held the *Pinewood Springs Gazette* and *The Everything,* a free paper where people could place ads for anything from fishbowls to cars, and then there was the personal section where men and women looked for true love.

As Belle stared mindlessly, a glimpse of yellow caught her eye, jerking her out of her thoughts. She rose and went to the window. Standing in front of the bakery was Harold's ex-mistress. She wore an expensive St. John's knit dress in lavender, and yellow-toned high heels that hurt Belle's feet just by looking at them. She appeared to be waiting for someone by the way she turned her head from side to side, staring down the street in each direction. *Why in the hell is she still in Pinewood? What's her angle?*

A loud rumble, like thunder, shook the windows of the diner, and Belle smiled, knowing the noise could only come from a Harley. Her pulse raced. Maybe Banger was coming in to see her and have a slice of her coconut cream pie. She knew he loved it, and she'd told him earlier that she was going to make it. She held her breath in anticipation as the rumble became louder and closer.

When she saw Scorpion's Harley, her excitement shifted to dread. *He* was the last person she ever wanted to see. Expecting him to swing into the parking space in front of the diner, he surprised her when he parked across the street, in front of the bakery. Megan came over to the bike and gave him a hug. Belle almost fainted. *What the hell? Megan with Scorpion? They certainly don't fit. Something isn't right here.*

He slithered off his bike and put his arm around her waist. They walked down the street, and Scorpion turned his head and stared at Belle. She quickly stepped to the side, trying to conceal herself behind a pillar, her hand on her mouth. She didn't dare look, so she stayed stuffed behind the pillar for several minutes until she craned her neck around the column to see if she could spot Scorpion. He was nowhere to be seen, and she breathed a sigh of relief, praying he wouldn't stop in at the diner.

A few people came in and business was slowly picking up, so she headed to the kitchen to brace herself for the lunch rush.

★ ★ ★

THE KNOCK ON her front door at nine o'clock in the morning made Belle's brow wrinkle. No one came by in the morning except for Holly when they'd go on their morning walk, but she knew it wasn't Holly. Belle had been miffed at Holly for letting Emily date Chad, who she'd found out was twenty-one years old. Holly kept calling, but she wanted to have a little distance from her friend until she cooled down.

Another knock.

Her stomach churned, imagining it was Megan, coming over to start something with her again. An icy shiver ran through her. What if Scorpion was with her, and they'd come over to do something to her? Seeing Harold's ex-mistress with him startled and frightened her. She didn't trust either of them.

She tiptoed to the front door, looking through the amber-colored glass triangle. It wasn't Megan or Scorpion—it was Detective Sanders. Belle groaned, debating whether she should pretend she wasn't home. Deciding that the persistent detective would only come back, she pulled the door open.

The portly man jerked his head toward her. "I have a few more questions I need to ask you, Mrs. Dermot. May I come in?"

Without answering, Belle held open the screen door, standing back when he slipped past her. She gestured toward the living room. "Have a seat." Taking a seat on the couch, she looked at him and asked, "What more do you want from me?"

He sat across from her, his knees spread open, a notebook and pen in his hand. "I have a few things I need to clarify with you. You told me you had never seen the syringe that I showed you in the photo, is that correct?"

"Yes," she snipped, irritated that her few hours before work had been ruined by his presence. "I hope you're not going to rehash the same questions you've already asked me."

"No. We got the results from the lab, and the substance inside the syringe tested positive for sux."

She stared blankly at him. "I don't know what that is."

"It's short for succinylcholine."

Shaking her head, she ran her fingers down her neck. "Okay, I still have no idea what that is. I'm presuming it's some kind of drug?"

Glaring at her, he leaned forward. "It's the drug given to patients during surgery. It's used as part of anesthesia 'cause it paralyzes the muscles, but during surgery, the docs hook the patient up to a machine to do the breathing. If they didn't do that, the patient would die because he wouldn't be able to breathe."

Belle crossed her legs, a feeling of dread crawling up her spine. "And what's the significance of telling me this?"

"It means that if your husband had been injected with this, it would've paralyzed him, and he would have had four minutes max before he suffocated. He wouldn't have been able to breathe. He would've been conscious, and seen who'd done it to him, but he wouldn't have been able to move—not even yell out." He settled back in the chair. "Did you hate your husband that much for screwing around behind your back?"

Belle's throat was dry, like she'd swallowed a glassful of sawdust. Her insides were shaky and dread spread through her. *Someone* killed *Harold? Who? Why? I can't believe he was murdered. I can't believe the detective thinks* I *did it.* Wiping at the corners of her eyes, she fixed her gaze on his face. "I didn't kill my husband. I can't believe you're accusing me. I cared for him, and I thought he'd died of a heart attack. I wouldn't have a clue as to where I'd find this substance you said was in the syringe."

"You were angry when you found out about Mr. Dermot's affair."

Her face flushed. "Of course I was. I think the majority of wives would be hurt, angry, untrusting, and bitter if they found out their husband had been banging another woman. It doesn't mean I killed him. It doesn't even mean I wanted him dead. This is crazy."

"Did you ever hire any caregivers to stay with your husband when you weren't at home?"

"No. Harold had bad diabetes, but he wasn't bedridden or in need of a caregiver. If he was sick, I took care of him."

Sander snorted. "Ironic, huh?"

Belle bristled. "Are you arresting me?"

"Not yet."

She stood. "Then I'll have to ask you to leave. I don't want to talk to you anymore. If you have any further questions for me, you'll have to call my attorney. Please go." She went to the front door and opened it, her head turned away from him. He trudged past her, entered his vehicle, and drove away. She watched him until he turned the corner, her body trembling. She closed the door and quickly dialed Cara's phone number.

"Law offices," a cheerful voice sounded.

"Cara, the cops think I killed Harold." Her voice broke—the words didn't seem real to her.

"What? Tell me what happened."

Belle sputtered out the details of her encounter with Detective Sanders. By the time she finished, she was a teary-eyed mess.

"Don't worry, it's a total long shot to place the syringe in your hands. Anyway, how do they know your husband died from it? Was there an autopsy?"

"No," she whispered. "Jessica, my stepdaughter, wanted one, but Harold had always told me he never wanted an autopsy done on him. It creeped him out to think about his body being cut open, so I refused to do one after he died." She sat on the stairs. "You don't think they'll exhume his body, do you?"

"Maybe, but they're going to have to come up with something more concrete for a judge to sign an order to exhume. A syringe found in your storage unit which many people had access to over a year after your husband died is weak at best. Anyway, the enzymes in the body break down sux almost immediately, that's why death is so quick. It'd be hard for a crime lab to find it in a person's body. It's not like arsenic, which stays in the tissues. There is a breakdown product that can be tested for, but after all this time, it would be extremely doubtful that it'd be in the body. They really don't have a case."

Belle's head was reeling. "Whether they have a good case or not, someone killed Harold. I can't believe he was murdered. What was the syringe doing in my purse in the storage unit?"

"I don't know. Getting your hands on sux is not easy unless you're a nurse or doctor, or someone who works in a medical or nursing facility where they have the drug. Why would someone want to kill your husband? Did he leave anyone a big life insurance payout?"

"No, but he stole a lot of money from his company, and it's never been found. Maybe he was blackmailed into stealing it, then the person killed him? I don't know. This is so disturbing. I don't know if I should tell the kids or not."

Belle then told Cara about spotting Megan with Scorpion, and the funny, scary feeling she had when she saw them together. After telling Cara everything, the heaviness lifted somewhat, and she wasn't as scared about getting arrested as she was earlier in the morning. She decided she'd wait to tell her children and looking at the clock, she rushed around getting ready for work, the knot in her stomach slowly untangling.

# Chapter Thirty

A FEW DAYS after the detective paid Belle a visit, she picked up the phone and called Holly. She'd missed talking to her best friend, and no matter what, Holly had a knack of turning the negative into something positive. She'd asked her to come and share a cup of coffee with her, and Holly readily agreed.

"Are you still upset with me?" Holly asked as she curled her fingers around the coffee mug.

"Not really, although I can't understand why you'd ever think it was okay for a sixteen-year-old to date a twenty-one-year-old man. I sent Emily to you to watch her. I guess I was just disappointed."

"If you'd ever given me a chance when we talked to explain, you'd know that wasn't true. She lied to me. She said she was going with another guy, someone in her class at school. Hell, the guy even came over and picked her up. I didn't know she was that cunning. How could you think I'd do that?"

"Emily said you *did* know."

"She would say that. She didn't want to get in trouble with you. Her track record on telling the truth isn't very good." Holly pushed back her chair, stretching her long legs in front of her. "Anyway, it's all in the past. I'm glad you called me. I didn't want to let our friendship go."

Belle shook her head. "That won't happen. I needed a little space, that's all, especially with that damn detective coming around. He's positive Harold was murdered." She crossed her arms around her as she shuddered. "Isn't that awful?"

Holly nodded. "Poor Harold. Even though he was a sonofabitch and couldn't keep his pants zipped, he didn't deserve to die. Do they have any idea who did it?"

Belle pointed a finger to herself. "Me. I don't think they're looking at any other possible suspects. They've decided I did it all because that damn syringe was in my storage unit. I have no fucking clue how it got there unless someone's trying to frame me, but who? And why? Doesn't make sense. Harold's death was ruled a heart attack, so there was no reason to plant the syringe." She rubbed the back of her neck. "Doesn't make sense to me."

"It's probably that slut who tried to break up your marriage."

"Oh, that reminds me. I saw your brother with her the other day. I was shocked. I didn't even know he knew her. What do you know about that?"

Holly rose to her feet then went over to the counter and grabbed the coffee pot, refilling each of their cups. "What can I say? He's fucking horny. He saw her last time he was in town, and was taken with her. I'm pissed as hell at him for it. I told him who she is, but he doesn't give a shit. Men always think with their dicks." She laughed.

"Really? I didn't think Scorpion had been back after the… Well, you know, the incident with Banger."

"Yeah. He's been back a couple of times. He just steered clear from you. Speaking of, how's it going with Banger?"

Heat rose to her face. "Great. He's a real sweetheart, and Ethan adores him. Emily is getting a little better. At least she's not glaring at him all the time."

She and Holly spent the morning laughing, gossiping, and complaining, and it was wonderful. They walked out to her friend's car and before leaving, Holly hugged her and whispered, "It's all going to be okay, you'll see."

Belle waved as Holly pulled away from the curb. She was happy she'd called her friend and asked her to come over. She walked slowly back to the porch, thinking how lucky she was to have such a good friend, her kids, and Banger in her life. A smile crossed her lips when her phone rang and Banger's name flashed on her screen.

"Hi, handsome," she said.

A deep chuckle. "I love the way you answer a phone. How are you? No fuckin' badges around?"

"No, and I hope it stays that way. I asked Holly to come over, and it was good. We're back on track."

"Her fuckin' brother better not be around."

Belle decided not to share the fact that he'd been in town a couple of days before; she had more than enough drama in her life without adding to it. "So, what're you doing?"

"Helping Hawk in his shop. Whenever the weather gets nice, the shop is fuckin' busy with customers who are itchin' to ride their bikes. They all want tune-ups. Mark Saturday on your calendar. We're going to my sister's for a barbecue. Kylie's gonna be there. Bring Ethan and Emily."

She groaned. "Your sister *and* Kylie at the same time? I'm going to be so nervous."

"They'll like you. I've already told my sister 'bout you, and she can't wait to meet you. Kylie may be kinda unfriendly, but she won't be rude—she wasn't raised to be disrespectful. You gotta give her some time. The good thing is she called me late last night and said she'd come for the barbecue at her aunt's house."

"Okay. It's going to be scary, but if you stick with me, I'll do my best to charm everyone."

"I'll stick by you, babe."

★ ★ ★

ALL SATURDAY MORNING, Belle ran around like a madwoman, making sure her baked beans came out perfectly, and she tried on so many outfits that she was exhausted. She finally settled on a black jean skirt, a long-sleeved black knit top with a spattering of silver grommets around the scooped collar, and black mid-calf boots. As she pulled out her beans from the oven, the smoky scent of bacon tantalized her nostrils.

"Did you make my favorite beans?" Ethan asked as he came into the kitchen. "We only have those in the summer."

"I thought I'd make them since we're going to our first barbecue of the year. I hope the weather stays pleasant."

"Can I try a spoonful?"

Belle laughed. Ethan was so crazy for the baked beans. The summer before Harold died, they'd all come home from the company's barbecue, and Belle had put the leftover beans in the refrigerator. The next morning, she'd discovered a spoon in the sink, the empty bowl of beans, and Ethan, who'd moaned all day from a major tummy ache. She thought he'd never eat them again, and he hadn't for a good year, but it seemed like that day had become a distant memory in his young mind.

"Mmm... real good, Mom."

"Make sure you don't eat them all. They're rich with the hamburger, bacon, and cheese in them." She pointed to the dishwasher. "Your spoon goes in there, not the sink." He dutifully placed it in the dishwasher then ran out to the porch.

Soon, Banger came by and picked Ethan and Belle up to head over to the barbecue. Emily didn't want to go, and Belle was disappointed, but she pretended to be fine with her daughter's decision. She had been looking forward to spending a nice afternoon with her kids and Banger, and she also wanted Emily to meet Kylie since they were only three years apart. After helping Belle and Ethan in the car, the trio took off to his sister's.

Amelia lived on an acre of land surrounded by forests of evergreens and pine trees. When they walked into the backyard, a large honey-colored brick patio had three round tables on it, and two large grills. Outdoor chairs and table trays were spattered on the grass, which was still mostly brown from the long, cold winter. The aromatic hickory scent mingled with the sweet smell of beer. There were about thirty people milling about, talking and laughing with beers in their hands. Thin wisps of weed smoke curled above their heads as the pungent aroma permeated the yard. Belle noticed a few older men sporting the same cut Banger had, and surmised they were members of his club.

"There're a bunch of kids here," Ethan said excitedly. Belle was happy to see that there were many who seemed to be around Ethan's age for him to hang out with so he wouldn't be so bored with the adults.

A woman who looked a few years older than Banger came up to them, a wide smile spread across her face. Her skin looked like she'd spent a lot of time in the sun, and her ocean-blue eyes were copies of Banger's. She was a fit, attractive woman, her blonde hair hanging loosely around her shoulders. With an outstretched hand, she said, "You must be Belle. I'm Amelia. I'm happy to finally meet you. I've been bugging my brother about it for a while now." She playfully poked Banger in his side.

"It's nice meeting you too. This is my son, Ethan. I brought baked beans. Where do you want me to put them?"

"You didn't have to bring anything, but they do smell good. I'll show you." She walked a few steps then stopped and winked at Banger. "You go on and get a beer. You don't need to be following Belle everywhere. I'll take good care of her. Why don't you take the boy and introduce him to Tyler and Cory?" Amelia motioned Belle to follow her. Shrugging at Banger, she followed his sister.

In the kitchen, several women stood around, slicing tomatoes, making salad, chopping onions, and filling platters with deviled eggs, carrot sticks, olives, and other veggies. They laughed and talked as they worked, taking sips from beer cans and mixed drinks in between. Amelia introduced her to the women, and their friendliness warmed and embraced Belle. After placing her beans on a very low heat, she went to the bathroom to wash her hands. When she came out, she rounded the corner and slammed into a very pretty young lady who had long, glossy blonde hair, a cute figure, and piercing blue eyes. *She must be Banger's daughter. Shit.* Belle smiled, and the girl smiled back.

"I'm sorry," Belle said. "I should've been looking. I hope I didn't hurt you."

"No, I'm okay. I wasn't looking either. I just got here, and I was going outside to look for my dad. I don't know you, but Aunt Amelia always has some new people at her barbecues. I'm Kylie."

Belle licked her lips and took a deep breath. "Nice meeting you, Kylie. I'm Belle."

Kylie's smile disappeared, and she stared at her. "Oh." She turned around and walked out to the patio. Belle watched after her, her heart sinking. *Well, that fucking sucked. What if Kylie never accepts me? I want to tell her that I have no intention of taking her mother's place.* Belle walked over to the picture window and looked out at the forest of trees. Maybe this thing with Banger wasn't going to work. The only one who was cool with it was Ethan. How could she isolate Emily, and have him do the same to Kylie? It seemed like their relationship was doomed.

"Why don't you come out and join the party?" Banger's deep voice breathed, making her insides melt. He pulled her back into his chest, his arms wrapped tightly around her. "I'm missing you." He kissed the side of her face. "You okay?"

She shrugged. "I bumped into Kylie. She was super friendly until I told her my name. How's this ever going to work?"

He swung her around, his hands on her shoulders. "Stop. I told you it's gonna take some time with Kylie, just like it's going to with Emily. We both love the fuck outta our kids, but what we have is between you and me. You do things to me that I'm not willing to give up." Cupping her chin, he tipped her head back and kissed her deeply. "Now, stop overthinking. Let's go back outside and get you a drink."

Belle nodded and pressed into him. "You're pretty special to me." She kissed him gently on his Adam's apple, and his throat vibrated when he groaned. She took his hand and said, "Come on. Introduce me to your people."

As the day wore on, Belle had a wonderful time, and Banger's club brothers, his nieces, nephews, and siblings welcomed her and Ethan into their fold. Throughout the meal, she spotted Kylie sneaking glances at her, and even when she came over to talk with her dad, Belle saw her darting her eyes in her direction. When Banger introduced her to Kylie, his daughter muttered, "We already met," then changed the subject, turning her back to Belle. Banger didn't push his daughter, and by the time everyone was ready to leave, she noticed Kylie smiled at her for a few seconds when they all said good-bye. It wasn't much, but it was better than throwing daggers out of her eyes.

As they sat on the couch in her house, Ethan snuggled in his bed upstairs, Belle pulled Banger's face to hers and kissed him passionately. "Thank you for today. It was wonderful sharing that part of your life."

"I loved having you and Ethan with me. You know what Kylie whispered in my ear when she hugged me good-bye?" Belle shook her head. "She said you're 'pretty and seemed nice.' That's a big step for my little girl."

"I so want all of it to work out, but I know this isn't a romance novel or one of the fairy tales I used to read to my kids. Life has so many fucking bumps in it."

"It does, babe, but the key is how you take them."

"Maybe. Sometimes things are so fucked and you don't have control over them. Like Emily. Where the hell is she? I gave her space today, didn't make her come to the barbecue with us even though I really wanted her to go, and she's way past her curfew. She drives me crazy! I don't know what her fuckin' problem is. I'm trying so hard with her."

Banger held her close and stroked her hair. Belle leaned her head on his shoulder, happy she wasn't alone waiting for her daughter to come home. The back door slammed and Belle jumped. Emily staggered into the foyer and waved at her mom and Banger. "Hiya," she said in a loud, slurred voice.

"Why are you home at two in the morning? And why are you drunk?" Belle rose to her feet and marched over to her, but Emily just ignored her and stomped up the stairs.

Belle began to follow when Banger said, "Leave it alone, babe. Nothing good's gonna come out of you confronting her when she's like that. Things will turn bad, and you'll both be sorry come morning. Come over here."

Belle hesitated, her eyes fixed at the top of the stairs, then she slowly padded over to Banger's waiting arms. "She was doing so well, and now we're right back where we started," she lamented.

"You can't expect change overnight. She's got some demons that'll take time to work themselves out."

"But when? I just want my little girl back. I'm so scared she's going to get herself in some serious trouble. You know, she's back with her old group of friends, and they're a bad influence on her. I'm nervous all the time about it."

"Maybe she needs to go through some bad shit to appreciate the good stuff she has. I know the worst thing for a parent is to see their kid go through hell and not be able to help or prevent it, but maybe that's what it'll take for her to see what she's got."

"I don't know. I'd die if I knew she was living on the streets, or with a man who hurts her. I can't even think about it."

Banger laid her head on his shoulder. "She's stronger than you think. I see the fight in her, the determination. She'll be all right. She may have a tough go of it, but she'll come out okay."

"Can you stay with me tonight?"

"What about your kids?"

"We can stay here on the couch and hold each other. I need to be in your arms tonight. I don't want to be alone."

He kissed her. "I'm here for you, baby." She reached over and grabbed an afghan she kept by the couch for cold nights. He kicked off his boots, took off his cut, and stretched out on the couch, drawing her to him. She threw the afghan over their legs then brought it up over them as she cuddled against him, safe in his embrace. His arms wrapped around her calmed the storms in her heart.

# Chapter Thirty-One

Belle smiled when she saw Banger and Ethan holding their baseball mitts, walking down the sidewalk toward the house. As promised, Banger had come over and taken Ethan to the nearby park to practice throwing and catching the baseball in preparation for summer Little League. Heat radiated through her chest, and she found herself humming one of the catchy jingles she'd heard numerous times on television.

For the previous two weeks, she'd felt more at peace than she had in years. Emily and Belle talked a long time the day after Emily came home drunk, and continued the discussion in their therapy session. Emily seemed better since she'd found a part-time job at the hair salon. Earning some money on her own seemed to boost her self-confidence, and she'd started hanging around a better caliber of people. Taking the therapist's advice, Belle fought the school to place her daughter in advanced classes, even though her grades weren't that good. The harder classes seemed to have helped because Emily was enjoying school more, and she'd even been talking about applying for colleges. Belle kept her fingers crossed every time her daughter walked out the door.

Ethan had invited a few friends over for video games and pizza, and two of them waited anxiously for him in his room. Belle wanted to make Banger a good meal, to show he was such a wonderful addition to her life. She loved him madly, and she longed to hear him tell her he loved her. She was pretty sure he did from the way he looked at her, made love to her, and cemented himself in her and her kids' lives.

Belle pulled out the pork loin from the oven just as Banger and Ethan came through the back door. "Fuck, something smells awesome,"

Banger said as he entered the kitchen. She saw his eyes sparkle, lips curving up into a smile, and she couldn't help but smile back.

"I thought you said we were having pizza." Ethan hung his head down.

"You and your friends are. I made this for me and Banger. Luke and Peter are in your room, and Blake's mom called to tell me they're on their way."

"Thanks, Mom." Ethan dashed out of the room, his loud footsteps on the stairs making Banger and Belle laugh.

"So, what are you making for us?" Banger asked as he leaned over and smelled the roasted pork.

"We're having pork loin, scalloped potatoes, asparagus with cherry tomatoes, biscuits, and a roasted pear salad with goat cheese and walnuts. I know you loved it when I made it at the diner."

He drew her into his arms and whispered in her ear, "You like spoiling me, don't you?"

She laughed softly. "I wanted to make you a nice dinner to show you how much I appreciate everything you're doing for us. You've been wonderful with Ethan. You can't imagine what that means to him… and to me."

Banger kissed her. "I love spending time with you and your family. You're a part of my life."

"Am I?"

"You know you are, woman. Fuck, I spend more time here than I do at my own house, and the guys are wondering why in the hell I don't go to the parties more often."

"Because of me?"

He pressed his lips together, nodding. "I'm crazy about you, Belle, and I think you are 'bout me."

She circled her arms around his neck, pulling his face close to hers until his warm breath fanned over her cheeks. "I'm *fucking* crazy about you." She ran her finger across his lips and he caught it, sucking it hungrily into his mouth. A small, breathless whisper escaped from her.

His thumb caressed her cheek, then his mouth covered hers; she drew his tongue into it as their breaths intertwined.

Pulling away, he said softly against her cheek, "I love you, babe."

Warmth radiated throughout her body, and she hugged him close to her. "I love you too." They kissed passionately, her hands rubbing his back, his cupping her ass cheeks. "I've been waiting my whole life for you," she murmured against his lips.

"For the past six years, I've been half a person, and now I'm whole." They kissed again, only pulling apart when Ethan shouted at the top of the stairs that they wanted their pizza ordered. They laughed, and Belle plugged in the pizza parlor's phone number while Banger grabbed a beer out of the refrigerator.

After dinner, they sat together on the couch, watching a zombie movie. Belle was still buzzing from Banger's declaration of love, and she thought spending a chunk of her paycheck on the dinner she'd prepared had been worth it. Her phone rang, and she turned down the television. It was Holly.

"Am I bothering you?" her friend asked.

"No, I'm just watching a low-budget zombie movie with Banger." She mouthed, "It's Holly," in response to his quizzical face.

"I won't keep you. We need a girls' day out with plenty of shopping and good booze. You've been working too hard and worrying too much, and I've just been bored out of my fucking mind. Darren works so many hours, and I'm alone a lot of the time. I want to have some fun. I also haven't shopped for a long time."

"Sounds like something we could do some time."

"Some time, my ass. When's your next day off?"

"Tuesday, but I'm doing something with Banger."

"Okay, then after that."

"Thursday."

"Thursday it is, then. We'll touch base before then. I thought we'd go to Aspen to look around and have lunch."

"Aspen? I can't afford *anything* there. It'd be too depressing."

"What about Silverplume?"

"It's so cute and quaint there, and there are a ton of affordable shops and antique stores. Sounds fun."

"I'll pick you up at eleven o'clock so we can do some shopping before lunch."

"I'll be looking forward to it. Great idea."

"I'll let you go. Bye."

Belle hung up, saying, "Holly's concocted a girls' day out. It should be a good time."

"When you going?"

"Next Thursday." She turned up the volume and settled back in Banger's arms.

Emily came home from her job at The Last Tangle Hair Salon. "Anything to eat?" she asked, standing by the entrance to the living room.

"Yes. I made a pork loin, and there are potatoes and asparagus in the fridge. I also bought cold cuts, if you want to make a sandwich. How was work?"

"Good. I'm so tired. I'm gonna eat something then crash." She shuffled to the kitchen.

Belle turned to Banger. "Am I going to see you before we go out on Tuesday?"

"Wish we could, but I got some club business I need to take care of that's gonna take me outta town tomorrow and Monday. I'll call you."

"Is it going to be dangerous?" She scanned his face.

He smiled and kissed her forehead. "Don't be fretting 'bout this the whole time I'm gone. I'll be fine."

She nestled back against him, but worry settled inside her. She knew she wouldn't feel at ease until he was back in Pinewood and in her arms.

★ ★ ★

BELLE HAD BEEN anticipating the arrival of Tuesday for the past two days, and it had finally come. Dressed in jeans and a turquoise t-shirt, she waited on the front porch, listening for Banger's Harley. From a distance, the bike's roar rolled over the breeze, and she smiled when he came into view a few seconds later. Her step was light as she ran down the sidewalk to greet him, and they kissed passionately. She hadn't seen him for the previous two days, and she'd missed him so much. Even though he'd called each day, it wasn't the same as being with him.

"I missed you, babe," he said.

"Me too." She buried her head in his chest. Then he helped her on his Harley, and they took off.

They wound around parsley-green mountain hills then dipped into valleys where colorful wildflowers sprung up from the lush grass. As the bike sped along the mountain roads, the spring winds caressed their faces and ruffled their hair. Slender ribbons of light came down from the sky, and Belle tilted her head back, loving the warmth on her face. She didn't have a clue where he was taking her, but it didn't matter; the only thing that was important was that he'd come home safely.

They crossed over the peak of a mountain, and a small town lay below. Its inhabitants, cars, streets, and stores looked like miniatures that grew larger the closer they came. Banger drove down what Belle presumed was the business district, where the storefronts were made of brick and had an Old West feel to them. He pulled the Harley into a parking place, and the two of them headed into a rustic-looking café. Belle had to wait several seconds for her eyes to adjust to the dimness of the lights, then she scanned the eatery, amazed at how much it looked like a set for an old Western. Alan Jackson's soulful voice singing "Remember When" flowed through the speakers as they sat down at a small table.

Ordering a beer and a glass of white wine, they clinked their glasses together, their eyes locked on one another's. Banger held Belle's hand and kissed her, the depth of his emotion shimmering on his face when he moved away. They sat silently, listening to the song, holding hands, and staring into each other's eyes. When the waitress brought their food, Belle sighed, sorry to break the quiet connection they were sharing.

After lunch, they walked up and down Main Street, which consisted of two blocks on either side of the road. They climbed back on the Harley, and Banger asked, "You ever been to Arrowhead Canyon?" Belle shook her head. "That's where we're going. I know you'll like it." He turned his head and they shared a kiss before he revved the engine and they were off.

Arrowhead Canyon took her breath away. Crystal-clear water from Red Fern Peak's watershed had shaped the natural box canyon, the steep walls enclosing it. Towering pillars of granite flanked the canyon, a cascading waterfall cutting through them—a wall of blue satin threaded in silver. Dismounting, they stood in the canyon, and Belle leaned back as she looked up at the massive stone columns, a pinkish tint to them in the afternoon sun. The cliffs and waterfall surrounded the couple, and the gushing water danced in a twirling downward ballet. Pine trees loomed above the granite pillars while a few sprung out from the rock formations. The tumbling water crashed around them, a light, cool mist dampening them, several miniature rainbows shimmering among it.

Banger pulled her to an area that had some smooth rocks to sit on. "You like it?"

"I love it. It's so serene here, and gorgeous. I've never seen anything so beautiful."

"I'm glad you like it." He squeezed her hand and looked deeply into her eyes. "I never expected to give my heart to any other woman. You've captured my heart and driven away the loneliness by filling the void that has been in my life since Grace died." He kissed her then gently wiped a tear from the corner of her eye. "Babe, I want to spend the rest of my life with you. You're the only woman for me, and I'd be mighty pleased and honored if you'd agree to spend your life with me."

Belle stared at him, her pulse racing, heart fluttering. "What are you asking me?"

"I'm asking you to be my old lady and to marry me." He reached inside his cut and took out a small box. Opening it, he took the ring out. It was a simple white-gold band with a three-carat black, pear-shaped diamond. Around the stone, round diamonds sparkled, catching the light from the sunbeams.

Belle's hand trembled, and her insides exploded. *He's asking me to marry him! I can't believe it.*

He placed the ring on her finger then cupped her face. "Life's a long, winding road, and I want you by my side. You've brought me back to life, babe, and I want you to ride with me all the way to the end."

Belle looked into his clear, blue eyes, brimming with tenderness and love for her, and her heart lurched. She loved this biker, totally and completely. She bobbed her head up and down, the lump in her throat making it difficult for her to speak. Tears trickled down her face as she threw herself at him, hugging him and peppering his face with kisses.

"So, it's a yes?" he joked.

She laughed. "Yes. I'd be honored to be your wife. I love you so much, and I need and want you in my life. I want to share my life and my children's lives with you. But are you sure you want an old lady who has a troubled teen, a pre-teen, and a murder charge hanging over her head?"

Banger's eyes twinkled. "Is that all you got for me, woman? Fuck, that's nothing."

They held each other, listening to their hearts beating in tandem with the waterfall as it rushed over the rocks.

Later that evening, Banger took Emily, Ethan, and Belle to Big Rocky's Restaurant for steak and barbecue. When they were all seated, Belle looked at her kids, inhaled deeply, and said, "Banger has asked me to marry him, and I've accepted."

"Yes!" Ethan said, which made her insides sing, and brought a chuckle from Banger.

Emily smiled. "I'm happy for you, Mom. I'm cool with it." She scrunched her face and looked at Banger. "But there's no way I'm calling you Dad."

"I don't give a damn what you call me, as long as it's respectful. The nasty shit you wanna say, keep it to yourself, or say it behind my back." He curled his lip, but from the tinge of amusement lacing his eyes, Belle knew he was teasing Emily.

Emily looked surprised at first, then a wide grin crossed her face. "That's fair," she said.

They ate their steaks and burgers, and an air of gaiety surrounded them. *Besides my kids being born, this is one of the happiest days of my life.* During dinner, the couple stole glances at each other, and Banger kept his hand on her knee. She couldn't stop looking at her beautiful engagement ring. It just didn't get better than this.

Life was very good.

# Chapter Thirty-Two

The following afternoon, Banger sat at the clubhouse's bar and threw back a shot of Jack, the amber-colored whiskey creating a burn that dragged all the way into his stomach. He jerked his chin to Puck for another. As he threw back his second shot, Hawk slid onto the barstool next to him. Banger motioned Puck to bring a couple more shots. When the prospect set the two glasses in front of the patched members, Banger lifted his and hit it against Hawk's.

Hawk raised his eyebrows. "What are we celebrating?"

"I'm gettin' married. Fuck." He threw his drink back, a buzz growing in his head.

Hawk downed his shot and stared at Banger. "Fuck, now Cara will never let me forget that she was right in setting you up. I was against it. Thought she was meddling, but she's gonna have me eating crow for quite a while on this one." Hawk clapped Banger on the shoulder. "Congrats, man. You deserve to be happy, and Belle seems like a good, loyal woman."

Banger nodded. "She is, and she'll make a fuckin' good old lady. I already told her she'll be the head old lady since she's marryin' the prez. She doesn't get the world, but she will in time. Fuck, man, I never thought I'd marry again after Grace died. I never thought I could love another woman. It's good."

"How's Kylie taking it?"

"I haven't told her yet. She's coming down for a visit in a couple of weeks, and I'll tell her then. I suspect she's not gonna be too happy 'bout it, but she'll learn to like Belle."

"Yeah. She's growing up, and soon she'll find a man of her own."

Banger's jaw clenched. "She's got plenty of time for that. I know one thing, I don't want her with a biker."

Hawk shrugged. "You know how it is. When that one person grabs you, you're fuckin' hooked. When you two getting hitched?"

"Not sure. Belle wants to wait for the kids to get outta school. I want a full biker wedding, so I wanna do it while the weather is still good. Maybe September."

"We need to party tonight, dude. Fuck, I'm gonna announce it now." Hawk stood up and told Puck to cut the music, several brothers playing pool cursed loudly in response. Hawk raised his hand. "Stop your fuckin' complaining. I got news. Our president has found an old lady, and they're gonna get married."

The burst of whistles, applause, and hoots was deafening, and Banger cocked his head to the side and leaned against the bar, warmth spreading inside him. He knew it wasn't entirely from the whiskey; his brothers were the best. They had each other's back through good and bad times, and he wouldn't trade life in the brotherhood for any other. His brothers made him proud to be an Insurgent.

"We gotta celebrate, man," Bruiser said from the corner of the room. Loud voices in agreement bounced off the walls.

"Tonight is party time." Throttle came over and clapped Banger on the shoulder. "Congratulations, brother. You're gonna make a lot of the club whores and hoodrats sad. For some reason, they loved your cock."

Banger laughed. "The only one who's ever gonna get it is my old lady."

They all agreed that party time would begin at eight o'clock, and the only old lady allowed would be Banger's; this was a party to celebrate and support his decision, and the brothers wanted the freedom to fuck freely without judging eyes. Some of the brothers who had old ladies, like Tigger, Ruben, and Billy, liked new pussy every once in a while, so they definitely didn't want any of the brothers' wives or girlfriends informing on them. The old ladies and the brothers would have a family party to welcome Belle into the fold, and to congratulate Banger, and then the club women would be relegated to the outer fringes of the club. Old ladies and club women *never* mixed.

Lola and Kristy walked over to Banger, Hawk, and Throttle. "What's all the hooting about?" Lola asked as she pushed her barely contained tits against Banger's arm. Kristy stood close to Hawk.

"Banger's got an old lady. We're partying tonight."

Lola's eyes widened, and she pouted. "You're hitched?" She ran her long nails down the front of his shirt. "Who's gonna take care of me?"

Banger chuckled and gently moved her hands away. "I think you got plenty of brothers who love your tits and ass, Lola. Don't think you're gonna be lonely."

"Congratulations," Kristy said, and she leaned over and kissed his cheek.

"Thanks," Banger replied as he squeezed her hand. He had a soft spot for Kristy. She'd been with the Insurgents for the past seven years, and she was a great listener. She'd lost her sister to breast cancer a couple of years before she joined up with the MC, so she knew what Banger was going through after Grace. He spent many hours talking with her, and she provided him a warm body and a great fuck when he needed that as well. He'd known she was sweet on Hawk, so when he hitched up with Cara, she'd been real sad. She'd confided in him that she had hoped Hawk would have made her his old lady, since she'd been one of his favorite fucks at the club, and she found solace in Banger's arms. He had never loved Kristy, but he thought she was a damned nice woman, and a great club girl.

"I still can't believe you're gonna be off-limits, unless you're gonna have pussy on the side like Ruben and some of the other brothers." Lola's eyes lit up with hope.

"Nope. Not gonna happen."

"I'm not hitched," Throttle said as he yanked Lola next to him, grabbing the ass cheek peeking out from under her short skirt. He crashed his mouth on hers and kissed her.

"Hey, here comes Rock." Throttle motioned for Rock to come over.

Hawk and Banger watched in amusement.

"Congrats, prez. I heard the news," Rock said. Banger tilted his chin up. "What's up, Throttle?"

"I got a couple of bitches here who want some down-and-dirty fun. You game?"

Banger watched as Rock's eyes went straight to Kristy's large tits. "Yeah." He grabbed her wrist and pulled her to him, and she giggled when his large hands kneaded her breasts. "Let's go to my room," he said to her and Throttle.

"Later," Throttle said to Hawk and Banger as he, Lola, Rock, and Kristy walked toward the staircase.

"I'm not gonna miss *that*," Banger stated as he took out his phone. "You ever miss it?"

Hawk shook his head. "Nah. Cara's enough for me."

Banger dialed Belle, a tingle shooting through him when he heard her voice.

"Hey, honey. How are you?"

"Okay, babe. Be ready at seven thirty 'cause I'm picking you up for a party they're giving me at the clubhouse. Wear somethin' sexy."

"Like what?"

"Wear your short black dress. You know, the one that hugs all your delicious curves. It fuckin' turns me on."

A soft giggle touched his ears. "I didn't know you liked it that much. I'll be ready when you come by. Will Cara be at the party?"

"No old ladies at this one. The family one, sure."

"Aren't I an old lady?"

"Different 'cause the party is for us, and I want you to meet the brothers. In the future, you'll only be able to go to the family stuff at the club. I'll tell you how it is as time goes. See you soon, babe."

★ ★ ★

BELLE'S NERVES WERE on edge when she walked into the great room, and she held Banger's arm tighter as all the men stared at her. Self-consciously, she pulled her dress down, sorry she'd let Banger talk her into wearing it in a club full of men. She'd heard stories from Holly about the wild parties the Deadly Demons had, and she had no doubt the Insurgents had the same type.

"Want a drink?" Banger asked as he led her to a large, wraparound bar.

"A glass of white wine, if you have it." She settled onto a cushioned barstool.

As she sipped her wine, she looked around the great room and saw a sea of denim and leather on the men, and the skimpiest outfits she'd ever seen on the women. Many of the women were young and pretty, showing off their assets in barely-there tops, and short skirts or shorts that revealed more of their butts than they covered. She blushed when she spotted a pretty woman on her knees, sucking a member's dick while he pulled on her exposed breasts.

Banger had forewarned her that she'd see some things that she'd probably never seen in her life. He explained how the brothers and the women were open about having a good time, and giving and receiving pleasure wasn't always done behind closed doors. *Knowing* and *seeing* were two different things though, and Belle couldn't help but stare in disbelief and embarrassment when she spotted men and women touching and screwing in front of everyone. It made her uncomfortable, and she couldn't help but wonder if Banger was down for this type of lovemaking.

He put his arm around her. "You doing okay?"

"Not really. I've never been to anything like this. It's like a big orgy with a bunch of drunk people." He laughed and kissed her hair, clutching her shoulder. "Are you into the sex in public thing?"

"Nope. Always liked privacy. Not all the brothers are. It's up to the person."

"Do women get a say in it?"

"Oh yeah, but the club whores and the hoodrats like the lifestyle, that's why they're here. No one is forced to come to the parties or be a part of the Insurgents MC. The club whores live at the club, wear the property patch, and we protect them and give them room and board and a stipend, but they can leave whenever they want. The hoodrats line up every weekend to let loose at one of our parties. It's the way it is. As long as everyone's a consenting adult, I don't fuckin' mess with it."

"I guess if they're all on the same wavelength, then it's cool. It would never be *my* scene though." Belle spotted a couple of pretty women in their late twenties, talking and pointing to her. "I think I'm upsetting your fan club by being here." She jerked her head toward the women.

Banger chortled and pulled her closer. "You're the only fan who matters."

"Did you have something with them?"

He moved in front of her and placed his hand under her chin, tilting her head back. "You gotta understand that none of these women ever meant shit to me. Did I fuck 'em? I did, but you knew that. I don't want you thinkin' for a minute that I want to be with them, or that they were better than you in bed, or any of that insecure shit. I'm with you. You're going to be my wife. What I did before doesn't have anything to do with what we have now. I never fucked around on Grace, and I won't on you. When I love, it's forever. Never doubt my love or loyalty to you." He kissed her passionately, and she circled her arms around his neck, drawing him closer.

Throughout the night, brothers came over to congratulate their president, never saying a word to her. It was like she was the invisible woman, except when they'd throw side glances at her, lingering on her breasts, which creeped her out. No one gawked at her overtly, and they behaved themselves, but Belle figured it was because she was with their president, and they wouldn't do anything to disrespect him.

The club brought in barbecued beef brisket, pulled pork, corn on the cob, mashed potatoes, and coleslaw from Big Rocky's, and Belle sat close to Banger on a wood bench of one of the many picnic tables strewn around the yard. Tunes from bands such as AC/CD, Bon Jovi, Lynyrd Skynyrd and others played over the speakers strategically placed around the yard. All the members had come up to them, bringing shots to Banger, who shared them with her. Belle tipped her head back and saw the stars flashing with the brilliant, polar-white pallor of strobe lights against black satin. The breeze had a chill to it, and she snuggled closer to Banger, her head tucked under his chin.

He ran his hand over her hips before slowly gliding it under her dress, squeezing her inner thigh. Desire flared in her like a flaming torch. She squirmed in her seat, and he slipped two fingers inside her panties and wiggled them between her juicy folds. "Fuck," he muttered under his breath. He placed her hand on top of his crotch, his hardness pulsing. "Let's go to my room, woman." He stood up, taking her with him.

His room was on the third floor, where all the officers of the club had one. Being president, he had the largest room, located in a corner, the windows providing views to the incredible landscape surrounding the club. Closing the door behind them, he swung her around and gave her gentle, sweet pecks on her lips. She pressed closer to him, her finger inching down to the top of his jeans. Slowly, she undid his belt, the heel of her hand grazing his crotch. He pulled her hand up and brought it to his mouth, kissing it. "I got a favor to ask you," he whispered in her ear, his lips brushing her earlobe and sending shivers through her.

"What?"

"Let me make love to you."

It was like his words released a million fluttering butterflies inside her. She swallowed the lump in her throat. "Okay," was all she could get out; her emotions had surpassed her. His mouth returned to her lips, this time pressing against them, his tongue gently prodding her mouth open. He slipped it inside, caressing hers as his hands slowly slid down her body. "You taste like whiskey and honey, babe," he said between kisses.

After kissing her for several minutes, slow and sensual, he ran his mouth down her neck, nipping and licking it. He pulled down her dress to reveal her shoulder then pressed his mouth on her soft, delicate skin.

His hands slid down further, and hers ran down the length of his back, landing on his butt. They took their time undressing one another, her carefully unzipping his pants, him deliberately unclasping her bra. As he removed her clothes, he kissed and stroked the just-revealed spot before moving on to the next; by the time she stood naked before him, her body hummed with excitement, every nerve zapping pleasure through her.

Gently, he lay her on his king-sized bed and hovered over her, his eyes catching hers in an intense gaze of desire and love. They kissed deeply and passionately, and his hardness rested against her throbbing mound. For a long time, they kissed and caressed each other until he rose up. "I'll be right back," he said, then went to the bathroom.

She watched him shuffle away, his taut ass flexing with every step. *Simply magnificent.* Her breathing deepened. She knew he wasn't searching for a condom since they'd stopped using them when she started using the pill. In a few seconds, he came out with a small glass filled with a bit of water. "You thirsty?" she asked.

With a smoldering look, he nodded. He leaned over her again and kissed her, his hand cupping and massaging her breast. He took the glass and drizzled warm water over her breasts, slowly licking it up. The sensual surprise made her flesh tingle. His hands and mouth explored every part of her, connecting them through touch.

"You're the only one for me," he whispered against her skin.

"I love you so much," she replied, gliding her hands down his spine, then running her fingers along the crease where his thigh met his groin. He moaned as he continued exploring her body with his lips, tongue, and hands. Closing her eyes, she relaxed and reveled in the exquisite pleasure he was giving her.

When he moved back up her body, his lips landed on hers and they kissed, deep and wet. She pushed up on her elbows and rested her hands on his shoulders, gently guiding him onto his back. "I want to *feel* you," she said in a low voice as she kissed him softly along his forehead, moving down his face. Peppering his neck with kisses, she ran her fingers against his firm skin, loving its smooth texture. She lay her head against his chest and listened to his pounding heart as his arousal escalated, then she nuzzled him all over, inhaling his essence.

"You are so beautiful," he said as his eyes locked with hers, his fingers tangling in her hair.

Belle kept his gaze and rubbed her tits on his chest, capturing his lips. Slowly, she pulled up, her talons scratching down his torso until her fingers wrapped around his stiff dick. He sucked in his breath, and she saw desire and heat in his eyes. She lifted her ass and stroked his hardness with her mound, his cock's head parting her wet lips, brushing next to her throbbing clit.

Straddling him, she glided his dick deep inside her, her eyes fixed on his as she pulled his hardness out. Over and over, his cock went in and out of her as she leaned in slightly, her tits swaying. Banger grabbed her breasts and played with them, tweaking her marble-hard beads, and she bent down and kissed him as her pussy swallowed then released him. Leaning back, she fingered her clit then put her finger in his mouth. He sucked her juices off as his gaze held hers. "You taste and smell fuckin' awesome, babe."

She bent over again and kissed his lips, tasting herself on them. He placed his hands on her hips and thrust into her, rocking and bucking until his legs tightened. She felt his warm seed filling her while her pussy clenched tightly around him as he came, milking every last drop from his dick. They locked their gazes as he came, followed by her own crashing waves of ecstasy. At that moment, when Belle held his eyes, she felt truly bonded to him; she knew that, no matter what happened in life, they would always have each other.

"I love you." His voice was low and gruff, and she felt his body relax.

"You're wonderful," she whispered against his neck as she lay across his chest. It seemed like forever passed before she rolled off his body and tucked herself in to him, her back molded against his stomach. He curled his arm around her and hugged her tightly.

"I'm so fuckin' lucky I found you. You're the half that makes me whole." Banger moved her hair away from her face and kissed her.

"I never thought I'd ever find my soulmate. You're my rock, my love, my world." Belle brought his hand up to her lips and kissed it.

They lay, sated, his leg draped over her, arms around her. As she listened to his deepening breaths, she knew she'd been blessed with a loving man who would be a wonderful husband and a great father to her kids.

Life didn't get any better than this one solitary moment.

# Chapter Thirty-Three

On Thursday morning at eleven o'clock, Belle heard Holly's car horn as she scrambled around, throwing sunscreen, lipstick, and sunglasses into her tote. She ran out of the house and jumped into Holly's car, panting. "Sorry, I had a late start this morning. This is gonna be so much fun!"

Holly picked up a thermos, shook it, and said, "I brought refreshments. It's time we have some fun without the men." She handed it to Belle.

"You're so bad." Belle laughed as she unscrewed the thermos and a strong whiff of tequila stung her nostrils. "I'm gonna be blasted off my ass before we even get to Silverplume."

"We got all day to shop. If we get too drunk, hell, we'll spend the night. We're just two free agents today." Holly glanced at Belle. "I still can't believe you're engaged to the president of the Insurgents. Fuck, that's badass. I still can't see you as a biker chick."

"I know. Sometimes I can't believe it, either. I mean, I was head of the Ladies Society of Roses back in Lakeview. Fuck, I was a Girl Scouts' leader for Emily's troop. Now I can't wait to wrap my arms around Banger and speed down the highway on his Harley. I never pictured this." Belle stretched her arm out in front of her, her diamond-encrusted ring gleaming in the sun. "Want to see my ring again?"

Holly rolled her eyes. "I've only seen it a ton of times. It's beautiful. I bet it cost plenty. How many carats are in that damn thing?"

"The solitaire is three carats and the rest are about two. I never saw a black diamond before. I love it. I love my ring. I love Banger. I love life, and I especially love this 'punch' you made." Belle giggled and took a big swig of the syrupy-sweet drink.

With the windows down, the radio blasting eighties tunes, the two women zipped down the highway. "How's Banger in bed?" Holly asked as she turned the radio down.

Belle's face lit up. "Awesome!"

Holly looked over, her expression hard. "Really? Too bad you're not into sharing. I wouldn't mind trying him out. Darren is strictly a 'missionary with the lights off' kind of guy. Banger doesn't strike me like that."

"Not at all. He's just so fucking good. He's the best." Belle blushed and covered her mouth. "I don't think he'd want me talking about our lovemaking. He's a very private person."

"All one percenters are private. You know, all that 'club business' bullshit."

They sped on and Belle laughed, taking another swig of alcohol punch as Holly cranked up the radio and they sang along to Mötley Crüe's "Girls, Girls, Girls."

★ ★ ★

BANGER FINISHED TURNING the last screw in the bookcase that Belle had given him to assemble for Ethan's room when his phone rang. He took it out of his pocket and was surprised to see Cara's name on the screen.

"What's up, Cara?"

"I have some disturbing news I want to share with you. I've been trying to get a hold of Belle all morning, but I can't get through."

"She went to Silverplume to do some shopping. Reception is the shits in some areas on the drive up there. What's going on?"

"I had my private investigator digging around in the death of her husband. I know the cops are chomping at the bit to arrest her, so I wanted to see what I could find before anything like that happens. I looked at everyone who's connected with her, her husband, and the two of them as a couple."

"Okay…."

"I found out that her best friend, Holly, was a suspect in a murder case back in her hometown of Overton, Texas, and in Colorado Springs, she was a suspect in an attempted murder charge."

His body stiffened and a heavy feeling punched through his stomach. "What the fuck?"

"It gets worse. Dean Wesley, my private eye, went to Colorado Springs and met up with the victim. She positively identified the picture of Holly, only Holly was going by the name Leeann back then. The woman said she was down on her luck, and Leeann took her in and helped her get back on her feet, and she was so grateful to her. Then Leeann had her sign some paperwork so, in case she got sick, Leeann could help her out. The victim was so appreciative of all that she'd done, she signed without reading the paperwork."

"What the fuck did she sign?"

"A life insurance policy making Leeann the beneficiary. She and Leeann went out for a ride one day, and the victim said Leeann gave her something to drink that was drugged. Then she pulled onto a small road, and there was another car parked by the train tracks. A guy, who she recognized as Leeann's brother, was leaning against it."

"Fuck. I bet it was that sonofabitch Deadly Demon."

"She said he always wore a leather vest with a patch, and he was in a motorcycle club, but she wasn't sure the name of it. I bet you're right, Banger."

"What the fuck did they do to her? Did the fucker rape her?"

"No, he didn't. He pulled her out of the car and slammed her head hard with something. She was semi-conscious. They positioned her behind the wheel of the car and placed it on the train tracks. She pretended to be totally knocked out, so they left. She was so groggy she couldn't muster the strength to move. She heard the train whistle, and she claimed a guardian angel helped her, because as the train approached she was able to move the car a bit. The car was still hit, but not full-on. She spent a year in rehab and will always walk with a limp."

Banger shook with rage.

"And get this. Holly—or Leeann, or whoever the fuck she is—worked in a hospital both in Colorado Springs and in Lakeview. She would totally have had access to sux. I'd bet anything she killed Belle's husband, but I'm not yet sure why. I'll have to dig a bit deeper. When you see Belle, tell her to stay far away from Holly; she's dangerous and crazy. Also, tell her to call me right away."

"Fuck, Cara, Belle's with the bitch. *She* arranged the trip today. Fuck, my woman's in danger."

"Do you know if Belle signed any papers for Holly?"

"I don't know. Emily went to live with her for a bit, maybe Belle signed something then. I don't know, but my gut tells me I gotta act fast. Fuck!"

"Do you have any way to track her? The trip to Silverplume is full of side roads. God, I'm so scared for her. I have to call Hawk, he'll get the guys together to help you. Oh, God, Banger. I can't—"

"I insisted that we install a tracking app on our phones. I can track her, I just hope it's not too fuckin' late. Tell Hawk to get the guys ASAP, bring his SUV, and come to my place. Move it!"

Banger slammed his fist on the bookshelf, cracking it in half. *If anything happens to Belle, I'll fuckin' lose it.* Within ten minutes, Hawk, Axe, Throttle, Bruiser, Rock, Chas, Puck, and Johnnie were ready to go. Banger said they'd take his and Hawk's SUVs since the Harleys would be heard a mile away. He told Puck and Johnnie to bring the pickup truck and meet them at the spot, and they sped out of Pinewood Springs. Banger gripped the steering wheel, his knuckles turning white. As they drove, Hawk filled the brothers in on what was happening, and Banger cursed under his breath, swearing he'd track Holly and Scorpion down and make them suffer a slow and painful death if they hurt his woman.

# Chapter Thirty-Four

Belle held her head as the landscape spun around her; she was woozy as hell, and she felt way drunker than she ought to have been, considering she hadn't even drunk half a glass worth of the punch Holly made. "Damn," she slurred. "Did you use moonshine? The drink was too strong. I feel sick." She looked at Holly, who kept fading further and further away. She lifted her hand to put the thermos down and ended up dropping it to the floorboard; her hand muscles were weak and uncoordinated. *I feel so sluggish and tired. It's like I've been drugged or something.* She moved her head, and it flopped to the side. With bleary eyes, she noticed that they'd left the highway and were driving on a dirt road. "Where're we going?" she managed to get out of her dry mouth.

Holly laughed and stomped on the brakes, throwing Belle forward, her knees slamming into the glove compartment. Belle looked ahead and saw they were parked at the bank of the Colorado River.

"Did you drug me?" she asked her friend incredulously.

"You really are a fucking stupid bitch!" She shoved Belle back against the seat.

Her friend's words came slowly at her, as Belle tried to understand why Holly was yelling at her. *Why are we at the river when we're supposed to go shopping?* In her foggy mind, she couldn't think clearly. Near the car, she noticed a Harley—it was Scorpion's. Panic grabbed hold of her, and she tried to open the car door, but her damn muscles weren't working right; she couldn't move her limbs normally. "Why's Scorpion here?" she asked raggedly.

Ignoring her, Holly slipped out of the car. Scorpion came over to the passenger's side and threw open the door, dragging Belle out. Trying to push him away, her lack of muscle control made her no match for him. He slammed her against the hood of the car, kissing her roughly on the lips as his hands rubbed over her breasts, squeezing them tightly. "I want what you're giving that sonofabitch Insurgent. You owe me, cunt."

"Scorpion! *That* isn't why you're here," Holly yelled at him.

"Shut the fuck up. I'm gonna have some fun before I get rid of her." He pushed his face against Belle's. "You up for that? No?" He guffawed. "That's okay, you just relax. I'll do all the work." He grabbed the hem of her shirt.

"Holly? What's going on? Why aren't you stopping this?" Her tongue was thick, and everything was spinning faster. She was afraid she was going to pass out.

Holly came over, punched her brother in the arm, and shoved him away from Belle. "I told you, you're not here for *that*. When you do your job, you can go back to town and fuck whatever slut you want."

"Holly?" Belle said weakly as she collapsed on the ground.

Pulling her up by the hair, Holly propped her against the car. Crouching down, she brought her face inches from Belle's. "You want to know what's going on? You're going to die. Your ass is worth a million dollars, and I'm ready to collect."

Belle shook her head, as if that would help clear the fogginess slowly taking over her entire brain. "Money…?"

"Yeah. Remember that life insurance policy you signed when you brought your brat daughter over to stay with me?"

Belle closed her eyes, forcing her brain to bring out a memory from one of the clear corners of her mind. She vaguely remembered Holly telling her that if something happened to Belle, Emily and Ethan wouldn't be provided for. Holly suggested that she take out a life insurance policy, making her the beneficiary since Ethan and Emily were minors. Belle agreed, thinking it was a good idea, that her friend was so kind for agreeing to take her kids in if anything happened to her. She remembered thinking that she trusted Holly with her life. *How fucking ironic.*

"I can see from the look in your eyes that you do remember. It was too easy. Did you really think I'd want to take care of your fucked-up daughter and puny son? Fuck. You're so stupid. I banked on your stupidity when I fucked Harold behind your back for three years."

*Money…? Harold…? What the fuck is she talking about?*

"I became friends with you for a reason. I knew your hubby was rich, and the way you acted with him told me that I could be fucking him in no time. You gave him a home, kids, good meals, but you didn't fuck him like a slut. All men want that. He knew you weren't interested in him sexually. He'd tell me, and I'd pretend I gave a shit."

"Come on, either let me fuck her or kill her, but your fuckin' talking is getting on my nerves." Scorpion threw his cigarette butt in the dirt and stubbed it out.

"You shut up. I had to put up with this whiny cunt for years, acting like I was her friend just to get to Harold so we could make some real money. I want her to know I was sucking and fucking her husband, and he loved it." She bent down and hissed in Belle's ear, "He fucking loved having sex with me. He bought me expensive presents, took me on his business trips, and stole the money from the business. All for me. *Me.* Then that cunt, his secretary, grabbed hold of his cock and tried to take away all the hard work I'd done. He even told me it was over between us. Can you imagine that? He wanted to give *her* the money I'd worked so hard for. Then you found out, and I was so glad because I thought you'd have a fucking backbone and would throw him out. But being the weak woman you are, you forgave him, and he left Megan *and* me, decided that he really loved you, and he was going to make everything all right and return the money. What a stupid asshole!"

The world was quickly fading. Holly was still chattering about Harold and the secretary and the money. *The money! Holly stole the money.* "You killed Harold?"

"Damn right, I did. He fucking screwed me over. No one dumps me. Ever. When I told him I wanted one last hurrah, that he owed it to me for all the good times I gave him, he relented. I knew he hadn't returned the money yet. He was going to do it after the weekend. I knew where he kept it, so I gave him a push—or should I say a prick—into the next world." She laughed loudly and cruelly. "Now you can join him, bitch." She jumped up and motioned to Scorpion. "Your turn."

"About fuckin' time. Damn, you got a mouth."

"My kids and Banger know I'm out with you," Belle croaked.

"Yeah, well, people disappear all the time, sweetheart. After I weigh your body down, you won't ever be found. They'll think the slut did something to you, or you ran off instead of being convicted for your husband's murder."

Scorpion dragged her to her feet, and she fell in to him.

"I promise to play the bereaved best friend to the hilt. Banger's going to be so sad that you ran away, but don't worry, I'll console him real good." Holly laughed. "Let's finish this bitch off."

"Not until I get what I want." Scorpion lifted Belle's top, pressing his mouth over her breasts before he pulled down her jeans. She felt sick, and knew the only hope she had was to pretend she was unconscious. She hung her head laxly and closed her eyes.

"You fucking perv. She passed out. Find another slut to fuck. We gotta get this over with. I'm not going to risk getting caught because you want to fuck her." Holly pushed her brother out of the way then pulled up Belle's pants. "Help me get her to the river. She's out cold. You can drown her then we'll weigh the body down. Get a move on."

Scorpion hoisted Belle over his shoulder and slammed her face down on the bank of the river. Belle tasted copper from her bleeding lips. Even though she wasn't unconscious yet, moving her body was extremely difficult. At that moment, she knew she was going to die. No one knew she was there. Banger had a tracking app on her phone, but why would he ever think anything was amiss? She'd told him she was going out with her best friend for a day of shopping, after all.

She wondered if Harold felt as sad and panicked as she did while he was dying. Tears burned behind her eyes. Sadness for a life she could have had with Banger, and not being able to watch her children grow into adults, coursed through her body. After all she had been through, her life would end in the middle of nowhere, in the deep, cold waters of the Colorado River. *What a sad and terrible way to die.*

The water flooded her nose and mouth and she flailed like a beached fish, striving to breathe. Again her head was dunked in, just before she gasped for more air. Through the rush of water, she heard Scorpion's muffled voice.

"You didn't give her enough of that shit. She's still conscious. Fuck, can't you do anything right?"

"Just hold her head down, she'll go. You like a fight, so why are you griping?" Holly snapped.

Her lungs were filling with water, and black spots floated in front of her eyes. *Here I go....*

Muted yells and screams echoed in the background as she gave herself up to her watery grave. Then she was spitting and coughing as someone leaned over her, pressing her chest and bringing his mouth to hers, breathing life into her water-laden lungs. The brackish liquid spewed from her as she coughed, and through the slits of her barely opened eyes, she saw shadows and black boots. Then several hands picked her up and placed her in the back of a vehicle, and she gave in to the darkness that engulfed her.

# Chapter Thirty-Five

"GET HER TO the hospital, now!" Banger turned back to a bloodied and bruised Scorpion and stabbed the final blow into his heart. Scorpion's small black eyes widened then went flat as the life seeped out of him. "Get rid of this piece of shit," Banger ordered. "When you're done, bring his bike back to the clubhouse. No reason to destroy a Harley."

Puck and Johnnie, the two prospects, dutifully wrapped Scorpion's body in a large tarp, threw it in the flatbed of the pickup, and sped away to dispose of it where it would never be found.

Holly stared wild-eyed at the group of bikers. "You gonna kill me too?"

Banger gritted his teeth and fought down the urge to gut her. "Nah. It's not that I'm soft, because I'd love to give you an Insurgents' death—slow and painful—but I gotta clear my old lady's name. Your ass is gonna be stuck in a cell, bitch. In your case, living is gonna be worse than dying." He turned to Chas and Rock. "Tie this cunt up and throw her in the back. We'll drop her off at the fuckin' badges' door."

After they tied her hands and feet, they tossed her in the back of the SUV. Holly cussed up a storm.

"Will someone gag the bitch?" Banger demanded. "I'm not listening to that shit all the way back to Pinewood."

When they got to the police station, Detective Sanders was waiting for them. Cara had called ahead and told him what was happening, along with sharing her information about Holly. Banger let Hawk deal with the detective; he had to go to the hospital and see his Belle.

When he entered her room in the emergency department, Belle was propped against a bevy of pillows holding a large glass, her teeth crunching on something. He rushed over and kissed and hugged her.

She pulled away. "I look a mess."

He kissed her bruised face, whispering, "You're the most beautiful mess I've ever seen. Whatcha got in the cup?"

"Chipped ice. The doctor says water flushes will push the drugs out of my system. I'm still woozy, but not like I was earlier today. Damn, I can't believe any of this."

"I know. Fuck, I knew there was something I didn't like about the cunt, but I couldn't pinpoint what it was. I didn't like how she kept flirting with me, you being her friend and all. I knew something wasn't right."

"She killed Harold." Her voice hitched. "And they had an affair for a long time. How did Harold do that to me, and with my friend? I thought Megan was the only affair he had, and I chalked it up to midlife-crisis shit. I don't understand any of this. I can't wrap my head around it, because everything I knew and believed for the last five years has turned out to be nothing but a big, fucking lie."

He bent down and drew her close to his body. "Harold was a fuckin' idiot to have looked at any other woman when he had you in his life. And Holly is a grifter. She conned and scammed for money, and if murder was the way to get it, that's what she did. She was never your friend."

"But how could she act like we were best friends, sharing our thoughts, our dreams, our jokes—everything? How could she do it?"

"She's a pro. She banked about two million from your husband and would've gotten another from you." He stopped, a lump forming in his throat. He'd been so close to losing the woman he adored. "We got Cara to thank for saving you," he said in a low voice.

"I'll have to thank her. If she hadn't looked into this, I wouldn't be here."

"Let's be happy you are. The past is over. We got a whole lifetime ahead of us." He went over and closed the door then came back to her.

Drawing a chair close to the bed, he said, in a hushed voice, "That fuckin' badge is gonna be over here real soon to talk to you 'bout what happened. Tell him everything except that Scorpion was there."

"What happened to him?"

"You don't need to worry about that. It's club business. Just don't mention the fucker. It was only you and the cunt. Got it?"

She nodded just as someone knocked on her door.

"Remember, babe." Banger kissed her gently on the lips then went over and opened the door. Detective Sanders stared at him. Banger moved aside. "Come on in."

Sanders entered the room. "I'd like to speak with Mrs. Dermot alone."

"I want Banger to stay," she said. "I can't talk too long. I'm still groggy."

He sat down on the chair at the foot of her bed while Banger plopped on the one next to her.

The questions went on and on and on, and Banger could see Belle's face was a mask of exhaustion. He'd give the fuckin' badge a few more questions, but then he was outta the room.

Once again, Sanders asked, "Was anyone with you besides your friend, Holly?"

Belle stuck with her story. "Only Holly was there. She drugged me. The toxicology report will prove that. I also left most of the punch, so I'm sure it's still there in the thermos in her car."

"Was her brother, Scorpion, there?"

She shook her head. "No. I haven't seen Scorpion since the time I spotted him with Megan, my late husband's mistress. That was about two or three weeks ago."

"Did you witness a fight between your fiancé—" his chin jerked to Banger "—and Scorpion?"

With a sweet, innocent face, she replied, "No, I never did. They didn't even know each other."

Sanders stared hard at her, and all she did was smile and put another spoonful of chipped ice in her mouth. Then Sanders looked at Banger's expressionless face. Inwardly, he was laughing his ass off. *She's gonna make a kick-ass old lady.*

"We did a search on your supposed friend's house, and we found all sorts of fake IDs, the life insurance you signed, and a multitude of sedatives. She had them buried in the corner of her closet."

In a small voice, she asked, "Did she kill Harold?"

"It appears that way. She planted the syringe in your unit knowing your stepdaughter would find it and put the blame on you. She got her brother to cozy up to Megan Ryan so if your body ever turned up, she'd be the likely suspect."

"Did Darren know anything about what Holly was doing?"

"No, he was duped just like everyone else who was pulled into her web." He closed his notebook pad. "You take care of yourself. The Lakeview district attorney will be getting in touch with you. I suspect the Gilpin County DA will too, since you were in their county when she tried to kill you."

Belle nodded. "Thanks."

Sanders's eyes darted from Belle to Banger, then he walked out. Banger muttered under his breath, "Fuckin' badge."

"Be nice. He's just doing his job, and he was nice to me even though he knew I was lying through my teeth."

"Mom? Can we come in?" Emily stood by the doorway, tears glistening in her eyes. Ethan sprinted into the room and hugged his mom.

Belle squeezed him tight to her as she smiled and motioned her daughter to come in. Emily headed over and Banger rose to his feet, walking to the corner of the room. He wanted to let her have a few minutes with her kids before she conked out.

Belle told them parts of the story, and Emily started to cry. "I'm so sorry for being such a pain in the ass. I can't believe I might have lost you too."

Belle stroked her hair, and the kids lay their heads on her shoulders, their arms wrapped around their mother. Emily lifted her head. "I can't believe Au—Holly did all this to you. And she killed Dad." She wrung her hands. "I know about Dad. About everything, I'm so sorry that I blamed you for all the bad stuff that happened to us. I know now that you were the one who made our lives run smoothly, despite everything you were going through. Those women…"

"What women?" asked Ethan.

"Friends of your father. Your father was a wonderful man who loved being a daddy to both of you. He loved you very, very much. Don't ever forget that." Belle glanced at Banger, who had been listening and observing the scene. She smiled and he gave her a wink.

He loved the way she protected her late husband even though he was a fucking asshole who'd done her wrong. From everything she'd told him, Harold *was* a good father, and she didn't want her kids to forget it. She was quite a woman.

Belle was pale as a ghost, but Banger knew she'd die before she asked her kids to leave. He cleared his throat. "Your mom's had a very rough day, and she's exhausted. She'll probably be released, but that could take hours. I know she wants to rest. Why don't you say good-bye, and I'll call you later with an update."

"The doctor said he wants to keep me overnight for observation," Belle said. "I am exhausted, but I don't want you two staying alone. I'd be too nervous."

"I took care of it. They're staying at Hawk and Cara's until you get home."

"How wonderful it is that everyone bands together in the club," Belle said.

"We're a family, and now you and the kids are too."

After they hugged their mom for the umpteenth time, they headed out. Emily paused at the doorway then said in a low voice, "Thanks for saving my mom."

"It was nothing." Banger clasped her on the shoulder, and she smiled then shuffled away, holding Ethan's hand.

Belle pushed her head further down on the pillows, her eyelids fluttering. "You can go. I'm sure you're tired. I'll be fine."

"I'm not going anywhere, babe. My ass is on this chair until you're released, then I'll take you home." He held up his hand when she opened her mouth. "No fuckin' argument, woman."

Smiling, she said, "I was only going to tell you I love you."

In three long strides, he was by her side, his face hovering over hers. "Then talk away, woman. I love you more than you'll ever know." He leaned down and kissed then held her hand.

"When Scorpion held my head underwater, my last thoughts were of you and my kids. I thought I would never see you again. I feel like I've been given a second chance to live my life with you, and watch my kids grow."

Banger sat close to her, holding her hand until she drifted off to sleep. Staring out the window at the Rocky Mountains, he felt like he'd been given a second chance as well, and he had no intention of ever taking her or their life together for granted.

After six years of pain and loneliness, he was happy and whole again, and there was nothing in this life that would ever change that for him.

# Chapter Thirty-Six

*Two weeks later*

BANGER KEPT GLANCING at the clock Belle had put up in his kitchen, wondering what was taking Kylie so long to arrive. It was quiet in the house, and he'd wanted to talk to her without an audience. Ethan was over one of his friend's house, and Emily and Belle were at work. Even though Banger had told Belle she didn't have to work anymore, she insisted on keeping her job at the diner until they were married. He reluctantly agreed, but he hated seeing her come home dead tired, her feet aching. She was a stubborn woman, so he knew arguing with her would just piss them both off. One thing he'd learned being married for so long, is that the small stuff definitely could be overlooked.

His ears perked up when he heard the garage door open. It had to be Kylie. He hadn't told her yet about him and Belle's engagement, and he hoped she would understand where he was coming from, and open up to Belle. He felt like a fucking fool pacing in the kitchen, his mouth dry and his heart pounding. He was the president of the national Insurgents MC, and he was nervous as hell to tell his daughter he was remarrying. Shaking his head, he chided himself on being a pussy, and he grabbed a bottled water out of the refrigerator and gulped it. He'd be damned if he'd let Kylie see him like that when she came in.

The door slammed, and he heard her soft footsteps on the terra cotta tiles in the laundry room. "Hi, Dad," she greeted him, her long hair swishing around her. "Sorry I'm late, but I stopped at the club for a few minutes."

Banger narrowed his eyes, "What for? I told you I'd be home." He went from nervous to pissed in a few seconds. He wasn't stupid, he'd seen the looks Jerry and Kylie gave to each other, but he'd be damned if he'd let his little girl hook up with any of the Insurgents, especially Jerry. The guy was fucking different women all the time, and one woman usually wasn't enough for him. There was no way he wanted Kylie mixed up with him, or with any biker. He sent her to college to get an education, and he hoped she'd meet a decent man, someone who wasn't an outlaw and a player. "Did you go there to see someone?"

Kylie had her back to her dad, her head buried in the refrigerator. "Since when do you have broccoli and asparagus in your fridge? And watercress? What's going on?" She swiveled around, a slice of cold sausage and black olives pizza in her hand. She took a bite.

"You didn't answer my question. Why did you go to the clubhouse?"

"Oh, Cara asked me to stop by to pick up the pictures she put together for me. I forgot to get them the last time I was home."

"Did you see anyone else?"

"Yeah. A lot of brothers were there, and a few of the club girls." She took another bite.

"Did you see and talk to Jerry?" Banger pressed his hands together.

Swallowing, she shook her head.

"You sure? 'Cause you know how I feel 'bout that shit."

She popped open a Coke and took a sip. "Dad, I've known Jerry for years, just like I know Jax, Axe, Chas, Bear, and a bunch of the other guys. I don't know Rock so well—he's kinda scary. Anyway, what's the deal with you?"

"None of the brothers except for Jerry look at you in a way that makes me want to hurt them. You stay away from him. I'd hate to hurt a brother."

She giggled. "Okay, Dad. Now, are you gonna answer me about why you have so many healthy foods in your fridge? Did Belle buy them for you?"

"Get me a beer." Banger took the green bottle from Kylie's hands. "Sit down."

Dragging her feet, she sat down and rocked slightly on the chair.

"What? All of a sudden you look weird."

"Belle brought the stuff in the fridge to me. Sometimes she comes over and cooks for me."

Kylie licked her lips. "That's nice of her. I'm glad she's serving you something other than meat and potatoes."

Banger stared at her flushed face, her blue eyes avoiding his look. For a minute, his heart ached for her, and he didn't think he could tell her. Then she gazed at him. He exhaled, leaned back in the chair, and crossed his leg over the other one. "I wanted to tell you in person. You know Belle had some shit with that bitch who claimed to be her best friend, right?"

"You told me a little bit about it, but Cara filled me in on the rest. I couldn't believe someone would pretend to be your friend and do all that crap behind your back. And then try and kill you. Damn, that's cold."

"Yeah. Well, I been kinda busy with all that shit, and Belle getting better. Anyway, I wanted to tell you last week, but I had a lot of shit going on with her and the club. The thing is I know this is gonna be hard for you, but I want you to hear me out before you fuckin' flip out." He saw the muscles around her mouth twitch, and her eyes stared at him. "Belle and I are gonna get married. I asked her, and she said yes."

Banger had expected Kylie to jump up, red-faced from anger, and give him a piece of her mind, but she just sat there, her lips trembling slightly. His heart twisted. *Fuck. I wish she'd jump up and scream. I wish she'd do* anything *but just sit there like her world has ended.* "Honey?" He reached over and placed his hand over her cold one. She slid it away, pushed back her chair, and stood up.

"I have to put my things away." She picked up her suitcase and walked out of the kitchen.

Banger followed her into her room. "We gotta talk about this, Kylie. I know it's a shock to you, and I'm figuring the way you're acting that you're madder than hell at me, but I want you to understand where I'm coming from. By me loving and marrying Belle doesn't mean I don't still love your mom."

"Yes it does," she whispered as she pressed her forehead against her closet door, her tops bunched up in her hands.

"Oh, sweetheart." Banger came over and placed his arms on her shoulders and rubbed them lightly. "Don't ever think I've forgotten about your mom. Grace was my light, my rock, my love while we were married, and I thought I was gonna lose it when she died. I probably would have, but I knew I couldn't. I had to be strong for you."

Kylie's shoulders slumped, and he continued to rub them. "How can you marry someone else if you still love Mom? I don't see how you can replace her."

"I'm not replacing your mom. I never could, but I'm letting Belle into my life and my heart. Your mom has a part of my heart no one ever will. I will never stop loving her, but my heart is big enough to love Belle too."

In a voice he could barely hear, Kylie said, "It's like Mom is dying all over again. You and I used to sit and share memories about her. Now that's gone."

He spun her around and held her close to him, his hand stroking her hair. "Your mom will always live in your heart, my heart, and in our memories of her. Just because I'm marrying Belle doesn't mean I'm cutting Grace out of my life. You and I will still talk about and remember your mom. Fuck, she'll always be a part of our memories."

He paused a moment, letting his words wash over and soothe his little girl. "Life goes on, sweetheart. Look where you are now compared to where you were when your mom died. You still remember her and are sad she's not around, but you spend good times with your friends, you're in college, and you've got a lot going on. That's normal. It's what your mom would want. She didn't want us dying with her."

Kylie pulled back a little and looked at him. "I know you have a right to be in love and be happy. I guess I was being selfish in never wanting things to change."

"You're not being selfish. Change is fuckin' scary, and I fought it until I couldn't anymore." He chuckled. "It was probably your mother kicking me in the ass and calling me 'a fuckin' fool' like she used to."

Kylie sniffled and laughed. "She *did* call you that, but you never got mad. You'd just smile and it would make her stop and laugh. I forgot about that." She hugged her dad.

"Your mom will always be with us, don't you forget it. And Belle isn't planning on replacing your mom. It's just that she makes your old dad a fuckin' happy man, and I want to spend the rest of my life with her. I want to know that you're good with it. Maybe not right now, but that you get where I'm coming from. Maybe you can accept Belle when you get to know her better."

They stood, hugging each other for a long while until Kylie broke away, wiping her cheeks and nose with a tissue. "You know, Dad, since you met Belle, you seem happier, and I'm glad for you. It will take me some time, but I'm good with you. I love you." She leaned over and kissed his cheek. "Now what are we gonna have for dinner? I'm starving."

He laughed. "Finish up in here, and I'll take you to El Tecolate for dinner. I feel like Mexican. You good with that?"

Beaming, she said, "That sounds perfect."

# Chapter Thirty-Seven

*Six months later*

THEY WERE IN the final phase of their house, and Belle and her two kids couldn't wait to move in. Banger walked around the house, checking to make sure his changes had been implemented.

"Does everything look all right?" Baylee asked as she followed the couple around their soon-to-be new residence.

Nodding his head, Banger smiled. "You did a fuckin' good job of designing our home and making sure it was done well. It's fantastic. What do you think?"

Belle cocked her head to one side, a whisper of a smiling playing on her lips. "It's absolutely beautiful. I didn't think I was going to love the stone on the outside since I love brick so much, but it's simply gorgeous. It definitely looks like a French chalet." She slipped her hand in his. "I thought Banger was crazy wanting so much space: six bedrooms, seven baths, a basement, and a theater room. But, I'll have to admit, when it's all done, it'll be simply beautiful. My favorite room is the gourmet kitchen, of course. You overdid yourself, Baylee."

Baylee blushed and continued walking through the house, her heels clacking on the wooden sub-floor. Belle liked the young woman who was already partner in a very prestigious Denver architect firm. She wanted to get to know her better, and since Belle was now an old lady, she'd have the chance to socialize and form friendships with the others. She and Cara had already become good friends, and Addie had begun joining them on their shopping trips. Belle wanted to designate one night a week for all the old ladies to go out for dinner, have a few drinks, and a good time. She'd pick a night when their husbands were at the club. No reason for the women to sit home while their men were having fun.

"It's perfect for us, isn't it?" Banger kissed her forehead, and she nodded.

As Banger and Baylee went through the house, the sounds of hammers, drills, and saws became too much for Belle, and she stepped out through the French doors onto a massive brick patio overlooking the stunning scenery. Deer walked slowly by, and Belle couldn't believe that this would soon be her home. She and her kids had been staying at Banger's house since the wedding. She closed her eyes, and let the cool autumn breeze skate over her as she remembered their special day.

They had had a true biker wedding on a bright, summer afternoon in early August. It had been an outside ceremony on the clubhouse property among the wildflowers, the gurgling stream, the majestic evergreens, and the delicate aspen trees. All the bikers had ridden their Harleys, and the noise and look of fifty guys in leather and denim on gleaming bikes had been something that had taken her breath away. She'd never seen the likes of it.

Emily had been her maid of honor, and Hawk had been best man. Belle had ridden to the ceremony on the back of Banger's bike wearing black jeans, a white T-shirt, and her leather cut with the proud words "Property of Banger" embroidered in white on the back. He had looked sharp in his black jeans, black shirt, and cut, his long hair free and flowing. He hadn't wanted to wear it like that, but Belle insisted since she loved his silky strands so much; he'd relented for the ceremony, but promptly pulled it back in a leather tie for the reception they'd had at the clubhouse.

The yard had been decorated with white and gold paper lanterns that shimmered and shone in the moonlight. Tables with gold linen tablecloths—at Cara's insistence—had filled the yard, and three tables laden with more food than anyone could have eaten had stood off to the side. The seven-tiered wedding cake had been beautiful with all the cascading fondant flowers.

After a night of drinking and dancing, the married couple had spent the night at the Palace Hotel. The next day they'd taken Ethan, Emily, and Kylie on a family trip to Hawaii. The two girls had hit it off—something which pleased the married couple to no end—and Ethan and Banger had enjoyed horseback riding and body surfing in the blue waters of the Pacific. Belle had been content shopping and spending time at the spa with the girls.

"This is the custom-made patio you ordered. I think it came out spot on." Baylee's voice, and the opening of the French doors, brought Belle back to the present. Her stomach fluttered when she saw Banger cross his arms across his muscular chest, his biceps flexing. He was so damn handsome, and he was all hers. It was like a dream come true, and she loved being Banger's old lady.

The day was perfect. It had started out with Cara calling to tell her that Holly, whose real name was Louella Cummings, had received life in prison for Harold's death, and a concurrent twenty-five year sentence for attempting to murder Belle. She was happy she didn't have to testify. Holly had taken the life in prison plea bargain so she wouldn't have had to face the death penalty. Of course, Holly had tried to blame everything on her brother, and had continued to insist that her brother was an accomplice and was the one who tried to drown Belle, but nothing corroborated her story. Like a good old lady, Belle had kept silent, sticking to her story that it had just been her and Holly on that fateful day.

Belle breathed a sigh of relief that Scorpion had never been found, and figured that the outlaw's disappearance was only noticed by his MC.

"Ready to go, babe?" Banger came over and put his arm around her, and she looped her arm around his waist. They walked to his car holding each other.

On the road, Belle's phone pinged and she looked at the text.

**Emily:** *Will b home later. I have to work 2 extra hrs to cover someone.*

**Belle:** *K. see u for dinner.*

Belle closed her phone. "It was Emily. Someone didn't show up at work, so she has to stay later." She stared straight ahead, feeling Banger taking her hand and kissing it.

"She's gonna be fine. We'll help her get through it."

She would've loved it if her whole life was a fairytale, but it wasn't. Emily had been trying real hard to stay on the straight path, but she'd relapsed right after they'd come back from Hawaii, and had just returned the previous week from an alcohol rehab center. She swore to her mom that she was never going back, and Belle hoped her determination would help to get her through, but she wasn't sure. Emily seemed to be taking the right steps: she'd dropped her loser friends, and she was study hard for her ACT and SAT tests. Belle prayed her little girl would keep the demons away; Emily had so much to give and receive from life.

"We have to swing by school and pick up Ethan."

"Okay," he said as he hung a right on Decatur Street. "I'll drop the two of you off, then I gotta go to the club to finish up some work. I'll be home around seven."

"Sounds good. I'll target dinner for around seven thirty."

Since the wedding, she'd given up the rental, and she and the kids stayed at Banger's house while they waited for their new house to be finished. Belle recalled how upset Kylie was when she and her dad had told her they'd wanted a house of their own, so they were moving. Belle's heart went out to her because she knew all of the memories Kylie had of her mom were in the house. Kylie eventually reconciled to the idea, and Belle was proud of her. Kylie had told the two of them that the brick and mortar weren't her mom, and that her mom lived in her heart, her memories, and in her soul.

At seven o'clock, Banger came home, and the family had a wonderful prime rib dinner with baked potatoes, a green salad, and peas and mushrooms. Since she had a lot of time on her hands, she made wonderful gourmet meals most nights of the week, something the brothers at the clubhouse kidded her and Banger about, saying that they always knew the only woman who could catch their prez would be a great cook.

Sometimes she missed cooking for the patrons at the diner. Banger had told her she didn't have to work because he had more than enough money for the family and then some. He told her he liked his woman at home, and she like being at home, especially for her kids, so she quit. But she'd left her recipes for Jerome, and when she and Banger would stop by for a bite to eat, Ruthie would tell them he was doing a great job.

"Ruben said Doris wants to know if you need help with planning the Christmas charity event this year." Banger buttered his roll.

"I totally do. I've never done this, and I feel like I'm in over my head," she answered. Being the president's old lady was a lot of work, and she was expected to oversee the charity functions the club participated in, arrange the family dinners, attend all bike rallies, go to Sturgis each year, and a bunch of other things she couldn't remember. She knew she'd eventually become an old pro at it, but for now, she felt like a deer caught in the headlights most of the time.

After dinner, Emily and Ethan went to their rooms to finish their homework, and she handed Banger a beer as she sat next to him on the couch in the family room. It was late October, and the cool winds had turned chilly, so Banger lit a fire; he drew her close to him as they watched the flames crackle against the wood.

"I have to talk to you about something," she said softly.

Looking down at her, he said, "Is something wrong?"

"I don't think so. I hope you don't."

"What it is?"

She turned sideways, her legs curled under her. "I'm six weeks pregnant."

He stared and moved back slightly.

She pressed her lips tight, her heart feeling as though it were shrinking. "I didn't plan this. I've been taking my birth control, but since we've been married, I may have forgotten one or two times. With all the ruckus with Emily, I couldn't even remember my name. I didn't think it was a big deal. I'm so sorry. I hope this doesn't change things between us."

He held her hands. "Why're you apologizing? I'm just fuckin' stunned. I didn't expect it, that's all. It never occurred to me that we could have a baby." A broad smile broke out over his face, and he tugged her toward him. "I'm fuckin' thrilled. Hell, I can't believe I'm gonna be a dad again. Fuck, I can't believe I'll be in my sixties when the kid will be twenty… Shit, that kinda sucks."

She kissed him. "You'll make a great dad. Ethan adores you, and you're so good with him. You're a wonderful father to Kylie, and you haven't given up on warming Emily's heart."

He nodded, his eyes sparkling. "You know, I'll be happy to experience the early years. With Kylie, I was young, and Grace was with her a lot while I was busy running the club, partying, going to bike rallies, and hanging with the brothers. Grace never complained, but I missed out on seeing Kylie grow."

"It's like you have a second chance." She kissed him again.

"Fuck yeah. I'm older and my partying days are few, especially since I met you. I like hanging with my brothers, but now I get home around midnight a couple of times a week rather than four in the morning, most days of the week, and drunk off my ass. Poor Grace, she had to put up with my shit when I was younger. See how lucky you are that I slowed down?" he joked.

She jabbed his arm playfully. "I never planned on another child either, but when I found out, I was elated. I'd hoped you would be too. We never discussed it, so I wasn't sure."

He hugged her close. "Woman, you made your man more than fuckin' happy. Now one of the bedrooms in our new house will be a nursery." He kissed her neck.

"I'm thrilled to have a baby with you. You make my life complete."

"You do the same for me, babe."

Breaking away, he took her hand and led her to their bedroom. Kissing her, he rubbed his hands over her body, nudging her backward to the bed. He gently eased her down on the bed, lifted her top over her head, then slid off her skirt and panties. He leaned over her, his face inches from hers, and she could see her desire reflected in them.

"You're so beautiful, and I can't believe you're mine." He bent down and licked her hardening nipple then took it between his teeth and pulled it. A single jolt of intense desire zapped her from her tingling nipple down to her aching pussy.

Moaning, she pulled out his leather tie and ran her fingers through his blond hair. "No man has ever made me as happy as you have. I've never been in love with any man before I met you. You are the love of my life."

He growled and crushed his mouth against hers and they kissed. Hard. Wet. Deep. With urgency, she tugged at his shirt, pushing it up over his head then she unzipped his jeans, pulling them down until his dick poked her, and she giggled. He shrugged them off then bent down and kissed her nipples, chuckling as she squirmed underneath him, his breath blowing against her. She licked her lips while gliding her fingers over his sculpted pecs, admiring the way he was so muscular. She'd never get tired of the feel, the scent, the taste of his body.

Her husband moved his mouth to her neck, kissing her softly, then more ardently as his hands moved down the sides of her body. Dipping to the softness between her legs, she opened them wide, and he kissed her inner thighs while his fingers spread her swollen lips. She took a deep, staccato breath, then his tongue licked her, and he slipped inside her gently. Bringing her legs up and back, he pushed into her harder and deeper as small grunts escaped through her lips.

A thousand sparks zapped her as she climaxed, and his guttural moans told her he was on the same pleasure journey as she was. Their bodies shook and shuddered together as their orgasms bonded them even closer. He collapsed on top of her, and she let out a deep breath, her fingers absently rubbing his back. Lifting his head, he kissed her passionately, then rolled off, pulling her close to him. They twined their legs together, wrapped in each other's arms. She squeezed him.

"I love you," she murmured into his skin.

Holding her chin, Banger tipped her head back, brushed his lips against hers, and said, "I love you too."

With her head on his chest, Belle laced her fingers with his, as a warm glow spread through her body. This was her life now, and she had no desire to be anywhere else than in her husband's arms.

**The End**

Make sure you sign up for my newsletter so you can keep up with my new releases, special sales, free short stories, and other treats only available to newsletter readers. When you sign up, you will receive a FREE hot and steamy novella. Sign up at:

http://eepurl.com/bACCL1

Visit me on Facebook
facebook.com/Chiah-Wilder-1625397261063989

Check out my other books at my Author Page
amazon.com/author/chiahwilder

# Acknowledgments

I have so many people to thank who have made my writing endeavors a reality. It is the support, hard work, laughs, and love of reading that have made my dreams come true.

**Thank you** to my editor, Kristin, for all your insightful edits, excitement with the Insurgents MC series, and encouragement during the writing and editing process. I truly value your editorial eyes and suggestions as well as the time you've spent with the series. You're the best!

**Thank you** to my wonderful beta readers, Kolleen, Paula, Franci, and Barb—my final-eyes reader. Your enthusiasm for the Insurgents Motorcycle Club series has pushed me to strive and set the bar higher with each book. Your dedication is amazing!

**Thank you** to my proofreader, Amber, whose last set of eyes before the last once over I do, is invaluable. I appreciate the time and attention to detail you always give to each book.

**Thank you** to the bloggers for your support in reading my book, sharing it, reviewing it, and getting my name out there. I so appreciate all your efforts.

**Thank you** to Carrie from Cheeky Covers. You put up with numerous revisions until I said, "Yes, that's Banger!" Your patience is amazing, and you never said, "Again?!" when I'd tell you I just wasn't feeling test book cover #28. You totally rock. I love your artistic vision.

**Thank you** to the readers who support the Insurgents MC series. You have made the hours of typing on the computer and the frustrations that come with the territory of writing books so worth it. You make it possible for writers to write because without you reading the books, we wouldn't exist. Thank you, thank you!

## Banger's Ride: Insurgents Motorcycle Club (Book 5)

Dear Readers,

Thank you for reading my book. I hope you enjoyed the fifth book in the Insurgents MC series as much as I enjoyed writing Belle and Banger's story. This rough motorcycle club has a lot more to say, so I hope you will look for the upcoming books in the series. Romance makes life so much more colorful, and a rough, sexy bad boy makes life a whole lot more interesting.

If you enjoyed the book, please consider leaving a review. I read all of them and appreciate the time taken out of busy schedules to do that.

I love hearing from my fans, so if you have any comments or questions, please email me at chiahwilder@gmail.com or visit my facebook page.

To hear of **new releases, special sales, free short stories**, and **ARC opportunities**, please sign up for my **Newsletter** at http://eepurl.com/bACCL1.

A big thank you to my readers whose love of stories and words enables authors to continue weaving stories. Without the love of words, books wouldn't exist.

Happy Reading,

*Chiah*

# JERRY'S PASSION

## Book 6 in the Insurgents MC Series

## Coming in June, 2016

**The first time Jerry saw Kylie, he was taken by her beauty and innocence, but he stayed away because she was too young.** A member of the Insurgents MC, Jerry's life revolves around the club, his Harley, and easy sex. Women clamor for the rugged, tatted outlaw's attention, and he obliges, but his sights are set on the pretty, young blonde who is all grown up now—sweet curves and all….

Kylie fills his thoughts, and he dreams of his fingers tangling in her glossy hair, her legs wrapping tightly around his waist, her full lips quivering as she comes.

Too bad he can't have her.

But… he can't stop himself from craving her, and if he acts, it'll surely cost him *everything*.

His resistance is waning….

**Kylie McDaniels is the pretty daughter of Banger—President of the Insurgents MC.** She grew up in the outlaw biker life, but her father shielded her from the dark side of it, and she still has an innocence he prefers she keep. Banger is very protective of his daughter, and he's made up his mind that she won't fall in love with a biker, especially Jerry.

She'd listen to her father, but the hot, muscular biker makes her want to do some not so innocent things.

Her insides melt, and her brain turns to mush whenever he looks at her with his hungry, brown eyes.

Damn. Why does he have to be so sexy?

As Kylie maneuvers her budding sexuality and attraction to Jerry, and trying to stay on the good side of her dad, someone is out there, watching her, waiting to make his move. He's come for retribution, and Kylie is the pawn in his scheme. Will Jerry be able to stop the madman before he strikes?

Can their forbidden love survive the chaos of the world around them?

The urge to make Kylie *his* is too strong, and Jerry will let nothing or no one take her away from him.

**The Insurgents MC series are standalone romance novels. This is Jerry and Kylie's love story. This book contains violence, sexual assault (not graphic), strong language, and steamy/graphic sexual scenes. It describes the life and actions of an outlaw motorcycle club. If any of these issues offend you, please do not read the book. HEA. No cliffhangers! The book is intended for readers over the age of 18.**

# Excerpt

## Jerry's Passion

Note: This short excerpt is a ROUGH DRAFT. I am still writing the story about this bad boy. It has only been self-edited in a rudimentary way. I share it with you to give you a bit of an insight into Jerry's Passion.

# Prologue

*Mid-March, 2016*
*Red Rocks University*
*Crested Peak, Colorado*

HE STOOD IN the shadows behind the bush, as he stared intently at the window on the second floor. A glimpse of her made his heart race and he licked his lips, ripping off the dry skin with his front teeth. She was so damn beautiful. When he'd decided to seek her out, he had no idea how pretty and innocent she was. Since she was the daughter of the president of the Insurgents MC, he'd figured she'd look tough and used up. But she was a lovely angel with blonde hair that touch the top of her ass, rounded tits that would fit perfectly in his hands, and large blue eyes that sparkled with innocence.

He inhaled sharply. Seeing her had changed his plans somewhat. Watching her come and go for the past several weeks, he'd grown attached to her. As crazy at it sounded, he wanted to get to know her, become a part of her world.

"Mary, come on up. Taylor and I aren't ready yet." Kylie yelled out her dorm window, her hair framing her face.

The girl she'd yelled out to bounced up the flight of concrete stairs then entered the three story Gothic-style building. It had taken some time for him to find which dorm Kylie lived in. The university had more than fifteen thousand students, but he'd persevered and he found her. She lived with a dark-haired roommate—Taylor—in room number two twenty-two, on the second floor in the middle of the hall. A perfect location for him to watch her as she sat at her desk and studied, glanced down at her phone, or just stared out the window looking at the Rocky Mountains in the distance, a faraway look in her blue gaze.

The man had been driven to find her, hate and retribution had fueled him on, but then he saw her and his pants grew tight, and he knew his plan had changed. He buried himself further in the bush when the large wooden doors of the building opened and Kylie, Taylor, and Mary filed out, laughing and talking like young college students do. He breathed out when the trio passed by the greenery which hid him. The scent of vanilla, lavender, and patchouli lingered as they scurried down the brick path. Not knowing which scent belonged to his Kylie—he had started thinking of her as *his*—the young man made a note to find out which aroma was hers.

Slipping out from his hiding place, he shoved his hands in his pockets, keeping his distance as he followed the young women. Each time Kylie's hips swayed, his pants grew tighter, and he willed himself to focus on the goal of his plan.

A broad shouldered young man approached the girls. "Hey, Ricky." The slight breeze carried Kylie's sweet voice.

"Hey. What're you guys up to?" he asked.

"We're going to grab a burger at the University Café, then check out the show for Thursday Thrills." Kylie moved closer to Ricky. Her stalker growled when he saw her arm rub against the college boy.

"There's a hypnotist. Everyone's raving about him. Want to join us?" Mary asked.

He watched as the three women flirted and fawned over Ricky who kept staring at Kylie in a way that made his blood boil. *Note to self—*

*Ricky's fuckin' history!*

"Sure, why not?" Ricky looped his arm with Kylie's, and the four students ambled toward the café.

Wrapping his leather jacket tighter around him, he leaned against the wall of the Student Center. He'd wait…he *had* to. The man wanted to make sure Ricky fuckface didn't spend the night with Kylie. She was his, and no one would take her away from him. Just thinking about running his hands through her silky hair, and touching her skin—he'd imagined it would be soft as velvet—made his dick jab hard against his jeans. It wasn't time yet, but soon, he'd have her legs wrapped around his waist as he plunged his hardness into her tight heat. Their fucking would be sweet and nasty, and she'd cry out his name as she came all over his cock.

Then he'd hurt her real bad. Maybe even cut her delicate throat.

He had to.

Retribution fucking sucked sometimes.

# Chapter One

*April, 2016*

JERRY LEANED AGAINST the trunk of the evergreen as he watched Kylie and three friends amble on the sidewalk. Kylie's hair shone in the moonlight like liquid gold, and he sucked in his breath when she threw her head back and laughed, covering her lips with her hand. He knew her lips well since he'd been studying them for the past three years. He loved the way she'd lick the sugar off them whenever she ate the donuts the club always had in the kitchen. So many times he wished he were those granules on her lips as her pink tongue skimmed over them.

Kylie stopped and checked her phone, the glow of it casting a white sheen over her face. "Ari says she's going to meet us," she said, then giggled uncontrollably. The other two women started laughing with her, then all three of them bent over, holding their stomachs, laughing and gasping for air.

A smile brushed over Jerry's lips. *She's fuckin' plastered.* His amusement quickly turned to anger when he saw the guy, who'd been walking with them, wrap his arm around her as she leaned into him, swaying and stumbling. She didn't seem like she cared that the young man's hand slowly rode up her shirt, but Jerry cared. He cared a whole fucking lot.

Propelling himself with his boot against the tree trunk, he came behind her. "Kylie," he said in a low, deep voice. From the way she jumped at her name, he knew he'd startled her. She whirled around, and, at first, she peered at him, her face blank, her eyes narrowed as she scrutinized his face. Then a broad smile rolled over her mouth, as he saw recognition dawning on her.

"Jerry, I didn't recognize you because… you're *here*. What are you doing on campus?" her eyes didn't quite focus on his.

"I came up to visit some friends who live near the university. I thought I'd come by and see you." His gaze roamed up and down her body, and when it landed on the guy's hand, fierceness replaced softness. "How are you?"

"Great." She pushed the man's hand away, and Jerry smiled, letting his eyes linger on her mouth. Her full lips shone under the full moon, and he imagined she was wearing lip gloss tasting like cotton candy or watermelon. How he yearned to taste those lips.

"That's good." He leaned in close and caught a whiff of lavender and patchouli as it wafted around him, landing on his dick. With his fingers, he brushed her hair back from her face, and it felt soft like a whisper.

She looked up at him and blinked. "You're so sweet." She pressed against him. "You made a special trip to say hi to me." She curled her arm around his neck, pulling him down toward her. "Thanks," she breathed, her lips grazing his ear.

*Fuck!* Jerry looped his arms around her small waist and held her close, loving the way she felt in his arms. He'd fantasized about holding her for too long. With her long, silky hair, round tits, and curvy hips, she was his perfect wet dream. And what the hell was up with the way his nerves were sparking? He'd held a ton of women before, but he never felt this connected, this emotional with any of them. Then again, none of them were Kylie.

"Hey, are you coming with us?" one of the young women asked.

"Who's the hot guy you have wrapped around you?" the other woman said.

Kylie pulled away from Jerry, but he reached out and grabbed her as she nearly fell. "You've had too much to drink," he rasped against her ear. She giggled.

The young guy took hold of her hand and tugged her to him. "Let's go." He began walking away from Jerry with a swaying Kylie in tow.

Gritting his teeth, Jerry sprinted ahead of the group, then stopped abruptly, causing the guy and Kylie to crash into him. Putting his arm around her shoulder, he glared at the young man. "I'm taking care of Kylie. Her dad would want it that way." The guy looked Jerry up and down, then rushed over to the two girls, and hooked his arms around each of them.

Jerry was such a bullshitter because he knew Banger would be livid if he saw his precious daughter snuggled against Jerry's chest. He knew she was off limits because she was the president's daughter, and Banger had made it a point, on more than one occasion, to let Jerry know not to get near her. Hell, Banger didn't even want Jerry to talk to her, but he couldn't keep himself away from her. He was drawn to her and even though he knew it was wrong, and dangerous, and all kinds of stupid, he'd wanted Kylie so badly for too long.

"You want to come with us to the festival?" Kylie looked up at him, her pretty face so innocent and tempting.

*I want to kiss you hard, suck your pretty tits, and ram my cock in you. I hope you're not fuckin' that pansy-ass prick up ahead. If you are, I'll have to beat his ass.* "Sure. Where is it?"

"In the quad. It's the spring festival, and they have a band, beer, and everything." Her gaze was wide.

He laughed and fought down the urge to kiss her. She was so damned adorable. *Fuck, I'm playing with fire.*

"Wait up, guys." Kylie gestured her friends to stop. She looked up at Jerry. "I want you to meet some of my friends."

"Is the asshole prick a friend or boyfriend?"

"Ricky? We're just friends. Anyway, so what if he were my boyfriend?" She raised her chin in a defiant move.

"I don't give a shit, but your dad would."

"You're not going to tell my dad about me being tipsy, are you?"

"You're more like drunk, babe, but no, I'm not gonna tell him." *There's no fuckin' way Banger's ever gonna find out I've got my hands all over his daughter. Shit.*

"Thanks," she whispered.

They caught up to her friends, and Kylie introduced them to Jerry while he stared impassively at them. His thoughts were only on Kylie, and if she continued drinking at the festival, he would definitely have to carry her back to her dorm room, tuck her into bed, and give her a long, deep kiss goodnight.

"It's kind of awesome you being here. I never pictured you at my college." Her soft voice interrupted his thoughts.

"How come?"

She lifted her shoulders up and down. "I don't know. I just think of you as being at the club."

"So you think of me?" he teased, clasping her shoulder tighter. "I like that."

She punched him lightly in his side. "You know what I mean. I just picture you and all the other guys as living and breathing the club. I guess I never imagined you outside of the Insurgents' world."

"Yeah, well, I do step out sometimes. I wanted to say hi before I headed back to Pinewood." *I rode my ass up here to see you. Fuck, I go hard just thinking about you.* "You don't come to Pinewood that often."

"I know," she groaned. "When I first got here, I was so homesick, but now I'm busy with school, activities, and parties, that I never seem to have the time to go home and see dad, and all of you." She held him tighter. "I'm fucked up. I drank too much."

"I'd have to agree, but hold on to me. I'll make sure you're okay." *I love the way she feels around me. Hell, I've been fantasizing about this for too long. Like a goddamned love-sick teenager.* "Are we almost at the quad?"

She nodded, pointing in front of them. Jerry saw a crowd and heard the beats of the electric guitars as they approached a large, grassy area....

## Chiah Wilder's Other Books

**Hawk's Property: Insurgents Motorcycle Club Book 1**
**Jax's Dilemma: Insurgents Motorcycle Club Book 2**
**Chas's Fervor: Insurgents Motorcycle Club Book 3**
**Axe's Fall: Insurgents Motorcycle Club Book 4**

I love hearing from my readers. You can email me at chiahwilder@gmail.com.

Sign up for my newsletter to receive updates on new books, special sales, free short stories, and ARC opportunities at http://eepurl.com/bACCL1.

Visit me on facebook at:
www.facebook.com/Chiah-Wilder-1625397261063989

Printed in Great Britain
by Amazon